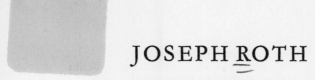

JOSEPH ROTH

THE RADETZKY MARCH

TRANSLATED BY EVA TUCKER
BASED ON
AN EARLIER TRANSLATION BY
GEOFFREY DUNLOP

THE OVERLOOK PRESS
Woodstock, New York

Joseph Roth: *Radetzkymarsch*
Copyright © 1932 by Gustav Kiepenheuer Verlag, Berlin
© 1950 by Verlag Allert de Lange, Amsterdam,
and Verlag Kiepenheuer & Witsch,
Cologne

This revised translation by Eva Tucker © The
Overlook Press and Penguin Books Ltd, 1974

Geoffrey Dunlop's translation, published by The Viking
Press Inc. in 1933 and Heinemann Ltd in 1934, has been
used by permission of the publishers.

The Overlook Press
Lewis Hollow Road
Woodstock, New York 12498

Library of Congress Catalog Card Number:
72–97581

ISBN: 0 8795 1015 3

Printed in Great Britain

PART ONE

Chapter 1

The Trottas were not an old family. Their founder's title had been conferred on him after the battle of Solferino. He was a Slovene and chose the name of his native village, Sipolje. Though fate elected him to perform an outstanding deed, he himself saw to it that his memory became obscured to posterity.

As infantry lieutenant, he was in command of a platoon at Solferino. The fighting had been in progress for half an hour. He watched the white backs of his men three paces in front of him. The front line was kneeling, the rear standing. They were all cheerful and confident of victory. They had eaten their bellyful and drunk brandy at the expense, and in honor, of their Emperor, who had been in the field since the previous day. Here and there a man fell, leaving a gap. Trotta leaped into every breach, firing the orphaned rifles of the dead and wounded; he would close up the thinned-out line or extend it; he cast his hyper-perceptive eye in many directions and strained after sounds on all sides. Amid the clatter of rifles his quick ears picked up his captain's intermittent, clear orders. His eyes pierced the grayish-blue haze in front of the enemy's lines. He fired with sure aim and every shot went home. His men sensed his glance, his hand, heard his voice and they felt safe.

The cease-fire order trickled along the front line, which stretched farther than the eye could see. Here and there a ramrod continued its clatter, a shot rang out, belated and solitary. The haze between the lines lifted a little, suddenly giving way to the silvery midday warmth of an overcast, stormy sun. Between the lieutenant and the backs of his platoon, the Emperor arrived, escorted by two staff officers. He was in the act of raising to his eyes a field glass handed to him by one of the escorts. Trotta was aware of the significance of the gesture. Even if it were assumed that the enemy was retreating, the rear-guard would nevertheless still be facing the Austrian army and the raising of a field glass might be interpreted as a challenge: and the challenger was the young Emperor. Trotta's heart pounded. Terror of the unthinkable, boundless calamity which might annihilate him, his regiment, the army, the State— the very world—sent burning shivers down his spine. The ancient grudge of infantry subalterns against staff officers, with their ignorance of the bitter realities of the front, inspired the action which stamped Trotta's name indelibly on the history of his regiment. With both hands he gripped the monarch's shoulders to push him down. No doubt the lieutenant's grasp was too rough. The Emperor fell at once. The escorts flung themselves on the falling man. That same instant a shot pierced Trotta's left shoulder—a shot aimed at the Emperor's heart. Trotta fell as the Emperor rose. Everywhere along the whole front the confused and irregular clatter of timid and newly awakened gunfire resounded. The Emperor, warned impatiently by his escort to leave the danger zone, nevertheless bent over the prostrate lieutenant to inquire, in accordance with Imperial duty, the name of the unconscious man who was unable to hear him. An army surgeon, an ambulance orderly, and two stretcher-bearers came running, backs bent, heads lowered. The staff officers pulled the Emperor down, then flung themselves on the ground beside him. "Here—the lieutenant," the Emperor called up to the breathless military surgeon.

Meanwhile the fire had died down again. Then, while a substitute cadet arrived to take over the platoon and announced in his shrill treble, "I'm taking over," while Francis Joseph and his escort rose, ambulance orderlies carefully strapped the lieutenant to a stretcher and all retired in the direction of regimental headquarters, where a snow-white tent spread over the nearest dressing station.

Trotta's left collarbone had been shattered. The ball lodged directly beneath the shoulderblade was removed under the eyes of the Supreme War Lord and amid the inhuman cries of the sufferer, whom pain had resuscitated.

A month later Trotta was healed. He returned to his South Hungarian garrison, promoted to Captain with the most distinguished of all decorations: the Order of Maria Theresa;

the prefix "von" was added to his name. Thenceforward he was called Captain Joseph Trotta von Sipolje.

As if his old life had been replaced by a strange new one, manufactured to order in some workshop, he would recite to himself every night before going to sleep and every morning after waking his new rank and his new status; he would stand in front of the mirror to make certain that his face and appearance were unchanged. Despite the clumsy heartiness of comrades seeking to bridge this sudden gulf opened by incomprehensible fate, and his own vain attempt to encounter all men as unconstrainedly as before, the titled Captain seemed in danger of losing his equilibrium. He felt condemned to wear another man's boots for the rest of his life, walking on slippery ground and pursued by secret murmurings—the object of uncertain glances. His grandfather had been a smallholder; his father an assistant paymaster, then sergeant-major of the gendarmery on the southern frontiers of the monarchy. Having lost an eye in a tussle with Bosnian border smugglers, old Trotta was now pensioned off as an invalid and was caretaker in the park at Schloss Laxenburg. There he fed the swans, trimmed the hedges, and in spring protected the laburnum and later the elder from pilfering hands; on mild spring nights he would root out homeless pairs of lovers from the benevolent shelter of dark park benches.

The rank and status of a plain infantry lieutenant had been natural and fitting enough to the son of a noncommissioned officer. But his own father felt a sudden chasm between himself and the titled Captain who moved in the strange, almost unearthly radiance of Imperial favor as if through a golden cloud. The measured affection which the young man offered the old seemed to call for a different manner, a new relationship between father and son. It was five years since the Captain had seen his father. Nevertheless, every other week when, in accordance with established routine he took his turn on the rounds, he had written the old man a short letter by the dim gusty light of guardroom candles—after he had inspected the sentries, and entered the times for relieving them, and had scribbled his bold, forceful *None* under the heading UNUSUAL INCIDENTS, thus denying even the remotest possibility of such occurrences. His letters were all the same, like army orders or regulation forms. They were written on yellowish, fibrous foolscap sheets, beginning "Dear Father" to the left, spaced four digits off the top margin and two off the side. They all gave the same brief intimation that the writer was in very good health, continued in the hope that the recipient was likewise, ended in the same formula, inscribed with flourishes in a fresh paragraph to the right on an exact diagonal with the beginning "Your truly respectful and grateful son, Joseph Trotta, lieutenant."

But how, now that his new rank no longer required him to go on the old rounds, was he to adapt the official letter form, designed to meet every requirement of the military curriculum; how was he to insert among the standard phrases extraordinary descriptions of circumstances which had become extraordinary and which he himself had scarcely managed to grasp? On that quiet evening when for the first time since his recovery Captain Trotta sat down at the table, much notched and scarred by the idle knives of bored privates, he realized that he would never get beyond the opening "Dear Father." So he leaned his sterile pen against the inkwell; nipped off an end of guttering wick as though expecting some happy inspiration from the soft light of the candle, some suitable turn of phrase, and drifted by degrees into vague recollections of childhood, his village, his mother, his military school. He observed the immense shadows cast by small objects on the bare blue walls; the gently curved shimmering outline of his sword hanging from its hook by the door, its dark ribbon tucked into the hilt. He listened to the ceaseless rain outside drumming on leaded window frames; and rose at last, having decided to go and see his father the following week, after the customary audience of thanks with the Emperor for which he was to be detailed in the next few days.

A week later, he took a cab to see his father at Schloss Laxenburg, immediately following the audience which had lasted a bare ten minutes—ten minutes of Imperial graciousness, ten or twelve inquiries read from a dossier to which it had been his duty, standing stiffly at attention, to fire the reply, "Yes Your Majesty."

He found the old gentleman in his shirtsleeves sitting in the kitchen of his quarters at a plain deal table covered with a dark-blue cloth edged in scarlet, a large cup of steaming, fragrant coffee in front of him. His notched cherrywood stick swung by its crook from the edge of the table. A creased leather pouch stuffed with shag lay half open beside the long white clay pipe which was stained a brownish-yellow, the colour matching his father's bristling mustache. Captain Joseph Trotta von Sipolje stood among these frugal, modest comforts like some military god in his gleaming officer's sash and lacquered helmet which generated a kind of black sunshine of its own; in smooth, finely polished riding boots with glittering spurs, two rows of bright, almost blazing buttons on his coat; and blessed with the superterrestrial effulgence of the Order of Maria Theresa. Thus the son approached his father, who rose slowly, as if to foil the young man's magnificence by the slowness of his greeting. Captain Trotta kissed his father's hand, bent his head to receive the paternal kiss on cheek and forehead.

"Sit down," said the old man.

The Captain unbuckled a portion of his glory and sat down.

"Congratulations," said his father, using the ordinary harsh German of army Slavs. His consonants rumbled like thunderbolts, the final syllables laden with small weights. Only five years previously he had addressed his son in Slavonic dialect, although the young man had merely a smattering of it and never used a word of dialect himself. However, to address his son in his mother tongue on this day, his son who by the grace of fortune and the Emperor had been removed so far from him, would have struck the old man as an impertinence not to be risked. The Captain, in the meantime, was watching his father's lips, ready to welcome the first sound of Slavonic like long-lost, familiar sounds of home.

"Congratulations, congratulations," the Sergeant-major thundered again. "It wasn't so easy to get on in my time. In my day Radetzky gave us a rough time."

It really is all over, thought the Captain. A leaden mound of military grades divided him from his father. "Do you still drink *rakija*, Father?" he asked, to acknowledge the last vestiges of kinship and intimacy. They drank, clinked glasses, drank again; after every glass his father groaned, gave himself up to endless coughing fits, turned purple, spat, then gradually subsided and began to tell anecdotes of his own days in active service, all with the unmistakable intention of belittling his son's career and merit. At last the Captain rose, kissed his father's hand, received his father's kiss on cheek and forehead, buckled on his sword, put on his shako, and left—aware that he had seen the last of his father in this life.

It was indeed the last time. He wrote the usual letters to the old man, but no other visible tie remained between them. Captain Trotta was severed from the long line of his Slavonic peasant forebears. With him fresh stock came into being. The years turned full circle, one by one, like smoothly running wheels. In accordance with his rank, Trotta married the no-longer-very-young niece of his colonel, daughter of a district commissioner. She brought him a dowry, and bore him a son. He settled down to enjoy the even tenor of a healthy military existence. He served in a small garrison, rode each morning into the barrack square, played chess with the notary in the same café every afternoon, grew into his rank, position, dignity, and reputation. He possessed an average talent for strategy, of which he demonstrated adequate proof at maneuvers each summer. He was a good husband, suspicious of women, was anything but a gambler, surly but just with subordinates, grimly opposed to all forms of deceit, unmanly conduct, cowardly safety, idle praise, ambitious self-seeking. He was as simple and blameless as his conduct sheet, and only the rage which occasionally shook him might have indicated to the observer of human nature that even in the soul of Captain Trotta black precipices loomed where storms sleep, and the unknown voices of nameless ancestors.

He was no great reader, Captain Trotta, and secretly pitied his growing son, who was beginning to have to cope with pencil, slate, sponge, ruler, and arithmetic; and for whom the inevitable reading books were lined up. As yet the Captain was convinced that one day his boy would be a soldier. It had never entered his mind that, from the battle of Solferino until the extinction of their line, a Trotta could follow any other calling. Had he had two, three, four sons (his wife was sickly, in constant need of medicines and doctors, and pregnancies were a hazard for her), they would all have become soldiers. That was how Captain Trotta felt in those days. There was talk of another war, and he was prepared for it. Indeed, it seemed almost certain to him that he was destined to die in battle. His unshaken simplicity accepted death in the field as the necessary consequence of a soldier's good name. Until one day when, out of idle curiosity, he picked up his son's first reader. The child

6

was just five and had a tutor who, reflecting the mother's ambition, was acquainting him far too early with the exigencies of school. The Captain read the morning prayer in verse—it had been the same for decades and he remembered it well. He read "The Four Seasons," "The Fox and the Hare," "The King of Beasts." Then he turned to the table of contents, where he found the title of a piece which concerned him personally: "Francis Joseph I at the Battle of Solferino." As he read it he had to find a chair. "At the battle of Solferino," the paragraph began, "our King and Emperor, Francis Joseph encountered extreme danger." Trotta himself came into it—but how transfigured! "Our monarch," it said,

had ventured so far forward among the enemy in the heat of battle that suddenly he found himself surrounded by enemy cavalry. At this moment of supreme danger a young lieutenant, mounted on a foaming chestnut horse, galloped into the fray, waving his sword. What blows he inflicted on the backs and heads of the enemy horsemen.

And further:

An enemy lance pierced the young hero's breast, even though most of the enemy had been killed. With his drawn sword in his hand, our young and fearless monarch had no difficulty in fending off their ever-weakening attacks. On that occasion all the enemy cavalry were taken. The young lieutenant—his name was Joseph von Trotta—was awarded the highest distinction our fatherland can give its heroes, the Order of Maria Theresa.

Clutching the reader, Captain Trotta went to the little orchard behind his house where his wife spent her time on mild afternoons. With blanched lips and in a very low voice, he asked her if she was acquainted with the outrageous story. She nodded smiling. "It's a pack of lies," yelled the Captain, and he flung the book down onto the damp ground. "It's for children," his wife replied gently. He turned his back on her. Rage shook him like a hurricane shaking a feeble shrub. He hurried back indoors, his heart pounding. It was time for his game of chess. He took down his sword from its hook, buckled it on with a vicious jerk, and left the house with long, uncontrolled strides. Anyone who saw him might have thought he was out to slaughter five dozen enemies. Without uttering a word, he sat in the café, four deep furrows drawn across his pale, narrow

7

forehead under the rough cropped hair. When he had lost his second game, he knocked the rattling chessmen aside with an angry gesture and said to his opponent, "I need your advice." Silence. "I've been grossly misrepresented," he began again, looking straight into the notary's flashing spectacles. But he realized that words were failing him. He should have brought the reader. With the odious object in his hands, things might have been easier to explain.

"What kind of misrepresentation?" asked the notary.

"I have never served with the cavalry," Captain Trotta felt himself constrained to begin, though he himself was aware that such a beginning was unintelligible. "And those unscrupulous compilers of school books have the temerity to say that I came galloping on a chestnut—'foaming chestnut horse,' to save the Emperor's life."

The notary understood. He knew the piece from his son's books. "Captain," he said, "you're taking it too seriously. Remember, it's for children." Trotta stared at him in horror. At that moment he felt the whole world was in league against him: the writers of school books, the notary, his wife, his son, his son's tutor. "All historical events," continued the notary, "are modified for consumption in schools. And quite right too. Children need examples which they can understand, which impress them. They can learn later what actually occurred."

"Bring me my bill," the Captain roared and rose. He went to the barracks, surprised Lieutenant Amerling (the officer on duty) with a young lady in the assistant paymaster's office, did the rounds himself, summoned the sergeant-major, ordered the NCO on duty to report for punishment, turned the company out for fatigue rifle drill in the square. The men obeyed him, frightened and confused. There were a few absentees in each platoon who could not be found. Captain Trotta ordered their names to be called. "All absentees for fatigue drill tomorrow," the Captain told the lieutenant. The privates panted at their drill. Ramrods clattered, rifle straps flew, sweaty palms slapped around the cool metal barrels, the heavy butts grounded on soft, dull clay.

"Load," ordered the Captain. The air vibrated with the rattle of blank cartridges. "Half an hour's salute drill," ordered the Captain. In ten minutes he changed his mind. "To prayers—kneel!" Appeased, he heard the thud of bony knees on clay, gravel, sand. He was Captain still and master of his company. He'd show these schoolbook hacks.

That night he avoided the mess, ate nothing, went to bed, and slept heavily without dreaming. Next day, at the officers' roll call, he rapped out his complaint to the colonel briefly and clearly. It was transmitted. And the martyrdom of Captain Joseph Trotta, Knight of Sipolje, champion of truth, began. Six weeks elapsed before the war office informed him that the complaint he submitted had been forwarded to the Ministry of Culture and Education; many more weeks passed before, one morning, the Minister's reply came. It read as follows:

Dear Sir,

In reply to your complaint with reference to reading lesson No. 15 in the authorized reading primer for Austrian elementary and secondary schools, composed in accordance with the Act of July 21, 1864, and edited by Professors Weidner and Srdehy, the Minister of Education most respectfully calls your attention to the fact that all pieces containing reading matter of historical significance, and in particular those which concern the august person of His Majesty the Emperor Francis Joseph, or indeed any other member of the Supreme Imperial House, have been adapted in accordance with the provisions of the edict of March 21, 1840, to suit the capacities of pupils for the best possible furtherance of all educational ends.

The said reading lesson No. 15 to which you draw the attention of the Ministry had already been submitted to the personal inspection of His Excellency the Minister of Culture, and by him approved as suitable for use in schools.

It is the heartfelt aim both of our higher- and lower-grade education authorities to set before the pupils of the Monarchy deeds of valor of all arms in such a fashion as may seem adaptable to the child's character and imagination, and to the patriotic sentiments of each new generation, without sacrificing veracity in the incidents described; yet at the same time eschewing a bare, dry style of narrative, devoid of imaginative stimulus or lacking incentive to patriotic feelings. In consequence of the above and other similar considerations, the undersigned most respectfully begs that you withdraw the complaint you have laid before us.

This document bore the signature of the Minister of Culture and Education. The colonel handed it to the Captain with a fatherly admonition to forget the whole thing.

Trotta received it without a word. A week later he had petitioned in the proper quarter for a private audience with His

Majesty, and one morning three weeks later he stood in the Burg face to face with the Supreme War Lord.

"Look here, my dear Trotta," said the Emperor, "it's a bit awkward, but you know, neither of us shows up too badly in the story. Forget it."

"Your Majesty," replied the Captain, "it's a lie."

"A great many lies are told," agreed the Emperor.

"I can't forget it, Your Majesty," gulped out the Captain.

The Emperor moved closer to him. He was not much taller than Trotta. Their eyes met.

"My ministers," said Francis Joseph, "know what they're doing, and I am obliged to rely on them. Do you understand, my dear Captain Trotta?" Then, after a silence, "We'll do something about it, you'll see."

The audience was at an end.

Although his father was still alive, Trotta did not go to Laxenburg. He returned to his garrison and sent in his papers. They retired him as Major. He moved to his father-in-law's small estate in Bohemia. But Imperial favor had not deserted him: a few weeks later he received the information that the Emperor had seen fit to bestow on the son of the man who had saved his life five thousand gulden out of the privy purse, for purposes of study. At the same time Trotta was raised to the rank of Baron.

Baron Joseph Trotta von Sipolje received these Imperial favors with an ill grace as though they were insults. The campaign against Prussia was fought and lost without him. He nursed a grudge. His temples were touched with silver, his eyes grew dull, his gait slow, his hand heavy and his tongue ever more silent. Though he was a man in the prime of life, he seemed to be ageing rapidly. He had been driven out of his paradise of simple faith in Emperor and virtue, truth and righteousness, and, fettered in suffering silence, he may well have recognized that the stability of the world, the power of the law, and the splendour of royalty are maintained by guile. Following a casually uttered wish of the Emperor, reading lesson no. 15 was expunged from the schoolbooks of the monarchy. The name of Trotta was now known only to the unpublished annals of his regiment.

The Major continued to vegetate, obscure subject of

ephemeral fame, like a fleeting shadow which is sent into the bright world of the living by some hidden agency.

He pottered on his father-in-law's estate with watering can and garden shears; and, like his father in the grounds of Laxenburg, the Baron trimmed hedges and mowed lawns. In spring he protected the laburnum and later the elder from pilfering hands. He replaced the rotten palings in the wooden fences with smoothly planed new ones, busied himself with household gear, harnessed his own bays, renewed rusty locks on gates and doors, wedged new, carefully whittled slats into sagging hinges, stayed out in the woods for days on end, shot small game and slept in the gamekeeper's hut. He tended poultry, crops, manure, fruit and espalier bloom, looked after groom and coachman. Stingy and suspicious, he made purchases fishing for coins with his fingertips in a skimpy leather purse which he thrust back quickly into his breast pocket. He became an insignificant Slavonic peasant. Occasionally the old rage would overpower him, shaking him as a hurricane shakes a feeble shrub. Then he would belabor the groom or the horse's flanks, bang doors into the locks which he himself had mended, threaten the farmhands with murder and destruction, push his dinner plate away with a growl and refuse to eat.

With him lived his sickly wife, in a separate room; his son, whom he saw only at mealtimes and whose school reports came twice a year for his inspection, evoking no word of praise or blame; his father-in-law, who gaily squandered his pension, had a weakness for young ladies, and stayed in town for weeks on end, though he was always in fear of his daughter's husband. A small, gnarled, Slavonic peasant, this Baron Trotta. He still wrote to his father twice a month, late at night by flickering candlelight on yellowish fibrous foolscap, the heading "Dear Father" to the left spaced four digits from the top and two from the side margin. He rarely received a reply. Indeed, the Baron sometimes thought of paying his father a visit. He had long been homesick for the caretaker, for the frugal, modest comforts, the stringy shag, the home-distilled *rakija*. But the son disliked spending as much as did his father, grandfather, great-grandfather before him. He now felt closer to the pensioner than on that day years ago when, in the fresh glamor of his nobility, he had sat beside him drinking *rakiia* in the narrow blue kitchen.

11

He never mentioned his origins to his wife. He felt that embarrassed pride would come between the daughter of a fairly old family of civil servants and a Slavonic sergeant-major.

One day, on a fine March morning, as the Baron stumped over frozen clods to see his steward, a farmhand came to him with a letter from the authorities in charge of Schloss Laxenburg. The pensioner was dead, had quietly passed away at the age of eighty-one. All Trotta said was, "Go to the Baroness. Ask her to have my trunks packed. I am going to Vienna this evening."

He went on to his steward's house, inquired after the spring sowings and discussed the weather. He gave orders for three new plows to be bought, for the veterinary surgeon to come on Monday and for the midwife that same day to attend a pregnant farmgirl. As he left he remarked, "My father has died. I shall be away in Vienna for three days." And he went, raising a negligent finger.

His trunk was packed, the horses harnessed to the carriage; it was an hour's drive to the station. Having gulped down soup and meat, he said to his wife, "I can't manage any more. My father was a good man. You never met him." Was it an epitaph? Or a lamentation?

"You're to come with me," he told his startled son. His wife rose to pack the boy's things. While she busied herself in the rooms above, Trotta said, "Now you'll see your grandfather." His son trembled and lowered his eyes.

When they arrived, the Sergeant-Major had been laid out. The corpse, with three glittering medals on its chest, its great bristly mustache, lay on a bier in the old man's living room. It was guarded by church candles six feet high and attended by two fellow pensioners in dark-blue uniforms. An Ursuline nun prayed in the corner by the single window, its curtains drawn. The pensioners stood at attention as Trotta entered. He was wearing his major's uniform with the Order of Maria Theresa. He knelt; his son, too, fell to his knees at the feet of the dead man, the soles of those great boots thrusting themselves into his young face. For the first time in his life Baron Trotta felt a tiny sharp pain somewhere in the region of his heart. His small eyes remained dry. A sensation of awkward piousness made him mutter three paternosters. Then he got to his feet, bent over the dead man, kissed the great mustache, and

12

waved his hand at the pensioners. "Come," he said to his son.

"Did you see him?" he asked outside.

"Yes," said the boy.

"He was only a sergeant-major in the gendarmery," his father said, "I saved the Emperor's life at the battle of Solferino. That was how we got the baronetcy."

The boy said nothing.

The pensioner was buried in the little cemetery at Laxenburg in the military section. Six comrades in dark-blue uniforms bore the coffin from chapel to grave. Major Trotta in full-dress uniform and wearing his shako kept one hand on his son's shoulder the whole time. The boy sobbed. The solemn noise of the military band, the priest's monotonous, dreary singsong which became audible with every break in the music, the drifting incense—it all choked the boy with a pain he could not understand. And the gun salute fired over the grave by a demi-platoon made him tremble with its reverberating finality. Martial greetings sped the old man's soul on its way to heaven, vanished forever from the earth.

Father and son returned home. The Baron said nothing all the way back. Only as they were getting off the train and into the carriage which was waiting for them behind the station garden did the Major say "Never forget your grandfather."

The Baron resumed his daily routine. The years slipped by. The Sergeant-Major's was not the last corpse he had to see underground. He buried first his wife's father, then, a few years later, his wife who had died quickly, unobtrusively, and without farewells after severe inflammation of the lungs. He sent his son to a boarding school in Vienna, having decreed that he should never become a regular soldier. He remained alone on the estate in the spacious white house still quick with the breath of the dead. He spoke only to the gamekeeper and steward, the groom and coachman. His rages became less and less frequent, but the servants were always aware of the weight of his hard peasant fist, and his wrathful silence lay like a yoke across the necks of all his dependents. Apprehensive silence, like the calm before a storm, preceded him.

Twice a month his son's dutiful letters arrived; once a month he answered in a couple of short sentences on scrappy strips of paper, torn from the margins of the letters he had received.

13

Once a year, on August 18th, the Emperor's birthday, he went in uniform to the nearest garrison town. Twice a year his son visited him, for the Christmas and summer vacations. Each Christmas Eve the boy received three hard silver gulden, for which he had to sign a receipt and which he was never allowed to take away with him. The gulden were put away that same night into a cashbox in the old man's safe. The school reports were kept with them. These spoke of his son's sturdy industry, his middling but always adequate capacities. The boy received not a single toy, no pocket money, not one book apart from the statutory schoolbooks. Yet he seemed to lack nothing. He possessed a neat, matter-of-fact, honest intelligence. His limited imagination made him wish for nothing more than to get through his school days as quickly as possible.

When he was eighteen, his father said on Christmas Eve, "This year you are not having three gulden. You can take nine out of the cashbox and sign a receipt for them. Be careful with women, most of them have got some sort of disease." And after a silence, "I've decided you're to go in for law. It will take you two years. There's no hurry for your military service. We can put that off until you're qualified."

The young man received his nine gulden as obediently as his father's wish. He seldom went after a woman, choosing with great caution, and he still had six gulden in hand when he came home for the summer vacation. He asked his father's permission to invite a friend. "All right," said the Major with some surprise. The friend arrived without much luggage but with a well-stocked paint box, which displeased the master of the house. "So he paints?" the old man asked.

"Yes, very well indeed," said his son Franz.

"Tell him not to mess up the house. He can paint the landscape."

The visitor did his painting out of doors but not of the landscape. He was painting a portrait, from memory, of the Baron. Every day at mealtimes he memorized his host's features. "What's he staring at me for?" Trotta asked. Both young men blushed and looked at the tablecloth.

Nevertheless, the portrait was finished, framed, and presented to the old man before they left. He examined it with deliberation, smiling, turning it around as if looking for details on the reverse which had been omitted from the front; he held it up to the window, then at arm's length; looked at himself in the mirror, compared himself with the portrait, and said at last, "Where shall we hang it?"

It was his first pleasure in many years. "You can lend your friend money if he needs it," he said quietly to Franz. "Be good to each other."

This likeness was the first and remained the only one ever taken of old Trotta. Later it hung in his son's study, and excited his grandson's imagination.

Meanwhile for the next few weeks it kept the Major in exceptionally good spirits. He hung it first on one wall then on another; examined with flattered satisfaction his bony jutting nose, pale, clean-shaven skin, tight-set lips, high cheekbones rising like hills under the small dark eyes; the low, heavily wrinkled forehead, thatched with a downward sloping crop of bristling close-cut hair. Only now was he getting to know his own face and sometimes he would hold silent conversation with it. It aroused in him thoughts he had never known and elusive memories—quickly fading shades of melancholy. He had needed this portrait to make him aware of his premature old age and his great solitude; they leapt out at him from the painted canvas, this old age and solitude. "Has it always been like this?" he asked himself.

Now and then he would make an unplanned visit to his wife's grave, look at the gray plinth and the chalky-white cross, read the dates of her birth and death and reckon that she had died too early, and admit that he could not recall her. He had forgotten, for instance, her hands. "Bitter tincture of iron" came to mind, a remedy she had taken for many years. Her face? If he shut his eyes he could still summon it, but it soon faded into the reddish twilight.

He grew gentle in the house and on the farm, sometimes stroked a horse or smiled at cows, treated himself to a glass of schnapps more often, and one day wrote a short letter to his son in addition to the usual monthly slip. People began to smile at him and he nodded pleasantly. Summer came, the vacation brought Franz and his painter friend. The old man took them to the inn in town, drank a few glasses of *slivovitz* and ordered an excellent meal for the young men.

His son passed his law finals, came home more often, began to look about the estate, and one day felt moved to give up law and manage it. The Major said, "It's too late for that. You're not cut out for farming and estate managing. You'll make a good civil servant. That's all." So the matter was settled. His son became a civil servant, assistant district commissioner in Austrian Silesia. Though the name of Trotta had vanished from authorized schoolbooks, it remained in the secret archives of higher bureaucrats, and those five thousand gulden allotted from the Emperor's privy purse assured Assistant District Commissioner Trotta of constant and benevolent supervision and protection from anonymous high places. His promotion was rapid. Two years before he was nominated Chief District Commissioner, the Major died.

He left a surprising will. Being assured, he wrote, that his son had no gift for agriculture, and since he hoped that the Trottas, indebted as they were to His Majesty the Emperor's continuing favor, might attain new honors and dignities and live more happily than he, the testator, had ever done, he had decided, in memory of his father, to bequeath the estate made over to him by his late lamented father-in-law, together with all its movable and immovable chattels to the administrators of the pensioner's fund at Laxenburg. The sole proviso was that the authorities of this beneficiary should accord the testator a plain headstone in the cemetery where they had buried his late father and, if convenient, in close proximity to his grave. He, the testator, requested a very simple funeral. All residuary moneys, five thousand florins with interest accrued, deposited in the Ephrussi bank in Vienna, as also any unallotted gold, silver, or copper coins found in his house after decease, together with the ring, watch, and chain of his late wife to go to the testator's only son, Baron Franz Trotta von Sipolje.

A Viennese military band, a company of foot soldiers, a representative of the Knights of the Order of Maria Theresa, some officers sent by the South Hungarian regiment whose modest hero he had been, all pensioners able to march, two officials from the Court and Cabinet Chancellory, a staff officer from the Military and Privy Cabinet, and an NCO bearing the Order of Maria Theresa on a black tasseled cushion, formed the official cortège. His son, Franz, walked apart, thin, black, solitary. The band played the same march they had played at his grandfather's funeral. On this occasion the salvos over the grave were louder and their reverberations greater. His son shed no tears. No one wept for the dead man. Everything remained contained and ceremonious. No graveside speeches. In close proximity to the sergeant-major of the gendarmery lay Major Baron Trotta von Sipolje, the champion of truth. They gave him a plain, military headstone on which, in small black letters beneath name, rank, and regiment, was engraved the proud addition, HERO OF SOLFERINO.

Little remained of the dead man but this stone, a faded glory, and the portrait. Thus in spring does a peasant tread the furrow, and later, in summer the traces of his feet are obscured by the fullness of the wheat he has sown. That same week Royal Chief District Commissioner Trotta von Sipolje received a letter of condolence from His Majesty in which two separate mentions were made of the "ever unforgettable services" rendered by the blessed deceased.

Chapter 2

Within the whole divisional radius there was no better military band than the one attached to infantry regiment No. X, in the little Moravian country town of W. Its bandmaster upheld the traditions of that race of Austrian military composers whose precise memories, ever alert to variations of old themes, enabled them to compose a new march every month. These marches were as identical as soldiers. Most began with a roll of drums, contained a tattoo accelerating to march time, and ended with a threatening roll of thunder from the kettle drums —that cheerful, brief storm of military music. What distinguished Bandmaster Nechwal from his colleagues was not so much the extraordinary fertile toughness of his compositions, as the gay and breezy vigor with which he practised his music. The slackness of other bandmasters, who allowed a drum major to conduct the first march, and waited for the second item before deigning to raise the baton, struck Nechwal as an indication of the decadence of the Austrian monarchy. As soon as the band had arranged itself in the prescribed circle and had stuck the elegant feet of the frail music stands into the black streaks of earth between the wide paving stones of the square, the bandmaster stood ready among his musicians, his ebony baton with its silver nob discreetly raised. These open-air concerts all took place beneath the Chief District Commissioner's balcony, and they all began with the Radetzky March. Although the march was so familiar to the members of the band that any one of them could have played it in his sleep without a conductor, their bandmaster nevertheless considered it essential to follow every note of the score. With a burst of musical and military zeal, as though they were trying it out for the first time, he would raise his head, his eye, his baton, and every Sunday direct their full force onto those segments of the circle (he stood in the center) which might need his direction. The bluff

18

drums rolled, the sweet flutes piped, clear cymbals crashed. Pleased and pensive smiles spread over the faces of his audience. Though they stood still, the blood tingling in their legs made them feel that they were marching. The younger girls held their breath, lips parted. The maturer men bent their heads and remembered maneuvers. The elderly ladies sat in the neighboring park with their little gray heads trembling. And it was summer.

Yes, summer. Only at dawn and sundown did the ancient chestnut trees opposite the District Commissioner's house stir their dark-green, ample leaves; the rest of the day they stood motionless, exuding a sharp fragrance, casting their wide, cool shade well out into the middle of the street. The sky never changed its bright blanket of blue. Invisible larks warbled unceasingly above the quiet town. Sometimes a cab jolted a stranger over the cobbles from the station to the hotel. Sometimes the hoofs of the pair which took Herr von Winternigg for a drive clattered lightly along the broad street, north to south, from that landowner's country house to his vast game preserve. Small, old, and shriveled, a yellow gnome with a tiny wizened face, Herr von Winternigg sat in his calash enveloped in an enormous yellow rug. Like a winter waif, he passed through the ripe summer. On high, noiseless, resilient rubber wheels, their brown polished spokes flashing in the sunlight, he rolled straight from his bed to his country riches. Great dark forests and fair-haired, green-clad gamekeepers waited for him. The townspeople raised their hats to him. He did not respond. Immobile, he travelled through a sea of greetings. The black coachman towered stiffly above him, his top hat almost brushing the boughs of the chestnut trees as he tickled the horses' backs with his supple whip. At regular intervals, a resounding crack issued from behind the coachman's firm-set lips like a ringing rifle shot and louder than the clip-clop of the horses' hoofs.

Summer vacation began at about this time. Carl Joseph von Trotta, the fifteen-year-old son of the District Commissioner, pupil of the Cavalry Cadet School in Moravian Weisskirchen, felt his native town to be a summer place: he and the summer resided there at the same time. For Christmas and Easter he stayed with his uncle. He came home only for summers, arriving always on a Sunday, in accordance with the wishes of his father, Baron Franz Trotta von Sipolje. No matter which day they were let out of school, at home the summer vacation had to begin on a Sunday. On Sundays, Herr von Trotta did not work. He could devote the whole morning from nine to twelve to his son.

Punctually, at ten minutes to nine, a quarter of an hour after early mass, the boy, in his Sunday uniform, stood waiting outside his father's door. At five to nine, Jacques came down the stairs in his gray livery, and said, "Your father's on the way, young master." Carl Joseph gave his tunic a last tug, adjusted his belt, took off his cap and set it against his thigh, as etiquette prescribed. His father arrived, the boy clicked his heels, the sound reverberating through the quiet old house. His father opened the door and then with a wave of his hand motioned his son before him into the room. But the boy stayed where he was, not acknowledging the invitation. His father went on ahead, Carl Joseph followed but remained waiting on the threshold. "Make yourself comfortable," the District Commissioner said, after a while. Only then would Carl Joseph approach the big red plush armchair and sit down opposite his father, knees drawn up stiffly, cap and white gloves balanced on them. Narrow rays of sunshine pierced the gaps in the Venetian blinds and fell on the crimson carpet. A fly buzzed, the clock began to strike. When the nine golden chimes had died away, the District Commissioner began.

"And how is Colonel Marek?"

"Very well, thank you, Papa."

"Are you still weak in geometry?"

"Thank you, Papa, a little better."

"Read all the books?"

"Yes, Papa."

"How's the riding? Last year it wasn't up to much . . . ."

"This year—" Carl Joseph began but he was immediately interrupted. His father had stretched out his narrow hand, half hidden by the round glossy cuff. The imposing square gold cuff link glittered.

"I said, 'not up to much.' It was," the District Commissioner paused and then said in an almost expressionless voice, "a disgrace."

Father and son were silent. However softly the word had been intoned, it lingered in the room. Carl Joseph knew that any severe paternal stricture must always be followed by a silence. The full force of censure had to be appreciated, pondered, stamped upon the memory, and imprinted upon heart and mind. The clock ticked, the fly buzzed. Then Carl Joseph began in a clear voice, "This year it was much better. The sergeant-major himself often said so. And first Lieutenant Koppel gave me a special mention."

"Delighted to hear it, I'm sure," observed the District Commissioner in sepulchral tones. He thrust his cuff back into his sleeve against the edge of the table, making a metallic tinkle.

"Go on," he said and lit a cigarette. It was the signal to relax. Carl Joseph put his gloves and cap on a little desk, got up, and began to give an account of all that had happened during the year. The old man nodded. Suddenly he said, "You're growing up. Your voice is beginning to break. Are you in love yet?"

Carl Joseph blushed. His burning face felt like a Chinese lantern, but bravely he turned it to his father.

"Not yet then, eh?" said the District Commissioner. "Go on. You needn't look so uncomfortable."

Carl Joseph gulped, his blush died down, suddenly he felt cold. He gave his news slowly, with many silences. Then he pulled his reading list out of his pocket and handed it to his father. "Quite an impressive list," the District Commissioner said. "Now tell me what *Zrinyi* is all about." Carl Joseph related the play, act by act. Then sat down, pale, tired, his tongue dry.

He stole a glance at the clock: it was only ten-thirty. The examination would go on for another hour and a half. The old man might well put him through classical history, or German mythology. His father paced the room, smoking, his left hand behind his back. The right-hand cuff rattled. The streams of sunlight grew stronger on the carpet, they crept nearer and nearer to the window. The sun must be high now. Church bells began to boom quite close, ringing into the room as if swinging immediately behind the closed blinds. Today the District Commissioner confined himself to literature. He had much to say on the true significance of Grillparzer and recommended Adalbert Stifter and Ferdinand von Saar to his offspring for light summer reading. Then he leapt back to military themes: sentry duty, Army Regulations Part II, the formation of an army corps, the full strength of the various regiments.

Suddenly he asked, "How do you define subordination?"

"Subordination," declaimed Carl Joseph, "is that duty of unconditional obedience which every subordinate owes his superior, and every—"

"Stop," interrupted his father. "Not 'and,' *just as.*"

Carl Joseph continued, "*—just as* every lower rank is duty bound to carry out the orders of a higher when—"

"*As soon as* . . ." corrected the old man.

"*—as soon as* such orders have been received." Carl Joseph drew a deep breath. The clock was striking twelve.

Now his vacation began. Another quarter of an hour and he heard the first noisy roll of drums from the barracks as the band turned out. On Sundays at about midday it played outside the official residence of the District Commissioner, who, here in this little provincial town, represented no less a personage than His Majesty. Carl Joseph, hidden by the thick vine trellis of the balcony, received this military concert like a tribute to himself. He felt in some small measure akin to the Habsburgs, whose power his father represented and was here to uphold, and for whom he himself would someday be ordered to march out to battle, and to death. He knew the names of all the members of the Imperial Royal House. He loved them all with a child's devoted heart. And above all, he loved the Emperor, who was kindly, great, illustrious and just; immeasurably remote, yet very close; and who felt a special affection for all his officers. The finest way to die for the Emperor was to the strains of a military band, and the easiest death of all came to the accompaniment of the Radetzky March. Rhythmically swift bullets hummed about Carl Joseph's ears. His drawn sword flashed as, heart and mind brimful of the gay brisk music, he gave himself up to its throbbing intoxication. His blood seeped out of him in a narrow crimson stream onto the dazzling gold of the trumpets, the deep black of the kettle drums, the victorious silver of the cymbals.

Behind him stood Jacques, clearing his throat. Lunchtime. During intervals in the music, a discreet chink of plates was audible from the dining room. It was separated from the balcony by two large rooms and lay exactly at the centre of the first floor. During lunch the music could be heard distinctly in the distance. How unfortunate it was not every day, for it was good and useful music and surrounded the solemn ceremony of the meal with mitigating gentleness; also, it prevented his father from starting up one of those embarrassingly terse conversations of which he was so fond. You could just listen and enjoy your food. The plates had narrow, fading blue-and-gold edges, Carl Joseph loved them. He often remembered them during the year. They, with the Radetzky March, the portrait of his dead mother (whom the boy did not remember), and the heavy silver ladle and fish tureen, the scalloped fruit knives and the minute coffee cups and the fragile little spoons, thin as thin silver coins—all these meant summer, freedom, home. He handed Jacques his belt, cap and gloves and went into the dining room. The old man entered at the same time and smiled at him. Fräulein Hirschwitz, the housekeeper, arrived a little later in her gray silk Sunday dress, head held high, her hair drawn back and gathered at the nape of the neck in a heavy bun, and wearing a great curved brooch across her bosom, like a kind of scimitar. She looked armed and fortified. Carl Joseph breathed a kiss into her long bony hand. Jacques drew back the chairs. The District Commissioner indicated the seats. Jacques vanished and reappeared presently wearing white gloves which seemed to transform him completely. They cast a snowy radiance over his already pale face, his white hair and side whiskers. Surely they surpassed in brightness all the world's bright things. Wearing these gloves, he held a dark tray. On it sat the steaming soup tureen. He set it down carefully, noiselessly, very deftly in the center of the table. According to long-standing custom, Fräulein Hirschwitz ladled out the soup. They received the plates proffered with arms outstretched and a grateful smile in their eyes. She returned the smiles. A warm effulgence shimmered in the plates: the soup. Noodle soup. Transparent over thin, pale-gold, interlacing noodles. Herr Trotta von Sipolje ate very fast, at times with set determination. It was as though he were disposing of course after course with cunning silence, aristocratic malice: he was simply annihilating them. Fräulein Hirschwitz only toyed with her food at the table, but when lunch was over she had it all served up to her again, from soup to dessert, in her own room. Carl Joseph swallowed timid, hurried hot spoonfuls of soup, big mouthfuls, so that they all finished together. No word was spoken unless Herr von Trotta broke the silence.

After the soup, the garnished roast was served, the old man's

Sabbath fare for countless years. The pleased preliminary scrutiny which he always bestowed upon this dish required more time than half the meal. Herr von Trotta's eye would linger tenderly, first on the garland of tender bacon embellishing this mighty roast, then on each separate little dish in which vegetables reposed: beets glowing dark red, spinach austere and richly green, gay spring-green lettuce, the acrid white of the horseradish, the faultless oval of new potatoes floating in melted butter and reminiscent of charming baubles. His attitude to food was peculiar. He devoured the most delicious morsels, as it were, with his eyes. His aesthetic sense took possession of the very essence of the food. The insipid remains which later found their way into his mouth were flavorless and to be swallowed with the utmost dispatch. The edifying appearance of his food gave the old man as keen a satisfaction as did its character of frugal simplicity. For he insisted on what is known as good, plain food, tribute exacted by his taste as well as by his world view, which he considered Spartan. His fortunate disposition managed, therefore, to combine the satisfaction of his desires with the demands of duty. He was a Spartan— albeit an Austrian one.

Now, as every Sunday, he set about carving the roast. He thrust his cuffs into his sleeves, raised both hands, and, as he set knife and fork to the meat, addressed himself to Fräulein Hirschwitz. "Do you see, dear lady, it is not enough simply to ask the butcher for a tender roast. It is necessary always to pay attention to the way in which it has been cut, whether horizontally or vertically. Nowadays butchers no longer know their own trade. The best meat is ruined simply by clumsy cutting. See here, dear lady. It's falling to pieces, simply crumbling away! As a roast it may no doubt be called tender, but these separate shreds will be tough, as you will see for yourself in a moment. Now, as to what you Germans call the garnishes, another time I should prefer the horseradish a little drier. Its flavour should never be lost in the milk. And it ought always to be prepared shortly before being served. This has been damp for too long. A mistake."

Fräulein Hirschwitz nodded ponderously, slowly. She had lived for many years in Germany and always spoke High German. It offended her predilection for the literary idiom that Herr von Trotta had directed his remark about garnishes. It cost her an obvious effort to loose the weight of her bun from the back of her neck, and so release her head in an indication of acquiescence. Her first eager amiability had in it now a hint of reserve—she seemed, even, to be on the defensive. So that Herr von Trotta found himself constrained to add, "I'm sure, dear lady, that I'm not mistaken."

He spoke the nasal German of higher civil servants and the Austrian upper middle class. It was somewhat reminiscent of the twanging of distant guitars in the night or the last peal of bells dying away: a gentle yet precise idiom, at once tender and malicious, in harmony with the speaker's thin bony face—his narrow aquiline nose a kind of sounding box for its resonant, rather melancholy consonants. Mouth and nose, when the District Commissioner spoke, were wind instruments rather than the features of a face. And, apart from his lips, nothing in his face moved. The black side whiskers—worn by Herr von Trotta as a token uniform, a badge to prove his fealty to the Emperor Francis Joseph, proof of his dynastic convictions—remained motionless when Herr Trotta von Sipolje spoke. He sat upright at the table as if he held reins in his hard hands. Sitting, he looked as if he were standing, and when he rose, straight as a dart, his full height came as a surprise each time. He wore dark blue always, summer and winter, Sundays and weekdays; a dark-blue coat and gray striped trousers, closely fitting his long legs, strapped tightly under polished, elastic-sided boots. He was in the habit of getting up to stretch his legs between the second and third courses. His true purpose, however, seemed to be to demonstrate to those with whom he lived how to rise, stand, and move without relinquishing immobility.

Jacques cleared the roast, catching a swift glance from Fräulein Hirschwitz admonishing him to have the remains warmed up for her. Herr von Trotta walked with measured steps towards the window, drew the curtains aside a little, and returned to the table. At this moment, cherry dumplings were borne in on an ample platter. The District Commissioner took one of them and cut it in half with his spoon and said to Fräulein Hirschwitz, "This, dear lady, is an exemplary cherry dumpling. It is of the correct consistency when cut and yet it immediately melts in your mouth." And turning to Carl Joseph, "I recommend you to take two." Carl Joseph took two. He devoured them swiftly, finishing the second before his father, and washed them down with a glass of water—wine was served only at dinner—sluicing them out of his gullet in which they might still be stuck, down into his belly. He folded his napkin with the same gestures as the old man.

They rose. The band outside was playing the overture to Tannhäuser. To its sonorous beat they followed Fräulein Hirschwitz into the study. There, Jacques brought them their coffee. Bandmaster Nechwal was expected. While down below the band re-formed to march back to barracks he entered in his dark-blue full-dress uniform with glittering sword and two sparkling gold harps on his collar.

"I'm delighted with your concert," said Herr von Trotta, today as on every Sunday. "It was quite outstanding today."

Herr Nechwal bowed. He had had his lunch an hour before in the officers' mess, but had had no time to wait for the black coffee. The flavour of the food was still on his palate and he longed for a black cheroot. Jacques brought him a bundle of cigars. The bandmaster took a lingering puff from the match which Carl Joseph held steadily to the end of the long black cigar, risking burnt fingers in the act. They settled down in comfortable leather chairs. Nechwal told them about the latest Lehar operetta in Vienna. The bandmaster was a man of the world. He went to Vienna twice a month, and Carl Joseph felt that hidden in the depths of Herr Nechwal's soul lurked many secrets of the great nocturnal underworld. He had three children and a wife "from an unpretentious background," though he himself stood in the brightest radiance of society, quite separate from his family. He told and enjoyed Jewish jokes with artful relish. The District Commissioner did not understand them, nor did he laugh at them, but said,

"Splendid! Very good indeed. . . . And how is your wife?"

It was his regular question; for years he had asked it. He had never seen Frau Nechwal nor did he ever wish to meet the lady of unpretentious background, but as Nechwal took his leave he would say, "Do please remember me to your wife. I've never met her, you know," and Herr Nechwal would promise to bear this greeting, with assurances that his wife "would be delighted."

"And how are the children?" asked Herr von Trotta, who always forgot whether they were boys or girls.

"The eldest boy is getting on well," said the bandmaster.

26

"And will he be a musician, too?" Herr von Trotta asked, with a certain nuance of condescension.

"Oh, no," said Nechwal, "next year I'm sending him to the cadet school."

"Oh, an officer? Splendid!" said the Commissioner. "The infantry . . ."

"Of course." Herr Nechwal smiled. "He's a clever boy, so perhaps he'll end up on the staff."

"To be sure, to be sure," said the District Commissioner. "It's been known to happen."

A week later, he had forgotten everything again. One didn't need to remember the bandmaster's children.

Herr Nechwal drank two small cups of coffee, no more, no less. With regret, he extinguished the last third of his cheroot. He had to go. It would not be proper to leave with a lighted cigar.

"It was quite outstandingly good today. Do please give my kind regards to your wife, whom I've never had the pleasure of meeting," said Herr von Trotta.

Carl Joseph clicked his heels. He ushered the bandmaster to the first flight of steps. Then he came back to the study, presented himself to his father and said, "I'm going for a walk, Papa."

"That's right, you have a good walk," said Herr von Trotta and waved his hand.

Carl Joseph went out. He intended to take a stroll, felt like ambling along to prove to his feet that he was on vacation, but he shaped up, as they say in the army, when he saw his first soldier. He began to march. He reached the outskirts of the town, the large, yellow Treasury building, basking comfortably in the sun. A sweet scent from the fields blew in his face and he heard the throbbing song of larks. To the west, the blue horizon ended in bluish-gray hills; the first peasant huts, thatched or covered with shingle, appeared. Winged throats beat on the summer stillness like fanfares. The land was asleep, lulled by the clear day.

Beyond the railway embankment stood a gendarmery post, with a sergeant-major in charge. Carl Joseph knew him, Sergeant-Major Slama. He decided to knock at the door. He stepped onto the veranda, knocked, rang the bell, but nobody came. A window was opened; Frau Slama bent out over her geraniums and called, "Who is it?" She saw it was little Trotta and said, "Coming!" She opened the hall door. Inside it smelled cool and faintly scented. Frau Slama had dabbed a drop of perfume onto her dress.

Carl Joseph thought of the Viennese night spots. He said, "Is the Sergeant-Major out?"

"On duty, Herr von Trotta," answered the woman. "But please come in."

Now Carl Joseph sat in the Slamas' best parlor. It was a low-ceilinged, red-tinted room, and was very cool. The high backs of the upholstered armchairs were brown-stained wood carved into leafy garlands which hurt to lean against. Frau Slama fetched cool lemonade and sipped it daintily, cocking her little finger, one leg thrown across the other. She sat beside Carl Joseph, turning towards him, beating the air with her foot, which was thrust into a small red-velvet slipper, bare, un-stockinged. Carl Joseph eyed the foot, then the lemonade. He would not look Frau Slama in the face. His cap lay on his knees, and he kept them stiff, sitting bolt upright beside the lemonade, as though it were his duty as an officer to drink it.

"What an age since we've seen you, Herr von Trotta," the Sergeant-Major's wife was saying. "You've grown quite big. Are you over fourteen?"

"Oh yes, well over."

He thought he'd get away as soon as he could. He would finish the lemonade in one gulp, bow politely, leave messages for her husband, and go. He stared helplessly at the lemonade; it seemed impossible to finish. Frau Slama filled it up again. She brought cigarettes; he was not allowed to smoke. She lit one for herself and exhaled the smoke, carelessly, with distended nostrils, beating the air with her foot. Suddenly, without a word, she snatched the cap from his knees, and put it on a table. She thrust her cigarette between his lips, her hand smelled of smoke and eau de cologne. The light sleeve of her flowery summer dress shimmered across his eyes. Politely he puffed the cigarette, wet from her lips, and eyed the lemonade. Frau Slama took back her cigarette, held it between her teeth and stood behind Carl Joseph. He was afraid to turn round. Both her bright sleeves were suddenly round his neck, her face heavy on his hair. He did not stir. But his heart thumped, a great storm beat up inside him, contained and cramped by his petrified body, the tight buttons of his tunic. "Come," Frau Slama whispered. She sat on his knee, kissed him quickly and looked at him roguishly. A bunch of her fair hair had somehow come loose over her forehead and she squinted up at it, trying to blow it back with pouting lips. He began to feel her weight on his legs, though at the same time he was suffused with new strength which tightened the muscles of thigh and arm. He clasped her, felt the cool softness of her breasts against the stiff cloth of his uniform. A gentle chuckle rose in her throat, a little like a sob, a little like a bird warbling. Tears stood in her eyes. Then she leaned back and with tender precision began to undo his tunic, button by button. She laid a cool, soft hand on his chest; she kissed his mouth with prolonged, systematic pleasure, and suddenly rose, as though a noise had startled her. He sprang up at once; she smiled, and drew him gently after her, with outstretched hands, walking backward, her head flung back, her eyes shining, to the door which she kicked open with her foot. They glided into the bedroom.

Through half-closed lids, like a powerless captive, he saw her undress him slowly, methodically, maternally. With some horror he noticed how, piece by piece, his Sunday uniform fell limply onto the floor, heard the dull thud of his shoes, and then, at once, felt Frau Slama's hand on his foot. Waves of warmth and coolness from below welled up in him and reached his chest. He let himself go limp and received the woman like a wave of bliss, of fire and of water.

He came to. Frau Slama stood over him handing him back his clothes, piece by piece. Hurriedly he began to dress. She ran into the parlor and brought back his gloves and cap. She straightened his tunic, he felt her steady gaze on his face but avoided looking at her. He clicked his heels resoundingly, pressed her hand, stubbornly gazing at her right shoulder, and left.

A tower clock struck seven. The sun approached the hills, blue now as the sky and scarcely distinguishable from the clouds. A sweet fragrance emanated from the trees by the wayside. An evening breeze combed through the grass at the edge of the meadow on either side of the road and it billowed and trembled beneath its soft invisible wide hand. Frogs began to croak in distant marshes. A young woman stared into the empty street from the open windows of a bright yellow house at the town's edge. Although Carl Joseph had never seen her before he bowed to her, stiffly and full of reverence. She nodded back a little shy, but grateful. He felt that only now had he taken leave of Frau Slama. Like a frontier post between love and life, the friendly unknown woman stood at the window. After he had greeted her, he felt himself restored to the world. He stepped out briskly and was home on the stroke of a quarter to eight, and announced his return to his father, pale, curt, decisive, as becomes a man.

The Sergeant-Major was on patrol duty every other day. He visited the District Commissioner's office daily with a bundle of documents. He never ran into the District Commissioner's son. Every other day, at four o'clock in the afternoon, Carl Joseph went marching to the gendarmery post. At seven o'clock in the evening he would take his leave. The scent he brought back with him from Frau Slama mingled with the scents of the dry summer evenings, clinging to his hands, day and night. At meals he was careful never to get nearer the District Commissioner than necessary.

"It smells of autumn here," the old man said to him one evening. It was a generalization. Frau Slama always used mignonette.

Chapter 3

The portrait hung in the District Commissioner's study facing the window, so high up that hair and forehead were almost obscured in the brown shadows under the old wooden ceiling. This fading shape and his grandfather's vanished fame filled the grandson with constant curiosity. Sometimes on quiet afternoons, the windows open, the dappled green shadow of chestnut trees from the park filling the room with the heady peace of summer afternoons when the District Commissioner was out of town on government business and old Jacques shuffled down distant stairs like a ghost in felt slippers collecting clothes to brush, boots to polish, ashtrays, silver candlesticks, and standard lamps—on such afternoons Carl Joseph would stand up on a chair to get a closer view of his grandfather's portrait. It disintegrated into deep shadows and bright highlights, into brush strokes and dots, the contours lost behind an intricate web of painted canvas, a hard iridescence of cracking oil paint. Carl Joseph climbed down from his chair. The reflections of leaves spotted his grandfather's brown coat. Brush strokes and dots rearranged themselves into the familiar yet unfathomable face. The eyes resumed their customary distant gaze, staring into the shadows of the ceiling. Every summer the grandson communed mutely with his grandfather. But the dead man revealed nothing. And the boy learned nothing. From year to year the portrait appeared to grow dimmer and more remote, as if the hero of Solferino were dying over again, slowly drawing his memory back into himself, as if the day must come when an empty canvas would stare down on his descendants from its black frame.

Below, in the yard, under the shade of the wooden balcony, Jacques was sitting on a stool in front of a military row of polished boots. Always when Carl Joseph got back from

Frau Slama, he would go to Jacques and perch on a ledge. "Jacques, tell me about Grandfather." Jacques would lay aside brushes and blacking as though to cleanse his mind of work and dirt before speaking of the dead man. And he would start off as he had on at least twenty previous occasions.

"I always got on well with him. I wasn't a young man when I first got a job at the castle. I never married. He wouldn't have liked that. He didn't like women about the place, except of course his own wife, but she died early, her lungs it was. We all knew he'd saved the Emperor's life at Solferino, but he never said a word about it, not a murmur. But that's why they put HERO OF SOLFERINO on his gravestone. He wasn't so very old when he died. About nine o'clock in the evening, must have been November. It had just begun to snow and that same afternoon he'd been out in the yard and said to me, 'Jacques, what have you done with my fur-lined boots?' I didn't know what I'd done with them, so I said, 'I'll fetch them at once, Herr Baron.' 'They'll do in the morning,' he said—and in the morning he didn't need them any more. No, I never got married."

That was all.

This was the last of the vacations; next year Carl Joseph expected his new rank would be made official. The District Commissioner said, on his last day, "I hope you'll get through without a hitch. You're the grandson of the hero of Solferino. Remember that, and you're bound to be all right."

The teaching staff remembered it, too, and the colonel, and even the NCOs, so that in fact Carl Joseph was "bound to be all right." Although not a very good horseman, weak in topography, and quite hopeless in trigonometry, he got through with a decent pass, was given his lieutenant's commission and assigned to the -th Uhlans.

Thus, one summer's day, Carl Joseph came before his father dazed by his own new splendor and by the graduation Mass, his ears ringing still with the thunderous farewells of his colonel. He was wearing an azure tunic with gold buttons, the little silver bandolier with its august gold eagles at the back, his shako with the metal chinstrap, a horsehair-plume in his left hand. He felt resplendent in flaming-scarlet riding breeches, highly polished boots, clanking spurs, the wide-hilted sword at his hip. This time it was not a Sunday. A lieutenant might arrive on a Wednesday. The District Commissioner sat in his study.

"Make yourself comfortable," he said, took off his pince-nez, screwed up his eyes, and inspected his son. He found everything in order. Then he embraced Carl Joseph. They kissed lightly on the cheek. "Sit down," said the District Commissioner, pressing the Lieutenant into a chair. He himself began to pace the room. He was thinking out a suitable opening. This time there seemed nothing to censure, and yet he could not bring himself to begin on a note of praise. "Well," he observed at last, "now you should read up on the history of your regiment and perhaps you might also look through the history of the regiment in which your grandfather fought. I have to go to Vienna on business for a couple of days. You can come with me."

He swung the bell on his table. Jacques came.

"Fräulein Hirschwitz," ordered the District Commissioner, "can arrange for some wine to be brought up, and, if possible, we might have a roast for luncheon, and cherry dumplings. We'll eat twenty minutes later than usual today."

"Very well, Herr Baron," said Jacques. He gazed at Carl Joseph and whispered, "Congratulations."

The District Commissioner went to look out of the window. The scene threatened to become emotional. He was aware of his son and servant shaking hands behind his back, Jacques was scraping his feet and muttering something unintelligible about the dead master. He did not turn round again until the servant had left the room.

"It's hot, isn't it," began the old man.

"Yes, Papa."

"Hadn't we better get some fresh air?"

"Certainly, Papa."

The District Commissioner selected his black ebony stick with the silver handle, not the yellow cane he usually liked to carry on fine afternoons. Nor did he dangle his gloves in his left hand, but put both of them on. He adjusted his silk hat and left the room, followed by the boy. Slowly, without exchanging a word, they walked in the summer peace of the municipal gardens. The policeman saluted them, men got up from their benches and bowed. Against the old man's drab sobriety, the jingling brightness of the young man seemed

33

even more splendid and noisy. In the avenue, beneath a red umbrella, an ash-blond girl sat serving raspberry soda. The old man stopped and said, "We could do with a cool drink." He ordered two plain sodas and watched the blond young lady with surreptitious dignity as she stared, passively enraptured, at Carl Joseph's colorful radiance. They drank and went on. From time to time the District Commissioner waved his stick a little, an indication of serene exhilaration. Although he was silent and serious as usual, to his son he seemed almost flippant. From his joyful breast issued occasional pleased little grunts, a kind of laughter. When saluted, he raised his hat in brief acknowledgment. There were bold moments when he became downright paradoxical, as when, for instance, he observed, "Politeness can become a little boring." Far better to indulge in such verbal excesses than to let his delight in the dazzled admiration of passers-by become apparent. As they approached their own front door again, he stopped, turned to his son, and said, "When I was young I wanted to be a soldier, but your grandfather expressly forbade it. Now I'm very glad indeed you aren't a civil servant."

"Yes, Papa," replied Carl Joseph.

There was wine. The roast and cherry dumplings had also been provided. Fräulein Hirschwitz entered in her gray Sunday silk and, on seeing Carl Joseph, relinquished the greater part of her severity.

"I'm so glad," she said, "and I wish you well with all my heart."

" 'Wish you well' is what we should call 'congratulate,' " remarked the District Commissioner. And they began to eat.

"No need to hurry," said the old man. "If I finish before you, I shall wait a moment."

Carl Joseph looked up. He realized that for all these years his father must have known how hard it was to eat at his pace. He felt that for the first time he had managed to penetrate the old man's armor, to see into the living heart, the secret web of his thoughts.

"Thank you, Papa," he said. The District Commissioner munched on quickly. He seemed not to hear.

Two days later they boarded the train for Vienna. The boy was reading a newspaper, the old man documents. Once the District Commissioner looked up and said, "We shall have to order you a pair of full-dress breeches in Vienna. You've got only two pairs."

"Thank you, Papa." They continued to read.

They were still fifteen minutes from Vienna when his father put away the documents. At once his son folded up his newspaper. The District Commissioner looked at the windowpane; then, for a few seconds, at his son. Suddenly he said, "You know Sergeant-Major Slama?"

The name beat on Carl Joseph's memory, an echo of a time past. At once he saw the road to the gendarmery post, the low room, the flowered wrap, the roomy, well-upholstered bed; his nostrils caught the scent of meadows and with it Frau Slama's mignonette. He paid attention.

"He lost his wife, poor fellow, this year," the old man continued. "It's very sad. She died in childbirth. You ought to call on him."

Suddenly it was unbearably hot in the carriage. Carl Joseph tried to loosen his collar. While in vain he strove for appropriate words, there arose in him the foolish, scalding, childish desire to burst into tears. It choked him, parched his throat as if he had gone without drink for days. He felt his father's scrutiny, stared strenuously at the landscape, grew conscious of their approaching destination as an intensification of his agony. He longed at least to be in the corridor, yet realized at the same time that he could not escape the old man's eye, or what he had to tell him. He used the last ebbing dregs of his fortitude to pull himself together for the time being and said, "I'll go to see him."

"You don't seem able to stand long railway journeys," observed his father.

"No, Papa."

Stiff and mute, assailed by an agony which he could not name, which he had never known and which felt like a mysterious disease from distant latitudes, Carl Joseph drove to the hotel. He could just manage to say, "Excuse me, Papa." He locked his door, undid his suitcase, drew out the blotter which contained a few letters from Frau Slama, in their envelopes, just as they had reached him, with the code address "Poste restante, Moravian Weisskirchen."

These sheets of paper were blue and they smelled of mignonette; fine black letters skimmed across the pages like

35

a slim and ordered flight of swallows. Letters of the late Frau Slama. To Carl Joseph they seemed heralds of her sudden death; they were informed with all the fragile grace which only dying hands can give to life—anticipatory greetings from the tomb. He had not answered her last letter. His examination, the speeches, leave takings, the ceremonial Mass, his commission, rank, and new uniform lost all significance beside this thin dark flight of letters on a blue background. He could still feel traces of the dead woman's caressing hands on his skin; within his own warm hands there was still the memory of her cool breasts; with closed eyes he could see the blessed weariness on her face fulfilled with love—her red lips parted, the white gleam of her teeth, her arm carelessly curved, and along every line of her body the flowing glory of desireless dreams and happy sleep. Now worms were crawling over her breasts and thighs and her face was rotting away. And the stronger these hateful visions of decay grew before the young man's eyes, the more they inflamed his passion. It seemed to reach far out to the incomprehensible infinity of those regions into which the dead woman had vanished. I should probably never have gone back to see her, thought the Lieutenant. I should have forgotten her. She was gentle with me, like a mother. She loved me and now she is dead. Clearly, her death was his fault. She lay, a beloved corpse, across the threshold of his life.

This was Carl Joseph's first encounter with death. He did not remember his mother. Nothing was left of her but her grave, her flowerbed, and two photographs. But now death touched him like black lightning, striking his harmless pleasure, singeing his youth, striking him down to the verge of that steep cleft which parts the living from the dead, so that a long life of mourning stretched before him. He braced himself to suffer it, resolute, pale, and manly. He put away her letters. He locked his suitcase. He went out into the passage, knocked at his father's door, entered, and heard the old man saying as through a thick glass wall, "You seem to be softhearted."

The District Commissioner was patting down his tie in front of the mirror. He had business at the municipal head office, the offices of the Chief of Police and Court of Appeal.

"You're coming with me," he said.

They drove in a two-horse cab on rubber tyres. The streets seemed more festive than ever to Carl Joseph. The ample, summery afternoon enveloped houses and trees, pedestrians and policemen, trolleys and benches, monuments and gardens. The smart clip-clop of hoofs rang out on the pavements. Young women glided past like soft lights. Soldiers saluted. Shop windows glittered. Summer drifted gently through the capital.

But all the beauties of summer passed unnoticed before Carl Joseph's listless eyes. His father's words hammered against his ears. The old man took note of a hundred changes: tobacco stalls which had moved, new kiosks, extended bus routes, changed trolley stops. Much had been different in his day. He fastened his precise recollections on all that had disappeared, on all that was still the same; with unaccustomed tenderness, his voice salvaged the minuscule treasures of buried days, his thin hand pointed in greeting to the places where once his youth had flowered. Carl Joseph was silent. He too had just lost his youth. His love was dead, but his heart was open to his father's melancholy. He began to suspect that beneath the District Commissioner's bony hardness, there dwelt another man, more secretive, yet more familiar, a Trotta, the descendant of a Slavonic pensioner and of the strange hero of Solferino. The more animated the old man's exclamations and comparisons grew, the more infrequently and softly came his son's obedient endorsements; the dutiful, wooden "Yes, Papas", which his tongue had practiced since early boyhood, began to take on a different sound—confidential, brotherly. His father seemed to be growing younger, the son older. They drew up at several government buildings, where the District Commissioner inquired after former colleagues, companions of his youth. Brandl was now the head of a police section, Smekal the chief of a department, Monteschitzky a colonel, and Hasselbrunner a Counselor of Legation. They went shopping, ordered dancing shoes at Reitmeyer's, glacé kid for court balls and audiences, a pair of full-dress breeches from Ettlinger, the court military tailor—and then the impossible occurred. The District Commissioner went into Schafransky's, the court jeweler, and chose a solid silver cigarette case, fluted down one side, an *objet de luxe*, on which he ordered the words IN PERICULO SECURITAS, YOUR FATHER to be engraved.

They found themselves at the Volksgarten and had some coffee. The round tables on the terrace shone white amid the deep-green shade. Blue-tinted syphons stood on the table-cloths. When the band ceased, they heard the jubilation of birds. The District Commissioner glanced upward and, as if culling memories from above, began: "Here in the Volksgarten I once got to know a little girl. Let me see, how long ago was that?" He immersed himself in silent calculations. Long, long years seemed to have slipped past since then. Carl Joseph felt as if a distant ancestor, not his father, were sitting next to him. "Her name was Mizzi Schinagl," continued the old man. As if she had been a little bird, he sought for the image of Fräulein Schinagl in the thick chestnut blooms.

"Is she still alive?" Carl Joseph asked out of politeness and as if to establish a criterion for the appraisement of a bygone age.

"I hope so. In my time, you know, we weren't sentimental. One took one's leave of a girl, of friends—" He interrupted himself suddenly. A stranger had come up to their table, a man in a wide slouch hat and flowing tie, in a very shabby gray morning coat with crumpled tails. Long thick hair curled over his collar, his broad, sallow face imperfectly shaved— obviously a painter. So *outré* and unmistakably the conventional artist type, he looked unreal, as though a cut out of some archaic illustration. The stranger had set his portfolio on the table and was about to offer sketches for sale with a haughty indifference which neither his gifts nor his poverty justified.

"Why, Moser!" said Herr von Trotta.

Slowly the painter raised his heavy eyelids, his large, bright eyes stared for a few seconds at the District Commissioner before he held out his hand and answered, "Trotta."

In the next instant he had shed both embarrassment and gentleness, clapped his portfolio together so that the glasses trembled, bawled three "*Donnerwetter*'s" so thunderously that he might have been evoking real thunderclaps, shot a triumphant glance at surrounding tables as if expecting their occupants to applaud, sat down, took off his hat, and flung it on the gravel beside his chair. He swept his drawings off the table with his elbow, dismissing them as rubbish, thrust his head toward the Lieutenant, frowned, leaned back, and inquired, "Is this your son, Governor?"

"My old friend, Professor Moser," the District Commissioner explained.

"*Donnerwetter*, Governor," Moser repeated. At the same time he clutched at the waiter's coat-tails, stood up, and whispered an order as if it were a secret, sat down again, but said nothing further, his eyes turned towards the waiters bringing the drink. At last a tumbler half full of *slivovitz*, clear as water, was set before him, which he passed to and fro several times under distended nostrils before putting it to his lips with a mighty gesture, as though it were a heavy goblet which he had to empty in one swallow. In the end he sipped a little, collecting the last stray drops from off his lips with the tip of his tongue.

"Here a fortnight, and you've not been to see me?" he asked with the sternness of a superior.

"My dear Moser," said Herr von Trotta, "we arrived today and leave again tomorrow."

The painter stared intently at the District Commissioner's face. He raised his glass for the second time and finished his drink with a gulp, like water. In trying to set it down, he missed the saucer and allowed Carl Joseph to take it from him. "Thank you," said the painter and pointed his finger at the Lieutenant. "Amazing, his likeness to the hero of Solferino! Only rather softer looking. A weak nose, drooping mouth. May change in time."

"Professor Moser painted your grandfather's portrait," remarked old Trotta. Carl Joseph looked at his father and at the painter and in his memory resurrected his grandfather's likeness, lost in the shadows under the study ceiling. He could not grasp the connection between his grandfather and this painter: it seemed impossible. His father's familiarity with Moser startled him, as he watched the stranger's broad, unwashed hand descend in a friendly pat on his father's gray striped trousers, and saw the District Commissioner withdraw his thigh in mild protest. The old man sat dignified as always, leaning back to avoid the alcohol-laden breath directed point-blank at his face and chest, yet smiling, accepting everything.

"You ought to get yourself smartened up," the painter was telling him. "You've let yourself run to seed. Your father used to look very different."

The District Commissioner stroked his side whiskers and smiled.

"Yes," the painter began again. "Old Trotta."

"My bill, please," said the District Commissioner quietly. "You'll excuse us, Moser, we have an appointment."

The painter did not get up; father and son left the Volksgarten. The District Commissioner tucked his arm under his son's. For the first time Carl Joseph felt his father's bony arm against his chest. The paternal hand, in dark-gray kid, rested confidingly, almost nestled against the blue sleeve of his tunic—the same hand which, scraggy and admonishing, cased round in stiff white linen, could warn and reprove, rustle papers with deft lean fingers, grimly jerk drawers back into their sockets, wrench the keys out so decisively that one felt they had been locked for all time. This was the hand which drummed with ominous impatience on a table edge if things were not to its owner's liking, on windowpanes when any awkwardness had arisen in the room. This hand could raise a skinny forefinger if anything had been left undone in the house, clench itself into a blind but never belligerent fist, pensively rest against the forehead, carefully lift a pince-nez off the nose, curve itself daintily round a wineglass, carry a black cheroot caressingly to the mouth. It was his father's left hand, so long familiar to his son. And yet only now did he perceive in it the hand of a father—a fatherly hand. Carl Joseph felt an impulse to squeeze this hand against his chest.

"You see," began the District Commissioner, "Moser . . .," he paused, searching for a fitting description, and said at last, "might have made something of himself."

"Yes, Papa."

"He was only sixteen when he painted your grandfather's portrait. We were both sixteen. He was my only friend in the class. He went on to the academy schools. Drink finished him. But all the same, he's . . ." The District Commissioner paused again and said after a few minutes, "Of all the men I've been seeing today, he remains my friend, no matter how . . ."

"Yes—Father."

It was the first time Carl Joseph used the term "Father." But he corrected himself at once. "Yes, Papa."

It was getting dark. Shadows gathered fast in the street.

"Are you cold, Papa?"

"Not at all." But the District Commissioner hastened his steps. Soon they were near their hotel.

40

"Governor!" The sound rang out behind them. The painter had obviously been pursuing them. They turned. He stood there humbly, hat in hand and head bent, as if to give the lie to his sarcastic exclamation. "Forgive me, gentlemen," he said, "but after you'd gone, I found I'd run out of cigarettes." He held out an empty tin case. The District Commissioner pulled out his cigar case. "I never smoke cigars," said Herr Moser.

Carl Joseph offered him a packet of cigarettes. With much ado, the painter set down his portfolio on the pavement at his feet, replenished his case, asked for a light, curved his hands around the tiny blue flame. His hands were red and clammy, too big for the wrists. They trembled a little, suggesting useless implements. His nails were like small black spades with which he had been grubbing in earth and dung, colored pulp, and tobacco juice. "So we won't be seeing each other again," he said, and bent to pick up his portfolio. He straightened his back, large tears were rolling down his cheeks. "Never again," he sobbed.

"I must go upstairs for a minute," said Carl Joseph, and went into the hotel. He ran up the stairs to his room and leaned out of the window, anxiously watching his father; he saw the old man pull out his wallet and then, two seconds later, the painter, with rejuvenated strength, slap down his loathsome hand on the District Commissioner's shoulder. He heard Moser call out, "Well, Franz, on the third, as usual."

Carl Joseph hurried downstairs again, feeling that somehow he ought to be protecting his father; the painter bowed, stepped back, and went off with a farewell wave, his head held high, with the confidence of a sleepwalker, across the trolley tracks, straight to the opposite pavement. There he turned and waved a last good-by before he vanished down a side street. But an instant later he was back again, bellowing, "Just a second," so loud that it resounded through the quiet street. He recrossed the tracks in wide bounds, incredibly sure-footed, until he stood again in front of the hotel as unconstrainedly as though he had only just met them, not taken his leave a moment before. He spoke in the melancholy accents of one who, after many long years, meets an old friend with his adult son.

"Sad to run across you like this. Can you remember how

41

we used to sit next to each other on the third bench? You were bad at Greek and I always let you crib. Come now, be honest and admit it in front of your boy. Didn't I always let you copy?" And to Carl Joseph, "He was a good chap, but always woolgathering. He didn't go after the girls, either, till very late. He'd never have managed it if I hadn't encouraged him. Be honest, Trotta. Tell him that it was me who took you!"

The District Commissioner smiled and was silent. Moser seemed to be preparing a long discourse. He set down his portfolio on the pavement, took off his hat, put one foot in front of the other and began.

"Remember that time during the summer vacation when I got to know your old man?" He stopped short, and with flurried hands felt all his pockets. Large beads of perspiration stood on his forehead. "I've lost it," he shouted. He swayed and trembled. "I've lost the money."

The hall porter emerged from the hotel. He bowed to the District Commissioner and Lieutenant with a vigorous sweep of his gold-braided cap, but his face was disapproving. It looked as if at any moment he might ask Moser to move on and desist from creating a disturbance in front of the hotel. Old Trotta put his hand in his breast pocket. The painter fell silent.

"Carl, could you lend me something?" his father asked.

The Lieutenant answered, "Let me go a bit of the way with Herr Moser. *Au revoir*, Papa."

The District Commissioner raised his silk hat and went into the hotel. Carl Joseph gave the painter a banknote and followed his father. Moser picked up his drawings and retreated with calculated dignity.

It was almost dark in the streets, the hotel foyer was also in darkness. The District Commissioner sat in a leather armchair, his stick and silk hat laid beside him; he was holding his bedroom key and had merged into the dusk. His son remained at a respectful distance, as if he had come to report officially that the Moser affair was disposed of. The lamps were not yet lighted. The old man's voice issued out of the twilight silence.

"We shall be leaving tomorrow at two-fifteen."

"Yes, Papa."

"That band in the gardens reminded me that you will have

42

to call on Bandmaster Nechwal. After you've been to see Slama, of course. Have you anything else you want to do in Vienna?"

"The breeches must be sent for and the cigarette case."

"Anything else?"

"Nothing, Papa."

"Well, tomorrow morning you'd better go and see your uncle. You seem to have forgotten him. How often were you his guest?"

"Twice a year, Papa."

"You see. Give him my kindest regards. And make my apologies. How is he by the way, old Stransky?"

"He looked very well last time I saw him."

The District Commissioner felt for his stick. He rested his outstretched hand on its silver handle as he did when he was standing; even sitting, it behooved one to maintain a certain *tenu* as soon as Uncle Stransky's name was mentioned.

"It must be nineteen years since I saw him. He was still first lieutenant in those days. Already in love with this Koppelmann woman. Irrevocably. A most disastrous business. Head over heels in love with a Koppelmann." He stressed the name, pronouncing each syllable separately. "Naturally, they could never manage to scrape up the requisite dowry. Your mother almost persuaded me to lend them half of it."

"Did he leave the service?"

"He did indeed. And then he got this job on the Northern Railway. What's his rank now? Still some sort of minor official, isn't he?"

"I think so, Papa."

"Well, there you are. Didn't he make a chemist of his son?"

"No, Papa. Alexander is still at school."

"Oh, indeed. I hear he limps."

"One leg is a bit shorter than the other."

"Of course," the old man concluded with satisfaction, as if he had foreseen nineteen years ago that Alexander would be sure to limp.

He rose. The lamps in the hall flared up, lighting his pallor. "I'm going up to get some money," he said. He approached the staircase.

"Let me go, Papa," said Carl Joseph.

"Thank you," said the District Commissioner.

43

"I advise you," he said a little later, as they sat over their pudding, "to have a look at these new Bacchus Rooms. They're supposed to be the latest thing. You may run into Smekal there."

"Thank you, Papa! Good night."

Between eleven and twelve next morning, Carl Joseph called on his Uncle Stransky. He was still in his office; his wife, née Koppelmann, sent her very best love to the District Commissioner. Carl Joseph walked slowly back via the Ring Corso to the hotel. He turned off into the Tuchlauben and asked them to deliver his new breeches, and went to pick up his cigarette case. The case was cool against his skin as it lay in the breast pocket of his thin tunic. He thought of the condolence call he would have to pay Sergeant-Major Slama and made up his mind not to enter that room on any account. "I'm so dreadfully sorry, Herr Slama," he would say, outside on the veranda. Invisible larks warble in the blue sky. The rasping stridulation of grasshoppers is audible. He can smell the hay and the late scent of acacias, the bursting buds in the little garden of the gendarmery post. Frau Slama is dead; Kathi. Katherina Luise on her birth certificate. She is dead.

For the first time Carl Joseph saw the District Commissioner's head laid supine, its thin bony nose with dilated nostrils, the dimpled cleft in the powdered smooth-shaven chin, the side whiskers brushed neatly back into wide symmetrical pinions. Already their outer edges were flecked with gray, age had just touched them and streaked the temples. One day he'll die, Carl Joseph thought, die and be buried and I shall be left.

They had the carriage to themselves. His father's slumbering face rocked peacefully in the reddish glow of the upholstery. His tight lips under the black mustache formed a single line; his Adam's apple protruded from his thin neck, between the shiny corners of his stand-up collar; his bluish, wrinkled eyelids trembled gently and incessantly; his broad, wine-colored tie rose and fell evenly; his arms lay crossed on his chest, his hands buried in his armpits. A great stillness emanated from his sleeping father. Quieted and appeased, his severity, too, was slumbering, embedded in the deep, straight furrow between nose and forehead, as a storm sleeps in a rugged valley between hills. Carl Joseph knew the furrow, knew it intimately. His grandfather's face on the study canvas displayed it, too, this same furrow, the wrathful insignia of the Trottas, the heritage of the hero of Solferino.

His father opened his eyes. "How much longer?"

"Two hours, Papa."

It began to rain. It was a Wednesday. On Thursday afternoon he would have to visit Slama. It was still raining on Thursday. A quarter of an hour after lunch, before they had finished their coffee in the study, Carl Joseph said, "I'm going to see the Slamas now, Papa."

"Unfortunately, there is only one," said the District Commissioner. "You're most likely to find him in at four o'clock." At that moment, two clear chimes could be heard from the clock tower. The District Commissioner, raising his forefinger, pointed in the direction of the sound. Carl Joseph blushed. It seemed that his father, the rain, clocks, people, time, nature herself were all conspiring to make his path still thornier. On those other afternoons, when he had been able to visit the living Frau Slama, he had sat here straining his ears for the blessed chimes, impatient as he was today, only concerned *not* to run into the Sergeant-Major. Those afternoons seemed obscured by many decades. Death overshadowed and concealed them, death stood between this day and that and thrust its entire timeless obscurity between past and present. Yet the chimes striking the hours had not changed, and, now as then, they were sitting in the study over their coffee.

"It's raining," his father said, as if he had only just noticed it, "so perhaps you had better take a cab."

"I like walking in the rain, Papa." He would like to have said, "I want the walk to take a long, long time. Perhaps I ought to have taken cabs in the days when she was still alive."

There was silence, the rain drummed on the windowpanes. The District Commissioner rose. "I must go across," he said, meaning to the office. "I'll see you presently." He closed the door more gently than usual. It seemed to Carl Joseph that his father stopped a moment outside to listen.

The quarter hour struck from the bell tower, then the half. Two-thirty. Another hour and a half to wait. He went out

45

into the hall, took down his coat, spent a long time adjusting the two folds down the back, tugged his sword hilt through the slit in the pocket, put on his cap mechanically in front of the mirror, and left the house.

Chapter 4

He went the usual way past the open railway crossing, along by the yellow, somnolent revenue building. From this point on the isolated gendarmery post was visible. He went on. Ten minutes off, beyond, lay the small graveyard within wooden palings. He sensed that the rain fell more closely here to veil the dead. The Lieutenant touched the wet iron handle and went in. An unrecognized bird fluted desolately. Where was it hiding: did its song rise from a grave? He unlatched the cemetery keeper's door. An old woman with glasses on her nose was peeling potatoes. She let potatoes and peel fall out of her lap into the pail. She rose.

"I want Frau Slama's grave."

"Fourteen, last row but one, grave number seven," the woman said promptly, as if she had long been expecting this inquiry.

The grave was still quite fresh: a tiny mound, a small provisional cross, a dripping wreath of glass violets reminiscent of confectioners' shops. KATHERINA LUISE SLAMA, born, deceased. She lay down there, and the fat curly worms were settling cozily to work on her round white breasts. The Lieutenant shut his eyes, took off his cap. The rain caressed his parted hair with gentle wetness. He paid no heed to the grave. The rotting corpse beneath the mound had nothing to do with Frau Slama; she was dead. Dead, that meant out of reach, even if one did stand at her graveside. Her body, buried in his mind, was nearer him than the carcass under the mound. Carl Joseph put on his cap, pulled out his watch. Another half hour. He left the cemetery.

He reached the gendarmery post and rang, but nobody came. The Sergeant-Major was not back yet. Rain was spattering noisily on the thick wild vine that covered the veranda. Carl Joseph went up and down, up and down, lit a

47

cigarette, flung it away, felt he must look like a sentry, averted his head whenever his eyes strayed up to that window on the right out of which Katherina had always looked, pressed the white bell button again, waited.

Four muffled chimes came slowly from the church tower in the town. At the same time, the Sergeant-Major appeared. He saluted mechanically before he noticed who it was he was saluting. As if expecting not the Sergeant-Major's welcome but rather his threats, Carl Joseph exclaimed louder than he intended, "Hello, good day, Herr Slama," stretched out his hand, hurrying to seize the other's, as if springing to the assault. He waited impatiently as if standing to parry an attack on the Sergeant-Major's clumsy preliminaries: the concentration with which he peeled off his damp thread glove, his zealous attention to this, and his lowered gaze. At last the bare hand lay moist and broad and limp in the Lieutenant's.

"Thank you for having called, Herr Baron," said the Sergeant-Major, as if the Lieutenant had not just arrived but were already taking his leave. He pulled out a key, unlocked his front door. A gust of wind drove the spattering rain against the veranda. It seemed to sweep Carl Joseph into the house. The hall was in semi-darkness. Was that not a faint glint, a silver earthly trace of the dead? The Sergeant-Major opened the kitchen door; the silver streak was drowned in a flood of light. "Please take off your coat," Slama was saying, himself still in belt and greatcoat.

I'm so terribly sorry, thought the Lieutenant. I'll get it over quickly now and go. Slama stood with outspread arms, waiting to relieve Carl Joseph of his coat. Carl Joseph surrendered to these civilities, Slama's hand brushed against the Lieutenant's neck, touching the line of cropped hair above the collar at the very place where Frau Slama's hands had often met—the gentle clasp of a beloved chain. When, at what precise moment would he be able to utter his expressions of sympathy? As soon as they got into the parlor or not until they were sitting down? And should he stand up again to deliver them? It was as if he would not be able to utter a single sound until the idiotic formula had been released, this thing which he had brought along with him, carried all the way in his mouth. It lay on his tongue, a useless burden, leaving a taste of staleness.

48

The Sergeant-Major pressed the door handle. The parlor door was locked. He said, "Forgive me," as if it was not his fault. He fumbled in the pocket of his coat, which he had taken off—it seemed an age ago—and jingled the keys. Never once while Frau Slama was alive had this door been locked. So she isn't here, the Lieutenant suddenly thought, as if he had not come expressly because she was no longer here, and he realized that all the time he had cherished the secret illusion that she might be there, sitting in the parlor, waiting. Now it was quite certain that she was not here. She was indeed outside, in the grave he had just seen. There was a reek of dampness in the parlor, one of its two windows was curtained over. Through the other came the gray light of the sad day.

"Please come in," the Sergeant-Major said again. He was close on the Lieutenant's heels.

"Thank you," said Carl Joseph. He entered and went up to the round table; he knew the pattern of the corded cloth that covered it and the little jagged stain at its center, the brown polish, the curves of its twisted feet. Here was the sideboard with glass doors; behind them the electroplated cups, china dolls, and a little yellow pottery pig with a slit in his back for saved coins.

"Do me the honor of taking a seat," the Sergeant-Major murmured. He stood behind the back of a chair, clasping it with both hands, holding it before him like a shield. It was over four years since Carl Joseph had seen him last. Then he had been on duty; he had worn an opalescent plume of cock's feathers on his black helmet, straps across his chest, and his rifle had been grounded while he waited outside the District Commissioner's office. Sergeant-Major Slama: his name was synonymous with his rank. Cock's-feather plume and blond mustache alike had seemed to sprout from his face. Now the Sergeant-Major stood bareheaded, without his sword, belt, and straps. The greasy sheen on the corded fabric of his uniform over the slightly jutting belly was visible above the chair back, and he was no longer the Sergeant-Major Slama of those days. Now he was Herr Slama, a gendarmery sergeant-major on the active list, lately husband of Frau Slama. A widower now and master of this house. His close-cropped yellow hair, with the center parting, sprouted like a small double brush above the smoothness of his forehead,

49

unwrinkled, but striped with a livid weal from constant hard pressure of the service cap. The head looked orphaned without its cap or helmet. The face, with no peak over it, was a perfect oval filled in with cheeks, nose, mustache, and small, blue, stubborn, trusting eyes. He waited for Carl Joseph to sit, shifted his own chair, sat down and took out his cigarette case, which had a gaily colored enamel lid. The Sergeant-Major puts it in the middle of the table between himself and the Lieutenant.

"Will you have a cigarette?"

The time has come, Carl Joseph thinks. He stands up and says, "I'm so terribly sorry, Herr Slama."

The Sergeant-Major, sitting with both hands at the edge of the table, appears at first to not quite understand what it is all about, tries a smile, rises too late, just as the Lieutenant is about to sit down again. He takes his hands off the table and puts them to his trouser seams, inclines his head, lifts it again, and looks at Carl Joseph as if to ask what is to be done about it. They sit down again. It is over. They are silent.

"She was a fine woman, the late Frau Slama," says the Lieutenant.

The Sergeant-Major, stroking his mustache, says, with a wisp of it between his fingers, "She was beautiful, too. You knew her, didn't you, Herr Baron?"

"Yes, I knew her. Was her death an easy one?"

"It went on for two days. We sent for the doctor too late, or she would have lived. I was away on night duty, and when I got back she was dead. The wife of the financier from over the road was with her." And then, at once, "A glass of raspberry cordial, Herr Baron?"

"Oh, thank you, thank you," Carl Joseph says in a brighter voice, as if raspberry cordial might completely change the situation, and he watches the Sergeant-Major get up and go to the cupboard, and he knows that there is no raspberry cordial there. It is in the kitchen, in the white cupboard, behind glass, and it was from there that Frau Slama had always got it. Attentively, he follows the Sergeant-Major's every movement, his short, strong arms, in tight sleeves, reaching up to the top shelf in search of the bottle, then dropping helpless, as the tiptoeing feet fall back onto their heels. And Slama, as if back from unknown territory into which he has gone on some unnecessary, unfortunately unsuccessful journey of discovery, faces him again with pathetic helplessness in his sharp blue eyes, to report simply, "I'm sorry, I don't seem to be able to find it."

"Oh, it doesn't matter, Herr Slama," the Lieutenant consoles him.

The Sergeant-Major, however, seems not to have heard these words of comfort; and, as if under orders which, delivered explicitly from on high and no longer subject to modification by subaltern interference, he leaves the room. He can be heard busying himself in the kitchen, and then returns bearing the bottle; he gets glasses with decorated rims from the cupboard, puts a jug of water on the table, and pours the sticky ruby-red liquid out of the dark-green bottle.

"Do me the honor, Herr Baron."

The Lieutenant pours water from the jug into the raspberry cordial. They are silent. The water gushes out of the sloping mouth of the jug, splashes a little, and is like a small answer to the indefatigable pouring outside, which goes on ceaselessly. The rain seems to envelop the solitary house and to intensify both men's loneliness. They are alone. Carl Joseph raises his glass, so does the Sergeant-Major. The Lieutenant savors the sweet, sticky liquid. Slama empties his glass in one gulp; he is thirsty, oddly, inexplicably thirsty for this cool day.

"You're joining the -th Uhlans?" Slama asks.

"Yes, I don't know which regiment yet."

"I've a friend in the regiment, a sergeant-major, Assistant Paymaster Zenober. We served in the Jaeger together, but he got himself transferred. A good, well-educated family. Sure to get his commission one of these days. Our sort stays put. There aren't any prospects in the gendarmery."

The rain increases, the gusts of wind become stronger, beating again and again against the windows. Carl Joseph says, "Ours is such a difficult profession—the army, I mean." Slama breaks into unexplained laughter. It seems to please him immensely that his and Carl Joseph's profession is so difficult. He laughs rather more stridently than he intends— which is obvious from his mouth being open wider than the laugh requires and gaping longer than the laugh lasts. For an instant, the Sergeant-Major looks as if sheer physical compulsion is making it very hard indeed for him to force himself back into everyday seriousness. Is he really glad that he and Carl Joseph have such a hard life?

"The Herr Baron," he begins, "is kind enough to speak of 'our' profession. I hope you'll excuse me saying that mine is rather a different kettle of fish."

Carl Joseph has no reply to this. He felt vaguely that the Sergeant-Major nurses a grudge against him and perhaps against conditions in general in the army and in the gendarmery. They had never been instructed in the cadet school as to how an officer ought to behave in such circumstances. So Carl Joseph smiles, a smile which forces his lips apart and together again like an iron clinch. It makes him appear as niggardly of hilarity as the Sergeant-Major is lavish with it. The raspberry cordial, still sweet on the tongue, leaves a bitter-stale aftertaste—he would like to send a cognac down after it. That day the red-tinted parlor seems smaller, narrower than usual, compressed perhaps by the rain. On the table lies the familiar album with its hard, shiny brass edges. Carl Joseph knows every photograph in it.

"Allow me, please," says Sergeant-Major Slama, opening the album for his inspection. Here, photographed in civilian clothes, a young bridegroom, he stands beside his wife. "At that time I was still a corporal," he remarks with some bitterness, hinting perhaps that even in those days he had deserved a better post. Frau Slama sits beside him wearing a light, tight-fitting summer dress with a wasp waist, a wide-brimmed straw hat perched at an angle on her head. What's this? Has Carl Joseph not seen the photograph before? Why then does it look so new today? And so old? So strange? And so ridiculous? Yes, he smiles as if looking at some queer old picture of times long past, as if Frau Slama had never been close, never dear to him, as if she had died not a few months but many years ago.

"I can see from this how pretty she was," he says not as before, out of embarrassment, but in honest flattery. One has to say something nice about a dead wife to her husband when one calls to condole. Now he feels released and free from the dead woman, as if the whole business has been extinguished. Sheer imagination, all of it. He finishes his raspberry cordial, gets up, and says, "Well, I must go, Herr Slama." Without lingering, he turns round. The Sergeant-Major has scarcely had time to rise before they are both standing in the hall again. Carl Joseph, already in his coat, is pulling on his left glove slowly, luxuriously—suddenly he has time for this—and as he says, "Well, *au revoir*, Herr Slama," he notices with satisfaction a new supercilious note in his voice. Slama stands there, looking down at helpless hands, suddenly empty, as if an instant ago they had been holding something which had now irretrievably fallen from their grasp. They shake hands. Has Slama anything more to say? No matter.

"Perhaps another day, Herr Baron," he is saying, however. Surely he can't mean it? Carl Joseph has already forgotten Slama's face. He can see the golden-yellow braid on his collar, and the three gold stripes on the black sleeve of the gendarmery tunic.

"Well, good-by, Sergeant-Major."

It is still raining, a mild persistent drizzle with gusts now and again of a northeasterly wind. It feels as if evening should have come long since and yet cannot come. The driving wet grayness is eternal. For the first time since he has worn uniform, indeed, for the first time since he could think, Carl Joseph has the feeling that he ought to turn up his coat collar. And for a moment he raises his hands, remembers he is in uniform, and lets them drop again. It is as if for a moment he has forgotten his profession. Slowly, noisily, he walks over the crunching gravel of the front garden, enjoying his own slowness. No need to hurry. Nothing has occurred, it has all been a dream. What time can it be? His watch lies buried too deep in the little inside pocket of his tunic. A nuisance to have to undo his coat. Anyway, it will soon strike from the clock tower.

He opens the wicket gate. He steps onto the road.

"Herr Baron," the Sergeant-Major suddenly says behind him. Curious how silently he has been following. Yes, Carl Joseph is startled. He stops, but cannot make up his mind to turn round immediately. Perhaps a revolver barrel is pointing straight at his shoulderblades between the two regulation folds of his coat. Terrifying and childish thought. Is it going to start all over again?

"Yes?" he says still in a voice of supercilious indolence, a

53

kind of laborious sequel to his leavetaking that costs him great effort—and turns round.

Coatless and bareheaded, the Sergeant-Major stands in the rain, his wet hair sticking up like a cloven brush, thick raindrops on his smooth pale forehead. He is holding a small blue package tied crossways with silver thread. "This is for you, Herr Baron," he says with lowered eyes. "I hope you'll forgive me, it's the District Commissioner's orders. I took it to him at once after she died. The District Commissioner glanced at it and said I was to give it to you personally."

An instant's silence. Only the rain pattering down on the poor little pale-blue package, making it dark—it can't wait any longer, the poor little package. Carl Joseph takes it, thrusts it far down into his coat pocket, blushes, for a moment makes as if to take off his right-hand glove, thinks better of it, holds out his gloved hand, says, "Thank you very much," and leaves quickly.

He can feel the little package in his pocket. From it, up through his hand, along his arm, comes a strange heat making his face flush even redder. He now feels he would like to loosen his collar, just as before he had wanted to turn it up. The bitter aftertaste of the raspberry cordial is in his mouth again. Carl Joseph pulls the package out of his pocket. Yes, there can be no doubt. They are his letters.

It is time for the evening to come, and time for the rain to stop. Time for many changes in the world. Perhaps the setting sun will send out a dying ray. Through the rain, the meadows exhale the familiar scent and a strange bird sounds a lonely cry, one never heard here before, making it a strange country. He hears five o'clock striking. So it is exactly an hour, not more than an hour. Should he walk fast or slow? Time moves strangely, enigmatically. An hour is like a year. It strikes five-fifteen. He has scarcely gone a few steps. Carl Joseph begins to quicken his pace. He crosses the railway lines, the outlying houses of the town begin. His way leads him past a café, the only one in the little provincial town with up-to-date revolving doors. It might be a good thing to go in and have a brandy at the bar and then walk on again. Carl Joseph goes in.

"A brandy, please, quickly," he says at the counter. He stays in his coat and cap. A few customers get up. He can hear the chink of billiard balls and chessmen. Officers of the local garrison sit in the shade of the alcoves. Carl Joseph does not see them, does not acknowledge them. Nothing is as urgent as the brandy. He is pale. The yellow-haired, pasty-faced barmaid smiles maternally down from her high seat and, with benevolent hand, places a lump of sugar beside his cup. Carl Joseph drinks it at a gulp and at once asks for another. All he sees of the girl's face is a pale-blond sheen and the two gold-capped teeth in either corner of her mouth. He feels that he is doing something wrong, and does not know why it should feel wrong to drink a couple of brandies. After all, he is no longer a cadet. What makes the barmaid smile at him so oddly? Her sea-blue gaze makes him uncomfortable, and the black paint on her eyebrows. He turns and looks into the café. In the corner by the window sits his father.

Yes, it is the District Commissioner, but that is hardly surprising. He sits here every day from five to seven reading the foreign news and the *Civil Service Gazette* while smoking a cheroot. The whole town has been aware of it, for three decades. The District Commissioner sits there, looks at his son, and seems to be smiling. Carl Joseph takes off his cap and goes across to his father. Old Herr von Trotta looks up briefly from his paper without putting it down and says, "You've been to see Slama?"

"Yes, Papa."

"And he gave you the letters?"

"Yes, Papa."

"Do sit down."

"Yes, Papa."

At last, the District Commissioner puts down his paper, leans his elbows on the table, and observes, turning to his son, "That brandy she gave you is poor stuff. I always drink Hennessy."

"I must make a note of it, Papa."

"I don't drink it often."

"Yes, Papa."

"You still look rather pale. Take off your coat. Major Kreidl over there is looking at you."

Carl Joseph rises and bows to the major.

"Was Slama difficult?"

"No, quite a good sort."

"Well, then . . ."

Carl Joseph takes off his coat.

"Where have you put them?" the District Commissioner asks. His son takes the package out of his pocket. Old Herr von Trotta takes it, weighs it in his right hand, and says, "There seems to be a lot of them."

"Yes, Papa."

It is quiet, they hear the click of billiard balls and chess pieces. Outside, it continues to rain.

"The day after tomorrow you join your regiment," the District Commissioner says with a glance through the window. Suddenly Carl Joseph feels the hard dry hand of his father laid over his right hand. The District Commissioner's hand lies cool and bony, a hard shell, over the Lieutenant's.

Carl Joseph lowers his eyes to the table. He blushes. He says, "Yes, Papa."

"My bill, please," the District Commissioner calls, removing his hand.

"Tell that waitress that we always drink Hennessy."

They cross the café to the door in a straight line, the father and behind him his son.

Now only single drops are splashing and pattering softly from the trees as they walk slowly home through the damp garden. Outside the door of the District Commissioner's office is Sergeant-Major Slama, helmeted, with rifle and fixed bayonet, his service ledger under his arm.

"Good day, my dear Slama," says Herr von Trotta. "Nothing to report, I suppose."

"No, sir," Slama repeats, "nothing to report."

Chapter 5

The barracks stood to the north of the town. They blocked the broad, well-kept highway, which, once past their red-brick walls, took on a fresh life, stretching far away into the distance. These barracks might have been put in the middle of this Slavonic province by the Royal Imperial army as a reminder of the might of the Habsburgs. They obstructed the ancient high road, made broad and spacious by centuries of migrating Slavs. The high road had to give way to them. It took a bend round the barracks. Standing at the northern edge of the town, where the houses grew smaller and smaller, becoming at last mere village huts, the broad curved black-and-yellow barrack gates could be seen in the distance on clear days, raised toward the town like a mighty shield of the Habsburgs, at once in threat and in protection. The regiment was stationed in Moravia. Its men were not, as might be expected, Czechs but Ukrainians and Rumanians.

Twice a week, military exercises took place in the fields south of the town. Twice a week, the regiment came riding through its streets. The loud clear ring of trumpets interrupted at regular intervals the even clatter of horses' hoofs and the red-breeched legs of the mounted troopers astride the glossy brown backs filled the little town with blood-red glory. People stopped at the roadside, shopkeepers ran out of their shops, leisurely customers in coffeehouses left their tables, policemen on their beats and peasants at the market square, in from the villages with fresh vegetables, left their horses and carts. Only the few cabbies on their rank along the municipal gardens continued to sit motionless on their boxes. From above, they got an even better view of the military splendor than any spectator on the pavement. And their worn nags seemed to hail the arrival of their younger, sounder brethren with dull indifference. (The cavalry horses were distant relatives of these jades which for fifteen years had done nothing but pull cabs to and from the station.)

Carl Joseph, Baron von Trotta, took little interest in horses. Sometimes he fancied he could feel the blood of his forebears in him. They had not been horsemen. Their hard fists had guided furrowing ploughs; they had passed, step by step, over the earth. They had dug their sharp plowshares into fertile clods of grainland, moving with bent knees behind double-yoked oxen. They had urged their beasts with willow wands—not whips and spurs. They had swung their polished scythes, raised high in their hands, and harvested the blessing which they had sown. His grandfather's father had still been a peasant. Sipolje was the village from which he came. Sipolje: the name had an ancient meaning, though contemporary Slavs barely remembered it. Yet Carl Joseph felt he knew his village. He could see it whenever he thought of his grandfather's portrait, high up, under the study ceiling. The village lay cradled in unknown hills, burnished by the rays of an unknown sun, its low houses built of clay and wattle. A good village, a pleasant village. He would have given his whole career as an officer for it.

But he was not a peasant, he was a baron and a lieutenant in the Uhlans. Unlike the other officers, he had no private quarters in the town. Carl Joseph lived in the barracks, the window of his room looked out on the square. Opposite it were the men's quarters. Always, when he turned in on late afternoons, and the heavy double doors slammed behind him, he felt a prisoner. Never again would the doors open to set him free. His spurs rang icily on the bare stone staircase and his boots echoed on the caulked wooden floor of the passage. The whitewashed walls captured the last light of the dying day, and reflected it as though in their barren miserliness they saw to it that the government oil lamps in the corners might not be lit before the day had really failed—that at the proper time, the walls had gathered up the day to economize and dole it out as need arose, to darkness. He did not put on the light. He pressed his forehead against the glass which only seemed to separate him from the darkness and was in reality like the familiar cool outer wall of it. He looked down into the warm comfortable yellow glow of the men's quarters. He would gladly have changed places with any private. They sat there, half undressed, in their coarse, ochre army shirts, dangling bare feet over their cots, chattering, singing, playing their mouth organs. At this time of day (it was late autumn) an hour after lock-up and an hour before lights-out, the barracks felt like a great ship that rocked gently, the oozing tawny oil lamps and broad white shades rose and fell in a vague surge of uncharted seas. The men sang songs in a foreign language, a Slavonic dialect. The old peasants of Sipolje would certainly have understood them. Carl Joseph's grandfather, even, might have understood. His mysterious portrait faded under the study ceiling. Carl Joseph's memory clung to this portrait as the sole and final token bequeathed him by the long line of anonymous ancestors. He was their descendant. Since he had joined the regiment he had felt himself his grandfather's grandson rather than his father's son. Yes, he was the son of his remarkable grandfather. They played their mouth organs continuously. He could see the movements of their coarse brown hands distinctly, thrusting the instruments back and forth along their red lips, here and there he caught a glint of metal. The great melancholy of these instruments drifted through the closed windows into the square of the barrack yard, filling the dark with gentle reminiscence of homes and wives, children and farms. At home they lived in little huts, made their women fruitful by night and their fields by day. High white piles of snow surrounded their huts in winter. Golden and tall in summer the corn billowed about their thighs. They were peasants. Peasants! Thus had the Trottas lived, thus.

Autumn was already far advanced. In the morning, sitting up in bed, he could see the rising sun, like a blood orange, creep over the edge of the eastern sky. When physical training began out in the water-meadow—in the wide green clearing surrounded by dark pine trees—silvery mists rose slowly, torn asunder by the violent, regular movements of the dark-blue uniforms. Then the sun rose, pale and melancholy. Its dull silver broke through the branches, cool and strange. Frosty shivers, like a cruel comb, broke out over the chestnut flanks of the horses who whinnied from the nearby copse in dolorous cries for home and stable. They were doing exercises with the carbine. Carl Joseph could scarcely wait for their return to barracks. He dreaded the fifteen minutes rest accorded every morning at ten sharp; the talk with his brother officers who sometimes gathered in the neighboring pub for a glass of beer to await the arrival of Colonel Kovacs. Worse still was the evening at the club. Soon now, it would be evening. It was obligatory to put in an appearance. It was almost time for lights-out. Already the dark-blue clattering forms of returning troopers came hurrying through the dim light across the square. Already Sergeant-Major Reznicek could be seen emerging from his doorway over there, a guttering lantern in his hand, the buglers spotlighted in the darkness. The yellow brass instruments shone in front of the dark gleaming blue of the uniforms. From the stables came the drowsy neighing of horses. The stars twinkled copper and silver in the sky.

There was a tap on his door; Carl Joseph did not stir. It was his batman, he would make his way in. He was called Onufrij. How long it had taken to learn that! Onufrij. The name would have been still familiar to his grandfather. Onufrij entered. Carl Joseph pressed his forehead against the window. Behind him, he heard his man click his heels. Today was Wednesday. Onufrij had leave. He had to turn on the light and sign a pass.

"Turn on the light," Carl Joseph ordered without looking around. Over there they were still playing their mouth organs. Onufrij turned on the light. Carl Joseph heard the click of the switch by the door. The room behind him lit up, but there, outside the panes, spread the black square with the golden, flickering, cozy light from the barrack room beyond. (Electric light was reserved for officers.)

"Well, where are you going today?" Carl Joseph asked, his eyes still fixed on the men's quarters.

"To see a girl," answered Onufrij. This was the first time his lieutenant had asked a personal question.

"What girl?" asked Carl Joseph.

"Katherina," said Onufrij. His voice indicated that he was standing at attention.

"Stand easy," commanded Carl Joseph. Onufrij's right foot was heard scraping in front of the left.

Carl Joseph turned round. There was Onufrij, his big horse teeth shining between full red lips. He could never stand at ease without smiling.

"What's she like, your Katherina?" asked Carl Joseph.

"Please sir, if I may say so, large white breasts."

"Large white breasts"—the Lieutenant's fingers shut on to

60

his palms, feeling with them the cool memory of Katherina's breasts. She was dead, dead.

"Here, show me your chit," ordered Carl Joseph. Onufrij gave him the regulation form. "Where does she live?" asked Carl Joseph.

"She's out in service," said Onufrij. And, "Large white breasts," he added happily.

"Give it to me," said Carl Joseph. Onufrij clicked his heels again. The Lieutenant took the form, smoothed it out, signed. "Go to your Katherina," said Carl Joseph. Again Onufrij clicked heels. "Dismissed" ordered Carl Joseph.

He switched off the light, fumbled in the dark for his coat, stepped out into the passage. At the moment he closed the door downstairs, the final blast of lights-out sounded. Stars glittered overhead. The sentry presented arms. Behind him the gates clanged shut. The road gleamed silver in the moonlight. The yellow lights of the town welcomed him like fallen stars. His steps rang on the freshly frozen ground, darkly autumnal.

Behind his back he heard Onufrij's boots. The Lieutenant hurried, so as not to be overtaken by his batman. But Onufrij, too, quickened his pace. So they hurried down the lonely hard, echoing highway. One behind the other. Obviously Onufrij enjoyed keeping up with his lieutenant. Carl Joseph stopped and waited. Onufrij stretched distinctly in the moonlight; he seemed to grow; he raised his head up towards the stars as if to draw down strength with which to encounter his officer. His arms jerked backward and forward in rhythm with his legs, as though he were treading air with his hands. Three paces in front of Carl Joseph he halted, flung out his chest still further and saluted with a formidable click of booted heels, all five fingers glued together. Embarrassed, Carl Joseph smiled at him. Anyone else, he reflected, would have found something pleasant to say. It was touching the way Onufrij followed him. He had never really looked at him properly. For as long as he had been unable to remember the name it had seemed impossible to look Onufrij in the face, and so every day it had felt as if he had another servant. The others all talked of their batmen with the intimate ease of connoisseurs, just as they did of girls or clothes, or favorite dishes, or horses. But when the talk was of servants, Carl Joseph could only think of old Jacques at home, whose service dated back to his grandfather. Old Jacques was the only servant in the world. Now here was Onufrij, standing on the moonlit highroad, facing him, his broad chest flung well out, with gleaming buttons, boots polished to shine like glass, and on his broad face a look of glee at meeting his lieutenant—which he strove convulsively to suppress.

"Stand easy," said Carl Joseph. He would have liked to say something pleasanter. His grandfather would have said more pleasant things to Jacques. Onufrij's right foot clattered out in front of the left. His chest still jutted. The order had had no effect. "Stand as easy as you like," said Carl Joseph, a little sad and impatient.

"Excuse me, sir. I am standing as easy as I like."

"Does she live far from here, your girl?" asked Carl Joseph.

"Not far. An hour's march, Sir."

No, it didn't work. Carl Joseph could find no more to say. He choked over some unknown kindness, he didn't know how to handle his servant. Whom could he handle? His embarrassment was great. He stood tongue-tied even with his brother officers. Why did they all start whispering after he left them, or before he forced himself to go up to them? Why did he sit a horse so badly? Oh, he knew what he was like! He could see the figure he cut as though in a mirror, there was no point in pretending. The others whispered and tittered behind his back. He didn't understand their replies until they'd been explained to him, and even then he couldn't laugh, particularly not then. And yet Colonel Kovacs liked him. And certainly his record was immaculate. He lived in his grandfather's reflected glory, that was it. He was the grandson of the hero of Solferino: the only grandson. He could feel his grandfather's dark mysterious eyes on the back of his neck. The grandson of the hero of Solferino.

For a few minutes Carl Joseph and his servant Onufrij faced one another without a word, there on the glittering white highroad. The moonlight and the silence prolonged these minutes. Onufrij never budged; he stood like a monument, silvered by the moon. Carl Joseph suddenly turned and began to march. Exactly three paces behind him came Onufrij. Carl Joseph listened to the crunching of the heavy soles, the iron clank of spurs. It was fidelity itself that pursued him. Each booted impact hammered out a brief renewal of the soldier's oath of

62

loyalty to his officer. Carl Joseph was afraid to turn, and wished that the long straight road might suddenly branch off, present some hitherto unnoticed turning, an escape from Onufrij's persistent readiness to serve. The man was keeping step. The Lieutenant tried to keep time with the boots behind his back. He feared he might hurt Onufrij if by any chance he changed his pace. Onufrij's whole deeply plighted troth lay in these dependable tramping boots. Each step moved Carl Joseph anew. It was as if there, behind his back, a clumsy fellow with heavy soles were trying to knock at his master's heart: the helpless gentleness of a spurred and booted bear.

At last they reached the outskirts of the town. Carl Joseph had managed to think of something pleasant with which he might suitably take leave. He turned and said, "Have a good time, Onufrij." And he went quickly off down a side street. His batman's thanks reached him only as a distant echo.

He had to go the long way round. Ten minutes later he reached the club. It occupied the first floor of one of the best houses in the old Ring. As on every evening, its windows spread their light over the crowded Promenade. It was late, he had to pick his way adroitly through the gathered shoals of civilians out for an airing with their wives. Day after day he felt the same unspeakable discomfort at having to jostle—a marked figure, jingling and resplendent—among the drab citizens, pursued by inquisitive, malicious, or lustful stares, until he vanished like a god through the bright doorway of the club. He worked his way quickly in and out among the people. The Promenade was fairly long, and it took two minutes, a loathsome two minutes, to reach the end of it. He went up the steps two at a time. He didn't want to meet anyone, meetings on the stairs were to be avoided, they were unlucky omens. In the hall, warmth and light and the sound of voices reached him. He entered, exchanging greetings, and looked for Colonel Kovacs in his usual corner.

There every evening the Colonel played dominoes, every evening with a different gentleman. Colonel Kovacs was a domino enthusiast, perhaps because of an irrational terror of cards. "I've never held a card in my hand," he would tell them. Nor could he say the word "card" without repugnance, and, as he spoke he would indicate his hands, as though in them he held his blameless character. "Gentlemen," he would sometimes add, "I advise you all to play dominoes. It's a clean game and teaches you self-control." And sometimes he raised one of the black-and-white multi-eyed dominoes like a magical instrument by whose means all vice-laden cardplayers might be released from their demon.

Tonight it was Captain Taittinger's turn to give the colonel his game. Colonel Kovacs's face threw a crimson-bluish light on the sallow haggardness of the captain's. With a faint jingle, Carl Joseph stopped at the Colonel's table.

"Good evening," said the Colonel, without looking up from his dominoes. He was a comfortable man, the Colonel. For years he had cultivated a fatherly manner. Only once a month did he work himself up into an artificial rage, which he himself dreaded far more than the regiment. Any pretext would unleash it. Then he would shout until the barrack walls and the old trees round the water meadow shook. His purple face would blench to the lips, his switch flick untiringly against the leather of his riding boots. He would grunt and bellow unintelligible nonsense, punctuate disconnected frenzies with an ever-recurring "in my regiment," which always came out more quietly than the rest. He would stop for no reason, just as he had begun, and stamp off the parade ground, out of the regimental office, the club, or whatever background he had selected to stage his thunderstorm. Oh yes, they all knew Colonel Kovacs, a nice old boy. They could rely on the regularity of his outbursts like the phases of the moon. Captain Taittinger, who had twice had himself transferred, and possessed accurate knowledge of superiors, never tired of assuring everyone that the whole army could boast no more accommodating colonel.

At last the Colonel looked up from his dominoes to shake hands. "Eaten yet?" he inquired. "Pity," he continued, gazing into remote distance. "The cutlet tonight was first-rate." "First-rate," he repeated a little later. He was really sorry that Trotta had missed the cutlet. He would have enjoyed eating his over again or, at least, watching one being eaten. "Well, have a good time," he said at last and returned to his dominoes.

At this hour, the confusion was great and there were no comfortable seats to be found. Captain Taittinger, who for years had acted as their mess superintendent and whose ruling passion was pastries, had in the course of time transformed these rooms into an almost exact replica of the pastry shop

64

where he spent his afternoons. There, he was to be seen sitting behind the glass door dimly, immobile as some odd uniformed advertisement, the baker's chief customer and probably his hungriest. Without the least animation in his sad face, he devoured plate after plateful of pastries, sipped occasionally from a tumbler of water, and stared out through the glass door into the street, nodding gently when a passing soldier saluted him. Nothing at all seemed to be going on inside his bony skull with its thinned-out hair. He was a mild and extremely lazy officer. His duties as mess superintendent—cookery, cooks, mess orderlies, and wine cellar—were the only acceptable part of his profession. His extensive correspondence with distilleries and wine merchants kept no fewer than two army clerks occupied. He succeeded, over the years, in making the club identical with his well-loved pastry shop. He had had elegant little tables placed in the corners and the table lamps covered with pink shades.

Carl Joseph looked about for somewhere reasonably comfortable to sit. Comparative safety, he felt, might be found between rosy Lieutenant Kindermann (of German extraction) and Reserve Ensign Bärenstein von Zaloga, a rich, recently titled, lawyer. The ensign's slight paunch and sober years so ill-became his very junior rank that he always looked like a civilian at a fancy-dress ball. And his face, with its tiny coal-black mustache, was disconcerting now, because the eyes lacked the pince-nez which nature herself had imposed on them. He reminded Carl Joseph of a family doctor or an uncle. He alone in these two large rooms could sit convincingly and honestly—all the others gave you the impression that they were fidgeting about on their seats. The sole concession, apart from the uniform, which Reserve Ensign Bärenstein made to the army was to wear an eyeglass while on duty. At home, in his civilian life, he actually did wear a pince-nez.

Without doubt, Lieutenant Kindermann too was more reassuring than the others. He was made of some pink-and-blond transparent substance; one could almost have passed one's hands through him, as through a bright mist in the evening sunshine. Everything he said was insubstantial, translucent—breathed forth from his being without diminishing it. Even the earnest look with which he followed serious conversations had something smiling and sunny about it. He sat at the little table, a merry cipher. "Good evening," he fluted in the high voice which Colonel Kovacs said was a wind instrument in the Prussian Army. Reserve Ensign Bärenstein rose, as befitted his inferior rank, but ponderously. "Good evening to you Lieutenant," he said.

"Good evening, Herr Doktor," Carl Joseph answered him almost respectfully. "I'm not disturbing you?" he asked, and sat down.

"Dr. Demant will be back with us this evening," began Bärenstein. "I happened to run across him this afternoon."

"What a nice fellow he is," fluted Kindermann, and, against Bärenstein's strong, forensic baritone, it sounded like a zephyr, a rippling of harp strings. Kindermann, forever eager to atone for the very slight interest he took in women by attentions which he pretended to lavish on them, added emphatically, "And his wife, do you know her? So charming, such a delightful person." As he said "charming", he raised his hand, his wanton fingers rippled the air.

"I knew her as a young girl," said Bärenstein.

"Oh, really, *did* you?" said Kindermann. He was obviously putting it on.

"Her father used to be one of the wealthiest hat manufacturers," said the ensign. It sounded as though he were reading a document. He paused, a little scared by his own remark. This mention of "hat manufacturers" sounded too civilian to him. After all, he wasn't sitting among solicitors. He swore to himself from now on always to think out his remarks. That much, at least, he owed the cavalry. He tried to see how Trotta was taking it. But Trotta was sitting on his left and the lawyer's glass was in his right eye. The only person he could see clearly was Lieutenant Kindermann, and he didn't matter. In order to ascertain whether his familiar allusion to the hat manufacturer had made an unfavorable impression on Trotta, Bärenstein brought out his cigarette case, held it out to the left, then suddenly remembered that Kindermann was senior in rank and said, "Oh, excuse me," and turned quickly to the right again.

The three sat smoking in silence. Carl Joseph stared at the Emperor's portrait hanging on the opposite wall. There, in the flower-white of a general's uniform stood Francis Joseph, with the wide, blood-red sash across his chest and, at his throat, the Order of the Golden Fleece. His black imposing field marshal's helmet, with its shimmering dark-green heron's feathers, lay by the Emperor's side on a small rickety-looking table. The portrait seemed remote, much farther off than the wall. Carl Joseph remembered how the sight of the portrait had, in the first weeks after he joined the regiment, afforded him a kind of proud consolation. Then, it was as if the Emperor might at any instant have stepped out of the narrow black frame and down to him. But gradually the Supreme War Lord had taken on the indifferent, habitual aspect of his stamps and coins. His portrait in the officers' club room hung like some esoteric sacrifice offered to himself by a god. The eyes—once they had suggested the clear blue skies of summer vacation—were now composed of hard blue china. And yet it was the same Emperor. At home, this very portrait hung in the District Commissioner's study. It hung in the great hall of the Cadet School. It hung in the colonel's office in the barracks. The Emperor Francis Joseph was scattered a hundred-thousandfold, throughout the length and breadth of his Empire, omnipresent among his people as God is omnipresent in the world. The hero of Solferino had grown old and died. Now worms devoured him. And his son, the District Commissioner was also growing old. Soon worms would eat him also. The Emperor alone—the Emperor—seemed one day, within a given hour, suddenly to have aged for Carl Joseph, and since that hour to have lived encased in an icy and eternal, silvery and terrifying old age, within a container of awe-inspiring crystal. The years dared not approach him. His eye grew ever bluer and harder. His very favor which graced the Trotta family was like a load of crushing ice. Carl Joseph grew cold under the blue glance of his sovereign.

He remembered how at home, back for vacation, when before lunch Bandmaster Nechwal arranged his band in its regulation circle, he had been eager to let life drip out of him, in passionate, warm, sweet death. The legacy of his grandfather, to save the life of the Emperor, lived on in him. Again and again, if one happened to be born a Trotta, one had to save the Emperor's life.

Now he had been in the regiment scarcely four months, and suddenly it struck him that this Emperor, inappropriately housed in crystal, had no more need of Trottas. Peace had lasted too long. Death in the field was as unlikely for a cavalry lieutenant as the highest grade of military advancement. One day they would promote him to colonel and then he would die. Meanwhile, he went to the club room every evening and saw the Emperor's portrait. The longer Lieutenant Trotta stared at it, the more unapproachable grew his sovereign.

"I say," piped Lieutenant Kindermann, "Trotta can't take his eyes off the old man."

Carl Joseph smiled at Kindermann. Reserve Ensign Bärenstein had long since started a game of dominoes and was about to lose it. He considered it military etiquette to lose every game he played with regulars. In civilian life, he always won. Even among solicitors he was considered a formidable opponent. But on his annual military exercises he cast prudence to the winds and did his best to play the fool. "He keeps losing," Kinderman remarked to Trotta. Lieutenant Kindermann was convinced that civilians were inferior beings. They couldn't even win a game of dominoes.

The Colonel still sat in his corner with Captain Taittinger. A few gentlemen strayed desultorily among the little tables. They could not venture to leave the club before the colonel finished his game. A plangent clock whined out the quarters, very slow and clear, its soft voice interrupting the chink of dominoes and chessmen. Sometimes an orderly clicked his heels, hurried into the kitchen, and returned with a little glass of cognac set on an absurdly large salver. Sometimes there was a neighing guffaw and, at the table it came from, one might observe four heads bent close together—it was obvious that they were re-telling jokes. At the end of these jokes, these anecdotes, every-one else could tell whether the laughter had been genuine or merely polite. This divided the sheep from the goats: unless you could manage a genuine laugh, you were an outsider. No, Carl Joseph could not really hold his ground.

He had just made up his mind to propose a new, three-handed game when the door burst open and an orderly stood to attention with an unusually noisy click of the heels. Silence fell instantly. Colonel Kovacs lept from his seat and looked toward the door. It was none other than Demant, the regimental surgeon. He himself was taken aback by the commotion his entrance caused. He lingered in the doorway and smiled. At his side, the orderly was still standing to attention and this obviously embarrassed him. He waved to the man, who did not notice. The doctor's heavy spectacles were slightly filmed over by the mists of the autumn night outside. It was his habit to take off his spectacles and polish them when he entered a warm room out of the cold.

"Well, if it isn't the doctor," the Colonel bawled, as if straining to make himself heard at a noisy fair. The good man felt that short-sighted people must also be deaf, that their spectacles would become less opaque if their ears could be made to hear more distinctly. Colonel Kovacs's voice cleared a passage. The officers stepped back. Those few still sitting at tables rose. The regimental surgeon advanced gingerly as if he were stepping over ice. His glasses gradually cleared. Greetings from all sides assailed him. He had some difficulty in recognizing the gentlemen. He inclined his head to read their faces as if he were peering into books. He stopped at last in front of Colonel Kovacs and squared his chest. His stance looked much exaggerated as he threw back his perpetually stooping head on its reedy neck, trying with a jerk to straighten his narrow sloping shoulders. He had been ill so long they had almost forgotten him—him and his unsoldierly bearing. Now they stared at him in some astonishment. The Colonel hastened to bring the official ritual of greeting to an end. He bellowed until the glasses rang. "Why, the doctor's looking simply splendid!" as if he wished to inform the whole army. He thumped Demant's shoulder, trying, as it were, to force it back into position. His heart went out to the doctor. But the fellow was so deuced unsoldierly. Damn it all, if only he'd look a bit more like an officer there'd be no need for all these efforts to be nice to him. Why the hell hadn't they sent him a different doctor? Why his of all regiments! And so the perpetual inner conflicts which the Colonel's heart was forced to wage with his professional tastes on behalf of such a damned nice fellow were quite enough to fluster an ageing warrior. That doctor'll be the death of me, thought the Colonel whenever he saw Demant on horseback. He had even asked him if he would not mind riding through the town.

I must say something decent, he thought confusedly. "The cutlets were first rate tonight," was his inspiration. And he said it. The doctor smiled. Why, the fellow even smiles like a civilian, thought the Colonel. Suddenly he remembered that there was an officer whom Dr Demant had not met. Trotta, of course, he'd joined after the doctor went on sick leave.

"This is Trotta, our youngest," shouted the Colonel. "You don't know each other yet, do you?" And Carl Joseph approached the regimental surgeon.

"The grandson of the hero of Solferino?" asked Demant. No one would have credited him with such intimate acquaintance with army history.

"Our doctor knows everything, doesn't he?" cried the colonel. "He's a regular bookworm." And for the first time in his life this suspect term pleased him so much that he repeated it: "A bookworm," in the tender accents which he usually reserved for "An Uhlan".

They sat down again. The evening took its normal course.

"Your grandfather," the regimental surgeon said, "was one of the most remarkable men in the army. Can you remember him?"

"No, I never saw him," said Carl Joseph. "But we have his portrait at home. It hangs in the study. When I was young I often looked at it. And Jacques, his servant, is with us still."

"Which portrait is that?" the doctor asked.

"A student friend of my father's painted it," said Carl Joseph. "It's a strange portrait. It hangs rather high up, and when I was a boy I had to climb on a chair to look at it."

They said nothing for a few minutes. At last the doctor said, "My grandfather was a publican. A Jewish publican in Galicia. Have you ever been there?" Dr Demant was a Jew. All anecdotes contained Jewish regimental surgeons. There had been two Jews at the Cadet School. They had joined the infantry.

"Come on, we're going to Aunt Resi's!" somebody shouted suddenly. And the rest echoed, "To Aunt Resi's! Let's all go to Aunt Resi's! To Aunt Resi's!"

Nothing could have dismayed Carl Joseph more than this summons. For weeks he had anticipated it full of misgiving. Each detail of the last visit to Frau Horwath's brothel remained fresh in his mind. He remembered everything. The fizz made of camphor and lemonade, the flaccid, doughy flesh of the girls, the blinding-red and crazy-yellow of the wallpaper, the smell of cat in the passage, of mice and of lilies of the valley, and the indigestion twelve hours later. He had scarcely been a week in the regiment and it had been his first visit to a brothel. "Amorous maneuvers," Taittinger had said. He was the ringleader. It was one of his time-honored duties as mess super-

70

intendent. Pale and haggard, his sword hilt tucked under his arm, he had moved with long spidery, softly jingling steps about Frau Horwath's parlor going from table to table, a stealthy admonisher to sour joys. Kindermann almost fainted when he smelled naked women; the female sex made him positively ill. In the water closet Major Prohaska had stood making genuine efforts to thrust his stubby fingers well down his throat. Frau Horwath's silk had rustled all over the house at once. Her large black eyes had rolled, ubiquitous, aimless, in her broad and mealy face. White and large as piano keys, her teeth had gleamed in her wide mouth. Trautmannsdorff had sat eying her every movement from a corner, through squinting little greenish eyes. He had risen at last, to thrust a hand into her bosom. It lost itself there, like a white mouse among white mountains. And Pollak, the pianist, the slave of music, had sat humped at his black grand piano, the large cuffs clattering at his pounding wrists—hoarse cymbals accompanying the tinny sounds.

To Aunt Resi's. They were going back to Aunt Resi's. Down in the street, the Colonel left them. He said, "A very pleasant evening to you, gentlemen," and twenty voices filled the empty quiet: "Good night, sir," while forty spurs came together.

Dr Demant made a shy effort to excuse himself. "Must you go, too?" he asked Lieutenant Trotta quietly. "I'm afraid so," Carl Joseph whispered. And the regimental surgeon accompanied him silently. They brought up the rear of the straggling line of officers who clanked and jingled through the silent, moonlit town. They did not speak. Both felt that the whispered question with its whispered answer had united them so that further words were not necessary. Both were cut off from the whole regiment. Yet they had scarcely known each other half an hour.

Suddenly, without realising what made him say it, Carl Joseph said, "I used to love a woman called Kathi. She died."

The regimental surgeon stopped and turned to face him. "You'll love other women, you know," he said. And they went on.

From the distant station, night trains whistled, and the regimental surgeon said, "I'd like to go away, far away."

Now they were standing in front of Aunt Resi's blue lantern. Captain Taittinger knocked at the bolted front door.

71

Somebody opened it. The piano inside at once struck up the Radetzky March. The officers marched into the parlor. "Fall out singly," ordered Taittinger. The naked girls buzzed toward them, a bustling clutch of white hens.

"God be with you," Prohaska said. This time, Trautmannsdorff put his hand straight into Frau Horwath's bosom, while he was still standing. For the time being he left it there. She had kitchen and cellar to superintend and she suffered under the first lieutenant's caresses, but hospitality imposed sacrifices. She allowed herself to be seduced. Lieutenant Kindermann grew pale. His face was whiter than the powder on the girls' shoulders.

Major Prohaska ordered soda water. Those who knew him well could predict that tonight he would get very drunk. He was clearing a passage for the alcohol with the water, as streets are cleared for a royal entrance. "Has the doctor come along?" he asked loudly.

"It's his job to study diseases at the source," Captain Taittinger answered scientifically, pale and haggard-looking as always.

Reserve Ensign Bärenstein's eyeglass was fixed now on the eye of a pale blond charmer. He sat there with small, black peering eyes, his hairy brown hands creeping like queer little animals over the young lady.

Gradually, they all found their places. On the red sofa, between the doctor and Carl Joseph, two women perched with stiffly drawn-up knees, made shy by the desperate faces of the two men. The champagne arrived, brought in with ceremony by the stern housekeeper in black taffeta. Frau Horwath resolutely drew the first lieutenant's hand out of her bosom, setting it down again on his black breeches, as one who restores a borrowed object, and rose, imposing and firm. She extinguished the central chandelier. Only the small lamps were left on in the alcoves. The white powdered bodies gleamed in this pink twilight, gold stars glittered, swords shone silver. One couple after another rose and vanished.

Prohaska, who had long since reached the cognac stage, came over and said to the doctor, "You fellows don't need them. I'll take them off you." He took hold of the women and staggered between them toward the stairs.

So that all at once Carl Joseph and the doctor were left by

themselves. The pianist fondled the keys at the other end of the room. The notes of a soulful waltz came drifting timidly and thinly across the room. Apart from this, it was quiet, almost cozy, and the clock on the mantelpiece ticked away. "I don't think we need stay, do you?" said the doctor, and he got up. Carl Joseph looked across at the clock on the mantelpiece, it was too dark to see the time. He went over to it and drew back a step. In a bronze, flyblown frame stood the Supreme War Lord, a small version of the well-known ubiquitous portrait of His Majesty, in his white raiment with the blood-red sash and the Order of the Golden Fleece. Something's got to be done, thought the Lieutenant quickly, like a child. Something's got to be done. . . .

He could feel himself turn pale, and his heart was thudding. He grasped the frame, stripped off the black paper back and took out the picture. This he folded twice, then once again, and stuffed it away in his pocket. He turned. Behind him stood the regimental surgeon. The doctor pointed to the pocket in which Carl Joseph had stowed his Imperial Master. His grandfather had rescued him, too, Dr Demant thought. Carl Joseph blushed.

"Disgusting," he said. "What do you think?"

"Nothing," the doctor replied. "I was only thinking about your grandfather."

"I am his grandson," said Carl Joseph, "but I have no chance to save his life. Unfortunately."

They placed four silver coins on the table and left Frau Resi Horwath's establishment.

Chapter 6

Dr Max Demant had been with the regiment for three years. He lived just outside the town, on its southern edge, where the highroad leads to the two cemeteries, the old and the new. Both cemetery keepers knew the doctor well. He came a few times every week to visit the dead, those long since forgotten and those still remembered. And he would linger, sometimes for hours, among their graves, and here and there the light clatter of his sword could be heard chinking against a headstone. He was undoubtedly an odd man, reputed to be a good doctor, which in itself was an oddity among army surgeons. He avoided all social contact. Only official duty obliged him more frequently than he would have wished to show his face now and again among brother officers. He ought, by age and length of service, to have held a medical-staff appointment. No one could say quite why he did not. Perhaps he himself did not know. "There are careers with snags in them." This was one of the dicta of Captain Taittinger, who provided the regiment with its choice aphorisms.

Careers with snags. Demant had often thought of it himself. A life with snags . . . He said to Lieutenant Trotta, "Mine has been a life with snags. If fate had been kinder to me, I could have become assistant to the celebrated Viennese surgeon and then, probably, a professor."

The great name of the Viennese surgeon had early cast its glamor over his sombre, restricted childhood. While still a schoolboy, Max Demant had made up his mind to be a doctor. He came from a frontier village on the eastern border of the Monarchy. His grandfather had been an orthodox Jew, a publican, and his father, after twelve years in the militia, had become an official of medium rank in the post office of the neighboring little frontier town. He remembered his grandfather distinctly. He would sit at all hours of the day under the arched doorway of his inn. His vast, crinkled, silvery beard hid his chest and reached down to his knees. The scent of manure and milk and horses and hay wafted around him. He would sit in front of his inn, a venerable king among publicans. When farmers, back from the weekly pig-market, stopped in front of his inn, the old man would rise majestically like a mountain in human guise. Since by then he was deaf, the little farmers had to shout their orders up into his ears through hands hollowed in front of their mouths. He would only nod. He had understood. He granted his customers their orders as though they had been favors conferred, not paid for in good hard cash. With powerful hands he unharnessed their beasts and led them to the stables. And while his daughters set brandy with dried salted peas before the guests in the wide, low-ceilinged taproom, he foddered their horses in the stable and soothed them with kindly words. On the Sabbath he sat bent over large pious tomes and his silver beard hid the lower half of the black print on the page. Had he known that one day his grandson would walk the earth in the uniform of an officer, murderously armed, he would have cursed his age and the fruit of his loins. Even his son, Max Demant's father, the post-office official of medium rank, was as far as the old man was concerned an abomination, whom he affectionately tolerated. The inn, left him by his ancestors, had to pass into the hands of his daughters and sons-in-law, while his male issue were destined to become officials, intellectuals, underlings, and fools. Down through the ages: that was hardly apposite. For the regimental surgeon had no children. Nor did he want any. For his wife. . . .

At this point, as a rule, Dr Demant would break off his reminiscences. He would think of his mother: she had lived in perpetual flurried quest of some kind of supplementary income. His father, after office hours, spent his time in little cafés. He played Tarot and lost and owed bills. He wanted his son to get through four secondary-school grades and then become a civil servant with the post office, of course. "You always aim high," he used to say to Max's mother. No matter how disordered he was in civilian life, he was always absurdly tidy in respect of every article preserved from his days in the army. His uniform, that of an assistant paymaster sergeant on full service, with its gold triangles on the sleeves, its black

75

trousers and infantry shako, hung in the wardrobe like a tripartite and still surviving character, with its gleaming buttons polished every week. And the black, curved sword with the fluted handle, also polished every week, lay horizontally, supported by two nails along the wall, above the never-used writing desk, its faded golden tassel dropping from it, reminiscent of a rather dusty sunflower in bud. "If it hadn't been for you," his father would say to his mother, "I could have passed that examination and could have become paymaster sergeant." Every year, on the Emperor's birthday, Post Office Official Demant puts on civil-service uniform, with cocked hat and sword. On this day he does not play Tarot. Every year on the Emperor's birthday he resolves to begin a new life, free of debt. So he gets drunk. And he returns home in the small hours, draws his sword and issues orders to a whole regiment in the kitchen. The saucepans are platoons, teacups privates, plates companies. Simon Demant is the colonel, colonel in the service of Francis Joseph I. Max's mother, in lace nightcap and voluminously pleated nightgown, her bed jacket fluttering out behind her, gets out of bed to calm her husband.

One day, a day after the Emperor's birthday, his father had a stroke in bed. He had a gentle death and they gave him a magnificent funeral. All the postmen accompanied the coffin. His image, in his widow's memory, lived on as that of a model husband who had died in his Emperor's service and in the service of the Imperial and Royal Post. The uniforms—of Assistant Paymaster Sergeant and of Post Office Official Demant—still hung side by side in the wardrobe, preserved in constant splendor by his widow with camphor and brush. They looked like mummies. Every time the wardrobe was opened, the son felt that he saw two corpses of his father side by side.

He wanted, at all costs, to become a doctor. He gave lessons for a miserable six kronen a month, he wore torn boots. In rainy weather he left great wet footmarks on the clean polished floors of the well-to-do—torn soles leave larger footmarks. At last he got through his finals and became a doctor. But poverty faced him still, like a black wall against which he dashed himself to pieces. So he literally sank into the arms of the army. Seven years' food, seven years' drink, seven years' clothing, seven years' shelter, seven whole long years. He became an army doctor. And remained one. His life seemed to flow along much faster than his thoughts, and before he had made a decision he was an old man.

And he had married Fräulein Eva Knopfmacher.

Here, again, the regimental surgeon interrupted the flow of his memories. He walked back home.

It was already evening, when he reached his house. Unaccustomed festive lights shone from all rooms. "The old gentleman's come," the servant informed him. The old gentleman: his father-in-law, Herr Knopfmacher.

At that moment he stepped out of the bathroom in his long flowered dressing gown, razor in hand with cheerfully reddened freshly shaved fragrant cheeks. His face gave the impression of falling into two halves. It was held together only by the gray pointed beard.

"My dear Max," Herr Knopfmacher said, carefully laying his razor down on a side table. He extended his arm, allowing his dressing gown to flap open. They embraced with two hasty kisses and went into the study together.

"I'd like a cognac," said Herr Knopfmacher. Dr Demant opened the cabinet, looked at numerous bottles for a while, and then turned around.

"I don't quite know my way about these," he said, "I don't know what you like." He had ordered a selection of alcohol rather the way an ignorant man orders an assortment of books.

"You still haven't taken to it," said Herr Knopfmacher. "Well, what have you got, *slivovitz*, arrack, rum, cognac, liqueur of gentian, vodka?" he asked rapidly, in a manner ill becoming his dignity. He got up. Dressing gown flapping, he went over to the cabinet where, with a sure hand, he selected a bottle. "I wanted to give Eva a little surprise," began Herr Knopfmacher. "And, my dear Max, I feel I ought to mention this to you at once. You haven't been around the whole afternoon. Instead of you," he paused and stressed it: "Instead of you, I found a lieutenant here. An ass."

"He's the only friend," replied Demant, "that I've had since I began to serve in the regiment. He's Lieutenant Trotta. A very worthwhile person."

"Worthwhile person!" his father-in-law repeated. "I suppose I'm a worthwhile person, too, for instance. Well, I wouldn't advise you to leave me alone for one hour with a pretty woman, not if you valued her that much." Herr Knopf-macher joined thumb and forefinger, and, after a pause, repeated, "That much". The regimental surgeon grew pale. He took off his glasses and polished them for a long time. In this way he enveloped his surroundings in a beneficent mist in which his father-in-law in his dressing gown was an indistinct if extremely large white blur. And he did not immediately replace his glasses when he had finished polishing them, but kept them in his hand and talked into the mist.

"I really have no grounds whatever for suspecting Eva or my friend, dear Papa." The regimental surgeon spoke hesitatingly. The turn of phrase sounded completely foreign to him, taken from some remote manual, heard in some forgotten drama.

He put on his glasses, and at once old Knopfmacher, now distinct in circumference and contour, closed in on him. Now too, the phrase he had just used seemed to lie far behind him. It was certainly no longer true. The doctor was quite as well aware of that as his father-in-law.

"No grounds?" Herr Knopfmacher repeated. "But I have grounds. I know my daughter. You don't know your wife . . . . And I know lieutenants. And men, in general. Mind, I'm saying nothing against the army. Let's stick to the matter in hand. When my wife, your mother-in-law, was still young, I had plenty of opportunity of getting to know young men, both in and out of uniform. Yes, you're a strange lot, you. . . ."

He sought for a general designation of some group known only vaguely even to him to which his son-in-law and other fools might belong. He would have liked to say, "You intellectual academics." For he had become clever, well-to-do, and respected without recourse to studies. Indeed, he was expecting to be made a Commercial Councillor any day. He spun out a pleasing fantasy into the future, a fantasy of munificence, vast munificence, the inevitable consequence of such a title. If, for instance, he were to take Hungarian citizenship, he could come by the title even more rapidly. They didn't make life so difficult in Budapest. Besides, of course, it was always academics who made life difficult with their abstract notions; fools, all of them. His own son-in-law made things difficult. If the children were to get themselves involved in some sort of gossip, he'd have to forget about his title. He had to keep things on the straight and narrow—he, personally. He even had to keep his eye on another man's wife.

"My dear Max, before it's too late, I feel I ought to say to you straight out. . . . "

The doctor's face wilted at this insistence. He did not care for the truth at any price. Oh, he knew his wife just as well as Herr Knopfmacher knew his daughter. But he loved her, so what was he to do? He loved her. In Olmütz there had been District Commissioner Herdall; in Gratz, District Judge Lederer. So long as it wasn't a brother officer, the doctor could only thank his wife, and God! If only he could leave the army. . . . He was in constant, mortal danger. How often he had decided to make the attempt, to suggest to his father-in-law. . . . He tried once more.

"I know," he said, "there's always a certain element of risk about Eva, there has been for years. She doesn't stop to think, unfortunately, but she never goes to extremes." He stopped, then emphasized the words, "Not to extremes." With this phrase, he stifled the doubts which for years had given him no peace. He stamped out his own uncertainty and became convinced that his wife was not deceiving him. "Never," he said again, vehemently; he was quite sure now. "Eva's a nice person, in spite of everything. . . ."

"Certainly," his father-in-law reassured him.

"But," the regimental surgeon continued, "neither of us can stand this life for long. As you know, my work leaves me completely unfulfilled. What mightn't I have achieved by now but for the army. I should have an excellent position in society and Eva's ambitions would have been satisfied. Since, unfortunately, she is ambitious."

"She gets that from me," said Herr Knopfmacher, not displeased.

"She's dissatisfied," the regimental surgeon continued while his father-in-law replenished his glass. "She's dissatisfied and tries to find some diversion. I can't blame her."

"Well, you ought to keep her amused," interrupted his father-in-law.

"I'm . . ." Dr Demant could think of no word, was silent for a while and glanced at the brandy.

"Oh, come on, do have a drink," encouraged Herr Knopfmacher. And he got up, took a glass, and filled it. His dressing gown gaped, revealing his hairy chest and pleasant belly, which was as rosy as his cheeks. He held the glass in front of his son-in-law's lips. At last Max Demant drank it.

"And there's something else which may really force me to leave the service. When I joined, my eyes were quite sound. They're getting worse every year now. Now I have ... I can't ... I find it impossible to see anything distinctly without glasses. And so, strictly speaking, I ought to report it and resign."

"Yes?" asked Herr Knopfmacher. "And what ...?"

"What are we to live on?"

His father-in-law crossed one leg over the other, feeling suddenly chilly. He wrapped his dressing gown more closely around himself and held it together at his throat.

"Yes," he said, "do you really imagine I can provide for you? Every year since you two have been married—it so happens I know the exact amount—I've been letting you have three hundred kronen a month. Oh, I know, I know, Eva's extravagant. But she'd still be that if you started a new life. And so would you, my dear son." He became affectionate. "Ah, my dear Max, things aren't nearly as easy as they used to be."

Max said no more. Herr Knopfmacher felt that he had parried the attack, and so he allowed his dressing gown to fall open again. He had another brandy. He kept a clear head, he knew himself. These academic simpletons. Still, this one was a better son-in-law than the other, Hermann, Elizabeth's husband. His daughters cost him six hundred kronen a month. He knew the exact amount by heart. But supposing the regimental surgeon were to go blind ... he scrutinized the flashing glasses. He ought to be keeping an eye on his wife. It ought not to present any difficulty to someone short-sighted.

"What's the time?" he asked, very kindly and very innocent.

"Getting on toward seven," said the doctor.

"I'd better go up and dress," his father-in-law decided. He rose and nodded and made his way out of the door with measured dignity. The regimental surgeon remained. After the familiar loneliness of the churchyard, the loneliness of his house seemed overpowering, uncanny, almost threatening. For the first time in his life, he poured himself a brandy. It was as if he were having his first drink. Get things straight, he thought. He made up his mind to speak to his wife. He went out into the passage.

"Where's my wife?"

"In the bedroom," the servant told him.

Shall I knock, the doctor asked himself. No, proclaimed his resolute heart. He turned the handle. There stood his wife in front of the wardrobe mirror wearing blue panties and holding a large, rose-pink powder puff in her hand.

"Oh," she shrieked, holding a hand across her breasts.

The regimental surgeon stayed in the doorway.

"It's you?" asked his wife. It was a question which sounded like a yawn.

"Yes, me," the regimental surgeon said in a firm voice. It felt as if someone else were speaking. He was wearing his glasses, but he was talking into a haze. "Your father tells me," he began, "that Lieutenant Trotta was here."

She turned. She stood, in the blue panties, holding up her powder puff like a weapon against her husband, and said in a twittering voice, "Your friend Trotta was here. And father's come. Have you seen him yet?"

"Yes, precisely about that," said the regimental surgeon, and he saw at once that he had made a false move.

For a time there was silence.

"Why can't you knock?" she asked.

"I wanted to give you a pleasant surprise."

"You frighten me."

"I . . ." the regimental surgeon began. He wanted to say, I'm your husband. He said, "I love you."

He loved her, indeed. There she stood, in blue panties holding her pink powder puff. And he loved her.

I'm jealous, he thought. He said, "I don't like people coming to the house without my knowing."

"What a charming boy he is," his wife said, and slowly, lavishly, began to powder herself in front of the mirror.

The regimental surgeon went up to his wife and grasped her shoulders. He looked in the mirror. He saw his brown hairy hands on her white shoulders. She smiled. He could see it in the glass, the glassy echo of her smile. "Be honest," he implored her. It was as if his hands were kneeling on her shoulders. He knew at once that she would not be honest with him. And he repeated, "Please be honest." He saw her pale deft hands fluffing out the blond hair at her temples. An unnecessary gesture. It excited him. From the mirror, her gaze met his, a gray, cool, arid glance, swift as a steel dart. I love her, he thought. She hurts me, and I love her. He asked, "Did you mind my being out the whole afternoon?"

She half turned. Now she was sitting, her body disjointed above the hips, a lifeless creature, a wax dummy in silk underwear. From under her long black lashes her bright eyes appeared artificial, darting icy imitation lightning. Her thin hands lay on her drawers like white birds embroidered on a blue silk background. In a deep voice, which he thought he had never before heard from her, and which seemed still further to emphasize the clockwork in her breast, she said very slowly, "I never miss you."

He began to walk up and down without looking at his wife. He pushed two chairs out of the way. It was as though he had much more to push aside. Perhaps he ought to push the walls down, break through the ceiling with his head, tread the floorboards into the ground. Very faintly he heard his spurs clanking in the distance, as if someone else were wearing them. A single word galvanized his mind, rushed in and out, flew ceaselessly through his head. Over, over, over. A small word. Swift, feather-light, and heavy as iron, it flew through his mind. His pace increased, his feet kept pace with the winged pendulum beat of the word in his head. Suddenly he stopped.

"So you don't love me?" he asked. He was certain that she would not answer him. She will be silent, he thought.

She answered, "No," raising the black, fringed curtains of her eyelashes, and with naked, horribly naked eyes, looked him up and down before she added, "You're drunk."

He realized that he had had too much to drink and thought with relief, I'm drunk and I'm glad I'm drunk. And he said in a strange voice, as though it were now his duty to be drunk, "I see." So vague were his notions about the words a drunk man would use in such a situation, and how he would hiccup. He went one better: "I'll kill you," he said very slowly.

"Go on, kill me," she tittered in her usual bright voice. She got up. She got up quickly, silkily, her powder puff still in her right hand. The slim rounded outline of her silken legs reminded him of the limbs of dummies in fashionable shop windows, the whole woman is made up of fragments.

He no longer loved her, he no longer loved her. He was filled with a malice which was repugnant to him, a rage which had crept upon him. It was an unknown enemy from distant regions which now had possession of his heart. He said out loud what he had thought an hour earlier, "I'm going to put things straight. I shall put things straight."

She laughed with a resonance unknown to him. A theatrical laugh, he thought. An uncontrollable urge to prove to her that he could keep her in order gave his muscles strength, his weak eyes unusual penetration.

"I'll leave you to your father. I'm going to find Trotta," he said.

"Run along, run along," said his wife.

He left. Before leaving the house, he went back into the study to have another drink. For the first time in his life, he was returning to alcohol as to a secret friend. He poured himself a glass, then another, then a third. He left the house with jingling steps. He went to the club and asked the orderly, "Where is Lieutenant Trotta?"

Lieutenant Trotta was not at the club.

The regimental surgeon turned off onto the long, straight highroad which led to the barracks. The moon was already on the wane, but it still shone clear and silver, almost a full moon. Not a breath stirred on this quiet country road. The meager shadows of the bare chestnuts on either side of the road traced confused patterns over the slightly arched crest of the road. His steps rang out hard and frosty. He was going to find Lieutenant Trotta. From the distance he could see the massive wall of the barracks in bluish-white and he marched against it, the enemy stronghold. The brassy, frozen blare of lights-out came toward him. Dr Demant walked straight through the metallic sounds, he stepped on them. Soon, at any moment, Lieutenant Trotta would appear. He detached himself, a thin black line, from the powerful white of the barracks, and approached the doctor. Another three minutes. Now they were facing each other. The Lieutenant saluted. Dr Demant listened to himself asking, as from far away, "You spent the afternoon with my wife, Lieutenant?"

The question re-echoed from the glassy blue dome of the sky. For some weeks now they had been calling each other by Christian names. But now they faced each other as enemies.

83

"Yes, doctor, I called on your wife this afternoon," the Lieutenant said.

Dr Demant came up close to the Lieutenant. "What is there between my wife and you, Lieutenant?" The doctor's thick glasses glinted. The regimental surgeon no longer had eyes, only glasses.

Carl Joseph was silent. It was as if in the whole wide world there was no answer to Dr Demant's question. One might have looked for decades for an answer; as if human speech were exhausted, dried up for all time. His heart pounded in quick, dry, hard beats against his ribs. Hard and dry, his tongue cleaved to his mouth. An immense, cruel emptiness sang in his head. He felt he was standing close up against a nameless peril which had already engulfed him. He was standing at the edge of a gigantic black precipice whose darkness had already closed above his head. Dr Demant's words rang from frozen, icy distances, dead words, corpses of words.

"Answer me, Lieutenant Trotta."

Silence. Nothing. Stars glitter, the moon shines. "Answer me, Lieutenant."

"Lieutenant." He meant Carl Joseph.

He summoned the miserable vestiges of his strength. A thin, worthless sentence threaded its way through the roaring emptiness in his mind. He clicked his heels (a military instinct, but also simply in order to hear some sound). The jingling of his own spurs steadied him. And he said very quietly, "There is absolutely nothing, Dr Demant, between your wife and me."

Nothing. Silence. Stars glitter, the moon shines. Dr Demant said nothing. He stared at Carl Joseph through dead lenses. The Lieutenant said again, very quietly, "Absolutely nothing, Dr Demant."

He's taken leave of his senses, thinks the Lieutenant. And: It's gone. It's gone. It is as if he can hear the dry splintering sound of something breaking. "Broken faith," he remembers having read the phrase. "Broken friendship." Yes, it is a broken friendship.

Suddenly he knows that for weeks the army surgeon has been his friend. A friend. They have been meeting every day. Once he went to the cemetery with the regimental surgeon and walked with him among the tombs. "There are so many dead," the regimental surgeon said to him. "Do you feel that we live on the dead?" "I live on my grandfather," Trotta said. He saw the portrait of the hero of Solferino, fading at home under the study ceiling. Yes, some ring of brotherhood sounded in the doctor's voice; brotherhood glowed in his heart, like a small flame. "My grandfather," Demant had said, "was a tall old Jew with a silver beard." Carl Joseph saw a tall old Jew with a silver beard. They were grandsons, both of them were grandsons. When the regimental surgeon mounted his horse he always looked a little ridiculous, even more minute than on foot, as if he were carried by his horse like a bag of oats. Carl Joseph rides just as badly. He knows exactly what he looks like. He can see himself as in a mirror. They are the two officers in the regiment behind whose backs the others titter and jibe. Dr Demant and the grandson of the hero of Solferino. The only two in the whole regiment. Two friends.

"Your word of honor?" the doctor asks.

Without answering, Trotta holds out his hand. The doctor says, "Thank you," and accepts the hand. They walk back together along the road. Ten, twenty paces, and they do not speak.

Suddenly the regimental surgeon begins, "You mustn't hold it against me. I've been drinking. My father-in-law arrived today. He saw you. She doesn't love me. She doesn't love me. Do you understand? . . . You're young," says the regimental surgeon after a pause as if he means that he has spoken in vain. "You're young."

"I understand," says Carl Joseph.

They march in step, their spurs jingle, their swords clatter. The familiar yellow lights of the town beckon them. Both would have liked to continue forever along this road. They would have liked to march side by side like this, on and on. Both of them have something they would like to say, both are silent. A word, a word so easily spoken. But it remains unspoken.

This is the last time, thinks the Lieutenant, we shall ever walk together like this. Now they have reached the outskirts of the town. The regimental surgeon needs to say something before they turn into the town. "It's not because of my wife," he says. "All that's become unimportant. I've got over that. It's on your account." He waits for an answer and knows that none would come. "Thank you, it's all right now," he says very quickly. "I'm going to the club. Are you coming?"

No, Lieutenant Trotta is not going to the club that evening. He is going back.

"Good night," he says and returns to the barracks.

Chapter 7

Winter arrived. It was still dark in the mornings when the regiment rode out. The thin ice crumbled under the horses' hoofs. Gray smoke streamed from the animals' nostrils and from the mouths of their riders. A faint breath of frost collected in drops on the sheaths of the heavy swords and the barrels of the light carbines. The small town grew even smaller. The muted, frozen bugle calls enticed none of the usual spectators on to the pavement. Only the cabmen at their rank raised their bearded heads each morning. They used sleighs when a lot of snow had fallen, and the little bells of their horses' harnesses jingled, set in constant motion by the restlessness of the shivering horses. The days were as alike as snowflakes. The officers of the regiment of Uhlans waited for some unusual incident to break the monotony of their lives. But no one knew what form it might take. Yet some terrible surprise seemed to be buried in the uneasy bowels of the winter. And one day it burst upon them like crimson lightning from out of the winter snow.

On that day Captain Taittinger was not sitting alone behind the glass door of his pastry shop. Since early afternoon, he had been in the room behind the shop, surrounded by the junior officers. He looked paler and more haggard to them. Indeed, they were all pale. They drank a lot of liqueurs, but their complexions became no ruddier. They were not eating anything. In front of Captain Taittinger only was piled the usual mound of pastries. Indeed, perhaps he was indulging himself even more than on other days. For grief was gnawing at his innards, hollowing them out, and he had to keep himself going. So while he put pastry after pastry into his wide open mouth, he repeated his story for the fifth time to his ever-eager audience.

"Well now, gentleman, the main thing to remember, absolute discretion with civilians. When I was in the Ninth

Dragoons we had one of those fellows who can never keep their mouths shut. In the reserve, of course, loaded with money, too, by the way, and the business had to happen almost the very day he joined. Well, of course, when we came to bury poor Baron Seidl the whole town knew why he'd died so suddenly. So, gentlemen, I hope that on this occasion we shall get a more discreet . . ." He wanted to say "funeral" but stopped short, tried for another word but found none. He gazed at the ceiling; up around about his own head and the heads of his audience, a frightful silence reigned. The Captain finished at last, "A more discreet proceeding." He took a breath, swallowed a pastry, and finished his glass of water in one gulp.

They all felt that he had summoned death. Death hovered above them and was by no means familiar to them. They had been born in peacetime, had become officers during peaceable maneuvers and exercises. They were unaware then that a few years later all, without exception, were to encounter death. Not one of them there had sharp enough ears to discern the whir of the vast machinery which was already beginning to manufacture war. Snowy peace reigned in the little garrison. Death, crimson and black, fluttered above them in the dusk of the small back room.

"I can't understand it," said one of the young men. They had all said much the same, over and over again.

"But haven't I just told you umpteen times?" answered Taittinger. "What started it was that touring musical comedy. The devil induced me to turn out that night and the—what do you call it now? I can't even think what the thing was called—*Rastelbinder*, that's it. Well, as I say, that's what it all started with. As I'm coming out of the theater, there's Trotta, standing around in the snow, all by himself, looking as though he'd just lost a coin. Fact is, I'd come out before the end. Always do, you know. Can't hold out till the end. I can usually tell by the time they've come to the third act that it's going to have a happy ending, and then I let them get on with it and get away as quietly as I can. Besides, I'd already seen the thing three times. Anyway, as I say, there is poor old Trotta standing around in the snow like a lost sheep. I say, 'Quite a decent show.' And then I mention Demant's strange behavior, that he'd hardly looked at me, leaves his wife alone in the second act, and simply doesn't come back. He could have handed her over to me, but just to get up and go, just like that. Seemed almost indecent. And so I say all this to Trotta. 'Well,' he says, 'it's ages since I've spoken to Demant.' "

"For weeks they went about together," somebody exclaimed.

"Of course, I know. That's just what made me tell Trotta how oddly Demant had behaved. All the same, I wasn't going to get myself mixed up in anything that wasn't my business. So I simply ask Trotta if he'd care to come over here with me. 'No,' he says, 'I have an appointment.' So I go. And naturally, it would be just the evening when this place has early closing. Fate, gentlemen! Of course, I go straight over to the club. Then, without the slightest notion, I happen to tell Tattenbach, and anyone else who happened to be around the story about Demant and how Trotta has an appointment outside the theater. I can still hear old Tattenbach whistling. 'What's up?' I say to him. 'Never you mind,' he says. 'Keep your eyes open, that's all I say. You keep your eyes peeled.' And he starts singing, 'Trotta and his Eva, Trotta and his Eva,' over and over again, like a music-hall song. And I don't know any Eva, I think he must mean the one in Paradise, that is to say, symbolically and generally speaking—see what I mean, gentlemen?"

They all saw what he meant and confirmed it with nods and exclamations. Not only had they understood the Captain's story, they knew it all from beginning to end. Yet they made him tell it over and over, since, in the deepest, most fantastic place in his heart, each hoped that Taittinger at last might change the facts and leave a loophole for some less unpropitious sequel. So they asked him over and over again, but nothing he said sounded different. Not the smallest of the depressing details changed.

"And now?" one asked.

"The rest you know," the Captain replied. "At the very minute we're leaving the club, Tattenbach, Kindermann, and I, Trotta, with Frau Demant on his arm, literally comes barging into us."

" 'Look here,' says Tattenbach, 'didn't Trotta say he had an appointment?' "

" 'It could be a coincidence,' I say to Tattenbach."

"And so it was. That I know now. Demant's wife came out of the theater by herself. Trotta felt he ought to see her home.

He'd had to miss his own appointment. None of this would ever have happened if Demant had handed his wife over to me in the intermission, none of it."

"No," they echoed, "none of it."

"Well, and then next evening Tattenbach is drunk in the club as usual. So as soon as Demant comes in he gets up and says, 'Good evening, Doctor Ikey.' "

"That started it."

"In bad taste," two of the others observed simultaneously.

"Bad taste, of course. But drunk, so what could you do? I say, 'Good evening, doctor,' quite civil. But Demant says to Tattenbach, in a voice I wouldn't have credited him with, 'Captain Tattenbach, you know how to address me.' Tattenbach says, 'If I were you, I should stop at home and keep my eyes peeled.' And he holds on to the chair. Incidentally, it was his birthday. Did I mention that?"

"No," they all cried.

"Well, it was. It happened to be his birthday."

Greedily they absorbed this new item. The information that it had all happened on Tattenbach's birthday might, it was felt, lead to a more hopeful outcome of the wretched business. And they all tried to think of a way of utilizing the fact that it had been Tattenbach's birthday. And little Count Sternberg, through whose head thoughts always flew like isolated birds through thick clouds, leaving no trace, at once expressed his premature relief by exclaiming, "Well, but that makes all the difference, doesn't it? I mean, it's quite a different matter if it all happened on his birthday."

They looked at little Count Sternberg, puzzled and disconsolate and yet ready to take recourse in nonsense. Sternberg's notions were extremely foolish, but perhaps if one scrutinized the facts closely they might reveal some hope, some consolation. The hollow laughter to which Taittinger gave vent at once overwhelmed them with new fears. With parted lips, inchoate sounds on their inarticulate tongues, eyes wide open yet unseeing, they stared, struck dumb and blind. For a few seconds they had believed they could hear the accents of consolation, and see hope shine forth. Now silent darkness surrounded them. In the whole wide, freezing, inarticulate world, piled high with snow, there seemed to be nothing save Taittinger's five-times-told, eternally unalterable tale. He continued.

"Well, so Tattenbach says, 'If I were you, I should stay at home and keep my eyes peeled.' And Demant sticks his head out at him as if he'd been inspecting the sick and says, 'You're drunk, Captain Tattenbach.' So Tattenbach gurgles 'I'd stop at home and look after my wife. Senior officers shouldn't let their wives go walking around with lieutenants at midnight.' And Demant says 'You're drunk and you're a scoundrel.' And then, just as I am getting up and before I can manage to move, Tattenbach starts bellowing like mad at him, 'Jew, Jew, Jew!' eight times running, he says it. I had the presence of mind to count."

"Good for you," says little Sternberg, and Taittinger nods to him.

"And," continued the Captain, "I also had the presence of mind to yell out, 'All orderlies out of the room.' What business had they to be there?"

"Bravo," applauded little Sternberg again and they all nodded approval. They grew silent again. From the pastry cook's kitchen they heard the hard clatter of plates and dishes, and from the street the bright jingling of a sled. Taittinger stuffed another pastry into his mouth.

"So now the fat's in the fire," exclaimed little Sternberg.

Taittinger swallowed the remains of his pastry and simply said, "Seven-twenty, tomorrow morning."

Seven-twenty, tomorrow morning, they knew the conditions. Service pistols, simultaneous discharge at ten paces. Swords had been out of the question for Demant, he couldn't fence. At seven in the morning the regiment would be on its way to the water meadow for exercises. It was scarcely two hundred paces from the meadow to the so-called green clearing behind the old castle where the duel was to take place. Every officer knows that tomorrow during exercises he would hear two shots. They could all hear them already. Death's wings, crimson and black, hovered above them.

"My bill," Taittinger called out. And they left the pastry shop.

It was snowing again. They straggled forth, a mute, dark-blue pack, across the mute white snow, wandering in pairs or alone. Each was anxious not to be alone and yet found it impossible to stay with others. They strove to lose one another in the alleys of the little town and were forced to encounter each other again a few minutes later. The twisting alleys brought them together. They were trapped in the little town and in their great perplexity. Each time one unexpectedly came across another, he was taken aback by the other's fear. All longed for dinner and at the same time dreaded the approaching evening at the club, where tonight not all would be present.

Indeed, not everyone was at the club. Tattenbach was not there, nor Major Prohaska, the doctor, nor First Lieutenant Zander, nor Lieutenant Christ, nor any of the seconds. Taittinger was not eating. He sat at a chessboard, playing himself. They were all quiet. The orderlies stood by the doors, stony and rigid. They heard the slow, crisp ticking of the grandfather clock; to the left of it the Supreme War Lord stared down through hard, china-blue eyes onto his silent officers. No one ventured to leave alone, or ask anyone to come with him. So they all stayed where they were. Where two or three were sitting together, their words dropped heavily, one by one, from their lips. A great leaden silence weighed between question and answer. They all felt the silence on their backs.

They thought of those who were not with them as if they were already dead. They all remembered Dr Demant's arrival a few weeks earlier after his long sick leave. They could see his hesitant walk and shining glasses. They could see Count Tattenbach. His short, stout body on bandy riders' legs, his ever-crimson head with its short, fair hair parted in the middle and his red-rimmed, pale little eyes. They could hear Demant's low voice and the Count's loud one. And although the words "honor" and "death," "shooting" and "killing," "death" and "grave" had been familiar in their hearts and minds ever since they had been able to think and feel, it seemed incredible to them on this day that they were perhaps cut off forever from the Captain's loud voice and the doctor's quiet one. Whenever the melancholy chimes of the big clock sounded, the men felt that their own last hour had struck. They would not trust their ears and glanced at the wall. It was true, time had not stopped. Seven-twenty, seven-twenty, seven-twenty. It hammered in every head.

They rose, one by one, hesitant, shame-faced. As they left each other, they felt they were betraying each other. They left almost without a sound. Their spurs did not jingle, their swords did not clatter; mutely their feet trod on the silent earth. The club was empty before midnight. And at a quarter to twelve

First Lieutenant Schlegel and Lieutenant Kindermann reached
the barracks where they lived. On the first floor, where the
officers had their rooms, one lighted window cast down its
yellow rectangle into the darkness of the barrack square. They
glanced up at it together.

"That's Trotta," Kindermann said.

"Yes, it's Trotta," Schlegel repeated.

"We ought to look in on him."

"He won't want us."

Together they jingled along the passage, stopped outside
Trotta's door, and listened. There was no sound. First Lieutenant Schlegel grasped the handle but did not turn it. He drew
back his hand, and both men retreated. They nodded to each
other and went to their rooms.

Indeed, Lieutenant Trotta had not heard them. For nearly
four hours he had been struggling to write his father a detailed
letter, but could not get beyond the opening lines.

"Dear Father," he began, "through no fault of mine and
without my knowledge, I have become the cause of a tragic
affair of honor." His hand was heavy. It hung with quaking
pen, a dead, useless instrument, over the paper. This was his
first difficult letter. It seemed impossible to the Lieutenant
to await the outcome of the affair before writing to the District
Commissioner. Ever since the unfortunate quarrel between
Tattenbach and Demant, he had put off his letter from day to
day. Now it seemed impossible not to get it off that very night.
What would the hero of Solferino have done in his place? Carl
Joseph could feel his grandfather's compelling gaze at the back
of his neck. The hero seemed to be urging his weak, hesitant
grandson to act decisively, promptly. He must write at once,
here and now. Yes, he ought even, perhaps, to have gone
straight to his father. Between the dead hero of Solferino and
the vacillating grandson stood his father, the District Commissioner, guardian of the honor of the Trottas and sole defender
of their inheritance. Full and ruddy, the heroic blood of
Solferino still flowed in the veins of the District Commissioner.
By not informing his father in good time he was also trying
to hide something from his grandfather.

But in order to write such letters he needed to be as strong
as his grandfather, as simple and direct, as close to the peasants
of Sipolje. He was only the grandson. This letter broke in a

horrifying manner the leisurely series of routine epistles sent once a week by every Trotta from son to father now as always.

A gory letter. He had to write it.

So the Lieutenant continued:

All I did was to take a harmless walk at about midnight with the wife of our regimental surgeon. The circumstances made any other course impossible. Some brother officers saw us. Captain Tattenbach, who is, unfortunately, frequently drunk, made insinuations in the worst possible taste to the doctor about it. Tomorrow, at seven-twenty in the morning, they are going to shoot it out. It looks as if I shall be obliged to challenge Tattenbach if he survives, as I hope he will. The conditions are stringent.

Your dutiful son, Carl Joseph Trotta, Lieutenant

P.S. Perhaps I may have to leave the regiment.

Now, the Lieutenant felt, the worst was over, But when his thoughts strayed back to the study ceiling, he saw again hidden among its shadows his grandfather's admonitory face. And next to the hero of Solferino he felt he could see the white-bearded face of the Jewish innkeeper whose grandson was Regimental Surgeon Demant. And he felt the dead calling to the living, and it semed to him that he himself had a duel to face. He would fall and die . . . .

On those Sundays, long ago, when Carl Joseph had stood on his father's balcony while below Herr Nechwal's military band had delivered the Radetzky March, it had seemed a trifle to fall and die. Death had been a familiar notion to the pupil of the Imperial and Royal Cadet School, though a remote one. At seven-twenty in the morning, death was lying in wait for his friend Dr Demant and the day after, or some days later, for Lieutenant Carl Joseph von Trotta. Oh, horror and darkness, to be the cause of death's dark advent and finally become its victim. How many corpses strewed the road. Like milestones along the roads of other men, gravestones lay along Trotta's road. It was certain that he would never see his friend again, just as he had never again seen Katherina. Never again! Before Carl Joseph's eyes the words extended, without shore or limit, a dead sea of mute eternity. The little Lieutenant clenched his feeble white fist against the strong dark law which strewed his path with gravestones, the law which would set no barriers against the implacability of the nevermore, and which would not lighten eternal darkness. He clenched his fist and went to the window, to raise it in the face of the dark sky. But he raised only his eyes. He saw the cold glitter of the winter stars. He remembered the night when he and the doctor had last walked together from the barracks to the town. Never again. He had known it even then.

Suddenly a longing for his friend overcame him, and also the hope that it might yet be possible to save the doctor. It was one-twenty, Dr Demant still had six hours to live, six good long hours. To the Lieutenant these hours now seemed almost as overwhelming as limitless eternity had before. He rushed to the cupboard, strapped on his sword, hurried into his coat, ran down the passage, almost floated down the stairs, sped on across the nocturnal square, out of the gates, past the sentry, on again along the quiet highroad, and reached the little town in ten minutes. A few minutes later, he was sitting in the only sled which stayed out all night and, with a heartening jingle of sleigh bells, was gliding towards the southern outskirts of the town towards the doctor's house. The little house was asleep behind its gates, all its windows sightless. Trotta pressed the bell. Everything remained silent. He shouted Demant's name. Nothing stirred. He waited and made the coachman crack his whip. No one answered.

If it had been Count Tattenbach he had been looking for, it would have been simple enough to find him. The Count, on the night before a duel, was probably sitting at Resi's drinking his own health. But it seemed impossible to guess where Demant might be. Perhaps the regimental surgeon was wandering through the streets of the town. Perhaps he had gone to visit familiar graves, choosing his own among them. So, "To the cemeteries," Carl Joseph directed the startled cabby. The cemeteries were quite near, one next to the other. The sled pulled up in front of the old wall and the locked gates. Trotta got out. He went to the gates. Obeying the crazy notion that had urged him on, he cupped his hands round his mouth and shouted Demant's name across the graves in a strange voice which issued like a sob from his heart; and he thought as he shouted that he was calling one already dead. And he became afraid and began to tremble like one of the bare shrubs between the gravestones over which the wind of the winter-night storm whistled. The Lieutenant's sword clanked at his hip.

The cabman, perched on the box of his sled, felt afraid for his fare. He thought, simpleton that he was, that this officer was either a ghost or a lunatic. But he was also afraid to whip his horse and drive off. His teeth chattered, his heart thumped fiercely against his heavy coat of cat furs. "Lieutenant," he begged, "won't you get in again?"

The Lieutenant returned. "Back to the town," he said. He got off in the town and conscientiously walked the winding streets and across minute squares. The tinny sound of a pianola, blaring through the nocturnal silence, gave his steps some provisional goal. He hurried toward its metallic clanging. It was coming through the dimly lit glass door of a pub, not far from Frau Resi's establishment, a pub frequented by privates only and out of bounds to officers. Carl Joseph stood by the brightly lit windows and peered over the top of the reddish curtains into the bar. He could see the counter and the lean publican in shirtsleeves. At one of the tables three men, also in shirtsleeves, were playing cards; at another a corporal was sitting with a girl, glasses of beer in front of them. In the corner sat a man by himself. He was holding a pencil in his hand and bending over a sheet of paper. He wrote something, stopped, sipped a glass of brandy, and stared into space. Suddenly he turned his glasses toward the window. Carl Joseph recognized him: it was Dr Demant in civilian clothes.

Carl Joseph tapped on the glass door and the publican opened it. The Lieutenant asked him to send out the gentleman who was sitting by himself. The regimental surgeon stepped outside on to the pavement.

"It's me, Trotta," the Lieutenant said and held out his hand.

"So you've found me," the doctor said. He spoke quietly, as usual, but, Trotta felt, much more distinctly, for in a mysterious way the words sounded above the blare of the pianola. It was the first time Carl Joseph had seen him in civilian clothes. This familiar voice coming from the doctor's transformed appearance felt like a reassuring messenger from home. Indeed, the voice seemed even more familiar because Demant looked so strange. All the fears which had confused the Lieutenant that night fled at the sound of his friend's voice, a voice Carl Joseph had not heard for many weeks and which he had missed. Yes, he had missed it, he realized now. The pianola ceased its braying. They could hear the night wind howl from time to time and feel

96

the sting of the powdery snow which blew into their faces. The Lieutenant took another step towards the doctor. He felt he could not come close enough.

"You're not to die," he wanted to say. It flashed into his mind that Demant was standing out here without his overcoat on, in the snow, in the wind. In civilian clothes it isn't so obvious, he thought. And he said with concern, "You'll be catching cold."

At once Demant's face lit up with his familiar smile which pursed his lips and raised the black mustache a little. Carl Joseph blushed. He hasn't time to catch cold, the Lieutenant thought. At the same time he heard Dr Demant's gentle voice. "My dear friend, there's no time for me to fall ill." He could speak while he smiled. The doctor's words went right through his smile and yet the smile remained intact. It hung in front of his lips, a sad little white veil. "But let's go in," he continued. He stood in front of the dimly lit door, a motionless black shadow, casting another across the snow. Silver snow powdered his black hair, which was illuminated by the light from the pub. Above his head there was, as it were, the glow of celestial worlds. Trotta was almost prepared to go back. He wanted to say good night and go quickly.

"Come on, let's go inside," said Demant again. "I'll ask if you can come in unobtrusively," He left Carl Joseph and returned with the publican. They crossed a hallway and a yard and reached the kitchen of the pub.

"Do they know you here?" Trotta asked, and the doctor answered, "I come here occasionally—that is, I used to come here." Carl Joseph stared at him. "Are you surprised? After all, I had my own little ways."

Why did he say "had", thought the Lieutenant, remembering how in grammar that sort of thing had been called the past definite. "Had." What made the regimental surgeon say "had?"

The publican brought a little table and two chairs into the kitchen and lit a gas jet under a green globe. Out in the bar the pianola continued its blare, a potpourri of celebrated marches, among them the opening drumbeats of the Radetzky March, distorted by hoarse subsidiary noises but still recognizable. The familiar portrait of the Supreme War Lord in flower-white uniform was half visible through the greenish shadow spreading over the whitewashed walls. The Emperor's white uniform

97

was spotted with numerous fly marks, as if it had been riddled with minute grapeshot; and Francis Joseph's eyes, painted a hard china-blue in this portrait as in the others, were extinguished by the shadow of the lampshade.

The doctor pointed his finger at the portrait. "A year ago," he said "that was still hanging out in the bar. But now the landlord no longer feels inclined to give proof of his loyalty." The pianola stopped. At the same instant a clock on the wall chimed two hard strokes.

"Two o'clock," said the Lieutenant.

"Five more hours," said the regimental surgeon. The landlord brought some *slivovitz*. Seven-twenty: it hammered inside the Lieutenant's skull.

He took his liqueur glass and raised it and said, in the strong firm voice in which they had been taught to rap out their orders, "Your health! You must live!"

"Here's to an easy death," replied the regimental surgeon, and emptied his glass, while Carl Joseph put his down again.

"It's a pointless death," the doctor continued. "As pointless as my life has been."

"I won't have you die!" cried the Lieutenant, stamping on the tiles of the kitchen floor. "And I don't want to die either, and my life is just as pointless."

"Be quiet," replied Demant. "You're the grandson of the hero of Solferino. He almost died equally pointlessly. Though it does make some difference whether you die with as much faith as he had, or as feebly as we two." He was silent. "As we two," he began after a while. "Our grandfathers did not bequeath us much fortitude. Not enough to live. Perhaps just enough to die a pointless death. Oh," he pushed his glass away, and it was as though he were thrusting away the whole world, including his friend. "Oh," he said again, "I'm tired. I've been tired for years. Tomorrow I shall die like a hero, a nice little hero. Quite contrary to my nature, and the nature of my ancestors, and that of my race, and against my grandfather's wish. In the big old books he used to read there is the saying, 'Whosoever raises his hand against his brother is a murderer.' But tomorrow someone is going to raise his pistol against me, and I shall raise my pistol against him. And I shall be a murderer. But I'm short-sighted, I shall not take aim. I shall have my little revenge. If I take off my glasses, I can see nothing at all, nothing at all.

98

I shall fire without seeing. That will be more natural and more honest and quite fitting."

Lieutenant Trotta did not entirely take in what the regimental surgeon was saying. The doctor's voice was familiar, and—once he had got used to the civilian clothes—so were his shape and face. But Dr Demant's thoughts came from immeasurably remote regions, from that immeasurably distant region in which Demant's grandfather, white-bearded king of publicans, might have lived. Trotta tried hard to understand, as at school he had tried hard at trigonometry, but comprehended less and less. He could only feel his new belief in the possibility of still saving everything sink slowly, and feel his hope dying away to brittle ash, as frail as this dim, hissing gas mantle. His heart beat loudly, like the hollow, tinny chimes of the clock on the wall. He could not understand his friend. Perhaps he had come too late. He still had much to say to him. But his tongue lay heavy in his mouth. His lips parted. They were dry, they trembled a little, he could only just manage to close them again.

"You look as though you've got a temperature," the regimental surgeon said in precisely the voice he was accustomed to use with his patients. He rapped on the table, the landlord came in with fresh glasses. "And you haven't even finished your first."

Trotta emptied the first glass obediently. "I discovered drink too late," said the doctor. "A pity. You'll never believe me when I say I am sorry I never drank."

The Lieutenant made a tremendous effort, looked up, and for a few seconds stared into the doctor's face. He raised his second glass, it was heavy, his hand shook, spilling a few drops. He drank it at a gulp. Rage flared up in him, mounting to his head, flaming in his cheeks. "I'd better go," he said, "I can't stand your jokes. I was glad I'd found you. I went to your house. I rang. I drove to the cemetery. I stood and shouted your name through the gates like a lunatic. I've . . ."

He got no further. Vague words, mute words, mute shadows of words, trembled on his quivering lips. His eyes were suddenly scalding wet and loud sobs shook his chest. He wanted to get up and run away, for he was very much ashamed. I'm crying, he thought, I'm crying. But he was powerless, infinitely powerless, in the face of this incomprehensible power which forced him to cry. He was glad to give himself up to it, surrendered ecstatically to impotence. He heard his own sobs and reveled

99

in them, was ashamed but nevertheless relished his shame. He flung himself into the arms of sweet grief and repeated stupidly amid repeated sobs, "I don't want you to die, I don't want you to die. I don't want it, I don't want it."

Dr Demant got up, walked about the kitchen, stopped under the portrait of the Supreme War Lord, began to count the black fly marks spotting the tunic of his sovereign. Turning from this absurd occupation, he came over to stand beside Carl Joseph, set a light hand on the heaving shoulders, and bent his shining spectacles over the Lieutenant's light-brown head. Wise Dr Demant had already settled his account with life, had sent his wife to her father in Vienna, given his servant leave, shut up his house. He had been staying in the Golden Bear ever since the unfortunate business began. He was ready. Since, contrary to his custom, he had started to drink, he had even been able to see some hidden meaning in this pointless duel, had reached the point of invoking his own death as the lawful termination of his life, full of error. He could, indeed, apprehend some intimation of that other world in which he had always believed. Long before the peril in which he now found himself, he had been familiar with graves, the dead had been his friends. The childish love for his life was extinguished. Jealousy, which a few weeks ago had still flared so painfully in his heart, was now a little heap of cold ashes. His will, just made, addressed to the colonel, was in his breast pocket. He had nothing to leave and very few people to remember. And so nothing had been forgotten. Alcohol eased his thoughts, it was only the waiting which made him impatient. Seven-twenty, the appointed hour, which for days had been hammering its terror into the anxious minds of brother officers, chimed in his like a little silver peal. For the first time since he had donned uniform, he felt light-hearted, strong, full of courage. He enjoyed the proximity of death as a convalescent relishes the proximity of life. He had come to terms, he was ready.

Now he was standing here, short-sighted and helpless as always, at his young friend's side. Yes, there was still youth and friendship and tears, which were shed for him. Suddenly he began to long again for the dreariness of his life, for the nauseating garrison, his hated uniform, the dullness of routine inspections, the stink of assembled unclothed privates, the endless vaccinations, the smell of carbolic in the hospital, his wife's ugly moods, the safe constriction of his house. He longed for the ash-gray weekdays, yawning Sundays, agonized hours on horseback, stupid maneuvers, and his own grief at all this emptiness. Through the sobs and groans of the Lieutenant there broke the piercing cry of the living earth; so that, while striving for words to console Trotta, pity overwhelmed the doctor's heart and love's thousand flickering tongues sprang up in him. The indifference in which he had spent the past few days lay far behind him.

Then the kitchen clock struck three hard chimes. Trotta was suddenly quiet. They could hear the echo of the three chimes drown slowly in the hissing gas jets. The Lieutenant began to say, in a steady voice, 'Don't you see how silly the whole thing is? Taittinger bores me as he does everyone else. Well, that night in front of the theater I just said I had an appointment. Then your wife comes out alone. So then I have to see her home. And just as we're passing the club they all come bursting out into the street."

The doctor took his hand off Trotta's shoulder and wandered about the room again. He walked almost noiselessly, with gentle, attentive steps.

"And besides," said the Lieutenant, "I wanted to tell you, I could see at once there'd be trouble. I could hardly manage to say a civil word to your wife. And in the garden in front of your house the lantern was on, I remember seeing your footprints, clearly outlined in the snow on the path from the garden gate to the front door. And it gave me the odd idea, crazy idea. . ."

"Yes?" said the doctor.

"A funny idea. I thought for a second your footprints were a kind of special guard—I can't quite say what I mean, but I felt they were looking up off the snow and watching us, me and your wife."

Dr Demant sat down again, looked at Trotta closely and said slowly, "Perhaps you're in love with my wife and don't know it yourself."

"None of the whole business is my fault," answered Trotta.

"No, it's not your fault," the regimental surgeon confirmed.

"But it feels all the time as though it is," said Carl Joseph. "You know, I told you all about Frau Slama and what happened." He sat quiet, then whispered, "I'm frightened. I'm frightened, everywhere."

The regimental surgeon spread out his arms, shrugged, and said, "You, too, are a grandson."

At this moment he was not thinking of the Lieutenant's fears. He felt it quite possible, even now, that he might escape from all that threatened him. Disappear, he thought. Be dishonored, degraded, serve three years as a private, or flee the country. But not be shot. Lieutenant Trotta, the grandson of the hero of Solferino, was already a stranger, the inhabitant of a foreign world. He said loudly, giving relish to his contempt, "What simple-mindedness. This 'honor' which trails from the idiotic tassels on their swords. So that you can't so much as see a woman home. Can't you see how imbecilic it all is? Didn't you rescue *him*," he pointed at the Emperor's portrait, "from a brothel? Idiocy," he suddenly shouted, "infamous idiocy!"

There was a knock. The landlord brought two full glasses. The regimental surgeon drank. "Go on, drink," he said.

Carl Joseph drank. He did not quite understand what the doctor was saying, but he felt that he was no longer prepared to die. The clock ticked out its tinny seconds. Time did not stop. Seven-twenty, seven-twenty. Some miracle would have to come to pass if Dr Demant were not to die. Miracles never came to pass. That much, at least, the Lieutenant knew. He himself— fantastic thought—will appear tomorrow at seven-twenty and say, "Gentlemen, Demant went mad in the night and I'm going to take his place." Nonsense, ridiculous, impossible. He looked at the doctor again, helpless. Time did not stop, the clock stitched off its seconds ceaselessly. Soon it would be four o'clock. Another three hours.

"Right," said the regimental surgeon at last. It sounded as if he had come to a decision and knew precisely what to do. But he knew nothing precise. His thoughts made confused tracks, blind and unconnected through blinding mists. He knew nothing. A worthless, infamous, stupid, powerful, cast-iron law fettered him, sent him fettered to a foolish death. He heard late-night noises from the bar, obviously no one was left in there. The landlord was plunging chinking beer glasses into gurgling water, dragging chairs together, pushing tables about, jingling his bunch of keys. They would have to go. From the street, from winter, from the dark sky and from its stars. From the snow, perhaps, could come counsel and consolation. Demant went to the landlord, paid, came back in his black overcoat, wearing a soft black hat, and stood transformed again in front of the Lieutenant. He seemed to Carl Joseph to be far better armed than he had ever been in uniform with sword and cap.

They crossed the yard, back through the passage into the night. The doctor looked at the sky. No counsel came from the silent stars, they were colder than the snow. The houses were dark, the streets deaf and dumb, the night wind blew powdery snow in their faces. The Lieutenant's spurs jingled faintly beside the doctor's boots, crunching through the snow. They walked quickly, as if they had a specific destination. Disconnected ideas flew through their heads—thoughts, images. Their hearts beat like swift heavy hammers.

Without realizing it, the regimental surgeon indicated their direction and Trotta followed. They approached the Golden Bear. They stood in the arched doorway of the hotel. In Carl Joseph's imagination arose the picture of Demant's grandfather, that silver-bearded king among Jewish publicans. In just such a doorway, a much larger one in all probability, he had sat all his life. He had got up when the farmers stopped. Because he could no longer hear, the little peasants had bawled their orders through hands hollowed before their mouths. Seven-twenty, seven-twenty: he heard it again. At seven-twenty this grandfather's grandson would be dead.

"Dead," the Lieutenant said aloud. Oh, wise Dr Demant was wise no longer. He had been free and brave in vain for these few days: it became clear now that really he had settled no accounts. Things were not quite so easy to settle. His wise head, bequeathed by a long line of wise ancestors, could give him as little help as the simple mind of Lieutenant Trotta, whose forebears had been the simple peasants of Sipolje. A stupid cast-iron law left no loophole.

"My dear man, I'm a fool," said the doctor." I should have separated from Eva long ago. I haven't the strength to run away from this idiotic duel. I shall be a hero out of sheer stupidity, all according to the code of honor and the rules of the book. A hero!" He laughed, it rang through the night. "A hero," he repeated and stamped up and down in front of the arched doorway of the Golden Bear.

In the Lieutenant's youthful mind, willing to seize at once on any comfort, a childish hope flashed out: they will not fire at each other, they will be reconciled. Everything will be all right. They'll be transferred to other regiments. And I will, too! Foolish, ridiculous, impossible, he thought at once. And lost, despairing, with dull brain, dry mouth, and leaden limbs, he stood motionless while the doctor walked up and down.

What time was it?

He dared not look at the time.

Soon it would strike from the clock tower. He would wait.

"In case we don't see each other again," said the doctor; he stopped, and said a few seconds later, "I advise you to get out of the army." He held out his hand. "Good luck. Go home. I can manage by myself. Good-by." He tugged the bell wire. Inside the house the bell jangled. Footsteps approached. The door was unlocked.

Lieutenant Trotta seized the doctor's hand. In his everyday voice, a voice which surprised even himself, he said an everyday "Good-by." He had not even taken off his glove. Already the door slammed. Already Dr Demant had ceased to exist. Led by an invisible hand, Lieutenant Trotta took the usual road to the barracks. He did not hear the window on the second floor being opened. Demant leaned out, saw his friend disappear around the corner, closed the window, switched on every light in his room, went to the washstand, stropped his razor, tried it against his thumbnail, and soaped his face, leisurely as on every other morning. He washed, took his uniform out of the cupboard, got dressed, buckled on his sword, and sat waiting. He began to nod, fell quietly and dreamlessly asleep in the wide armchair beside the window.

When he awoke, the sky had brightened above the housetops, a bluish light shone from the snow. Soon they would be knocking. In the distance he could hear sleigh bells. They came nearer, stopped. Now the bell was ringing, now the stairs were creaking, now spurs came clanking, now there was a knock on his door. Now they were in his room, First Lieutenant Christ and Captain Wangert of the Garrison Infantry. They stayed near the door, the Lieutenant half a pace behind the Captain. The regimental surgeon glanced up at the sky. In a distant echo of distant boyhood the extinguished voice of his grandfather trembled, "Hear, O Israel." The voice was saying, "The Lord our God is one God."

"I'm quite ready, gentlemen," said the regimental surgeon.

They sat rather cramped in the little sled, the bells jingled gently. The brown horses raised their cropped tails to drop round, steaming, golden turds in the snow. The regimental surgeon, who had never in his life much cared for animals, suddenly longed for his horse. He'll survive me, he thought. His face revealed nothing. His companions sat silent.

They stopped about a hundred yards from the site. They went on foot to the green clearing. Morning was bright already, although the sun had not yet risen. The pines stood silent, slim and erect, proudly bearing the snow on their branches. Cock crowed to cock in the distance. Tattenbach spoke noisily to his seconds. The head surgeon, Dr Mangle, walked up and down between the groups. "Gentlemen," a voice was saying. At this moment, with all the customary ceremony, Dr Demant took off his glasses and set them down carefully on a broad tree stump. Oddly enough, he could still see his way quite clearly to the place where they told him he must stand, saw the distance between himself and Count Tattenbach, and saw Tattenbach himself. He waited to the very last moment, hoping for a mist. Yet everything remained as distinct as if the regimental surgeon had never been short-sighted. A voice was counting, "One." The regimental surgeon raised his pistol. He felt free and courageous again, even arrogant for the first time in his life. He took aim as once he had taken aim for target practice when he was doing a year's voluntary service, though even then he had been a very poor shot.

I'm not really short-sighted, he thought, I shan't ever need to wear glasses again. From the medical point of view, it seemed scarcely credible. The regimental surgeon resolved to brush up on his ophthalmic studies. Just as he had managed to remember a certain specialist's name, the voice said, "Two." The doctor could still see everything clearly. A shy bird of unknown species began to chirp, and from the distance came a bugle call. At this hour the regiment of Uhlans was due at its drilling ground.

Lieutenant Trotta rode in the second squadron as usual. Frost collected in drops on the sheaths of the heavy swords and the barrels of the light carbines and dulled them. Frozen trumpets roused the sleepy little town. Cabmen in their thick furs, waiting along their rank, raised their bearded heads. When the regiment had reached the water meadow and dismounted and the men were lining up as usual in double rank for early morning exercises, Lieutenant Kindermann came over to Carl Joseph and said, "Are you ill, have you any idea what you look like?" He pulled out a coquettish little pocket mirror and held it up to Trotta's eyes. In the small shining rectangle Lieutenant Trotta saw an age-old face which he knew well: dark, narrow, glowering eyes, the sharp bony ridge of a great nose, gray sunken cheeks and a long narrow mouth tight-set and bloodless, like a long-healed sword scar, which separated chin from mustache. Only the little brown mustache looked unfamiliar to Carl Joseph. At home in his father's study, his grandfather's face in the shadows had been quite clean-shaven.

"Thank you," the Lieutenant said, "I didn't sleep last night." And he left the drilling ground.

He turned off to the left between the tree trunks where a field path branched on to the highroad. It was seven-forty. No shots had been heard. It's all right, it's all right, he told himself, there's been a miracle. In ten minutes at most, Major Prohaska will come riding along and they will know everything. He heard the hesitant noises of the little town waking up and the long scream of an engine from the station. When the Lieutenant reached the place where the path opened on to the highroad, the Major appeared on his chestnut. The Lieutenant greeted him. "Good morning," the Major said and nothing more. The little path was too narrow for a rider and pedestrian side by side, so the Lieutenant followed the Major. About two minutes' distance from the water meadow (they could hear the NCOs giving their orders), the Major pulled up, half turned in the saddle, and said, "Both of them." As he rode on, he added, more to himself than to the Lieutenant, "There was nothing anyone could do."

That day the regiment returned to barracks a good hour earlier than usual. Trumpets blared as they blared every day. That afternoon the sergeants on duty read out to the men Colonel Kovacs's announcement that Captain Count Tattenbach and Regimental Surgeon Dr Demant had died soldiers' deaths for the honor of the regiment.

Chapter 8

In those days before the Great War when the events narrated in this book took place, it had not yet become a matter of indifference whether a man lived or died. When one of the living had been extinguished another did not at once take his place in order to obliterate him: there was a gap where he had been, and both close and distant witnesses of his demise fell silent whenever they became aware of this gap. When fire had eaten away a house from the row of others in a street, the burnt-out space remained long empty. Masons worked slowly and cautiously. Close neighbors and casual passers-by alike, when they saw the empty space, remembered the aspect and walls of the vanished house. That was how things were then. Everything that grew took its time in growing and everything that was destroyed took a long time to be forgotten. And everything that had once existed left its traces so that in those days people lived on memories, just as now they live by the capacity to forget quickly and completely.

The deaths of Count Tattenbach and the regimental surgeon moved and troubled the minds of the officers and men of this regiment of Uhlans—and indeed, of the civilian population—for a long time. The dead were buried in accordance with the usual religious and military rites. Although (except among themselves) none of the soldiers had uttered a word as to the manner in which the two had died, nevertheless there was a rumor among the townspeople of the little garrison that both men had fallen victim to their rigid code of honor. So that, from that day on, it was as if each surviving officer bore upon his forehead the mark of close, violent death. To the shop-keepers and artisans of the little town these strange gentlemen became stranger still. The officers moved among them like incomprehensible worshippers of some remote, unappeasable god, whose gaily decked-out, gaudy victims they were. People shook their heads as they saw them pass, they even pitied them. They have all kinds of privileges, the people said to themselves, they can swagger about with their swords and attract women; the Emperor himself takes a personal interest in them and cares for them as if they were his sons. And yet, at any moment, if one insults the other, it has to be avenged in red blood.

Indeed, those of whom such things were being said were not to be envied. Even Captain Taittinger, who was rumored to have taken part in a few other fatal duels in other regiments, began to change his habits. Whereas the noisy and light-hearted became quiet and subdued, a strange restlessness took possession of the sweet-toothed, quiet, lean Captain. He could no longer sit for hours behind the glass doors of his little pastry shop devouring pastries, or play silent games of chess and dominoes with himself or his colonel. He was afraid of solitude. He literally clung to others. If no brother officer was about, he would go into a shop and buy something he didn't want. He would hang around for a long time and chatter foolishly to the shopkeeper, unable to make up his mind to leave the shop, unless, by chance, he saw a casual acquaintance passing in the street, in which case he would immediately run out. So changed was the world. The club was empty. The officers desisted from the companionable jaunts to Frau Resi's. The orderlies were less busy. Anyone who ordered a cognac thought, as he looked at his glass, that it might be the very one out of which Tattenbach had drunk a few days ago. They continued to tell the old anecdotes but these no longer evoked loud guffaws—smiles at most. Lieutenant Trotta was never about except on duty.

A deft magic hand had wiped every trace of youth off Carl Joseph's face. In the whole Royal and Imperial Army not another lieutenant like him could have been found. He felt the need for some extraordinary achievement, but near or far, he found nothing extraordinary to achieve. It went without saying that now he would leave the regiment and enter another. But he searched for some difficult task to perform. In fact, he was looking for a self-imposed penance. He could never have managed to say it, but we may, after all, say it of him: it oppressed him unspeakably to feel himself the instrument of misfortune. In this state of mind he wrote to his father, announcing the outcome of the duel, with news of his inevitable transfer to another regiment. He withheld the fact that at this point a short leave was due to him, since he feared to look his father in the face. But it turned out that he underestimated the old man. For the District Commissioner, that model of civil servants, was well up in military usage. And oddly enough, he seemed just as conversant with the griefs and perplexities of his son, as could clearly be read between the lines of his reply. It was as follows:

My dear son,

I thank you for your precise account and for your confidence. The fate which has overtaken your brother officers moves me deeply. They died like men of honor.

Duels were even more frequent in my time, and honor seemed far more precious to us than life. It also seems to me that in my time officers were made of tougher stuff. You, my son, are an officer, and the grandson of the hero of Solferino. You will know how to bear your innocent and involuntary connection with this tragic affair. No doubt you will be sorry to leave the regiment, but remember that wherever you may be serving, in whatever regiment of our entire army, you will be serving our Emperor.

Your Father
FRANZ VON TROTTA

P.S. The fortnight's leave to which your transfer entitles you you may spend either at home with me, or, better still, in your new garrison, which will give you time to become acquainted with your new surroundings.

F. v. T.

Lieutenant Trotta could not read this letter without a feeling of shame. His father had guessed everything. In the Lieutenant's eyes, the image of the District Commissioner swelled to fearsome dimensions: he assumed almost the stature of his grandfather. And if Carl Joseph had felt anxiety before at the thought of confronting the old man, now it was out of the question to spend his leave at home. Later, later when I get my regular leave, the Lieutenant thought. He was cast in a different mold altogether from the Lieutenants of the District Commissioner's youth. "No doubt you will be sorry to leave the regiment," his father wrote. Had he written it because he could sense the contrary? What was there that Carl Joseph did *not* want to leave? Perhaps this window with its view of the men's quarters? The men themselves, perched on their cots, the melancholy sound of their mouth organs and their singing, the remote songs which sounded like uncomprehended echoes of similar songs sung by the peasants of Sipolje? Perhaps I ought to go to Sipolje, thought the Lieutenant. He went over to look at the ordnance map, the one piece of decoration in his room. He could have found Sipolje in his sleep. The pleasant, quiet village lay in the extreme south of the monarchy. Traced on a lightly cross-hatched bronze-coloured background were the hair-thin, minute letters, faint as the breath of which the name Sipolje was composed. Near it were a draw well, a water mill, the little station of a light railway running its single track through a wood, a mosque, a church, a young plantation, narrow forest paths, solitary huts. It is evening in Sipolje. The women stand in the sunset by the fountains, the colored kerchiefs on their heads stained gold by the vanishing sun. Moslems pray in their mosques on faded carpets. The miniature engine of the railway puffs clanging into the dark-green gloom of pines. The water mill clatters; the stream murmurs. It was the familiar game he had played as a cadet. The familiar images rose at once. Above them all shone his grandfather's mysterious gaze. There was probably not a cavalry garrison near Sipolje. He would have to transfer to the infantry. Cavalry officers cannot regard their foot-slogging brothers without a certain element of pity. Not without a certain element of pity would they regard the transferred Trotta. His grandfather had been only a plain infantry captain. To march on foot across one's own native earth would almost be like a return to his peasant forebears. Their heavy feet had trodden the hard soil, they had dug their plowshares into the fertile soil of the fields and had scattered fruitful seed with gestures that were a blessing. No, the Lieutenant was not in the least sorry to leave the regiment and perhaps the cavalry. His father would have to give his consent. He would have to go through an undoubtedly rather tedious course of infantry training.

He had to make his farewells. An evening at the club. A round of drinks. A short speech by the Colonel. A bottle of wine. A firm handshake from his brother officers, who were already gossiping behind his back. A bottle of champagne. Who could say, perhaps it might even end up in a general turn out all together to Frau Resi's. Another round of cognac. Oh, if only the leave-taking were over and done with. He would take his batman Onufrij with him. He did not want to go through the trouble of getting used to another name. He would avoid visiting his father. Altogether, he would try to avoid as much as possible the unpleasantness usually connected with a change of regiment. There remained only the difficult visit to the widow of the late Dr Demant.

What a visit! Carl Joseph tried to tell himself that Frau Eva Demant had gone back to Vienna to her father after her husband's funeral. He would therefore stand on the doorstep of the house, ring the bell for a long time and receive no answer, get her Vienna address, write her a letter as brief and sympathetic as possible. It was very convenient that he only had to write to her. I am not in the least plucky, the Lieutenant thought at the same time. Wasn't he constantly aware of the dark mysterious gaze of his grandfather, who knew how miserably he might have to lurch through this hard life. He grew brave only when he thought of the hero of Solferino. He had to keep going back to his grandfather for a little fortitude. So slowly, the Lieutenant set out on the difficult visit. It was three o'clock in the afternoon. Little shopkeepers looked miserable, freezing in front of their shops as they waited for their sparse customers. Creative, familiar sounds rang from the artisans' workshops. There was the sound of jovial hammering from the blacksmith, the plumber clanked forth his hollow, tinny thunderings, quick taps sounded from the cobblers' cellars, and the saws sang in the joiner's workshop. The Lieutenant knew all the sounds and faces of these workshops. Every day from the saddle he had seen them over the tops of the faded blue signs. Every day he had caught morning glimpses of first-floor rooms, the unmade beds, the coffeepots, and men in shirtsleeves, women with their hair still down; the flowerpots along the window sills; dried fruit and pickled gherkins behind ornamental ironwork.

Now he was on the doorstep of Dr Demant's house. The front door creaked. He went inside. The servant let him in. The Lieutenant waited. Frau Demant arrived. He trembled a little. He remembered the condolence visit he had paid Sergeant-Major Slama. He could feel the man's heavy, moist, cold, loose handshake. He could see the dark hall, the reddish parlor. He had in his mouth the stale aftertaste of the raspberry cordial. So she's not in Vienna, the Lieutenant thought—but only until the actual moment he saw the widow. Her black dress came as a surprise. It was as if he had only just been informed that

Frau Demant was the widow of a regimental surgeon. The room, too, which he now entered was not the same as the one he had been in when his friend was still alive. On the opposite wall, festooned in black, hung a large likeness of the deceased. It receded further and further, like the Emperor's portrait in the club: it was as though it were not within sight and touching distance, as though it were immeasurably far beyond the wall— out of reach, as though he were seeing it through glass.

"Thank you for coming," said Frau Demant.

"I wanted to say good-by," answered Trotta.

Frau Demant raised her pale face. The Lieutenant saw the gray, clear beauty of her wide, shining eyes. They were turned straight on his face, two rounds of light, of glittering ice. In the winter-afternoon dusk of the room only the woman's eyes shone out. Quickly the Lieutenant glanced above them at her narrow white forehead, then at the wall, at the distant portrait of her dead husband. These preliminaries were taking far too long, it was high time she asked him to sit down, but she said nothing. Meanwhile, he could feel the gathering darkness of approaching evening close in on him through the windows, and he was childishly afraid that they might never turn the lights on in this house. No appropriate words occurred to him. He heard the woman's quiet breathing. She said at last, "But what are we standing like this for? Let's sit down." They sat down facing each other across a table. As before, at Sergeant-Major Slama's, he had the door behind him. As on that occasion, he felt the threat of the door. It seemed for no reason at all to open slowly from time to time and then noiselessly shut again. The dusk thickened. Frau Demant's black dress merged into the dusk, which now enveloped her. Her white face hovered naked, bared on the dark surface of the evening. The dead man's portrait had vanished from the wall opposite. "My husband," Frau Demant's voice was saying out of the darkness. The Lieutenant saw the gleam of her teeth—they were whiter than her face. Gradually, too he began to distinguish again the bright gleam of her eyes. "You were his only friend, he often said so. How often he spoke of you! If you only knew—I can't believe he's dead. And," she whispered, "that it is my fault."

"It is *my* fault," said the Lieutenant. His voice was very loud and hard and sounded strange to his own ears. There was no consolation for Demant's widow. "My fault," he repeated. "I ought to have taken you home more circumspectly. I ought never to have brought you along by the club."

The woman began to sob. Her white face bent lower and lower over the table, sinking slowly like a large white oval flower. Suddenly, to the right and left of it, white hands came up out of the darkness, receiving the sinking face, cushioning it. And now, for a while, for a whole minute, and then another, nothing could be heard except the woman's sobs. An eternity for the Lieutenant. I'd better get up and leave her to cry and go away, he thought. In fact, he got up.

Her hands fell back at once upon the table. In a calm voice which seemed to come from another throat, not the one with which she had just been sobbing, she said to him, "Where are you going?"

"To turn on the light," said Trotta.

She got up, went past him around the table, brushing him. His nostrils caught the faint whiff of her scent; she was past him, the scent dispersed. The light was hard. He forced himself to stare straight at the lamp. Frau Demant kept one hand in front of her eyes.

"Turn on that little lamp above the bracket," she told him. The Lieutenant obeyed. She waited by the door, shading her eyes. When the little lamp under its pale-gold shade was lit, she switched off the ceiling light. She took her hand from her eyes as if removing a visor. She looked very bold in her black dress with her pale face, which she turned full on Trotta. She was angry and brave. Her cheeks showed faint streaks of drying tears. Her eyes were shining, just as before.

"Sit down," ordered Frau Demant. "Over there, on the sofa." And Carl Joseph sat down. Soft, comfortable cushions seemed to be gliding against him, off the sofa back, out of the corners, sly and insinuating, from all sides. He felt that it was dangerous to sit here and moved decisively to the edge of the sofa. He put his hands on the hilt of his upright sword and watched Frau Demant advance upon him. She looked like the dangerous commandant of all these cushions. On the wall, to the right of the sofa, hung his dead friend's portrait. Frau Eva sat down. A smooth little cushion lay between them. Trotta did not stir. He was doing what he always did when he could see no way out of one of the numerous awkward situations he always

113

seemed to be slipping into; namely, he told himself that he could go.

"So they're going to transfer you?" asked Frau Demant.

"I've applied to be transferred," he told her, his eyes on the carpet, his chin on his hands, and his hands on his sword hilt.

"Must you?"

"Yes, I must."

"I'm sorry, very sorry."

Frau Demant sat like him, her knees supporting her elbows her chin on her hands, her eyes on the carpet. She was probably expecting a word of comfort and charity. He was silent. He enjoyed the luxurious sensation of cruelly avenging his friend's death by a callous silence. Stories of dangerous, murderous, pretty little women, an ever-recurring theme of his brother officers, came back to him. She most probably belonged to the dangerous sisterhood of weak murderesses. He must take good care to keep clear of her. He began to get ready to leave. At that instant, Frau Demant changed her position. She removed her hands from under her chin, cautiously, and softly her left hand felt its way along the silk braid of the sofa's edge. Her fingers, along the narrow, glossy path, slowly advanced, then steadily retreated, and again advanced on Lieutenant Trotta. They slid into his field of vision. He longed for blinkers. The white fingers were involving him in a voiceless but quite inevitable conversation. A cigarette—splendid inspiration. He pulled out his cigarette case and matches. "Will you give me one?" asked Frau Demant.

He was forced to look into her face as he held the match. He disapproved of her smoking, as if the enjoyment of nicotine were unseemly for someone in mourning: And the way she inhaled her first puff—her lips set in a small coral round which sent out a soft bluish cloud—was vicious and arrogant!

"Haven't you any idea where they'll transfer you?"

"No," the Lieutenant said, "but I shall do my best to get sent as far away as possible."

"Far away? But where, for instance?"

"Perhaps to Bosnia."

"Do you think you'll be happy there?"

"I don't think I shall ever be happy anywhere."

"Oh, I hope you will." Glib, far too glib, it seemed to Trotta.

She stood up, came back with an ashtray, and put it between them on the floor.

She said "So I suppose we're never likely to meet again."

Never. That word, the dread and shoreless ocean of soundless eternity. He could never see Katherina again, nor Dr Demant, nor this woman. Carl Joseph said, "No, I suppose not, unfortunately." He would have liked to add, "And I won't see Max Demant again." Widows should be burnt. Trotta remembered one of Taittinger's daring phrases as he spoke.

The front doorbell rang; there were sounds in the passage. "That's my father," said Frau Demant. Herr Knopfmacher was already in the room.

"Oh, it's you, it's you," he said, bringing a sharp tang of snow with him. He unfolded a large snow-white pocket handkerchief and blew his nose resoundingly. He stowed the handkerchief carefully in his breast pocket like a precious object, thrust out a hand toward the door and switched on the ceiling light. He came up to Trotta, who had risen at Knopfmacher's arrival. In his handshake, Herr Knopfmacher indicated all the grief that needed to be expressed at the death of the doctor. Already he was saying to his daughter, pointing to the ceiling lamp, "I'm sorry, I can't stand these artistic glooms." It was as if he had flung a stone at the crape-enveloped portrait of the dead man.

"Well, you aren't looking too grand," Knopfmacher said the next instant in an exultant voice. "It's taken a lot out of you, I suppose, this terrible affair, yes?"

"He was my only friend."

"You know," Knopfmacher said and sat down at the table— "Oh, please stay where you are"—and he went on when the Lieutenant had settled on the sofa again, "that was just exactly what he said about you when he was alive. What a business!" He shook his head a few times and his full, rosy cheeks quivered a little.

Frau Demant drew a wisp of lace from her sleeve, dabbed her eyes, got up, and hurried from the room.

"Who knows how she'll get over it," said Knopfmacher. "Well, I talked to her long enough beforehand. But, of course, she wouldn't take any notice of me. You see, my dear Lieutenant, every profession has its dangers. But an officer! An officer—forgive me—really ought never to marry. Between you and me, though of course he's certain to have told you, he'd thought of sending in his papers and devoting all his time to science. I can't tell you how pleased I was to hear it. He'd certainly have become a famous doctor. Dear, kind Max." Herr Knopfmacher raised his eyes to the portrait, allowed them to linger on it, and ended his obituary. "An authority."

Frau Demant brought her father's favorite *slivovitz*.

"You'll have a drink?" Knopfmacher asked, filling some glasses. With cautious hand, he carried the brimming glass across to the sofa.

The Lieutenant rose, the stale taste of raspberry cordial still in his mouth, as on the previous occasion. He finished the alcohol in a gulp.

"When did you see him last?" inquired Knopfmacher.

"One day before."

"He asked Eva to go to Vienna without giving her any hint. She went in complete ignorance. Then we got his farewell letter. I saw at once there was nothing to be done."

"No, there was nothing to be done."

"I hope you won't mind my saying that this code of honor seems out of date. After all, we're in the twentieth century. Why, we've got the gramophone, you can telephone hundreds of miles away, and people like Blériot go flying about in the air. I don't know if you're much of a newspaper reader, are you at all interested in politics? But everyone seems to be saying that the whole constitution is going to be radically changed. Here and abroad, all sorts of things have been happening, since universal secret suffrage was brought in. Our Emperor, God bless him and keep him, isn't nearly as old-fashioned as some people think. Of course, these conservatives may not be altogether wrong, things have to be done slowly, cautiously, step by step. No use rushing things."

"I don't know anything about politics," said Trotta.

Knopfmacher was beginning to feel irritated. He was angry with the whole stupid army and its idiotic institutions. His child was a widow, his son-in-law dead. He'd have to find a new one, a civilian this time, and he'd probably have to wait for his councilorship. It was high time to stop such nonsense. These young, frivolous lieutenants must not be allowed to get out of hand, not in the twentieth century. The nations were insisting on their rights, and so were the citizens. Down with aristocratic privileges. Social democracy might be a bit risky, but it was a good counterweight. There was a lot of talk about war, but no doubt there wouldn't be one. They'd show them. The times were enlightened. In England, for instance, the king had no powers at all.

"Naturally," he said, "there's no use for politics in the army. But he. . . ." Knopfmacher indicated the portrait. "Well, anyway, he knew something about it."

"He was very wise," said Trotta very quietly.

"There was nothing to be done," Knopfmacher repeated.

"Perhaps," said the Lieutenant, and was himself aware that he was speaking with borrowed wisdom, wisdom hidden in those vast tomes of the silver-bearded king of publicans, "perhaps he was very wise and quite alone." He turned pale. He could feel Frau Demant's barefaced glances. He would have to leave. It grew very quiet. There was nothing more to be said. "Father, we won't see Baron Trotta again, they're going to transfer him," said Frau Demant.

"You'll keep in touch," asked Knopfmacher.

"You will write to me?" said Frau Demant.

Carl Joseph rose.

"Good luck," said Knopfmacher. His hand was large and soft, it felt like warm velvet.

Frau Demant went on ahead. The servant came to hold his coat. Frau Demant stood next to him. She said very rapidly, "You will write? I will want to know what becomes of you." It was a swift, warm breath, dispersed immediately. The servant was opening the door, he was out on the steps. The gate appeared in front of him, just as it had when he had left Sergeant-Major Slama.

He hurried back to the town, stopped at the first café he passed, stood at the bar and drank a brandy, then another. "We only drink Hennessy," he could hear the District Commissioner saying. He hurried on, to the barracks.

Outside the door of his room, Onufrij was waiting, a dark-blue streak against bare whitewash. The office orderly had brought him a package, by colonel's orders. It stood in the corner, a long, narrow brown-paper object. On the table lay a letter. The Lieutenant read it:

"My dear Friend, I leave you my sword and my watch. Max Demant."

Trotta unpacked the sword. From its hilt dangled Demant's smooth silver watch. It was not going. The hands stood at ten to twelve. The Lieutenant wound it and held it to his ear. Its quick quiet voice ticked consolingly. He opened the case with his pocket-knife, inquisitive and playful, like a boy. On the inside were the initials M.D. He drew the sword from its sheath. With his penknife, Dr Demant had scratched a clumsy line of sprawling letters on the steel. LIVE IN HAPPINESS AND FREEDOM the inscription read. The Lieutenant hung the sword in his cupboard. He held up the sword hanger. Its wired silk glided through his fingers like cool gold rain. Trotta shut the cupboard. He was closing a coffin.

He switched off the light and lay down fully dressed on his bed. The yellow glow from the men's quarters opposite spilled on the white lacquer of his door, its reflections caught by the glittering handle. From across the way came the hoarse sighing music of mouth organs accompanying the men's deep-throated roar. They were singing the Ukrainian song which tells of the Emperor and his Empress. The Empress had long been dead, but Ruthenian peasants thought she was still alive.

PART TWO

Chapter 9

Eastward to the frontiers of the Tsar, the Habsburg sun shot forth its rays. It was the same sun which had fostered the growth of the Trottas to nobility and esteem. Francis Joseph had a long memory for gratitude and his favor had a wide reach. If one of his favorite children was about to commit some folly, the servants and ministers of the Emperor intervened in good time to force the erring child into prudence and reason. It would scarcely have been fitting to permit the sole heir of this recently created baronetcy of Trotta von Sipolje to serve in the native province of the hero of Solferino, the grandson of illiterate Slovenian peasants, the son of a gendarmery sergeant-major. This young nobleman might, of course, if he chose, exchange his service in the Uhlans for a modest commission in an infantry regiment; it merely proved him faithful to the memory of his grandfather, who had saved his Emperor's life as a plain lieutenant in the line. But the prudence of the Imperial and Royal Ministry of War avoided sending the bearer of such a title, a title identical with the actual Slovenian village in which the first baron had been born, to serve in the neighborhood of the village. The District Commissioner, son of the hero of Solferino, agreed with the authorities. Though with a heavy heart he allowed his son to transfer to the infantry, he was not at all pleased with Carl Joseph's request to serve in the Slovenian province. He himself, the District Commissioner, had never felt any desire to see the home of his fathers. He was an Austrian, civil servant of the Habsburgs, his home the Imperial Hofburg in Vienna. Had he entertained political notions of any useful reshaping of the great and multifarious monarchy it would have seemed fitting to him that all the crownlands should simply form large and colorful outer courts of the Imperial

Hofburg; and to see in all the nations of the monarchy subjects of the Habsburgs. He was a District Commissioner; within his district he represented the Apostolic Majesty. He wore the gold collar, cocked hat, and sword. He had no wish at all to drive a furrow into the blessed Slovenian earth. His final decisive letter to his son contained the following sentence: "Fate has raised our stock from peasant frontiersmen to Austrians. Let us remain such."

So it came about that Carl Joseph, Baron Trotta von Sipolje, found the southern frontiers inaccessible. He had only the choice between serving in the interior of Austria or on its eastern border. He chose a battalion of Jaeger stationed not more than two miles from the Russian frontier. Near it was the village of Burdlaki, Onufrij's home. This district was akin to the home of Ukrainian peasants, their melancholy concertinas and their unforgettable songs; it was the northern sister of Slovenia.

For seventeen hours Carl Joseph sat in the train. In the eighteenth there came into sight the last eastern railway station of the monarchy. Here he got out. His batman came with him. The Jaeger barracks stood at the center of the small town. Onufrij crossed himself three times before they entered the barrack square. It was morning. Spring, which had long since reached the inner provinces of the Empire, had only recently arrived here. The laburnum glowed on the arches of the railway viaduct. Violets flowered in the moist woods. Frogs croaked in the endless marshes. Storks circled above the low-thatched roofs of the village huts in search of old wheels to use as foundations for their summer nests.

At that time the borderland between Austria and Russia in the north-eastern corner was one of the most remarkable areas of the monarchy. Carl Joseph's Jaeger battalion garrisoned a town of ten thousand inhabitants. It lay around a wide circular market-place at whose center two main roads intersected, east to west, north to south. One led from the cemetery to the railway station, the other from the castle ruins to the steam mill. About a third of the town's ten thousand inhabitants were craftsmen of various kinds; another third lived in poverty off meager small holdings. The rest engaged in trade of a sort.

We call it "trade of a sort" since neither the goods nor the business methods corresponded in any way to the notions which the so-called civilized world has formed of trade. In these parts the tradesmen made their living far more by hazard than by design, more by the unpredictable grace of God than by any commercial reckonings in advance. Every trader was ready at any moment to seize on whatever floating merchandise heaven might throw in his way, or even to invent his goods if God had provided him with none. The livelihood of these traders was indeed a mystery. They displayed no shopfronts, they had no names. They had no credit. But they possessed a keen, miraculous sharp instinct for any remote and hidden sources of profit. Though they lived on other people's work, they created work for strangers. They were frugal. They lived as meanly as if they survived by the toil of their hands. And yet the toil was never theirs. Forever shifting, ever on the road, with glib tongues and clear, quick brains, they might have had possession of half the world if they had had any notion of the world. But they had none. They lived remote from it, wedged between East and West, cramped between day and night, themselves a species of living ghosts spawned by the night and haunting the day.

Cramped? The character of their native soil left them unconscious of it. Nature had forged endless horizons for these dwellers on the frontier, drawing around them a mighty circle of green forests and blue hills. When they walked in the twilight of pinewoods, they might even have felt themselves privileged by God, had their daily cares for the sustenance of wives and children left them time to perceive His goodness. But they entered their forests only to gather wood to trade with native shopkeepers as soon as winter drew near. For they also dealt in wood. They dealt in coral for the peasant girls of nearby villages and for those other peasants over the border, on Russian soil. They dealt in feathers for featherbeds, in tobacco, in horsehair, in bar silver, in jewelry, in Chinese tea, in fruit from the south, in cattle and horses, poultry and eggs, fish and vegetables, jute and wool, butter and cheese, woodlands and fields, Italian marble, human hair from China for making wigs, raw-silk and finished-silk merchandise, Manchester cotton and Brussels lace, galoshes from Moscow, Viennese linen, lead from Bohemia. No cheap bit of goods or splendid merchandise thrown up by the earth in profusion was unknown to the tradesmen of this district. What the law forbade them to come by and to sell, they would get one way or another in defiance of it—slick and secretive, adroitly prudent and bold. Some traded in live human flesh. They shipped off deserters from the Russian army to America and peasant girls to Brazil and Argentina. They had shipping agents and business connections with foreign brothels. Yet, with it all, their gains were meager, and they had no inkling of the vast superfluity in which a man may live. Their senses, so acutely edged for the sniffing out of petty gain, their hands which could strike gold from gravel like sparks from a flint, were not capable of bringing pleasure to their hearts or health to their bodies. The people in this district were swamp-begotten. For evil swamps lay far and wide to either side of the highroad and over the whole face of the land. Swamps that spawned frogs and fever, deceptive grass, dreadful enticements to a dreadful death for the unsuspecting stranger. Many had perished in the swamps with no one hearing their cries for help. But all who had been born here were familiar with the malignity of the marshland, and they themselves were tinged with this same malignity. In spring and summer, the air was thick with the deep and endless croaking of the frogs. Under the sky, equally jubilant larks rejoiced. It was an untiring dialogue between sky and marshland.

Many of these traders were Jews. A *lusus naturae*, perhaps a mysterious law obeyed by some secret branch of the legendary tribe of Khazars, determined that many among these frontier Jews were red-headed. The hair flamed from their heads. Their beards were like torches. On the backs of their nimble hands wiry hairs bristled like minute spears. And delicate reddish wool burgeoned out of their ears, like fumes of the red fires which might be glowing in their heads.

A stranger who settled here was bound to degenerate in time. No one was as strong as the swamp. No one could hold out against the borderland. At this time gentlemen in high places in Vienna and St Petersburg were already beginning preparations for the Great War. The people at the frontier were conscious of its approach sooner than others, not only because they sensed the future out of habit, but because from day to day they observed omens of disaster. They turned these preparations to profit. Many lived by espionage and counterespionage, drew Austrian gulden from the Austrian police and Russian rubles from the Russian. The isolation and swampy boredom of the garrison sometimes drove an officer to despair, to gambling, to debt, and into the company of sinister men. The cemeteries of the frontier garrisons concealed many young corpses of weak men.

But here, as in every garrison in the monarchy, privates drilled. Every day the Jaeger battalion, bespattered with shiny mud, their boots gray with slime, turned back to barracks. Major Zoglauer rode at their head. Lieutenant Trotta was in charge of the first platoon of the second company. A long sober blast from the bugler set the pace for the marching Jaeger—not the proud fanfare which had pierced the clattering hoofs of the Uhlan horses, and had checked and surrounded them. Carl Joseph tramped along, persuading himself that he preferred it. Around him crunched the hobnail boots of the Jaeger, over sharp-edged gravel freshly strewn week after week in spring, by request of the military authorities, only to be sucked down by the swampy highroad. All the stones, millions of them, disappeared into the insatiable ground. And everywhere triumphant silver-gray shiny mud oozed up out of the depths, devouring mortar and gravel, slapping up around the stamping boots of the men.

The barracks stood behind the municipal park. Next to it on the left was the District Court, and facing it the official enclosure of the District Commissioner's office buildings. Behind those ornate but crumbling walls stood two churches, one Roman Catholic, the other Greek Orthodox. To the right of the barracks stood the grammar school. The town was so small you could cross it in twenty minutes. The major buildings clustered together in irksome proximity. Like convicts in their prison yard, the townspeople exercised every evening round and round the unbroken ring of their park. It was a good half hour's walk to the station. The mess of the Jaeger officers was situated in two small rooms of a private house. Most preferred to eat in the station restaurant, including Carl Joseph. He was glad to tramp through the oozing slime if only to see a station. This was the last of all stations in the monarchy, but even so, it displayed two pairs of glittering lines stretching away without break into the heart of the monarchy. Like all the others, this station had shining signals of brightly colored glass, ringing with gentle messages from home; and there was a Morse keyboard ticking away incessantly on which the confused, delightful voices of a lost and distant world were hammered out, stitched as on some busy sewing machine.

This station, like all others, had its porter and this porter swung a clanging bell and the bell signified "All aboard, all aboard!" Once a day, at lunchtime, he went swinging his bell alongside a train on its way to Cracow, Oderberg, Vienna. A cozy, nice train. It stood there, almost the whole of lunchtime, just in front of the first-class refreshment-room windows, behind which the officers sat. Not until the coffee arrived did the engine whistle. Gray steam rolled against the windows. By the time it had begun to collect in drops and run down in streaks, the train had departed. They finished their coffee and went back in a slow, disconsolate group, through the silver slime. Even generals on tours of inspection took care not to come here. They did not come, nobody came. Only twice a year the one hotel in the town where most of the Jaeger officers were billeted was visited by rich hop merchants from Nuremberg and Prague and Saaz. When they had completed their incomprehensible deals, they hired a band and played cards in the only café, which belonged to the hotel.

Carl Joseph could see the whole town from his room on the second floor of the Hotel Brodnitzer. He could see the gable roofs of the District Court, the little white tower of the District Commissioner's offices, the black-and-yellow flag over the barracks, the double cross of the Greek church, the weathercock on the municipal building and all the slate-gray shingled roofs of the little, one-storied houses. The Hotel Brodnitzer was the tallest building in the area. It was as much a landmark as the church or the municipal and government buildings. The streets had no names and the little houses no numbers, so that anyone in search of a specific place had to find his way by vague description. So-and-so lived behind the church, so-and-so just opposite the jail. So-and-so somewhere to the right of the District Court. They lived like villagers. The secrets of the people in these low houses leaked out through chinks and rafters into the slimy streets and even into the ever-inaccessible barrack yard. So-and-so's wife had betrayed him, so-and-so had sold his daughter to a Russian

124

cavalry captain; in this house they dealt in rotten eggs, the whole family over the way lived by contraband; so-and-so had been in jail, but the other had got off scot free. So-and-So lent officers money, and his neighbor collected a third of the pay. The officers, mainly middle class, of German parentage, had been stationed in this garrison for years. They were used to it and accepted the inevitable. Cut off from their homes and the German language, which here became merely an official language, exposed to the endless desolation of the swamps, they took up gambling and drank the fiery local brandy manufactured locally and sold under the label NINETY PERCENT. From the harmless mediocrity to which cadet schools and drill had educated them, they sank into the corruption of the area—already overcast by the vast breath of the hostile empire of the Tsars. They were scarcely fourteen kilometers out of Russia. Not infrequently Russian officers from the frontier garrison came across in their long pale-lemon and dove-gray army coats, with heavy gold and silver epaulettes on their broad shoulders, and shiny galoshes drawn over their shimmering top-boots in all weathers. Indeed, there was a certain amount of friendly exchange between the garrisons. Sometimes they would go in little canvas-roofed baggage carts across the frontier to watch the Cossacks display their horsemanship and drink the Russian brandy. Over there, in the Russian garrison, spirit casks stood on the edge of the wooden pavements, guarded by Russian privates with grounded rifles and long, triple-edged fixed bayonets. At dusk, these little casks rolled and bumped along uneven streets, kicked by Cossack boots to the Russian club, a soft slap and gurgle from inside betraying their contents to the townspeople. The officers of the Tsar showed the officers of His Apostolic Majesty what Russian hospitality really meant. And none of the Tsar's officers and none of His Apostolic Majesty's officers knew at that time how, above the goblets from which they drank, death was already crossing his haggard invisible hands.

In the open space between the two frontier woods, the sotnias of Cossacks galloped and wheeled like winds in military formation, uniformed winds on the swift little ponies of their native steppes, flourishing their lances above their tall fur caps like streaks of lightning on long wooden stems, coquettish blades with graceful pennons. On the soft swampy ground the clatter of hoofs was almost inaudible. The wet earth gave no more than a low sigh under the flying thud of their hoofs. The dark-green meadow grass scarcely bent beneath them. It was as though these Cossacks hovered above the plain. And when they crossed the dusty, coppery highway, there rose up a tall, bright-yellow, fine-grained sandstorm, glittering with sunlight, drifting wide, sinking to earth in myriad tiny clouds. The guests sat watching them from rough wooden stands. These riders' movements were almost quicker than the eyes of the watchers. The Cossacks ducked from their saddles to snatch blue and scarlet handkerchiefs off the ground in their strong tawny horse teeth, suddenly falling right under the bellies of their mounts in full gallop, their legs still pressing the flanks in glistening riding boots. Others flung their lances high in the air, and, far beyond them, the shafts glittered and twirled, to fall obediently back in the riders' hands, returning, as falcons might, to their masters. Others again, crouching down flat across their horses' backs, their mouths pressing the beasts' soft muzzles fraternally, jumped through iron hoops, astonishingly narrow, each just wide enough to girt a small beer keg. The horses stretched all four feet out from their bodies, their manes soared like wings, their tails acting as rudders, their narrow heads like the slim bows of canoes skidding along. Another could jump his beast over twenty beer barrels set edge to edge. The horse whinnied before taking them. The rider came galloping from a distance; a gray speck, he grew in scorching speed to a streak. The body, the rider, became a huge, legendary bird, half-horse, half-man, a winged centaur, until at last, after the jump, he stood stock-still a hundred paces beyond the casks: a monument, a lifeless image. Others again fired at flying targets as they sped like arrows, themselves looking like arrows, targets which were held up to them on big white rounds by riders galloping away. The marksmen galloped, fired, and hit. Many tumbled to the earth. The men, coming from behind, sped gently across their bodies, no hoof touched them. There were riders with horses galloping beside them who could leap in full gallop from saddle to saddle, return to the first, suddenly tumble back into the second, until at last, with one hand set on each horse, their legs dangling down between the galloping bodies, they pulled both up with a jerk at the given stopping place, reining them in to stand there motionless, like steeds in bronze.

Such displays of horsemanship were not the sole diversion provided by the outpost between the monarchy and Russia. A regiment of Dragoons was also stationed in the garrison. Between Jaeger officers, Dragoons and the gentlemen of the Russian regiment, Count Chojnicki established intimate relations. He was one of the wealthiest Polish landowners in the district.

Count Wojciech Chojnicki, a connection of the Ledochowskis and Potockis, a cousin of the Sternbergs, a friend of the Thuns, was a man of the world. Forty years old (though he might have been any age), a cavalry captain in the Reserve, a bachelor, he was frivolous and at the same time melancholy, a lover of horses, alcohol, society, both flippant and serious. He spent his winters in cities and in the gambling casinos of the Riviera. But he returned like a migrating bird to the home of his ancestors when the laburnum began to bloom on the railway bridges. He brought with him a faintly scented whiff of society and tales of gallantry and adventure. He was the kind of man who can have no enemies but no friends either; he had only associates, boon companions, or casual acquaintances. Chojnicki, with his pale, intelligent, rather prominent eyes, his shining baldness smooth as a pebble, his wisp of a yellow mustache, and his narrow shoulders, his thin, disproportionately long legs, could attract whomever he chose or whomever chance had set in his way.

He lived alternately in two houses, known to the townspeople and respected by them, as the old and the new Schloss. The so-called old Schloss was a huge dilapidated hunting lodge which, for mysterious reasons, the Count refused to put into repair. The new Schloss was a spacious, two-storey country house, the upper storey often filled with strange and sometimes rather shady-looking visitors. These were the Count's poor relations. The closest possible study of family history would never have enabled Count Chojnicki to trace the exact degrees of kinship of his guests. Gradually they had made it a habit to arrive and stay the summer at the new Schloss, as family pensioners and connections. Having rested and fed, sometimes clothed in new suits provided by the Count's local tailor, these guests departed when starlings twittered in the night and the time of cuckoo weed was approaching—back into the unknown regions from which they had come. The master of the house noticed neither their arrival, nor their presence, nor their departure. His Jewish steward had standing orders to examine their family credentials, regulate their habits, and get rid of them at the approach of winter. The house had two entrances. While the Count and any guest who was not a kinsman used the front door, the relations had to go the long way around, across the fruit garden and in by the little side door in its wall. Apart from this, these uninvited guests were free to do anything they pleased.

Twice a week, on Mondays and Thursdays, Count Chojnicki held his little evenings, and once a month he gave a party. On little evenings only six rooms were lit up, for the parties twelve. On little evenings the footmen wore drab yellow livery and no gloves. Parties meant white-gloved footmen in dark-brown coats with silver buttons and velvet facings. All occasions began with vermouth and dry Spanish wines from which the guests passed on to Burgundy and Bordeaux. Then it was time for the champagne, which was followed by cognac. An evening ended with a fitting tribute to local patriotism—namely the local product, Ninety Percent.

The officers of the ultrafeudal Dragoons and the chiefly middle-class Jaeger swore lifelong friendship with great emotion at Count Chojnicki's parties. Through the wide curved windows of the Schloss, summer dawns would witness a colorful confusion of infantry and cavalry uniforms. Toward five a.m. a swarm of despairing batmen came running to the Schloss to wake their masters; for regimental parades began at six. The host, in whom alcohol engendered no fatigue, had long since gone to his little hunting lodge. There he would fiddle about with weird test tubes, chemical apparatus, and minute flames. Local gossip had it that Chojnicki was trying to make gold. Indeed, it certainly looked as though he were occupied with some foolish experiment in alchemy. However, even if he failed to produce gold, he was certainly making money at roulette. Sometimes he would drop hints about infallible systems passed on to him by a deceased gambler.

For years he had been a deputy to the Reichsrat, always re-elected by his district, quelling any local opposition by money, influence, or sudden attack. He was the spoilt darling of every government and despised the parliament he served in. He had never made a speech nor asked a question. Unbelieving and contemptuous, fearless and without scruple, Chojnicki was in the habit of saying that the Emperor was a thoughtless old man, the government officials a set of fools, the Reichsrat a well-meaning assemblage of pathetic idiots, the Civil Service venal, cowardly, and indolent. German-Austrians were waltzing apes, Hungarians stank, Czechs were born lick-spittles, Ruthenians treacherous Russians in disguise, Croats and Slovenes, whom he always called Crovots and Schlaviners, were tinkers, peddlars, and sots. His own nation, the Poles, were snobs, hairdressers, and fashion-plate photographers.

After every return from Vienna, or any other part of that society in which he kicked his heels up so familiarly, the Count would give an ominous lecture, somewhat as follows:

"The monarchy is bound to end. The minute the Emperor is dead, we shall splinter into a hundred fragments. The Balkans will be more powerful than we are. Each nation will set up its own dirty little government, even the Jews will proclaim a king in Palestine. Vienna's begun to stink of the sweat of democrats—I can't stand the Ringstrasse any more. The workers all wave red flags and don't want to work any more. The mayor of Vienna is a pious shopkeeper. Even the parsons are going red, they've started preaching in Czech in the churches. At the Burgtheater all the performances are filthy Jewish plays. And every week another Hungarian water-closet manufacturer is made a baron. I tell you, gentlemen, if we don't start shooting pretty soon, it'll be the end. You just wait and see what's coming to us."

His listeners laughed and had another drink. They couldn't see what the fuss was all about. Now and again, of course, you did some shooting, at election times, for instance, to secure the safe return of Count Chojnicki, which proved that things were not being allowed to go to the dogs just like that. The Emperor was still alive. He would be followed by his successor. The army continued to drill, resplendent in every regulation hue. The people loved their dynasty and acclaimed it, in many different kinds of peasant costume. Chojnicki was a joker.

But Trotta was more sensitive than his comrades, sadder than they, his mind forever full of echoes, darkness, and the rustling wings of death he had already twice encountered. Lieutenant Trotta could sometimes feel the dismal force of these prophecies.

Chapter 10

Every week when he went on barrack duty, Lieutenant Trotta wrote his monotonous letters to the District Commissioner. The barracks had no electric light. In the guardrooms they still used government candles, just as they had in the time of the hero of Solferino. Nowadays they were less rough and ready, were called Apollo candles, they were made of snowy tallow with well-plaited wicks and a steady flame. The Lieutenant's letters home gave no hint of his changed mode of life or the unusual conditions at the frontier. The District Commissioner avoided all questions. The replies which he posted so regularly on every fourth Sunday of the month were as monotonous as the Lieutenant's letters.

Every morning old Jacques brought the post into the room where, for many years, the District Commissioner had breakfasted. It was a rather remote room, not used during the day. Its windows faced east, ready to welcome impartially all mornings, warm or cool, sunny or overcast, frosty or rainy. Winter and summer alike, the window was open at breakfast. In winter the District Commissioner's legs would be wrapped in a warm rug, his breakfast table drawn up beside the stove, and in the stove would be a crackling fire, which old Jacques had lit half an hour before. Every year on April 15th Jacques stopped lighting fires in the stove. Every year, rain or shine, Herr von Trotta would begin his summer-morning walks on April 15th. At six o'clock the barber's assistant, still sleepy and unshaven himself, came into Herr von Trotta's bedroom. By six-fifteen the District Commissioner's chin lay smooth and powdered, flanked by his side whiskers streaked with gray. His bald scalp, still a little flushed from the few drops of eau de cologne rubbed into it, shone ready, massaged for the day. Every superfluous hair had been removed, any that might have sprouted out of the nostrils, inside the ears, or perhaps along the nape of the neck, over the high starched collar. Then the District Commissioner took his light walking stick and gray silk hat and set out for the municipal gardens. He wore a white waistcoat with gray buttons, cut very low, and a dove-gray morning coat. His narrow, uncreased trousers were fastened down by gray elastic over pointed, elastic-sided boots of softest glacé-kid, without seams or laces. The streets were still empty. The municipal water cart, pulled by two heavy brown horses, came rattling over cobblestones to meet him. The driver, on his high box seat, lowered his whip the instant he caught sight of Herr von Trotta, dropped his reins round the handle of his brake, and swung his cap so low that it touched his knees. He was the only man in the little town, indeed in the district, whom the District Commissioner ever greeted with a merry, almost jovial wave of the hand. The local policeman saluted him at the gates of the municipal gardens. To him the District Commissioner said a friendly, "Good day," without, however, raising his hand. He would proceed on his way to the blond owner of the mineral-water stand. Here he half-raised his gray silk hat, took a glass of tonic water, drew out a coin from his waistcoat pocket without removing his gray gloves, and continued his walk. Bakers and chimney sweeps, greengrocers and butchers met him. They all bowed. The District Commissioner replied with a gesture of the forefinger, gently touching his hat brim. Not until he met Kronauer, the chemist, who also indulged in morning walks, and was, moreover, a borough councilor, would he raise his hat. Sometimes he would say, "Good morning!" and stop to ask, "How are you?" "Very well," the chemist would answer him. "Delighted," the District Commissioner commented and went on again.

He was never back before eight o'clock. Sometimes he met the postman in the hall, or out on the steps. Then he would walk across the yard, for a few minutes, to his office, because he liked to find his letters all ready for him on the breakfast table. He found it quite impossible to see or speak to anyone at breakfast. Old Jacques might come in unbidden, on winter mornings, to stoke up the fire, or in summer, to shut the window, if the rain happened to be pouring in too gustily. Fräulein Hirschwitz was out of the question. Before one p.m. the sight of her was anathema to the District Commissioner.

One morning—it was the end of May—Herr von Trotta got back from his walk at five past eight. The postman must long since have come. Herr von Trotta sat down at the table in his breakfast room. His egg, medium boiled, stood as always in its usual place, in the silver eggcup. The honey shone golden, the fresh-baked rolls lay there fragrant and redolent of yeast and flame as every day; the butter gleamed yellow, laid on a huge dark-green leaf. The coffee steamed in gold-rimmed china. Nothing was missing. Or so it seemed to Herr von Trotta at first glance. But at once he got up again, put down his napkin, and inspected his table again. His letters were not in their usual place! So far as the District Commissioner could remember, no day had ever passed without some official mail. First Herr von Trotta went across the room to open the window as if to make certain that the world still existed. Yes, the old chestnut trees in the park still wore their massive crowns of dark-green leaves. In them unseen birds chirped as on every morning. The milk cart, too, which drew up at about this hour at the District Commissioner's residence was there today, unconcerned as if this were a morning like all others. The Commissioner ascertained that outside nothing had changed. Was it possible that there had been no mail? Was it possible that Jacques had forgotten it? Herr von Trotta shook the handbell. Its silver notes pealed through the quiet house. No one came. For the time being, Herr von Trotta allowed his breakfast to go untasted. He shook the bell a second time. At last there was a knock. He was amazed, startled, and insulted when he saw his housekeeper, Fräulein Hirschwitz, come in.

She was encased in a kind of morning armor in which he had never seen her. A massive apron of smooth, shiny, dark-blue oilcloth protected her from neck to feet. A white cap sat tightly on her head, displaying her large and fleshy ear-lobes. She seemed extraordinarily repulsive to Herr von Trotta. He could not bear the smell of oilcloth.

"This is most annoying," he said without responding to her greeting. "Where is Jacques?"

"Jacques is unwell today."

"Unwell?" repeated the District Commissioner, who had not understood at once. "Ill, do you mean?" he continued.

"He has a temperature."

"Thank you," said Herr von Trotta and waved her off. He sat down at the table. He only drank the coffee. The egg, the honey, the butter, the rolls he left on the tray. Certainly he understood now that Jacques had fallen ill and was therefore not able to bring his letters. But why had Jacques fallen ill? He had always been as well as—as the mail, for instance. If suddenly the post had refused to deliver any letters it would scarcely have been more surprising. The District Commissioner himself was never ill. If you were ill, it meant that you were going to die. Illness was nothing more than a device of nature to accustom men to dying. Epidemics—in the Commissioner's youth cholera had still been feared—could with luck be withstood by certain individuals; other diseases which might creep upon a man overnight he had to succumb to, no matter how many different names they were called. Doctors—he thought of them as medical officers—pretended that they could cure illness. But only so as not to have to starve. In theory, of course, people who were ill might always recover, but never, so far as he remembered, had Herr von Trotta been in personal contact with them or even heard of them.

He rang again. "I should like my letters," he told Fräulein Hirschwitz, "but please send someone over with them. What do you think can be the matter with Jacques?"

"He has a temperature," said Fräulein Hirschwitz. "I fancy he must have caught a chill."

"A chill? In May?"

"He's not as young as he used to be."

"Get Dr Sribny to come." This was the District Medical Officer. He was on duty every day from nine to twelve in the District Commissioner's offices. He would soon be here. In the District Commissioner's opinion, he was a decent sort of man.

Meanwhile, the office porter came with the mail. The District Commissioner only glanced at the envelopes and gave them back, with orders to put them on his desk. He stood looking out of the window and could not cease to be surprised that the outside world should take so little note of all the changes in his house. Today he had neither breakfasted nor read the mail! Jacques had succumbed to a mysterious illness. And yet life continued as usual. Very slowly he walked across the yard, preoccupied with many fuzzy reflections. Twenty minutes later than usual he sat down at his desk. His assistant came in with a report. Yesterday again there had been another demonstration of Czech workmen. A Sokol outing had been announced. Delegates from Slavonic states—the report meant Russians and Serbians but in official jargon these must never be mentioned by name—were due to arrive the next day; and German-speaking Socialists were attracting attention. A workman in the local spinning factory had been given a thrashing by his mates for having, according to the agent's report, refused to join the Red Party. All this upset the Commissioner, it wounded him. All these projects of disobedient subjects, these attempts to undermine, to insult, whether directly or indirectly, His Majesty the Emperor, to render laws weaker than they were already, to disturb the peace, scoff at officials, set up Czech schools, return opposition delegates—they were all aimed at the District Commissioner personally. At first he had been merely contemptuous of these nationalists with their self-determination, these workers demanding rights. Gradually, he came to hate them, the ranters, the agitators, the trouble makers. He gave his assistant stringent orders to break up at once any meeting which seemed likely to pass a resolution. Of all the words which had lately become fashionable, that was the one he hated most. Perhaps because its current implications brought it so close to the most shameful of all words: revolution, a word which had no place in his vocabulary, he had expunged it completely. He never used it, even in official correspondence. And if in a subordinate's report there occurred, for instance, the expression "revolutionary agitator" in connection with some rampant Socialist, he would cross it out, and write over the top of it in red ink the emendation "suspicious character." In other districts of the monarchy revolutionaries might possibly be found. In Herr von Trotta's there were none.

"Send Sergeant-Major Slama to me this afternoon," said Herr von Trotta to his assistant. "Request gendarmery reinforcements to deal with these Sokolists. Make out a brief report for the District Council and submit it for my inspection tomorrow morning. We ought perhaps to get in touch with the military authorities. In any case—as of tomorrow—the gendarmery is to hold itself in readiness. I should be obliged for a précis from the last ministerial instructions dealing with precautionary measures."

"Certainly, sir."

"Good. Has Dr Sribny come yet?"

"He's just been called across to see Jacques."

"I should like to have a word with him."

The District Commissioner dealt with no more official papers. Years ago, in the quiet years when he had begun to get his bearings in the District, there had been no Socialists and relatively few "suspicious characters". In the slow course of years he had scarcely noticed their increase, how their influence spread, how dangerous they grew. But Jacques's illness had made Herr von Trotta suddenly aware of all the evil changes in the world, as if Death, which might even now be sitting at the bedside of the old servant, was not threatening him alone. If Jacques dies, it occurred to the District Commissioner, then the hero of Solferino would, in a sense, die all over again, and perhaps—his heart stood still—perhaps he too would soon be dead, whose life that hero had once saved. Ah, not only Jacques had fallen ill that day. The letters still lay unopened on the District Commissioner's desk. Who knew what they contained? Sokolists were banding themselves together within the monarchy under the very eyes of officials and police. Sokols—he called them Sokolists, reducing, with a single syllable, a major portion of the Slav population of the Empire to the level of a cranky minority—these Sokols pretended to be mere gymnastic associations, harmlessly engaged in strengthening their muscles. In reality they were spies or rebels in the Tsar's pay. Even yesterday's *Foreign News* had informed him how in Prague German-speaking students occasionally sang "The Watch on the Rhine", that Prussian hymn of Austria's ally and arch-enemy. Who was there left to rely on? The District Commissioner shivered. For the first time since he had worked in this office he got up from his desk to close the window, on an undeniably sunny spring day.

The District Commissioner asked the District Medical Officer, who entered at that moment, how old Jacques was. Dr Sribny said, "If it turns into pneumonia I don't think he'll pull through. He's very old. His temperature is high. He's been asking for the priest."

The District Commissioner bent over his desk. He was afraid the doctor might notice some change in his expression, and indeed he could feel that something in his face was beginning to change. He pulled out his drawer, took out a box of cigars, and offered the doctor one. Silently he waved at the armchair. They both smoked.

"So you haven't much hope?" Herr von Trotta finally inquired.

"Very little, I'm afraid, to tell you the truth," the doctor answered. "At his age. . . ." He didn't finish the sentence and scrutinized the other's face as though he were trying to decide how much younger the master was than the servant.

"He hasn't ever been ill," the District Commissioner pleaded. It was a kind of extenuating circumstance, with Dr Sribny as the Supreme Court on which final sentence would depend.

"Yes, yes," was all the doctor would say. "It's often like that. Exactly how old is he?"

The District Commissioner pondered his reply. "Somewhere between seventy-eight and eighty."

"Yes," Dr Sribny said, "that's just about what I estimated— that is, today. So long as anyone's up and about we tend to think they'll live forever."

After which the doctor rose and went back to his work. Herr von Trotta scribbled on a slip: "I am over in Jacques's cottage." He put the paper under his paperweight and went out into the yard.

He had never been inside Jacques's cottage before. It was a tiny house with a chimney far too tall for the little roof built against the back courtyard wall. It had three walls of yellowish brick and a brown door in the middle, which opened onto the kitchen; then came the glass-paneled door into the living room. Jacques's pet canary stood on the knob of its domed cage, next to the window, which was covered with a rather short white curtain which made the pane look faded. A deal table stood against the wall. A blue oil lamp, with its round tin reflector, hung above it. On this table, solidly framed, rather like the framed likeness of a relation, stood a picture of the Holy Mother of God. Jacques lay in bed, his head toward the window, in a snowy mound of pillows and sheets. He thought it was the priest, and drew a long breath of satisfaction, as though grace were approaching him.

"Oh, Herr Baron!" he said.

The District Commissioner went up close to the old man. His own grandfather, the gendarmery sergeant-major, had been laid out in just such a room, in the pensioners' quarters at Laxenburg. The District Commissioner could still remember that small, enclosed room, with its yellow glow from tall white candles, and the vast hard soles of a booted and ceremoniously uniformed corpse seemed again to thrust themselves in his face. Was it Jacques's turn now? The old man propped himself up on his elbow. He wore a dark-blue woolen nightcap, and through its tightly knitted stitches his hair gleamed silver. His clean-shaven face, reddened by the fever, had a look of ivory about it.

Herr von Trotta sat down on a chair beside the bed and said, "Well, the doctor tells me there isn't anything much the matter. It's just a sort of cold in the head."

"Yes, Herr Baron," answered Jacques, with a feeble effort to bring his heels together under the blankets. He sat up. "I'm very sorry," he added, "I hope I'll be better in the morning."

"Of course. In a few days at most."

"I'm waiting for the priest, Herr Baron."

"Yes, yes, yes," said Herr von Trotta. "He'll be coming, there's plenty of time for all that."

"He's on his way now," answered old Jacques, in the accents of one who could perceive the priest's approach. "On his way now," he said again suddenly, and seemed to have forgotten that the District Commissioner was sitting beside him. "When the old master went," he continued, "none of us knew anything about it. That morning, maybe the day before, he came out into the yard and he said to me, 'Jacques, where are those boots?' Yes, it was the day before, and then, next morning, he didn't need them any more. After that, winter set in, it was a very cold winter, I think I can hold out till winter. It isn't so very long till winter. July, June, May, April, August, November, and then Christmas, and that'll be the end, dismiss, company dismiss." He stopped and looked with wide blue glittering eyes through Herr von Trotta as through glass.

Herr von Trotta tried gently to press the old man back onto his pillows, but Jacques's body was rigid and did not give. Only his head trembled, and with it the dark-blue nightcap trembled unceasingly. Tiny beads of perspiration stood out on his high, bony, sallow forehead. From time to time the Commissioner dried them with his handkerchief, but fresh ones kept glistening forth. He took old Jacques's hand and looked at its broad red back, scaly and chapped, and the powerful outspread thumb. Then he put it carefully back on the sheet and returned to his office to tell the porter to go for a priest and nursing sister, leaving a message for Fräulein Hirschwitz that she was to sit with Jacques until they came. He asked for his stick, hat, and gloves and went out into the park at this unusual hour, to the surprise of all who happened to be there.

But he was soon driven back into the house, out of the deep shade of the chestnut trees. As he approached his door, he heard the tinklings of the priest administering the Blessed Sacrament. He took off his hat, bent his head, and waited, standing outside his own front door. A few passers-by also stopped. Now the priest was coming out of the house. A few people waited until the District Commissioner disappeared into his hallway and crowded inquisitively after him, to learn from the office porter that Jacques was lying on his deathbed. He was well known in the town. They bestowed a few minutes' respectful silence on this old man who was about to depart from them.

Herr von Trotta went straight across the yard and into the room of the dying man. He looked around in the dark kitchen for a place to put down his hat, stick, and gloves, found room for them at last on the dresser shelves among jugs and plates. He sent Fräulein Hirschwitz away and sat on the bed. By now the sun stood so high that the whole wide yard was bathed in sunlight and it shone in through the window of Jacques's room. The short white curtain hung like a gay little apron, sun-drenched in front of the windowpane. The canary sang gaily and without stopping, the bare smooth deal boards gleamed in the sunlight. A wide silvery ray of sunshine fell over the foot of the bed so that the lower half of the white counterpane lay bleached to an almost celestial white, while a sunbeam climbed up the wall by the bed. From time to time a gentle breeze blew through the few old trees out in the yard planted against the wall, as old as Jacques or maybe older, which had sheltered him in their shade every day. The breeze blew and the trees rustled and Jacques seemed to know it, for he raised himself and said, "Herr Baron, the window, if you please. . . ."

The Commissioner unlatched the window and at once the pleasant sounds of May penetrated into the little room. They could hear the soughing of the trees and the soft breath of the little breeze, the loud buzz of the glittering Spanish flies, the throbbing of larks from distant blue heights. The canary flew out but only to show he could still use his wings. He was back in a few minutes, perched on the window sill and sang twice as hard as before. The world was gay, inside and out. And Jacques leaned forward in his bed, listening, rigid, the beads of perspiration on his forehead glittered, his thin lips opened slowly. At first he only smiled, without a sound. Then he blinked; his flushed, bony cheeks had begun to pucker against the cheekbones. Now he looked like an old rogue, and a thin titter came from his throat. He laughed without stopping. He could not stop laughing. The pillows trembled gently and even the bedstead groaned a little. The District Commissioner smiled, too. Death was coming to old Jacques like a laughing girl in spring. Jacques opened his venerable mouth and let her see his sparse yellow teeth. He held his hand up, pointing to the window and shook his head, continuing to titter.

"It's a lovely day," remarked the District Commissioner.

"Look out there, he's coming. Here he is, here he is!" said Jacques "All in white and riding on his white horse. What is it makes him ride so slowly, look, look, how slowly he's riding. Good day, good day, wouldn't you like to come a little closer? Why don't you come? Why don't you come? It's nice today, isn't it?" He drew back his hand and stared at the District Commissioner and said, "How slowly he's riding. That's because he's from over there. He's been dead so long he's not used to riding over the stones any more. Once you knew—remember how he used to look? I'd like to see the picture. I want to find out if he's really changed. Bring the picture, please, bring it Herr Baron."

The District Commissioner understood at once that he meant the portrait of the hero of Solferino. He went out obediently. He even went up the stairs two at a time, hurried into his study, climbed a chair, and took the portrait of the hero of Solferino from its nail. It was a little dusty. He blew on it and wiped it with the handkerchief which he had used to wipe the forehead of the dying man. Still the District Commissioner smiled. He was happy. It was a long time since he had felt so happy. He hurried back across the yard with the big portrait under his arm. He approached Jacques's bed.

Jacques took a long look at the portrait, stretched out his index finger, and stroked the face of the hero of Solferino and said at last, "Hold it up in the sun." The District Commissioner did as he was asked. He held the portrait up across the foot of the bed in the shaft of sunlight. Jacques sat upright and said, "Yes, that was just how he looked . . ." and lay down again on his pillows.

The District Commissioner stood the portrait on the table next to the Holy Mother of God and came back to the bed.

"I'll soon be up there," said Jacques, smiling and pointing to the ceiling.

"Plenty of time for that," replied the District Commissioner.

"Oh no," said Jacques, laughing very brightly. "There's been plenty of time for that long enough. Now it's time I was up there. You might just look and see how old I am. I've forgotten."

"Where shall I look?"

"Under there," Jacques said, pointing to a drawer in the bedstead. This the District Commissioner pulled open. He found a little brown-paper package, neatly done up in bits of string and a box with a highly colored but fading picture of a shepherdess in a white wig on its lid. He recognized it as one of those boxes of chocolates which in his childhood had so often lain under other boys' Christmas trees. "That's the little book," said Jacques. It was his army paybook.

The District Commissioner put on his pince-nez. "Franz Xavier Joseph Kromichl," he read. "Is this your book?"

"Of course it is," said Jacques.

"But is your name Franz Xavier Joseph?"

"Seems to be."

"Then why have you always called yourself Jacques?"

"He told me to."

"I see," said Herr von Trotta and read the date. "Well, you'll be eighty-two next August."

"Eighty-two in August. And what's today?"

"Today's May 19th."

"And how long will it be till August?"

"Three months."

"I see," said Jacques quite peacefully, and he leaned back. "I shan't see that. Open the box." The District Commissioner opened the box. "Inside you'll find St Anthony and St George. You can keep those. Then," Jacques continued, "there's a special bit of root to keep off the fever. Give that to your son Carl Joseph, send him my greetings. Might come in useful. That's a swampy sort of place he's in. And now shut the window. I want to sleep."

It was midday. The bed was now completely flooded in sunshine. Big Spanish flies stuck immobile to the window-panes and the canary had stopped singing and was pecking sugar. Twelve chimes resounded from the town-hall tower and their golden echo died in the yard. The District Commissioner went into his dining room.

"I'm not eating," he told Fräulein Hirschwitz. He glanced round the dining room. That was the place where Jacques had always stood, dish in hand; he had come round there along the table, and handed it a certain way. Herr von Trotta could not eat today. He went down again into the yard and sat under the overhanging balcony to await the arrival of the nursing sister.

"He's asleep now," he told her when she came. The gentle breeze fanned past him from time to time. The shadows of the beam grew broader and longer. The flies buzzed round the District Commissioner's side whiskers. From time to time he flicked them off and his cuff clattered. For the first time since he had been in his Emperor's service he sat idle on a weekday. He had never felt he wanted to go on leave. It was his first experience of a day off. He kept on thinking of old Jacques and was nevertheless happy. Old Jacques was dying and yet he seemed to be celebrating a great event in honor of which the District Commissioner had his first holiday.

Suddenly he heard the Sister of Mercy come out of the door. She said that Jacques, apparently quite clearheaded and free from fever, had got up out of bed and was in process of getting dressed. And indeed, the District Commissioner immediately saw the old man at the window. He had set out his soap and brush and razor on the ledge just as he always

142

did on normal days. His bit of mirror dangled from the window knob, and now he was beginning to shave. Jacques opened the window and called out in his ordinary voice, "I'm quite well, Herr Baron, I feel very well. I hope you'll excuse me, please don't put yourself out."

"So all's well. I'm delighted, really delighted. Now you must begin a new life as Franz Xavier Joseph."

"I'd much rather stick to Jacques."

Herr von Trotta, pleased indeed at such a miraculous occurrence but at the same time a little at a loss, returned to his seat, and asked the Sister of Mercy to stay, just in case, and inquired if she had known other instances of such speedy recovery in people of advanced age. With eyes lowered on her rosary and picking her reply out from among her beads she said that both sudden illness and quick recovery were matters in the hands of God, Whose will had often restored the dying to health with miraculous swiftness. A more scientific answer would have pleased the District Commissioner better, and he decided to ask Dr Sribny in the morning.

For the present, he went back to his office, relieved, it is true, of a heavy burden, yet full of an even heavier, inexplicable feeling of unrest. He could do no work. Sergeant-Major Slama, who had long been awaiting his arrival, received instructions for dealing with the Sokol outing, but they were given without emphasis or severity. The many dangers which threatened both the District of W. and the monarchy seemed less formidable now to Herr von Trotta than they had in the morning. He dismissed the Sergeant-Major but called him back at once and said, "Listen, Slama, have you ever heard anything like it? This morning old Jacques looked as though he were dying and now he's quite bright and up and about again."

No, Sergeant-Major Slama had never heard of anything like it. And to the District Commissioner's question whether he wanted to have a look at Jacques, he answered that he would willingly do so. They returned together into the yard.

Old Jacques was sitting on his stool with a soldierly row of boots in front of him, brush in hand, and spitting vigorously into a wooden box containing polish. He tried to rise when he found the District Commissioner at his elbow, but could not manage it quickly enough, nor before his master's hand was on his shoulder. He gave the Sergeant-Major a mock salute with his blacking brush. The District Commissioner sat down on the bench. Slama leaned his rifle against the wall and sat down, too, at a respectful distance. Jacques remained on his stool and polished the boots, albeit more gently and slowly than usual. Meanwhile, the Sister of Mercy prayed in his room.

"I've just remembered," said Jacques, "how I ordered the Herr Baron about this morning. I've suddenly thought of it. . . ."

"Doesn't matter, Jacques," said the District Commissioner. "You had a temperature."

"Yes, everything I said then I said as a corpse. And now, Sergeant-Major, you'll have to lock me up for false pretences. Because I'm called Franz Xavier Joseph, though I'd sooner have Jacques on my gravestone. My savings book's under the army paybook. There'll be enough for the funeral and a mass. They call me Jacques in that one, though."

"All in good time," the District Commissioner said. "There's no hurry."

The Sergeant-Major laughed out loud and wiped his forehead. Jacques had polished every boot until it shone. He shivered a little, went indoors, and came out again, wrapped in his winter fur coat, which he also wore in summer when it rained, and sat down again on his stool. The canary followed him; it darted above his silver hair, circling around for a place to perch on until it settled at last upon the crossbeam over which some rugs were hanging and started to sing. Its song roused a hundred sparrows' voices in the leaves of the few trees, and for several minutes the air was full of a twittering, piping, gay confusion. Jacques raised his head to listen with a certain pride in the triumphant voice of his canary, which outsang them all. The District Commissioner smiled. The Sergeant-Major laughed, his handkerchief up to his mouth, and Jacques tittered. Even the Sister of Mercy had left her prayers and now stood smiling at the window. Already the golden afternoon sun lay on the wooden beam and played in the high green treetops. Evening gnats danced in and out, clustering in thin, tired swarms; an occasional heavy May fly passed the sitters, humming its way to destruction in the leaves, probably straight into the sparrows' gaping beaks.

The wind blew up a little. Now the birds were all silent. The vault of sky was deepening its blue, its small white clouds were tinged to rose.

"It's time you went to bed," said Herr von Trotta to Jacques.

"I must just take that picture upstairs," the old man mumbled. He went to fetch the portrait of the hero of Solferino and vanished in the dark of the staircase.

The Sergeant-Major watched him go and said, "Strange."

"Yes," replied Herr von Trotta. "Very strange."

Jacques returned and came up to the bench. He sat down, without a word, rather surprisingly between the Sergeant-Major and the District Commissioner, opened his mouth, drew a deep breath, and even before they had both turned toward him his old head sank against the wood, his hands fell on to the seat, his fur coat gaped open, his outspread legs stretched stiff and wide, the upward-pointing toes of his slippers thrust into the air. A strong short gust of wind swept through the yard. The sun had disappeared behind the wall. The District Commissioner's left hand supported his servant's silver head, with his right he felt for the heart in the lifeless body. The startled Sergeant-Major stood beside him; his black cap lay on the ground. The nun came out in long, hurrying strides. She took the old man's hand and held it between her fingers, laid it gently back on to the fur coat, and made the sign of the cross. She looked quietly at the Sergeant-Major. He understood, and raised Jacques up under the armpits. She held his legs. So they carried him back to his little room and laid him out on the bed, folded his hands, twisted the rosary around them, and set the Holy Mother of God by his head. They knelt down at his bedside and the District Commissioner prayed. He had not prayed for a long time. A prayer came back to him from the buried depths of his childhood, a prayer for the souls of dead relatives and this he whispered. He stood up and glanced down at his trousers, brushed the dust off his knees and went outside, followed by the Sergeant-Major.

"My dear Slama," he said—instead of his usual, "Good day to you"—"that's just how I'd like to die when my time comes."

He wrote the instructions for the laying-out and funeral of his servant on a large sheet of official paper, point by point, section and subsection, like a master of ceremonies. Next morning he went out to the cemetery to choose a grave, bought a headstone, and ordered the inscription HERE RESTS IN GOD FRANZ XAVIER JOSEPH KROMICHL, KNOWN AS JACQUES, AN OLD SERVANT AND A TRUE FRIEND. He arranged for the most expensive kind of funeral, with four black horses and eight liveried mourners.

Three days later he followed the hearse on foot, as sole mourner, with Sergeant-Major Slama walking at a respectful distance behind him, and many others who joined the cortège because they had known old Jacques, but especially because they were seeing Herr von Trotta on foot. So that a respectable number of people followed old Franz Xavier Joseph Kromichl, known as Jacques, to the grave.

From this time on his house seemed changed to the District Commissioner, no longer like a home. He found no letters, now, next to his breakfast tray, but could never decide to give the office porter new instructions. He no longer touched any of the numerous little silver bells, and if, in forgetful moments, he happened to stretch out his hand toward one of them, he would only stroke it but never ring it. Sometimes in the late afternoon he fancied he could hear old Jacques's ghostly shuffle on the stairs. Sometimes he went to the little room in which Jacques had lived and pushed a lump of sugar between the bars of the cage for the canary.

One day, when the Sokol outing was almost due and his official presence in the office was not without importance, he came to a surprising decision.

Chapter 11

The District Commissioner decided to visit his son in his distant frontier garrison. This was no easy undertaking for a man such as Herr von Trotta. He had extraordinary notions of what the eastern borders of the monarchy were like. Two of his schoolmates had, on account of embarrassing lapses from duty, been transferred to those far regions on the borders where Siberian wolves could probably be heard to howl. Bears and wolves and even more vicious monsters, such as lice and bedbugs, threatened the civilized Austrian. Ruthenian peasants sacrificed to pagan gods and Jews raged cruelly against the homes and possessions of strangers. Herr von Trotta packed his old six-chambered revolver. Not that adventure frightened him; rather it reawakened in his blood that intoxicating sensation from his long buried boyhood which had sent him and his old friend Moser out hunting in the mysterious wooded depths of the paternal estate and into churchyards at midnight.

Cheerfully he took brief leave of Fräulein Hirschwitz, in the vague bold hope that he might never see her again. He went alone to the station. The booking-clerk said to him, "A journey at last. I wish you a pleasant trip."

The stationmaster came hurrying out on to the platform. "Are you traveling officially?' he inquired.

And Herr von Trotta in that expansive mood in which we rather enjoy arousing conjectures, replied,

"More or less officially, Stationmaster. Yes, one might say officially."

"For a long time?"

"I can't tell yet."

"I suppose you'll be visiting your son?"

"If I can manage it."

The District Commissioner stood at the window and waved his hand. He was taking cheerful leave of his district. He did not think of his return. He checked all the stations off against the timetable. "Change at Oderberg," he repeated to himself. He compared the scheduled times of arrival and departure with the actual ones, and set his watch by all the station clocks they passed. Oddly enough, each irregularity refreshed, even elated him. In Oderberg he let one train go by. Curious and examining everything, he walked along the platform and went through the waiting rooms and even a little way down the road into the town. Back on the platform, he pretended he had missed his train unintentionally and actually said to the porter, "I've missed my train." He felt disappointed that the porter was not surprised. In Cracow he had to change again. He welcomed it. If he had not told Carl Joseph when to expect him or even if that "dubious place" had boasted two through trains a day, he would willingly have broken his journey to take a look at the world. Still, even through the windows, it could be viewed. Spring welcomed him all along the line. He arrived in the afternoon.

He stepped off the footboard with sprightly calm, with that "elastic step" with which the newspapers were always crediting the old Emperor, and which in the course of years had been acquired by many of his elderly civil servants. For at this time there was in the monarchy a quite distinctive and now forgotten way of getting out of carriages and trains, going up front-door steps to pay a call, encountering relatives and friends, dictated, perhaps, by the tight trousers these old gentlemen wore, which were held down by bits of elastic over their elastic-sided boots. With this distinctive gait, Herr von Trotta left the railway carriage. He embraced Carl Joseph, who had planted himself in front of the footboard. That day, Herr von Trotta was the only passenger to get out of a first- or second-class coach; out of the third came a few privates back from leave, workmen from farther up the line, and Jews in long black fluttering robes. Everyone looked at father and son. The District Commissioner hurried to the waiting room. There he kissed Carl Joseph on the forehead. At the bar, he ordered two brandies. On the wall behind the shelves of bottles hung a mirror. While they drank, father and son scrutinized each other's face.

"Is that mirror over there so impossible," asked Herr von Trotta, "or do you really look so wretched?"

"Have you really gone so gray?" Carl Joseph would have liked to ask. For he noticed the many silver hairs which glittered in his father's dark side whiskers and around the temples.

"Let's have a look at you," the District Commissioner continued. "No, it certainly isn't the mirror. It's the conditions here, perhaps. Are they bad?"

The District Commissioner ascertained that his son's appearance was by no means all that a young lieutenant's should be. He may be ill, the father thought. Over and above the illnesses from which one died, there were only those appalling maladies which, according to hearsay, not infrequently assailed officers. "Are you supposed to be drinking cognac?" he asked, in the hope of getting at the facts by circumlocutory methods.

"Oh, yes, certainly, Papa," said the Lieutenant. This voice which had, so long ago on quiet Sunday mornings crossexamined him, still rang in his head, the civil servant's nasal voice, severe, always a little surprised and curious, a voice before which any lie perished on the tongue.

"Do you like it in the infantry?"

"Very much, Papa."

"And what about your horse?"

"I brought him with me, Papa."

"Do you ride him much?"

"No, not often, Papa."

"Don't you enjoy it?"

"No, I never did, Papa."

"Oh, stop that 'Papa,'" Herr von Trotta suddenly exclaimed. "You're big enough, and I'm on leave."

They went into the town.

"Well, really, it isn't so fierce here, after all," observed the District Commissioner. "Is there, are there, many amusements?"

"Oh yes," said Carl Joseph, "at Count Chojnicki's. We all see each other there. You'll meet him. I like him very much."

"The first great friend you've ever had?"

"The regimental surgeon, Max Demant, was too," answered Carl Joseph. "Here is your room, Papa," said the Lieutenant. "All the others live here, too, and sometimes they make a racket late at night. But there isn't another hotel. And they'll be a bit more careful while you're staying here."

"Doesn't matter, doesn't matter," said the District Commissioner. He unpacked a round tin box and opened the lid. He showed it to Carl Joseph. "It's some kind of root. It's supposed to be very good against bog fever. It's from Jacques."

"How is he?"

"He's gone now." The District Commissioner pointed to the ceiling.

"Gone," the Lieutenant echoed. To the District Commissioner it sounded like an old man's voice. His son must have a good many secrets. And he knew nothing of them. They said "father and son," but between them lay many generations, like great mountains. He didn't know much more about Carl Joseph than about any other lieutenant. He had been assigned to the cavalry and transferred into an infantry regiment. He wore the green facings of the Jaeger instead of the scarlet facings of the Uhlans. Well, that was all he knew about him. He was obviously growing old. An old man. He no longer wholly belonged either to the service or to his duties. He belonged to Carl Joseph and to Jacques. He brought this weatherworn, petrified root from one to the other.

Still bending down over his suitcase, the District Commissioner opened his mouth. He spoke into the case as into an open grave. But he did not say, as he had intended, "I love you, my son," only, "He had an easy death. It was a real May evening, and all the birds were singing. Do you remember the canary? It sang loudest of all. Jacques was polishing boots, and then he died out in the yard, sitting on the bench. Slama was with me at the time. He'd only been feverish since the morning. He said I was to remember him kindly to you. . . ."

Then the District Commissioner looked up from the case at his son's face. "I'd like to die like that eventually."

The Lieutenant went into his room, opened the cupboard, and put the root into the top drawer, with Katherina's letters and Max Demant's sword. He consulted the regimental surgeon's watch. He felt that the thin black second hand ran faster around its minute circle than on any other watch he knew and that its resounding tick was more violent. The hands had no goal, the ticking no meaning. Soon I shall hear father's watch ticking, too, he will leave it to me. I shall hang grandfather's portrait in my room and Max's sword and an heirloom of his father's. It will all be buried with me. I'm the last Trotta.

He was young enough still to draw sweet voluptuousness from his grief and from the certainty that he was the last, a painful honor. From the nearby marshes came the loud rich croaking of the frogs. The sinking sun reddened the furniture and walls of the room. Then the trundling wheels of a light dogcart were heard and soft clumping hoofs on a dusty road. The dogcart drew up, a straw-colored britska, Count Chojnicki's summer vehicle. Three times the cracks of his whip cut across the chorus of frogs.

Count Chojnicki was curious. No passion other than curiosity urged him on his journeys through the world, kept him chained to the tables of large gambling rooms, locked him behind the doors of his old hunting lodge, impelled him to take his seat in parliament, drew him back home again every spring, inspired his parties, barred his way to suicide, solely his curiosity kept him going. He was insatiably curious. Lieutenant Trotta had told him that he was expecting his father, the District Commissioner, and though Count Chojnicki knew a good dozen chief officials in Austrian districts and innumerable fathers of lieutenants, he was nevertheless eager to meet District Commissioner Trotta.

"Your son and I are very great friends," said Chojnicki. "You're my guest. Your son has told you? And surely we've met somewhere, haven't we? Aren't you a friend of Swoboda's at the Ministry of Commerce?"

"We were at school together."

"Well, there you are. He's a close friend of mine, Swoboda. A little timeworn, but a fine man. May I be completely frank? You remind me of Francis Joseph."

There was a short silence. Never had the District Commissioner uttered the name of the Emperor. On festive occasions you said "His Majesty." In everyday life you said "the Emperor." But this Chojnicki said "Francis Joseph," just as a minute ago he had said "Swoboda."

"Yes, you remind me of Francis Joseph," Count Chojnicki repeated.

They drove off. On either side croaked the interminable chorus of frogs and stretched the interminable blue-green marshes. Evening drifted toward them, violet and gold. They heard the soft rolling of the wheels on the soft sand of the country road, and the sharp creaking of the axle trees. Chojnicki pulled up outside his little hunting lodge.

Its back wall was built along the dark fringe of the pinewood. A small garden and stone gateway divided the house from the narrow road. The hedges, flanking the short path untidily from gateway to house, had stood long untrimmed and burgeoned in savage arbitrariness across the pathway, inclined their branches toward each other and did not permit two people abreast to pass at the same time. So the three men walked in single file, the horse obediently following, pulling the dogcart and apparently quite used to the pathway—at home here, like a human being. Beyond these hedges stretched wide plains overgrown with clumps of thistle, guarded by the broad dark-green faces of dock leaves. To the right stood a broken stone column; it might have been the remains of a tower. It rose to the sky, embedded like a strong broken tooth in the garden mold, patched with moss, streaked with soft, dark-edged fissures. A heavy wooden door displayed the Chojnicki arms: an azure shield, divided in three with three golden stags, their antlers interlocking. Chojnicki put the light on. They stood in a low, wide room. The last light of day was still glinting through the narrow slats of the Venetian blinds. The table under the lamp was set with plates, bottles, jugs, silver cutlery, and dishes.

"I have given myself the pleasure of preparing a light meal for you," said Chojnicki. He filled up three liqueur glasses with Ninety Percent, clear as water, handed two to his guests, and raised the third. They drank them down. The District Commissioner was somewhat uneasy as he put his little glass back on the table. At any rate, the reality of the food contradicted the mysterious nature of the lodge, and the District Commissioner's hunger was greater than his uneasiness. Brown *foie gras* dotted with pitch-black truffles stood in a glittering garland of freshly ground ice; the tender breast of a pheasant rose solitary on its snowy dish surrounded by a colourful accompaniment of green, red, white, and yellow vegetables, each on its little crested platter, rimmed blue and gold. A capacious crystal jar contained myriads of dark-gray beads of caviar, encircled by yellow rounds of lemon slices. And the round pink slices of ham guarded by a large three-pronged silver fork lay in obedient rows on a long platter, accompanied by red-cheeked radishes reminiscent of crisp little village girls. Stewed, roasted, and marinated with sour-sweet onions, sleek pieces of carp lay in a flat dish, while slender slippery pike were displayed in glass, silver, and china. Round loaves of bread, black, brown, and white, rested in simple rustic plaited baskets like children in cradles, the slices artfully pieced together so that the loaves looked undivided. Among these dishes stood full-bellied flasks, tall, narrow, square, or hexagonally cut carafes of crystal, as well as smooth round ones, some with long slender necks, others with short ones, with and without labels; all followed by a regiment of wine and liqueur glasses.

They began to eat.

The District Commissioner found the unaccustomed way of taking a meal at an unaccustomed hour a most agreeable indication of the extraordinary customs of the frontier district. In the old Imperial and Royal Monarchy even such Spartan creatures as Herr von Trotta were remarkable gourmets. It was a long time since he had eaten a festive meal. The last had been on the occasion of Prince M.'s farewell dinner, given on the eve of that local magnate's departure on a distinguished mission to the newly occupied border provinces of Bosnia and Herzegovina, an honor conferred upon the prince in recognition of his noted accomplishments as a linguist and his supposed capacity to break-in uncivilized populations. Yes, on that evening the District Commissioner had indeed eaten and drunk elaborately. And that day, with other days of revelry and feasting, remained as lively in his memory as days on which the Ministry had praised him officially, those days on which his appointment as First Assistant District Commissioner, and later District Commissioner, had been announced.

He enjoyed all the excellence of the food with his eyes, as others relish it with their palate. His gaze traveled a number of times over the amply supplied table and lingered here and there in enjoyment. He had almost forgotten the mysterious, somewhat uncanny surroundings. They ate. They drank of the various bottles. And the District Commissioner praised everything, saying, "Simply delicious," and, "Exquisite," as he sampled dish after dish. His face gradually reddened. His side whiskers stirred like restless pennons.

"I've brought you both here," Chojnicki said to them, "because if we'd gone to the new Schloss we wouldn't have been left undisturbed. There I keep open house, so to speak, and all my friends can come and go as they like. Generally, I keep this place to work in."

"You work?" asked the District Commissioner.

"Yes," said Chojnicki. "I work. In a sense, I work for my own amusement. But I carry on a family tradition all the same, though really I admit I don't take my work so seriously as even my grandfather did. The peasants round here thought of him as a potent magician, and perhaps he was. They think me one, too, but I'm not. So far I haven't produced a single grain."

"Grain of what?" asked the District Commissioner.

"Of gold, of course," Chojnicki answered, as if it were the most natural thing in the world. "I happen to know a little about chemistry," he continued. "It's a traditional family accomplishment. I have all the apparatus, ancient and modern, here on the walls." He pointed to the walls. The District Commissioner saw six rows of wooden shelves. On these stood mortars and large and small paper bags, glass jars like those in ancient pharmacies, strange-looking glass balls filled with many different-colored liquids, little lamps, retorts, tubes.

"Strange, very strange," said Herr von Trotta.

"And," Chojnicki continued, "I couldn't myself really tell you how seriously I take my experiments. I seem to get bitten with it, you know, when I come here in the early mornings and read my grandfather's book of formulae. Then, when I get to work, I begin to laugh at myself and go away. Yet I always come back and try again."

"Strange, strange," said the District Commissioner.

"No stranger," replied the Count, "than anything else I might try to work at. Shall I become Minister of Culture and Education? That was suggested to me. Or run a department in the Home Office? They wanted me to. Or shall I go to Court, into the office of the Comptroller of the Household? I could do that, too. Francis Joseph knows me."

The District Commissioner pushed back his chair a couple of inches. When Chojnicki spoke so familiarly of his sovereign, just as if he were some idiotic deputy of the kind that had invaded parliament ever since the franchise was extended, or

154

at best as though His Majesty the Emperor were already dead and an historical figure, it cut the District Commissioner to the core. Chojnicki corrected himself. "His Majesty knows me."

The District Commissioner drew up to the table again and inquired, "But why, excuse me, why should it seem just as superfluous to serve the Fatherland as to attempt to manufacture gold?"

"Because the Fatherland has ceased to exist."

"I don't understand," said Herr von Trotta.

"I thought you might not," said Chojnicki. "I mean that we've all ceased to live."

It was very quiet. The last light of day had long since vanished. A few stars might already have been poking through the narrow slats of the green blinds. Soft, metallic voices of chirping crickets had replaced the loud fat chorus of frogs. From time to time one heard the harsh call of the cuckoo. The District Commissioner, who was transported into a previously unknown, almost enchanted state by the alcohol, the strange surroundings, and the extraordinary utterances of the Count, cast a shy glance at his son, simply to rest his eyes upon a familiar, well-known person. But even Carl Joseph no longer looked familiar and well-known. Because Chojnicki had been right and they had indeed ceased to exist, the Fatherland, the District Commissioner, his son.

With great effort Herr von Trotta managed to frame the question, "I don't quite see what you mean. How can the monarchy not exist?"

"Of course," Chojnicki replied, "in the literal sense, it still exists. We still have an army," he indicated the Lieutenant, "and government officials," the Count indicated the District Commissioner. "But it's falling to pieces here and now. Falling to pieces? It has already. An old man with one foot in the grave whose life is endangered by any cold in the head keeps his ancient throne by the sheer miracle of still being able to sit on it. How much longer? How much longer? This age has no use for us. This age wants to form independent national states. People no longer believe in God. Their new religion is nationalism. Nations don't go to church, they go to independence meetings instead. Monarchy, our monarchy, is founded on piety, on the belief that God chose the Habsburgs to reign over a certain number of Christian peoples. Our

Emperor is the Pope's secular brother, His Imperial and Royal Apostolic Majesty—Apostolic! No other sovereign is that, so dependent on the grace of God and the piety of the people. The German Emperor could still reign even if God were to abandon him. Perhaps by the grace of his people. But the Austro-Hungarian Emperor must not be forsaken by God. And God *has* forsaken him."

The District Commissioner rose. He would never have believed it possible that there was anyone in the whole world who could suggest that God had forsaken the Emperor. Yet suddenly now it seemed to him, who had all his life left ecclesiastical matters to the theologians and who, incidentally, had thought of the church, of mass, the ceremony on Corpus Christi day, the clergy and even God himself as institutions of the monarchy, it seemed to him that Chojnicki's words pierced through the confusion which had been oppressing him for the last few weeks, especially since the death of old Jacques. To be sure, God had forsaken the old Emperor. The District Commissioner walked across the room, the old boards creaked under his feet. He went to the window and saw the narrow strips of the dark-blue night through the gaps in the blinds. Suddenly, all natural occurrences and all the events of daily life were imbued with threatening and incomprehensible significance. Incomprehensible the whispering chorus of grasshoppers, incomprehensible the glitter of the stars, incomprehensible the velvet blue of the night, and incomprehensible to the District Commissioner the journey to the frontier and his stay with this Count. He went back to the table and stood stroking his side whiskers, as he always did when he was somewhat at a loss. At a loss! Never in all his life had he felt so utterly at a loss.

In front of him stood a full glass. He drank it quickly. "So you think," he said, "that we . . . that we. . . ."

"That we're done for," completed Chojnicki. "We are done for. You and your son and I. I tell you, we're the last inhabitants of a world in which sovereigns rule by the grace of God, and eccentrics like myself make gold. Listen, look."

Chojnicki got up and clicked a switch. Light from the big central chandelier flooded the room.

"You see," he said, "it's the age of electricity, not alchemy.

And of chemistry too, you understand. You know what they call the stuff? Nitro-glycerine." He split it up into syllables: "Ni-tro-gly-ce-rine," the Count repeated. "Not gold any longer. And in Francis Joseph's palace they often still burn candles. You see? We will perish by nitro-glycerine and electricity. It won't be long, not long at all."

The glare spread by the electric lamps had streaked each test tube and glass and retort on the shelves with points of light, wide and narrow, igniting reds and greens and blues. Carl Joseph sat pale and quiet. He had been drinking the whole time. The District Commissioner eyed the Lieutenant; he was thinking of his friend Moser, the painter. And since he, too, had been drinking, the pallid shape of his tipsy son seemed to old Herr von Trotta to be hovering in the depths of an old, very much tarnished mirror, against a background of chestnut leaves in the Volksgarten, with a flapping soft hat on his head and a big portfolio under his arm. Somehow Chojnicki's gift of historical prophecy had been passed on to the District Commissioner so that he, too, could see into the future, his son's future. The plates, dishes, bottles, glasses were half empty and mournful. Magically, the lights danced in the globes and retorts along the walls. Two old side-whiskered footmen, both as like the Emperor Francis Joseph and the District Commissioner as two brothers, had come in to clear away the meal. From time to time the harsh call of the cuckoo fell like a hammer on the chirping of the grasshoppers. Chojnicki raised a bottle.

"You must have another glass of our native product"—it was his usual name for Ninety Percent—"there's only a swallow left." They emptied the last dregs. The District Commissioner pulled out his watch but could not discern the exact position of the hands. They seemed to be rotating so rapidly over the white face that there were a hundred hands instead of the normal two. It might be nine o'clock in the evening or midnight.

"Ten o'clock," said Chojnicki.

They left the house, gently guided by the whiskered servants. Chojnicki's large carriage was waiting. The sky hung very low, a good familiar, earthly bowl of blue glass, so close you could almost finger it. The stone column to the right of the pavilion seemed to touch it. Into this low-hung sky some earthly hand had pricked stars like flag pins stuck in a district map. At times the whole blue night shifted above the Commissioner's head, tilted an inch or so, and stood still again. The frogs croaked in the endless marshes. There was a damp smell of rain and grass. The coachman in his black coat towered over the ghostly white horses and black coach. The horses whinnied. Their hoofs, noiseless as cats' paws, scraped in the wet sand of the road. The coachman clacked his tongue, and they trundled away.

They went back the way they had come and turned off down the wide graveled birch-tree avenue, until they reached the lamps which marked the outer drive of the new Schloss. Silver-birch trunks shone brighter than the lamplight. The strong rubber wheels of the carriage ran smoothly and with dull murmurings over the gravel. Only the hard clatter of the horses' swift hoofs was loud. The carriage was roomy and comfortable. You could lean back in it, almost as on a sofa. Lieutenant Trotta was sleeping. He sat next to his father. His pale face lay vertically on the upholstery. Through the open window the wind brushed it, and from time to time it was illuminated by a lantern. Chojnicki, who was opposite his guests, observed the bloodless, half-open lips of the Lieutenant, his hard, jutting, bony nose.

"He's sleeping well," he said to the District Commissioner. Both felt like the Lieutenant's two fathers. The District Commissioner had been sobered by the night wind, yet a vague fear still troubled his heart. He had seen the end of the world, and it was his world. Chojnicki sat facing him still alive, so alive that his knees solidly bumped Herr von Trotta's shinbones, alive and yet uncannily dead. The old six-chambered revolver which Herr von Trotta had brought weighed down the back pocket of his breeches. Of what earthly use was a revolver? There were no bears or wolves at the frontier. There was only the end of the world.

The carriage drew up at the arched wooden gateway. The coachman cracked his whip. Its double portals drew back and the white horses went on, up a gentle slope in measured steps. Windows along the entire front of the house spilled their yellow light over the gravel and across the lawns on either side. They could hear voices and a piano. Without doubt, it was a big party.

They had already eaten. Footmen kept running in and out with large bottles of many-hued liqueurs. The guests were dancing and playing Tarot and Whist and drinking. Someone was making a speech to a knot of people who were not listening. Some lurched from room to room, others slept in corners. There were only men, dancing together. Black full-dress tunics of Dragoons pressed against the blue tunics of the Jaeger. In the new Schloss Chojnicki lit his rooms with candles. They rose, snow-white or waxen-gold, out of large silver candlesticks, set on stone shelves or moldings jutting from the walls, or held by footmen who were relieved every half hour. At times the night air shook out their flames as it rippled in gusts through the open window. Whenever the piano ceased to strum, one could hear the song of nightingales. Crickets whispered, and from time to time wax tears came splashing down with a soft thud on to the silver.

The District Commissioner was looking for his son. A nameless fear drove the old man from room to room. His son? What had happened to his son? He was not among the dancers, or the lurching drunkards, or the staid old gentlemen who sat about in corners gossiping. The Lieutenant sat alone in a distant room. A large, full-bellied bottle stood faithfully at his feet, half empty. It looked far too vigorous a companion for the meager, crumpled drinker—almost as if it could swallow him. The District Commissioner stood over the Lieutenant, just touching the bottle with the toe of his pointed boot. His son became aware of two, of several fathers, and every second their number increased. He could feel them closing in on him, and so it seemed to him idiotic to stand up and pay them all the respects which were really due to only one of them. There was no point. The Lieutenant remained in his odd position—that is, he sat, lay, and cowered all at the same time. The District Commissioner never moved. His brain worked very fast, it gave birth to a thousand memories all at once. He saw, for instance, the cadet who had sat in his study on Sunday mornings with such snowy-white gloves and a black cap on his knee, answering each question with a ringing voice and obedient, childlike eyes. The District Commissioner saw the cavalry lieutenant, just commissioned, entering the same room, this time in blue and gold and scarlet. But that young man was now very remote from Herr von Trotta. Why did it hurt him so to look at a strange, drunk Jaeger lieutenant? Why did it hurt so much?

Lieutenant Trotta did not stir. He was capable of remembering that his father had recently arrived and he could see that not one but several fathers were standing beside him. But he could neither grasp what had induced his father to come on this particular day nor why he was multiplying so prodigiously, nor indeed why he himself, the Lieutenant, was not capable of standing up.

For several weeks Lieutenant Trotta had got used to Ninety Percent. It did not go to his head; only, as connoisseurs used to say, into the legs. At first it engendered a pleasant warmth inside his chest. His blood tingled more rapidly through his veins, appetite dispelled any queasiness, any need to get up and vomit. So you had another. No matter how raw and overcast the morning, you turned out in the best of tempers, as if into the sunniest, happiest morning. In the break you had a snack with all the others in the frontier pub near the wood where the Jaeger drilled, and you put away another Ninety Percent. It ran like a swift flame down your gullet, a flame extinguishing itself. You scarcely knew you had eaten anything. Then you marched back to barracks, changed, and went over to lunch in the station. Although you had walked a good way, you didn't feel hungry. So you had a Ninety Percent to get up an appetite. You ate and you felt sleepy at once. You had a black coffee and a Ninety Percent to go with it. In short, the whole long, boring day scarcely gave one a chance not to imbibe spirits; on the contrary, there were many afternoons and evenings when it was absolutely *de rigueur* to be drinking brandy.

For life became simple as soon as you had had a drink. Oh, miracle of this frontier. Life here might be hard on the sober, but who was allowed to stay sober? When Lieutenant Trotta had had his fill he saw his subordinates, brother officers, and superiors all as very dear friends. The little town seemed as familiar to him as if he had been born and bred in it. He could go into the dilapidated little shops which were dug into the thick walls of the bazaar like dark, winding hamster burrows, stuffed full of all sorts of merchandise, and trade in a number of useless articles: artificial coral, cheap little mirrors, some abysmal soap, combs of aspenwood, and plaited dog leashes; all this because he loved following the cries of the red-headed hawkers. He smiled at everyone, at peasant women in colored head scarves, with big raffia baskets under their arms, at the dolled-up daughters of the Jews, at officials in the District Commissioner's office, at teachers from the local grammar school. A warm full current of kindly friendship flowed through this little world. Everyone appeared to greet the Lieutenant merrily. All harassment had vanished. No worries, on or off duty. You got through every day without a hitch. You could make out Onufrij's lingo. If, on occasion, you found yourself out in a nearby village, you asked the peasants the way back home and they answered in a foreign language, but you understood them. You never rode. You lent your horse to one or other of your friends, good riders, who really knew how to handle a mount. In a word, you were pleased with life. But Lieutenant Trotta had no idea that his gait became unsteady, that his tunic was stained and his trousers had no crease, that there were buttons missing from his shirt, nor that in the evening his face was yellow and in the morning ash-gray; and his gaze was aimless. He did not gamble: this alone reassured Major Zoglauer. There were times in every man's life when he had to drink. It was nothing, it would pass. Spirits were cheap. It was their debts that finished most of them off. Trotta did his job no worse than the others. He never kicked up rows like so many of them. On the contrary, the more he drank, the quieter he became. One day he'll sober down and marry, the Major thought. He's got friends in high places. He'll get on fast enough. He'll end up on the staff if only he wants to.

Herr von Trotta sat down carefully on the edge of the sofa beside his son, trying to think of something to say to him. He was not used to talking to drunkards. "You know," he began at the end of a long silence, "you ought to be far more careful with spirits. Take me, for instance, I never drank more than I could handle."

The Lieutenant made an immense effort to attain an upright position from his cowering one. It was no use. He looked at the old man. Now, thank the Lord, there was only one of him, who was having to make do with the narrow end of the sofa and had to keep himself steady by putting his hands on his knees. "What did you say, Papa?" he asked.

"You ought to be more careful with spirits," the District Commissioner repeated.

"What for?" asked the Lieutenant.

"Why, what do you mean?" said Herr von Trotta, somewhat consoled by the reflection that at least his son had grasped what he was saying. "Spirits will be the ruin of you, you know. Just think of Moser."

"Moser? Moser?" said Carl Joseph. "Oh, of course. But he's quite right. I remember him. He painted grandfather's portrait."

"You'd forgotten that?" said Herr von Trotta very quietly.

"I haven't," replied the Lieutenant. "I've always had an image of that portrait; I'm not strong enough for it. The dead, I can't forget the dead. Father, I can't forget anything, father. . . ."

Herr von Trotta sat next to his son, perplexed. He could not quite understand what Carl Joseph meant, yet he could feel that something more than drunkenness spoke out of him. Somehow or other his son was crying for help, and he could not help. He himself had come as far as the frontier to find a little help. For he was quite alone in the world. And this world was coming to an end. Jacques was gone, he was alone, he had wanted to see his son again. But his son, too, was alone and perhaps, since he was younger, nearer the end of the world. How simple it all was once, thought the District Commissioner. There were rules of conduct for every situation in life. When your son came home on vacation, you examined him. When he got his commission, you congratulated him. When he wrote his dutiful letters home, which contained so little, you answered them with a few appropriate lines. But how did you behave when your son was drunk? When he cried, "Father." When something in him cried out, "Father!"

He saw Chojnicki enter the room and got up more violently than was his habit.

"Here," said Chojnicki, "this telegram has just arrived for you. The hotel porter brought it." It was a service telegram. It summoned Herr von Trotta back home. "So they've sent for you already, what a pity," Chojnicki said. "I suppose it's to do with these Sokol meetings."

"Yes, that seems to be it," said Herr von Trotta. "There's unrest."

He knew now that he was too weak to do anything about the unrest. He was very tired. Only a few more years before they gave him his pension. But at this moment it occurred to him that he would retire soon. Then he could look after Carl Joseph, a fitting task for an old father.

Chojnicki said, "It's not easy to keep order with your hands tied, as they are in this hidebound monarchy. You only have to lock up a few of the ringleaders and you find yourself set upon by Freemasons and deputies and socialists, and the papers start such a hue and cry that they get let off. If you make them disband the Sokol association, you get rapped over the knuckles by the authorities. Autonomy! Just wait a bit. Here in my district every demonstration ends with bullets. Yes, and as long as I go on living here, I shall stand for parliament and get in. Luckily, this part of the world is too far removed from all the specious reports they think up in every dirty newspaper office."

He went over to Carl Joseph to say with the assurance of an expert quite accustomed to dealing with drunkards, "Your father has to go back home."

And Carl Joseph understood him at once. He could even get up. He looked around with glassy eyes in search of his father. "Father, I'm awfully sorry."

"I'm rather worried about him," said the District Commissioner to the Count.

"I'm sure you are," answered the Count. "We shall have to get him away from here for a bit. When he gets his leave I'll do my best to show him the world a little. Then he won't want to come back. He may fall in love."

"I won't fall in love," Carl Joseph said very slowly.

They drove back to the hotel. Only one word was uttered during the drive. "Father," Carl Joseph said. That was all.

Next day Herr von Trotta woke very late, to the bugle call of the returning battalion. His train was leaving in two hours. Carl Joseph arrived. Down below, Chojnicki was already cracking his whip to summon them. The District Commissioner ate in the station restaurant with the Jaeger officers.

An incredibly long time had elapsed since he had left his District of W. With an effort, he remembered that it was only two days since he had got into the train. Except for Count Chojnicki, he was the only civilian, and he looked somber and drawn among the colorful officers sitting at the long horseshoe-shaped table beneath the familiar, ubiquitous portrait of the Supreme War Lord in flower-white field marshal's uniform with the blood-red sash. Directly under the Emperor's snowy-white side whiskers, indeed, almost parallel, there hovered the dark, silver-tinged side whiskers of Herr von Trotta. The youngest officers, lunching at the lower end of the horseshoe, could observe the resemblance between his Apostolic Majesty and His Majesty's District Commissioner. Lieutenant Trotta, too, from where he was sitting, was able to compare his father's face with that of his sovereign. And for a few seconds it seemed to the Lieutenant that the canvas face up on the wall was really that of an older father, while a living Emperor in civilian clothes, grown slightly younger, sat at the table. And Emperor and father alike grew hazy and alien to him.

The District Commissioner, meanwhile, cast a despairing, searching glance around the table over the soft and practically hairless faces of the young officers, and the mustachioed ones of the older officers. At his side sat Major Zoglauer. Ah, how glad he would have been to have had a few minutes' anxious talk with him about Carl Joseph. But there was no time now, his train was being shunted outside the windows.

The District Commissioner was utterly dispirited. They were all drinking his health and wishing him a pleasant journey and success to his forthcoming official tasks. He smiled to the right and to the left, stood up, clinked glasses here and there; and his mind was laden with cares, his heart heavy with dire fore-bodings. What an immense stretch of time had elapsed since he had left the District of W. Indeed, the District Commissioner had set out with a light heart, his courage high, to this adventurous district and to his dear son. Now he was returning alone, from his lonely son, from this frontier where the end of the world could be discerned as clearly as a storm gathering on the edge of a town whose streets lie in happy ignorance under blue skies. The porter's clear bell was ringing, the engine screeching. The damp steam of the train was rolling against the restaurant windows and clung in small gray drops to the glass. The meal was over. They all got up. The whole battalion escorted Herr von Trotta on to the platform. Herr von Trotta felt the urge to say something special, but nothing suitable occurred to him. He directed a final, tender glance at his son, then became afraid lest the glance should be noticed and lowered his eyes. He pressed Major Zoglauer's hand. He thanked Chojnicki. He raised the dignified gray silk hat which he wore when traveling. He held his hat in his left hand and put his right arm around Carl Joseph's shoulder. He kissed his son on both cheeks. But although he would have liked to say, "Don't hurt me, my son, because I love you," he could only manage, "Keep well," for the Trottas were a shy race.

He was getting in, standing at the window. His bald head shone. Once more his anxious eyes sought Carl Joseph's face.

"Next time you come to see us, Herr von Trotta," observed the ever-cheerful Captain Wagner, "you'll find a little Monte Carlo here."

"How's that?" asked the District Commissioner.

"They're going to start a casino here," Wagner informed him. And before Herr von Trotta could call his son to give him heartfelt warning of the proposed Monte Carlo, the engine whistled, the buffers clashed resoundingly, and the train slid out of the station. The District Commissioner waved his gray glove. And all the officers saluted. Carl Joseph did not stir.

On their way back to the town, he walked beside Wagner. "It's going to be a first-rate casino," the Captain said. "A real casino. Lord, it's ages since I've seen a roulette. You know, I simply love the way it revolves; and the little click. I'm extremely pleased about it."

Captain Wagner was not the only one to welcome the opening of the new casino. All were impatient. For years the garrison had lived in expectation of the casino which Kapturak was to open.

A week after the District Commissioner's departure, Kapturak arrived. And probably his arrival would have caused a far greater stir had not a remarkable coincidence at the same time brought among them the lady who was to attract everyone's attention.

Chapter 12

On the frontiers of the Austro-Hungarian monarchy there were at that time many men like Kapturak. They began to circle about the old Empire like those dark and cowardly birds which catch sight of a dying man from far away. With sinister, impatient beating of their wings they await his end. With beaks of steel they swoop down on their quarry. Nobody knows where they come from nor into what regions their wings will carry them. They are the plumed brothers of mysterious death, his heralds, his companions and successors.

Kapturak was a short, insignificant-looking man. Rumors surrounded him, speeding along the intricate paths he trod, following the almost imperceptible traces he left behind him. He lived in the frontier inn. He had dealings with representatives of the South American shipping companies which year after year dispatched thousands of Russian deserters to a cruel new home. He enjoyed gambling and drank little. Nor was he lacking in a kind of sullen sociability. He recounted that for years he had been engaged in smuggling Russian deserters over the frontier and that he had had to leave home, wife, and children for fear of being sent to Siberia, when several officials and soldiers were arrested and sentenced. And to the question of what he intended to do here he replied a smiling and terse, "Business."

The proprietor of the hotel which lodged the officers, a certain Herr Brodnitzer of Silesian origin, who had taken refuge on this borderland for reasons of his own, proceeded to open the casino. He placarded his café windows with a gigantic poster. It announced facilities for games of every kind, a band which would perform all night long, and the special engagement of celebrated revue artistes. The renovation of the café began with the band, consisting of eight musicians, hastily assembled. Then came the "Mariahilf Nightingale," a fair-haired young lady from Oderberg. She sang waltzes from Lehár's operettas and that daring ballad "When from love's night I wander through gray morning," and for an encore the chanson "Under my skirt I've pink undies full of tucks." Thus Brodnitzer filled his patrons with mounting expectations. It turned out that, apart from the numerous large and small card tables, Brodnitzer had also put up a little roulette table in a dark corner of his café, screened off from the rest. Captain Wagner told everyone and fired their enthusiasm. These men who had served on the frontier for years thought of the little roulette ball (which many of them had never even seen) as one of those magical objects, part of the great world, by means of which a man could acquire beautiful women, expensive horses, and country estates all at the same time. Who might not make his fortune at roulette? They had all known impoverished school days, spent their adolescence in cadet schools and hard years of duty in the frontier garrison. They were waiting for war. In its stead had come partial mobilization against Serbia, from which they had returned without glory and with nothing to look forward to but routine promotion, maneuvers, drill, club, drill, and maneuvers. For the first time they heard the click of the little ball and they knew that Lady Fortune was in their midst waiting to confer her favors on one today, another tomorrow. Pallid, exotic-looking strangers sat in the café every night—people they had never seen before. Once Captain Wagner won five hundred kronen and next day he was clear of debt. That month, for the first time in years, he drew his full pay, the whole three-thirds of it. True, Lieutenants Schnabel and Gründler had lost a hundred each that same evening. Tomorrow they might win a thousand . . . When the little ball set off on its round, transformed into a milk-white ring drawn round a periphery of black and red spaces; when these spaces too began to fuse into a single rotating ring of uncertain color, then every officer's heart trembled and a strange roaring rose up in each head, as if a separate ball were rotating in every brain. Before their eyes the world turned red and black, red and black. Their knees buckled, although they were seated. Their eyes pursued the ball in desperate haste, unable to catch up with it. In obedience to its own laws, it began at last to totter, drunk with speed, and collapsed exhausted into its numbered space. All drew a long breath. Even the losers felt released. Next morning they would tell each other. And a great intoxication seized them all. More and more officers flocked to the casino

From inscrutable regions came strange civilians, to gamble in the café. It was they who set the pace, piled up the bank, drew large banknotes out of their pocketbooks, gold coins, watches and chains from waistcoat pockets, rings from their fingers. Every room in the hotel was occupied. The sleepy cabs which had always waited outside the station with yawning drivers on their boxes and broken-down horses between the shafts like figures in a waxwork show, began to wake up, and, lo and behold! their wheels could actually turn, the lean hacks could trundle away, clatter from station to hotel, hotel to frontier, and back into the little town. The sour-faced local tradesmen began to smile. Their gloomy booths grew brighter and the wares which they displayed gayer. Night after night the "Mariahilf Nightingale" caroled. And, as if her singing had reached the ears of slumbering sisters, new girls in gaudy clothes whom no one had ever seen before came to the café. They pushed the tables back and danced to the strains of Lehár waltzes. The whole world was changed.

Yes, the whole world. In other places, strange posters appeared of a kind never before seen here. In every tongue of the region they exhorted the workers in the brush factory to come out on strike. Brushmaking was the one poor industry in the neighborhood. Its workers were all poor peasants. Some of them lived by cutting wood in winter and bringing in the harvest in the autumn. In summer they were all forced to work in the brush factory. Others came from the lowest stratum of the Jewish community. They could not calculate or barter, nor had they learned a trade. For a twenty-mile radius there was no other factory.

Costly, inconvenient regulations hampered the manufacture of brushes. Owners did not willingly conform to them. They were supposed to supply their factory hands with masks designed to keep out the dust and germs, and to build large, well-lit workrooms; to burn the refuse twice a day; to take on new hands in place of any who began to cough. For all who worked at cleaning the bristles sooner or later began to spit blood. The factory was a dilapidated structure with narrow windows, a slate roof fallen into holes. Fenced all around with a burgeoning willow hedge, it stood in a derelict open space on which garbage had been dumped for generations, where dead cats and rats were flung out to rot among rusty tins and broken earthenware, side by side with old boots. To every side lay fields, full of the blessed, ripe corn, and humming with the chirp of crickets; and dark-green marshes stretched beyond the fields, resounding with the cheerful croaking of frogs. Swift swallows darted across the small gray windowpanes, opalescent dragonflies danced by, white and brilliant butterflies came fluttering as the workers sat indefatigably combing the tangled bundles of bristle with heavy iron rakes, gulping down the gray little clouds which filled the air with each new stroke, while the triumphant voices of larks reached them through the holes in the roof. It was not more than a few months since those workers had come from their free villages where they had been born and bred in the sweet odor of hay, the chill freshness of snow, the pungent reek of dung, and vibrant bird song in the ever-changing blessedness of nature. The workers now saw swallow, butterfly, and dancing midges through clouds of gray dust and grew homesick. When larks sang they grew discontented. Until that time they had never known that there were laws to protect their health, that there was a parliament within the monarchy, and that in that parliament there were deputies who had been workers. Strange men came, put up posters, called meetings, explained the constitution and its shortcomings, read newspapers out aloud, and spoke to them in all the local dialects. They were louder than the larks and frogs: the workers called a strike.

It was the first strike in this area. It frightened the civil authorities. They had for years been used to taking a leisurely census, to celebrating the Emperor's birthday, assisting in the annual recruitment, and sending identical reports to the government representative. Here and there they arrested some Russophile Ukrainian, an Orthodox Greek priest, a Jew caught smuggling tobacco, and spies. For decades bristles had been prepared here; and sent on to Moravia, Bohemia, Silesia to the brush factories, to be returned as completed articles. For decades the workmen had coughed and spat up blood, fallen sick and died in the hospitals. But they did not strike. Now, from all over the district the gendarmery posts had to be called in and a report had to be sent to the government representative, who in turn got in touch with the Army High Command. And the Army High Command sent word to the commander of the garrison.

The younger officers got it into their heads that "the people," that is to say, the lowest class of civilians, were demanding equal rights with high-grade officials, the aristocracy, and commercial councilors. If revolution were to be avoided, these could not possibly be conceded. And they did not want revolution. So there had to be some shooting before it was too late. Major Zoglauer made a brief speech in which all this emerged quite clearly. Certainly war is much to be preferred. An officer is not a policeman. But for the time being there is no war. Orders are orders. If necessary, he will advance with fixed bayonets and tell them to open fire. Orders are orders. Meanwhile, this need not prevent anyone from going to Brodnitzer's café and winning a fortune there. One day Captain Wagner lost heavily. A gentleman, a stranger, an ex-captain in the Uhlans, a landowner somewhere in Silesia with a high-sounding name, won on two evenings in succession, lent the captain money, and, on the third, was summoned back home by telegram. The full amount was two thousand kronen, a small matter for a cavalry officer. Not a small matter, however, for a captain of the Jaeger. He would have approached Chojnicki if he hadn't already owed him three hundred.

Brodnitzer suggested, "Why not borrow it over my signature, Captain?"

"Yes," said the Captain. "Who'd give me that much for something signed by you?"

Brodnitzer thought the matter over. "Herr Kapturak."

Kapturak arrived. He said, "So, you want two thousand kronen. Until when?"

"I haven't the vaguest idea."

"A lot of money, Captain."

"You'll get it back," answered Wagner.

"But how? In what instalments? You know you're only allowed to pledge a third of your pay. That's already been done by all the officers. I don't really see how I'm to do it."

"Herr Brodnitzer . . ." began the Captain.

"Herr Brodnitzer," Kapturak said, as though Brodnitzer were not in the room, "owes me a lot of money, too. I might let you have it through another officer who hasn't yet pledged his pay, if there's anyone who'll come to the rescue. What about Lieutenant Trotta, for instance? He used to be in the cavalry. He's got a horse."

"All right," said the Captain. "I'll have a word with him." And he roused Lieutenant Trotta.

They were standing in the long, dark, narrow passage of the hotel. "Sign it, quick," the Captain whispered. "They're waiting in there. They can see you don't want to." Trotta signed.

"Come on down straightaway," said Wagner, "I'll be waiting for you."

Carl Joseph stopped at the little back door which the hotel residents used to get into the café. For the first time he saw Herr Brodnitzer's newly opened casino. It was his first sight, indeed, of any gambling rooms. A dark-green curtain was drawn around the roulette table. Captain Wagner drew it back and slipped into another world. Carl Joseph could hear the soft velvety purr of the ball. He did not dare lift the curtain. At the end of the café, next to the street entrance, stood the stage and on it trilled the never-wearying "Mariahilf Nightingale." At the tables they were playing cards. Cards were slammed down on the imitation marble. People jerked out incomprehensible cries. In their uniform white shirtsleeves, they looked like a seated regiment of gamblers. Their coats dangled from the chair backs. The empty sleeves vibrated gently and ghostlike at every movement the players made. Above their heads lay a dense storm cloud of cigarette smoke. The tiny ends of the cigarettes glowed red and silver in the gray haze, sending up more and more fuel into the bluish thunder cloud above. And below the visible cloud of smoke there seemed to hang another of noise; a droning, humming, buzzing cloud. If you shut your eyes, you could fancy that a vast flock of grasshoppers had been released, with a fearful din, above the sitting people.

Captain Wagner returned from behind the curtain a changed man. His eyes were sunk in purple hollows. Above his mouth, his brown mustache dropped unkempt, one half seeming oddly foreshortened. On his chin sprouted reddish stubble, a luxuriant crop of minute lances. "Where are you, Trotta?" shouted the Captain, though he stood close against the Lieutenant. "Two hundred gone," he bellowed. "It's the blasted red. I've queered my pitch at roulette. I'll have to try my hand at something else." And he dragged Carl Joseph to the card tables.

Kapturak and Brodnitzer rose. "Any luck?" Kapturak asked, for he saw that the Captain had had none.

"Lost, lost," bellowed the Captain.

"Dear, dear, dear," said Kapturak. "Well now, just look at me, for example. I've lost any number of times, you know. I'd lost almost everything. But I got it all back. Change your game, keep changing your game. That's the main thing."

Captain Wagner unhooked his tunic collar. His face resumed its normal reddish-brown hue. His mustache readjusted itself of its own accord, as it were. He slapped Trotta on the back. "You've never touched cards, have you?"

Trotta watched Kapturak take a shining pack of virgin cards from his pocket and lay it gently on the table, as if anxious not to injure the bright face of the bottom card. He caressed the pack with his deft fingers. The backs of the cards gleamed like dark-green mirrors. The ceiling lights glimmer in their gently arched backs. Individual cards rise of their own accord, and straight up on their sharp edges, lie down, now on their backs, now on their bellies, gather themselves in a pile which fans out its separate leaves with a light clatter, as the red and black faces go rushing by, like a brief, multicolored thunderstorm, close in on themselves again, all back on the table, split up into smaller piles. From these, cards separate themselves, move tenderly up against each other, each covering half the back of the next, spread themselves out in a circle reminiscent of an oddly inverted and flattened artichoke; fly back into a single line and at last rearrange themselves into a pack. All cards obey the noiseless call of fingers. Captain Wagner follows this prologue with hungry eyes. He loved cards!

Sometimes those he had called came to him, sometimes they evaded him. It thrilled him when his mad desires went galloping hard upon the fugitives, at last, at last, forcing them to turn. Sometimes, of course, the cards in flight were faster, so that the captain's desires had to turn back, exhausted. Over the years, Captain Wagner had evolved extremely intricate tactical methods, which were difficult to review, and in which no means of compelling fortune had been neglected. He used conjuration, force, and sudden assault, fervent prayer, the tenderest, most extravagant enticements. On one occasion, whenever he needed an ace of hearts, the poor Captain had been obliged to feign despair and secretly assure the hidden fickle one that unless she came to him soon he would commit suicide that very day. Another time he considered it more politic to remain aloof and pretend indifference to the card he most vehemently desired. On a third occasion, it was strictly necessary, in order to win, to shuffle the pack with his own hand—with the left hand, moreover, a skill he acquired at last after long practice and by sheer iron resolution. His fourth tactic based all hope on sitting to the right of the bank. In most cases, however, it was advisable to combine these methods, or shift from one to the other very rapidly, and always, of course, in such a way that no one else at the table noticed. For that was important. "Shall we change places?" the Captain would say, for instance, quite innocently. And if, catching his partner's eye, he discerned there a smile of recognition, he would add with a laugh, "You're wrong, I'm not superstitious. I find the light here distracting." If other players were to observe these strategic feints of Captain Wagner, their hands would betray his intentions to the cards. They would, so to speak, get wind of his plan of attack, and so have time to elude him. So that, from the instant he sat down at the table, the Captain had to work like a whole staff of generals. And while his mind bent to its inhuman task, ice and fire alternately consumed his heart, hope and despair, jubilation and bitterness. He struggled, he fought, he agonized. Ever since they had established the roulette, his brain had been evolving deeply laid tactics to outmaneuver its wily ball. But he was well aware that it was harder to defeat than cards.

He nearly always played baccarat, though this game was not only prohibited, it was particularly penalized. But what did games which involved rational calculation and thought mean to him, when his speculations touched on the incalculable and the inexplicable, revealed it and often even made it yield to him? No, he wanted to encounter the mysteries of fate at first hand, do battle with them and resolve them. And so he sat down to baccarat. And, in fact, he won. He got three nines and three eights in succession, whereas Trotta had nothing but jacks and kings. Kapturak only had two pairs of fours and fives. But here Captain Wagner forgot himself. Although it was one of his basic principles never to let luck see how sure you felt about it, he suddenly tripled his stake. He hoped to rake in the loan all in one evening. That was the beginning of disaster. The Captain lost; Trotta had never stopped losing. In the end, Kapturak won five hundred kronen. The Captain had to sign another I.O.U.

Wagner and Trotta got up. They began mixing Ninety Percent with cognac, and this again with Okoêimer beer. Captain Wagner was ashamed of his defeat, as a general in retreat from a battle to which he'd taken a friend in order to share his triumph. But the Lieutenant shared the Captain's shame. They both knew that without alcohol they could never look each other in the eye. They drank slowly in regular little gulps.

"Your health," said the Captain.

"Your health," said Trotta.

Each time they repeated these good wishes they gave each other a glance of encouragement, proving to each other how little disaster concerned them. But suddenly it seemed to the Lieutenant that his best friend, the Captain, was the unhappiest man alive, and he began to weep bitterly.

"What are you crying for?" asked the Captain, and his own lips were beginning to quiver.

"Because of you, you," said Trotta, "my poor friend." And they gave themselves up to lamentation, both mute and vocal.

In Captain Wagner's memory an old plan revived. It concerned Trotta's horse, which he rode every day and which he loved and had at first intended to buy himself. It had struck him that if he had the price of such a horse he would doubtless be able to win a fortune at baccarat and so become the owner of several horses. He then thought of asking the Lieutenant for his horse, but only on loan, so as to make his fortune and then redeem it. Was that unfair? Whom could it harm? How long would it take? Two hours at cards and you had the lot. You are always most likely to win if you sit down to play without fear and without making any calculations. If only he could play like a wealthy, independent man just once! The Captain cursed his pay. It was so shabby that it never once permitted him to play with dignity. Now, as they were sitting together so moved and had forgotten the whole world around them, yet convinced that it had forgotten them, the Captain at last felt able to say, "Sell me your horse."

"I'll give it to you," said Trotta, moved. But one could not sell a present, not even temporarily.

The Captain thought and said, "No, sell it."

"Please, accept it," Trotta pleaded.

"I'll pay for it," insisted the Captain. So they wrangled for a few minutes. The Captain at last stood up, lurched slightly, and bellowed, "I order you to sell me your horse."

"Certainly, Captain," Trotta said mechanically.

"But I have no money," hiccuped the Captain, sat down, full of kindness again.

"That makes no difference, let me give it to you."

"No, that's precisely what I don't want you to do. And now I don't even want to buy it any more. If only I had some money."

"I might sell it to someone else," said Trotta. He glowed with joy at this unique inspiration.

"Excellent," the Captain agreed. "But to whom?"

"Well . . . to Chojnicki, for instance."

"Excellent," the Captain repeated. "I owe him five hundred kronen."

"Let me take that on," Trotta said.

Because he was drunk, his heart was full of pity for the Captain. The poor man had to be saved. He was in extreme danger. He knew him so well and liked him so much, good old Wagner. And besides, at this moment the Lieutenant felt it inescapably essential to say a few kind and consoling words, perhaps even really noble words, and to perform an act of friendship. Magnanimity, friendship, the desire to seem very strong and helpful mingled in his heart in three warm currents. Trotta gets up. Day is breaking. Only a few lamps are still on, already dimmed by the gray light of day, breaking powerfully through the blinds. Besides Herr Brodnitzer and his one waiter, there is no one in the café. Chairs and tables stand disconsolate and the platform on which the "Mariahilf-nightingale" has hopped all night long is abandoned. All the surrounding desolation arouses terrible images of a sudden departure which may have taken place here, as if the guests had left the café all at once in droves, surprised by danger. Long cardboard cigarette ends strew the floor, mixed with the short cigar butts. The remains of Austrian cigarettes and Russian cigars betray the fact that many foreigners have gambled and drunk here with the natives.

"The bill," the Captain shouted. He embraces the Lieutenant. He presses him long and tenderly to his breast. "Well—God bless you," he says, his eyes full of tears.

Outside it was full daylight, the early morning light of a small town in the East, full of the scent of chestnuts in bloom, of lilac bushes just come into flower, and the fresh sourish odor of black bread which bakers were delivering in their big baskets. The birds were singing, an unending ocean of twittering, a resounding ocean of the air. A pale-blue transparent sky stretched smooth and low above the gray crooked shingle roofs of the small houses. The little peasant carts trundled along gently and slowly through the still drowsy, dusty streets. They littered the ground with bits of straw, chaff, dry wisps of last year's hay. The sun rose rapidly above the long, clear horizon, to the east. Lieutenant Trotta strode out to meet it, sobered a little by the gentle morning breeze, and full of the proud resolution to save his friend. It was not easy to sell his horse without first asking the District Commissioner for permission. Still, he was doing it for his friend. It wasn't easy to offer the horse to Chojnicki—but, then, what in life did Lieutenant Trotta find easy? But the harder the undertaking seemed, the more firmly and defiantly the Lieutenant went striding on toward it. The hour was striking from the tower. Trotta reached the gates of the New Schloss the same moment when, booted and holding his riding whip, Chojnicki was about to get into his summer carriage. The Count noticed the unnatural glow on the Lieutenant's unshaven, puffy cheeks, his drunkard's rouge. It spread over the real pallor of his face as the light of a red lamp does a white tablecloth. He's falling to pieces, Chojnicki thought.

"I want to make you a proposition," said Trotta. "Would you like my horse?" The question frightened him. Suddenly he found it difficult to speak.

"I know, of course, that you don't like riding, and that you've left the cavalry. I suppose you find it rather a nuisance to have to look after a beast you don't care to use. Yes, but —won't you regret it?"

"No," said Trotta. He would keep nothing back. "I need the money." The Lieutenant felt ashamed. There was nothing either dubious or dishonorable, nothing at all that "wasn't done" in going to Chojnicki to borrow money. And yet, it seemed to Carl Joseph, this first request for a loan had also begun a new stage in his life, marked by his failure to ask his father's permission. He said, "As a matter of fact, you see, it's like this. I've had to sign an I.O.U. for a brother officer. A large sum. And besides, he's lost another, smaller sum during the night. I don't want him to be in debt to this café proprietor; on the other hand, I'm not in a position to lend him anything. Yes," the Lieutenant repeated, "it's quite impossible. This man already owes you money."

"But that's nothing to do with you," said Chojnicki. "It's not worth mentioning. You see, I'm . . . what people call rich. I'm not really interested in money. It would be exactly the same if you were asking me for a brandy. After all, just think how I'm placed. Just look," he pointed to the horizon, tracing a semicircle with his hand, "all those woods are mine. Not that it means anything really, only you mustn't go letting yourself get conscience-stricken. I'm grateful to anyone who'll offer to relieve me of something. No, really, it's absurd, it's nothing at all, it's a pity we have to waste so many words over it. Look, this is what I suggest. I'll buy your horse and leave you the use of him for a year. And in a year's time he's to be mine." Clearly, Chojnicki is getting impatient. Besides, it is almost time to be on parade. The sun is rising higher every minute. It is full day.

Trotta hastened toward the barracks. In half an hour the battalion was to turn out. He had no time to shave. Major Zoglauer was due at about eleven. He did not like unshaven platoon leaders. The one thing he still paid attention to after all these years at the frontier was cleanliness and neatness while on duty. Well, it was too late now. He hurried toward the barracks. At least he had sobered up. He met Captain Wagner before the assembled company. "Yes, it's settled," he said quickly and went to stand in front of his platoon. He gave the order, "Form two abreast, turn right, forward march!" His sword glittered. The trumpets blared. The battalion turned out for drill.

That day Captain Wagner paid for the so-called refreshments in the frontier pub. In the half hour's break there was time for two or three Ninety Percents. The Captain had no doubt at all in his mind that he had begun to be in control of his fate. He alone was in control. That afternoon he would be

177

in possession of two thousand five hundred kronen. You paid back fifteen hundred at once and sat down to baccarat quite calmly, quite unruffled, exactly like a rich man. You took the bank. You shuffled with your own hands. With your left hand. For the moment it might be advisable to pay back only a thousand and so sit down quite calmly, quite unruffled, exactly like a rich man with five hundred for roulette and a thousand for baccarat. That would be even better.

"Chalk it up to Captain Wagner," he shouted to the barman.

They got up, the break was over, it was time for field exercises. Luckily, Major Zoglauer disappeared after half an hour on that day. Captain Wagner instructed First Lieutenant Zander to take over, and quickly rode off to Brodnitzer. He asked whether he could count on finding players that afternoon at about four o'clock. Yes, there was no doubt about that. Everything augured well. Even the familiar spirits of the house, those invisible beings which Captain Wagner could sense in every room where gambling went on, and with whom he sometimes held inaudible converse, in a sort of secret language he had worked out over the years; today even these familiar spirits emanated sheer benevolence. To get them still better disposed, or at least to prevent them from changing their minds, Wagner decided to break his habit and have lunch in the Café Brodnitzer and not to stir from his place until Trotta arrived. So he stayed. At about three the first gamblers arrived. Captain Wagner began to tremble. Suppose this Trotta let him down and didn't bring the money until tomorrow? By then, his luck would have turned. He might never get another day like this. It was a Thursday, the gods were well disposed. But on a Friday! To expect to win on a Friday was like asking a staff surgeon to drill a company. The more time lapsed the fiercer grew the captain's opinion of the dilatory Lieutenant Trotta. So he wasn't coming, the young scoundrel. And it was for that he'd gone to all this trouble, cut drill, missed his usual lunch at the station, bargained so carefully with the familiar spirits and, up to a point, kept the lucky Thursday in position, only to be let down. The hands of the clock on the wall moved indefatigably forward. And no Trotta, no Trotta, no Trotta. Yes, he was coming. The door opened and Wagner's eyes glittered. He didn't shake hands with Trotta. His fingers trembled. All his fingers were like impatient thieves. The next instant they had closed round a glorious crackling wad of notes. "Sit down there," ordered the Captain. "I'll be back in half an hour at the latest." He vanished behind the green curtain.

The half hour passed, then an hour and another hour. It was dusk, the light had been turned on. Slowly Captain Wagner approached. At most, he was recognizable by his uniform—and even that had changed. Its buttons were undone, the black rubber neckband edged out of the collar, the sword hilt was pushed up under the tunic, the pockets gaped, cigar ash lay strewn all down the front. On the captain's head disheveled brown hair curled over the devastated parting and his lips sagged open under his rumpled mustache. "Every penny," the captain choked and sat down.

They had nothing more to say to one another. Once or twice Trotta attempted a question. Wagner implored silence with outstretched hand and eyes that seemed to reach out with it. Then he got up. He adjusted his uniform. He realized that his life had lost all point. He was going out to put an end to it. "Good-by," he said ceremoniously and left. Outside, however, a gentle summer evening enveloped him with a hundred thousand stars and a hundred sweet scents. After all, it was easier to stop playing than to stop living. He gave himself his sacred word of honor never to risk another game. Better rot than touch another card. Never again! Never seemed a very long time; he curtailed it somewhat. Say, not until August 31st? That he could see. Right. Word of honor, Captain Wagner.

And so, with a clean and tidy conscience and in all the first glow of his resolution, well pleased with the life he had just saved, Captain Wagner goes to call on Chojnicki. Chojnicki is standing at his door. He knows the Captain well enough to see at a glance that he has lost again, heavily, and that he has once again resolved never to play again.

"What have you done with Trotta?"

"Haven't set eyes on him."

"Everything?"

The Captain hangs his head and stares at his boots. He says, "I've sworn on my word of honor. . . ."

"Excellent," says Chojnicki, "about time, too." He is determined to rescue Lieutenant Trotta from his friendship with the crazy Wagner. He must be got out of here, Chojnicki thinks. In the meantime, I'll see to it that he has a few days' leave with Wally. And he drives into town.

"Yes," says Trotta without hesitation. He is afraid of Vienna and of the journey with a woman. But he has to go. He feels the distress which always overcomes him before any change in his life. He feels that a new danger threatens him, the greatest danger of all—namely, one for which he has longed. He dares not ask who the woman is. The faces of many strange women sweep past him, blue eyes, brown, black, fair hair, black hair, hips, breasts, legs, women he might have brushed up against as a boy, a youth—they sweep past him together, a marvelous, tender turmoil of strange women. He inhales their fragrance, he feels the cool hard tenderness of their knees; the sweet yoke of bare arms lies on his neck, and at the back of his neck he feels the bolt of clasped hands.

There is a fear of passion which is itself passionate, just as a certain kind of terror of death can itself be deadly. This fear now fills Lieutenant Trotta.

Chapter 13

Frau von Taussig was beautiful and no longer young. The daughter of a railway official, the widow of a young cavalry captain called Eichberg, she had married again a few years previously, this time a certain Herr von Taussig, a rich and ailing manufacturer. He suffered from mild attacks of so-called recurrent insanity. His fits recurred every six months and for weeks beforehand he could feel them coming on. Then he would go to a clinic on Lake Constance, where wealthy lunatics were cosseted by attendants, gentle as midwives. On the advice of one of those featherbrained fashionable specialists of the kind who prescribe "emotional outlets" for their patients as glibly as old-fashioned practitioners their doses of rhubarb and caster oil, Herr von Taussig had married his friend Eichberg's widow not long before. Taussig's "emotional outlet" was secured, but this did not prevent his fit from coming sooner and lasting longer than usual. His wife had made many friends in the course of her brief married life with Herr von Eichberg and after his death had refused several ardent proposals. People thought too highly of her to mention adulteries. The times were strict, as we know, but they recognized exceptions and even liked them. It was one of those aristocratic principles according to which ordinary citizens were considered to be second-class people, but according to which this or that ordinary officer might become the Emperor's personal equerry; according to which Jews could lay no claim to higher distinctions, yet individual Jews were knighted and became close friends of archdukes; women were to live by a traditional code of behavior, yet certain of them were permitted to philander like a cavalry officer. (They were the principles which today we describe as hypocritical, because we have become so much more uncompromising, honest, and humorless.)

The only one of Frau von Taussig's intimate friends who

had never proposed to her was Chojnicki. The world in which it might still be worthwhile to go on living was doomed to extinction. Whatever world might come after it no longer deserved decent inhabitants. It was therefore absurd to form permanent relationships, marry, and even beget descendants. Chojnicki gazed at the widow with melancholy pale-blue, rather prominent eyes, and said to her, "Please forgive me for not wanting to marry you." With these words he ended his visit of condolence.

So the widow married the madman Taussig.

She needed money, and he was easier to handle than a child. As soon as his fits had subsided, he would send for her. She arrived, allowed him to kiss her, and took him home. "Well, good-by till next time," Herr von Taussig would remark to the specialist who accompanied him to the other side of the railings of the enclosed section. "*Au revoir, à bientôt*," said his wife. She enjoyed her husband's illnesses. And they drove back home.

She had last stayed with Chojnicki ten years ago, before she had married Taussig, no less beautiful than now and ten years younger. She had not returned alone that time either. A lieutenant, young and sorrowful, like this one had escorted her. He had been called Ewald, had been an Uhlan (in those days there were Uhlans at the frontier). It would have been the first real sorrow of her life to have to return unescorted; she would have been disappointed even to have gone with a first lieutenant. She still felt far too young for senior ranks. In another ten years, possibly.

But age advanced with cruel silent step and sometimes in cunning disguise. She would count the days which slipped from her and the tiny wrinkles, fine nets spun by age around her unsuspecting eyes during the night. Her heart, however, was the heart of a girl of sixteen. Blessed with imperishable youth, it dwelt in her ageing body, a beautiful secret in a crumbling castle. Each new young man whom Frau von Taussig embraced was the guest so long expected and desired. Alas, he could get no further than the antechamber. She did not live, she only waited. One after another, she watched them go again with troubled, unappeased, embittered eyes. Gradually she got used to seeing men come and go, that race of childish giants, like clumsy mammoth insects, able to fly and yet of an immense weight, an army of gauche fools trying to flutter with wings of lead, warriors who fancied themselves conquerors when they were despised, fancied themselves possessors while they were being ridiculed; fancied they had had enjoyment when they had scarcely tasted it; a barbarian horde for whom she had nevertheless waited as long as she had lived. One day perhaps, perhaps, there would arise from the midst of their dark confusion a prince, light and shining with blessed hands. He did not come. She waited, he did not come. She grew old, he did not come. Frau von Taussig advanced men like pawns against the wily moves of time. Sheer dread of their appraising eyes made her go with her own eyes shut into her so-called adventures. She enchanted foolish men for her own ends, with her own desires. Unluckily, they never noticed. Nor did they transform themselves in the least.

She appraised Lieutenant Trotta. He looks old for his years, she thought. He's been very unhappy, but it hasn't made him any wiser. He would never make passionate love, but perhaps he would not be inconstant. He's so unhappy as it is that I could only make him happier.

Next morning Trotta was given three days' leave "for family reasons." At one in the afternoon he took leave of his fellows in the refreshment room. Surrounded by envy and acclamation, he got into a first-class carriage after Frau von Taussig, though he had to pay extra for this.

As night descended he grew afraid of the dark like a child and left the carriage to smoke—or rather he said he wanted to smoke. He stood in the corridor, full of vague and muddled thoughts, staring out through dark glass at the flying dragons shaped for a moment by the engine's glowing sparks, and dissolving again in a moment; he stared at the dense darkness of the forests, and the unhurrying stars on the vault of the sky. Cautiously he pulled the door and tiptoed back into their carriage.

"Shouldn't we perhaps have taken sleepers?" came the woman's unexpected terrifying voice through the darkness. "You can't stop smoking, can you? You may smoke in here, you know." So she wasn't asleep yet. His match illuminated her face. White, in the midst of untidy hair, it lay against the crimson upholstery. Yes, perhaps they ought to have taken sleepers. The cigarette end cast a red glow through the darkness. They were crossing a bridge, the train was clattering more noisily. "Bridges," said Frau von Taussig. "I'm always so afraid they'll collapse." Yes, the Lieutenant thought. Well, let them collapse. His only choice was between a sudden catastrophe and one that would creep upon him by slow degrees. He sat motionless opposite the woman, watching the lights from stations they sped through illuminate the carriage for a few seconds, and saw her pale face grow paler still. He could not utter a single word. He supposed he ought to kiss her instead of talking. After the next station, he told himself. But he kept on postponing the kiss. Suddenly the woman put out her hand, fumbled for the latch of the carriage door, found it, and clicked it shut. And Trotta bent over her hand.

Frau von Taussig loved him at that instant with all the ardor which, ten years ago, she had lavished on Lieutenant Ewald, on the same line at about this hour and, who knows, perhaps in this same compartment. But now that Uhlan was extinguished like those that had gone before and come after him. Desire flooded all her memories, sweeping away all traces. Frau von Taussig's first name was Valerie, and it had been abbreviated to the customary Wally. This name, whispered in her ear at each tender encounter, sounded quite new at each tender encounter. This young man had just rechristened her; she was a child and fresh as her name, yet now custom impelled her to tell him sadly and decisively that she was "so much older" than he, an observation on which she always ventured with her young men in a spirit of madly rash precaution. Besides, it was always a pretext for a whole new series of small caresses. All the familiar, tender words which came to her lips with so little effort were spoken now. Then, how well, alas, she knew the sequence, there followed the man's request, begging her not to speak of age or time. She knew how little such requests meant and she believed them. She waited. But Lieutenant Trotta sat there saying nothing, a hardhearted stubborn young man. She was in dread lest his silence be a judgement, and so, cautiously she began. "How much older than you do you think I am?" He hadn't a notion. This was the sort of question you didn't answer nor did it concern him. He could feel the rapid alternation of smooth freshness with heat as it moved along her skin; those sudden climatic changes which were one of the magical manifestations of life. In the space of an hour all the characteristics of all the seasons crowded onto one feminine shoulder. They do indeed revoke the laws of time. "I might be your mother," she was whispering. "Just guess how old I really am."

"I don't know," said the miserable Lieutenant.

"I'm forty-one," replied Frau Wally. It was a month since her forty-second birthday. But nature herself has forbidden some women to tell the truth, just as she forbids them to grow any older. Frau von Taussig would perhaps have been too proud to take a whole three years off her age. But to deprive time of one single, puny year, it was scarcely even petty theft.

"That isn't true," he said to her at last, very gruffly, out of politeness. And she embraced him in a fresh surge of gratitude. White station lights rushed past the windows, lit up the carriage and her white face, and seemed to strip her shoulders a second time. The Lieutenant lay at her breast like a child. She felt a benevolent, blessed, maternal pain. Maternal love flowed into her arms and filled her with a new strength. She wanted to spoil her love as though the lap which now received him had also borne him.

"My child, my child," she said over and over again. She was not afraid of growing old. For the first time, even, she was glad of the years which lay between them. And when day, a radiant day in early summer, broke in through the rushing windows, she showed the Lieutenant her face unfurbished without a qualm. True, she counted a little on the red sunrise. It so happened that their carriage windows faced east. To Lieutenant Trotta the world seemed transformed. And so he had no doubt that this was love—that is to say, the realization of what he had always imagined love to be. Really, he was only grateful like a satisfied child. "We'll stay together when we get to Vienna, won't we?" My child, my child, she kept on thinking. She gazed at him filled with maternal pride as though she had some claim to the virtues which he did not possess but which she ascribed to him.

She thought out a whole series of little treats. How lucky that they should be arriving just in time for the Corpus Christi procession. She would see about getting two seats on the grandstand. Together they would watch the gay procession which she loved, as did all Austrian women, of whatever class, in those days.

She got seats in the grandstand. The happy solemn pomp

of the procession lent her a warm and rejuvenating glow. From the days of her youth she probably knew all the phases, parts, and rules of the Corpus Christi procession as well as the master of ceremonies, as the old audiences in their family boxes knew every scene of their favorite operas. Her eagerness for the pageantry did not diminish, but rather increased, with her expert knowledge.

And in Carl Joseph the old, childish, heroic dreams which had filled him and made him happy at home on his father's balcony when he had heard the strains of the Radetzky March were resuscitated. The whole imposing majesty of the old monarchy swept past his eyes. The Lieutenant thought of his grandfather, the hero of Solferino, of his father's unshakable patriotism, which was like a small but firm rock among the soaring peaks of Habsburg power. He thought of his own sacred duty to die for the Emperor at any moment, on land or water or in the air, in short, to die for him everywhere. The words of the oath of allegiance which he had rattled out mechanically, became imbued with life. They rose, word by word, each an oriflamme.

The china-blue eyes of the Supreme War Lord, lifeless in so many portraits on so many walls throughout the monarchy, assumed a new fatherly solicitude, gazing down like a whole blue sky on the grandson of the hero of Solferino. The light-blue breeches of infantrymen shone forth. Like the very in-carnation of the whole of the science of ballistics, there followed the coffee-brown artillery. Blood-red fezzes on the heads of the sky-blue Bosnians shone in the sun like toy bonfires, lit by Islam in honor of His Apostolic Majesty. In black lacquered carriages sat the gold-decked Knights of the Golden Fleece and sober, apple-cheeked City Fathers. After them, like majestic hurricanes, fluttered the horsehair plumes of the infantry body-guard. Finally, the bells of St Stephen's Cathedral pealed the welcome of the Roman Church to the Roman Emperor of the German nation. The old Emperor got out of his carriage with the elastic step which all the newspapers praised, and went into the church, like any other man. He went to church on foot, the Roman Emperor of the German nation, accompanied by a peal of bells.

No Lieutenant of the Royal and Imperial Army could have observed this spectacle with indifference, and Carl Joseph was one of the most impressionable. He saw the golden glamor which emanated from the procession but did not hear the somber beating of vulture wings. They were hovering above the double eagles of the Habsburgs, these vultures, their sibling foes.

No, the world was not about to end as Chojnicki had told them, you could see with your own eyes that it was full of life. These citizens were thronging their broad Ringstrasse, the ardently loyal, jubilant subjects of his Apostolic Majesty, all so many courtiers around the throne. The whole city was a gigantic outer court of the Burg itself. In the baroque doorways of ancient palaces stood liveried porters with staves in their hands, gods among footmen. Black carriages on high imposing wheels, with rubber tires and slender spokes, drew up in front of the gates. The horses respectfully scraped at the cobblestones. Government officials in black cocked hats and with gold-embroidered collars and slender court swords came dignified and perspiring from the procession. White schoolgirls, blossoms in their hair and candles in their hands, walked home squeezed between their solemn parents, somewhat cowed and possibly even somewhat exhausted. Above the bright hats of the bright ladies who paraded their beaux as if on leads were spread the delicate canopies of their sunshades.

Announced by the thundering of the General's March, rose that Imperial and Royal anthem of earthly and yet Apostolic arch-cherubim, "May God keep him, God preserve him," high over the heads of the people standing in the streets, of marching troops, of gently trotting steeds, of carriages silently rolling on. It hovered above all heads, a paradise of sounds, a canopy of black-and-yellow sounds. The Lieutenant's heart stood still and at the same time beat violently, defying medical science. Cheers ascended, fluttering among these solemn strains, like clear white pennons between huge banners painted with coats of arms. The white horses of the Lippizaner came curvetting, majestically coquettish, as mettlesome as any of the breed of famous Lippizaner mares, reared in the Imperial and Royal stables. This was followed by the clattering hoofs of half a squadron of Dragoons in charming pageantry, their black and gold helmets glinting in the sunlight. High trumpet calls rang forth, the voices of eager heralds: "Clear the way, clear the way, the Emperor approaches!"

And the Emperor came: eight pure white horses drew his carriage. On these, in black coats with gold embroidery and wearing white periwigs rode the lackeys. They looked like gods and yet were only the servants of demigods. On either side of the carriage stood two Hungarian bodyguards with black and tawny panther skins slung over their shoulders. They were reminiscent of the guardians of the walls of Jerusalem, the Holy City, whose king the Emperor Francis Joseph was. The Emperor was wearing a flower-white tunic, familiar from all the portraits in the monarchy, and above his helmet fluttered a mighty crest of parrot plumes. The feathers fluttered gently in the breeze. The Emperor smiled in all directions. The smile rose on his old face like a little sun he himself had fashioned. Blue-and-brown and gold-and-silver decorated uniforms moved like exotic trees and shrubs broken loose from the soil of a tropical garden and striving to regain their distant home. The black fire of top hats flashed above zealous, crimson faces. Colored sashes—the rainbows of the bourgeoisie—stretched over broad chests, waistcoats and bellies. Across the roadway of the Ringstrasse the bodyguard extended in two wide lines of white capes with scarlet facings and white plumes, and glinting halberds in their fists. The trolleys, cabs, and even the automobiles pulled aside for them as for familiar ghosts of Austrian history. At the crossroad and at street corners fat flowerwomen with layers of aprons—urban sisters of the fairies —watered their glistening flowers from green watering cans. They smiled blessings at passing courting couples, tied up lilies of the valley, and let their old tongues wag. The brass helmets of the fire brigade marching to attend the display were bright reminders of danger and disaster. The air was redolent of hawthorn and lilac. The city noises were not loud enough to drown the whistling of blackbirds in gardens and the twittering of larks high in the air. All this the world lavished on Lieutenant Trotta. He sat in a carriage beside his mistress, he loved her, and it felt that he was traveling through the first good day in all his life.

And it was indeed as if life were beginning for him. He learned to drink wine as he had drunk Ninety Percent on the frontier. He took her to eat in that renowned restaurant whose proprietress was imperial in her dignity, whose rooms had the bright serenity of a temple—distinguished as a castle, and peaceful as a village hut. Here, at their own tables Archdukes had their meals and the waiters who served them looked so much like them that it was almost as if the servers and the served took turns. Here everyone called each other by Christian names as brother to brother, yet their salutations were those of princes. All were known here, the young, the old, the good rider and the bad, the gallants, the gamesters and the fops. The ambitious, the favorites, the heirs to an ancient, traditional, proverbial stupidity, consecrated by many generations and honored on all sides—and the wise who would be in power next. The sounds were those only of well-bred forks and spoons, and of the smiling murmurs at the tables which only the person to whom they are addressed can catch, but which the initiated neighbor nevertheless divines. Peaceful brightness emanated from the tablecloths, day poured in silently through curtained windows, the wine gurgled gently out of the bottles, and anyone who wished to call a waiter needed only to raise his eyes. For in this reverent quiet the blinking of an eyelid could be perceived as distinctly as a call elsewhere.

So that was how what he called "life" began, and what indeed really was life at the time: drives in a smooth carriage through the fragrance of a day in early summer by the side of a woman who loved him. Every time she glanced at him tenderly he seemed fully justified in his youthful conviction that he was an exceptional man of many aspects, indeed, even a first-rate officer in the sense in which the phrase was used in the army. He thought how nearly all his life he had felt depressed and shy; you might say "embittered." But as he recognized himself now, he could no longer understand why he had been depressed, shy and embittered. The proximity of death had frightened him. Yet even the melancholy thoughts with which he now remembered Katherina and Max Demant gave him a kind of pleasure. He felt that his life had been a hard one. He had earned the tender glances of a beautiful woman. Nevertheless, he looked at her anxiously from time to time. Wasn't it a mere caprice of hers to take him about with her like a boy and give him a good time for a few days? That he could never permit. As had been established, he was an exceptional person and whoever loved him had to love him entirely, honestly, and unto death, like poor Katherina. Who could tell how many other men this beautiful woman might have in mind, while she believed she loved only him, or pretended to love him? Was he jealous? Certainly he was jealous. And powerless, too, it now occurred to him, jealous and without the means of stopping here or going even further with her, without the means to hold her for as long as he cared to do so, to fathom and to conquer her. He was nothing but a shabby little lieutenant, with fifty kronen a month from his father. And he was in debt . . . .

"Do you gamble much in your garrison?" Frau von Taussig suddenly enquired.

"The others do," he said. "Captain Wagner does. He loses a lot."

"And you?"

"Not at all," said the Lieutenant. In that instant he saw his way to power. He rebelled against his mediocre fate. And he longed for a splendid one. If only he had entered the Civil Service, what chances might there not have been to turn the intelligence which he certainly possessed to useful account. He might have done well. What was an officer in peacetime? What had the hero of Solferino gained by his deed, even in war?

"Please don't ever play," begged Frau von Taussig. "You don't look the sort that ever wins."

That hurt his feelings. He wanted to show her at once that he was lucky, always. He began to plot secret plans for this very day, for this very night. His embraces were, in a sense, provisional only, a mere preliminary foretaste of the love which tomorrow he would lavish on her: the love not merely of a distinguished man, but of a powerful one. He wondered what the time was and looked at his watch, began to think how he could leave her, how to find an excuse to go early. Frau Wally sent him away herself. "It's getting late, you ought to go."

"Tomorrow morning?"

"Tomorrow morning."

The hotel porter told him of some gambling rooms quite near. They welcomed the Lieutenant with businesslike cordiality. He saw a couple of senior officers and froze into the prescribed rigidity in front of them. They waved an indolent forefinger at him, staring at him with incomprehension, as though unable to grasp the fact that they were being regarded as officers, as if they had ceased long ago to have any connection with the army and were only casual wearers of its uniform, and that this clueless greenhorn stirred in them distant recollections of a distant time when they had still been officers. They found themselves in another, perhaps secret, section of their lives with only their clothes and stars to remind them of their ordinary everyday life that would begin again at daybreak tomorrow.

The Lieutenant counted his ready money. It amounted to 150 kronen. In imitation of Captain Wagner, he stowed away fifty in his tunic pocket and put the rest in his cigarette case. For a while he sat at one of the roulette tables—he was not familiar enough with cards and dared not risk that—but he did not play. He was feeling perfectly calm, and surprised at his calm. He watched the piled disks—red, white, blue—increase and diminish, shift here and there. It never occurred to him that his object in being here at all was to make them wander in his direction. At last he decided to play, but only out of some sense of duty. He won. He staked half his winnings. And won again. He didn't bother about colors, still less about numbers. Calmly he played at random. He won. And staked the whole of his winnings. He won a fourth time. A major beckoned to him. Trotta got up. The major said, "This is your first time here? You've won a thousand kronen. You'd better leave at once."

"Yes sir," said Trotta and left obediently. But when he exchanged his disks he was sorry he had obeyed the major. He was angry with himself because he simply did what he was told by anyone who chose to come along. Why did he allow himself to be sent away? Why hadn't he the guts to go back? He felt dissatisfied with himself and his first winnings.

It had got late, and was so quiet that the footsteps of individual pedestrians could be heard in distant streets. Distant stars glittered peacefully in the narrow strip of sky between the tall houses. Around the corner a dark figure was coming toward the Lieutenant. It lurched toward him, obviously drunk. The Lieutenant recognized him at once: it was the painter Moser on his usual round of the night streets of the city centre, complete with portfolio and slouch hat. He touched his hat and began to offer his pictures: "All girls, in all sorts of positions."

Carl Joseph stopped. He felt that fate itself had guided Moser across his path. He was unaware that for many years at this same hour on any night of the week he might have met the professor in any street of the city center. He pulled out the saved fifty kronen from his pocket and gave them to the old man. He did it as though a silent voice had instructed him, as if he were carrying out an order. Like him, like him, he thought. He's quite happy, he's quite right. This reflection frightened him. He tried to find reasons why the painter Moser should be right, found none and became even more frightened, and felt a craving for alcohol, the drinker's craving, which is a thirst of the soul as well as of the body. Suddenly your vision becomes blurred like that of a short-sighted man, and you hear only vaguely, like a deaf man. You must get a drink, immediately. The Lieutenant turned back and stopped the painter. "Where can we get a drink?" he said.

Near the Wool Market an all-night bar sold *slivovitz*; unfortunately, it was twenty-five percent weaker than the Ninety Percent. The Lieutenant and the painter sat down and drank. Gradually Trotta realized that he had long ceased to be master of his fate, ceased to be exceptional, a man of many aspects. On the contrary, he was poor and miserable, full of melancholy at having obeyed a major who had prevented his winning a hundred thousand kronen. No. He was not cut out for victory. Everyone laughed at him, everyone: Frau von Taussig, the major in the gambling rooms. Only this one man, the painter Moser—it was quite safe to call him a friend—was upright, honest, and faithful. Ought he not to reveal his identity? This excellent man was his father's oldest and closest friend, his only friend. Why be ashamed of him? He had painted his grandfather.

The Lieutenant drew in a deep breath to draw courage from the surrounding air and said, "Do you realize we've known each other for a long time?"

The painter Moser jerked his head back, he allowed his eyes to flash under their bushy eyebrows. "We? A long time? *Known each other*, you say? Personally? . . . Of course, naturally, you know me as a painter. I'm known fairly extensively as a painter. I'm sorry—I'm very sorry—I'm afraid . . . you've made a mistake. Or . . ." Moser seemed troubled. "Is it possible you're taking me for someone else?"

"My name is Trotta," said Carl Joseph.

Moser stared at the Lieutenant with glassy expressionless eyes; he held his hand out. Then he burst into tumultuous jubilation. He clutched the Lieutenant's hand and pulled him half across the table, bent himself forward, and so, in the middle of the table, they met in a long, brotherly embrace.

"And what's your father doing?" asked the professor. "Still in his office? Have they made him a governor yet? Haven't heard a word from him since. Some time ago I ran into him sitting in the café in the Volksgarten. He let me have some money. He had his son with him too, the young—Oh, but that was you, of course!"

"Yes, that was me," said the Lieutenant. "How long ago it seems." He remembered how frightened he had been at the sight of that raw and clammy hand descending on his father's thigh. "I ought to beg your pardon," he said. "No, really, I mean it. I treated you very badly. Do forgive me please, dear friend."

"You did," said Moser. "Very badly. I forgive you. Not another word. Where are you staying? I'll see you home."

The bar was just closing. Arm in arm, they walked through the quiet streets. "I turn off here," muttered the painter. "Here's my address. You come and see me tomorrow, my boy."

He gave the Lieutenant one of the vulgar business cards which he handed out in all cafés.

Chapter 14

The day on which the Lieutenant had to return to his garrison was a sad one and, as it happened, also a dull one. He walked again down the streets through which two days ago the procession had passed. In those days, thought the Lieutenant, he had been proud of himself and his profession for a brief hour. Today, however, the thought of his return accompanied him like a jailer accompanying a convict. For the first time in his life he rebelled against the military law which governed his life. He had obeyed ever since his earliest boyhood. And now he wanted to obey no longer. True, he had no clear notion of freedom; but he felt that it must differ from leave much as war differs from maneuvers. This comparison came to him because he was a soldier and because war is the freedom of soldiers. It occurred to him that the ammunition essential for freedom is money. But the sum at present in his pockets was rather like the blank cartridges fired at maneuvers. Did he really own anything at all? Could he afford any liberty? Had the hero of Solferino, his grandfather, left any fortune? Would he inherit it one day from his father? Never before had such reflections occurred to him. Now, like a flight of exotic birds, they came circling around his head, building their nests in it, and fluttering restlessly about in them. Now he became aware of all the confusing calls of the great world. Since yesterday he had known that Chojnicki intended to go away earlier than usual this year, that he intended to travel south with his mistress that very week. And he knew what it means to envy a friend and he felt doubly ashamed. He was going to the northeastern frontier, but his friend and mistress were going south. And south, which until that day had been a geographical designation, glowed with all the maddening allure of an unknown paradise. "South" was in another country. It struck him that there were foreign countries not subject to the Emperor Francis Joseph I. Countries with armies of their own and thousands of lieutenants in large and small garrisons. In these other countries the name of the hero of Solferino meant nothing. Countries with their own monarchs, and monarchs who had their own heroes who had saved their lives. It was very confusing indeed to pursue such thoughts, as confusing to a lieutenant under the monarchy as it might be today, for instance, to reflect that the earth is only one among millions upon millions of similar bodies, each a world. That countless suns shimmer in the Milky Way, each with planets of its own. So that one is, oneself, a paltry individual, if not, to speak quite bluntly, nothing but a little heap of dust.

The Lieutenant still had seven hundred kronen of his winnings. He had not dared to visit another gambling room. Not only because he feared an unknown major who might, for all he knew, have been placed there by the city commandant to keep a sharp eye on all young officers, but for fear of renewing the memory of his ignominious retreat. Oh, he knew quite well that he would immediately leave the gambling rooms again at the barest indication of an order from a superior. And so, like a child during an illness, he lost himself in the painful knowledge that he had no power to force his luck. He felt extraordinarily sorry for himself, and self-pity did him good at this point.

He had several brandies and at once he felt at home with his impotence. And like a person going to jail or into a monastery, the money in his pocket seemed depressing and superfluous to the Lieutenant. He resolved to spend it all at once. He went into the shop where his father had bought him his silver cigarette case and bought a string of pearls for his mistress. Flowers in his hand and the pearls in his trouser pocket, he went to see Frau von Taussig, with a long face.

"I've brought you something," he told her, as if he were saying, "I've just stolen something for you". It seemed to him that he was mistaken to play an alien part, the part of a man of the world. And only at the instant when he was holding the present did it occur to the Lieutenant that it was a ridiculous piece of extravagance, degrading to him and perhaps insulting to this rich woman. "Please excuse it," he said. "I'd only meant to buy you some little thing but . . ."—it was all he could say. He blushed and cast down his eyes.

Oh, how little Lieutenant Trotta knew of women who see age approaching! He did not know how they receive every present like a magic gift which rejuvenates them and which their wise yearning eyes have the power to value. And Frau von Taussig adored his helplessness. The younger he looked the younger he made her feel. She flew, clever and impetuous, around his neck, kissed him like her own child, wept since she was to lose him, but laughed since she had him with her still and also a little because the pearls were so lovely. And she said through a charmingly vehement flood of tears, "You're a dear, dear boy." At once she regretted these exclamations. "Boy" made her sound so much older than actually, at that moment, she was. Luckily, she noticed at once that it made him as proud as a decoration awarded by the Supreme War Lord in person. He's too young, she thought, to know how old I am.

But in order to destroy her actual age, to root it out and drown it in the sea of her passion, she clasped the Lieutenant's shoulders, whose delicate warm bones at once began to confuse her hands, and she drew him to the sofa. She overwhelmed him with her mighty longing to become young. In violent, arched flames passion issued from her, shackling the Lieutenant and subjugating him. Her eyes blinked in gratitude and happiness at the young man above her. Looking at him renewed her youth. Her passion to be young forever was as urgent as his to be in love. For a while she felt she could never part from this lieutenant. All the same, at the next moment she was saying, "What a pity you've got to go back today."

"Am I ever going to see you again?" he asked her reverently, as young lovers do.

"Wait for me. I shall come back." And, "Don't deceive me," she added quickly, fearing inconstancies with her ageing woman's dread of unfaithfulness and the youth of others.

"I love only you," answered the honest voice of a young man to whom nothing seems so important as keeping faith.

Such was their parting.

Lieutenant Trotta drove to the station, got there too early, had a long time to wait. But he felt he was already travelling. Each further moment he might have spent in the city would have been painful, humiliating even. He mitigated the compulsion that was mastering him by starting his return a little earlier than he needed to. At last he could get into the train. He fell into peaceful, almost unbroken sleep and awoke just before they reached the frontier.

His batman, Onufrij, was waiting for him and announced that there had been rioting in the town. The brushmakers were holding a demonstration. The garrison had orders to be on guard.

Now the Lieutenant understood why Count Chojnicki had left so soon. Just now he was traveling south with Frau von Taussig—and here was he, an impotent prisoner who could not turn back at once, to go back on the train.

That day there were no cabs outside the station. So Lieutenant Trotta walked. Behind him, Onufrij carried his bag. They came to the town. The little tradesmen's shops were all shut up. Iron bars barricaded the wooden doors and shop fronts on the low houses. Gendarmes patroled with fixed bayonets. No sound was to be heard, apart from the usual croakings of the frogs in the marshes. The wind had driven up the sand which this dusty earth produced so tirelessly and strewn it plentifully over roofs and walls, palings and wooden pavements, and the occasional, isolated willows. Centuries of dust seemed to lie thick on this forgotten world. There was no one in the streets and one might have supposed the inhabitants had all been struck dead behind their barred doors, their shuttered windows. There was a double guard in front of the barracks. Yesterday all the officers had moved into them and Brodnitzer's hotel stood empty.

Lieutenant Trotta reported to Major Zoglauer. From his superior he learned that his journey had done him good. No journey could do anything else, in the opinion of a man who had for more than a decade served at the frontier. Then, as though this were mere routine, Zoglauer informed him that early tomorrow morning a column of Jaeger would turn out to take up positions on the highroad opposite the brush factory, and there hold themselves in readiness to proceed with arms, if necessary, against the seditious disturbances of brushmakers out on strike. This column was to be led by Lieutenant Trotta. As a matter of fact, there wouldn't be anything much to worry about, there was every reason to suppose the gendarmery amply staffed to keep these people properly respectful. All that was required was to keep a cool head and be careful not to advance before it was necessary. The final decision to use the men would rest with the civil authorities. It wasn't, of course, very nice for any officer to be at the beck and call of the local mayor. All the same, this rather ticklish job was, in its way, a kind of distinction for the junior lieutenant of the battalion; besides, no other officer had had leave, so that the elementary dictates of good fellowship would seem to suggest, etc., etc.

"Certainly, sir," said the Lieutenant and went away.

There was nothing to be said against Major Zoglauer. He had almost begged the grandson of the hero of Solferino instead of commanding him. And the grandson of the hero of Solferino had, after all, had unexpectedly splendid leave. He crossed the square into the mess. He was now convinced that a peculiarly treacherous, scheming fate had first accorded him the leave only in order to destroy him immediately afterward. It was for this that he had had himself transferred to a frontier garrison. The others were sitting in the mess and welcomed him with exaggerated jubilation, inspired more by their curiosity to hear about things than any heartfelt pleasure at having him back with them. They all asked at once what it had been like. But Captain Wagner said, "He can tell us about it tomorrow, when everything's over." Suddenly they all stopped talking.

"Suppose I get killed tomorrow," said Lieutenant Trotta to Captain Wagner.

"Damned rotten death," replied the Captain. "Rotten sort of a business altogether. After all, it's only a lot of poor idiots. And they may be right, you can never tell."

It had not yet occurred to Lieutenant Trotta that they were only poor idiots who might even be right. The Captain's remark seemed so splendid to him now that he no longer doubted that they were poor idiots. So he had two Ninety Percents and said, "Then I simply won't give the order to fire; or go at them with fixed bayonets either. Let the gendarmes do their own dirty work."

"You'll do what you've got to. You know that."

No. At that instant Carl Joseph did not know it. He drank, and soon reached the state in which he could see himself doing anything—refusing an order, leaving the army, making his fortune gambling. No more corpses should lie across his path.

"Get out of the army," Dr Max Demant had said to him. The Lieutenant had been a weakling long enough. Instead of getting out of the army, he'd had himself transferred to the frontier. All that was going to come to an end. Why should they degrade him tomorrow into a kind of superior policeman? The day after they'd be putting him on point duty, showing strangers the way to the next street. Ridiculous, all this playing at soldiers in peacetime. There wouldn't ever be any war. One would rot in the mess. But could he, Lieutenant Trotta, say whether a week from today he might not be basking in the south?

All this he told to Captain Wagner in a loud eager voice. A few officers stood around listening. Most would have been perfectly satisfied with rather higher pay, less uncomfortable garrisons, and slightly more rapid promotion. To some, Lieutenant Trotta appeared a bit strange and uncanny. He was well in, of course. Hadn't he just come back from this marvelous leave? Well, so he didn't like having to turn out in the morning. Was that it?

Lieutenant Trotta felt a silent animosity around him. For the first time since he had served in the army he decided to provoke his fellow officers. And since he knew what would hurt their feelings most, he said, "Perhaps I shall get myself sent to the staff college."

Quite so. Why not? the officers said. Hadn't he come from the cavalry regiment? Why shouldn't he be able to get to the staff college? He'd be sure to pass his examinations and get himself made a general out of turn at an age when people like themselves might just be expecting to be promoted to captain and wear their spurs. It could do him no harm to turn out tomorrow for a bit of a carouse.

He had to turn out very early the next day. For the army itself regulated the sequence of the hours. It took possession of time and accorded it the rank it deserved according to military judgement. Although sedition was not expected before midday, Lieutenant Trotta set off at 8 a.m. along the wide dusty highroad. His men lay, wandered, or stood about behind the tidy piles of rifles, looking at once peaceful and dangerous. Larks sang, the crickets chirped, flies buzzed. Colored scarves on the peasant women's heads shimmered in the distant fields. They were singing. And sometimes the soldiers, who came

199

from this district, replied with the same songs. They would have known what to do in the fields over there. But what they were waiting for here they did not understand. Was it war already? Were they to die at noon today?

There was a small village inn in the neighborhood. Lieutenant Trotta went there for a Ninety Percent. Its low-ceilinged taproom was full. The Lieutenant saw that these were the workmen due to assemble at twelve in front of the factory. They all stopped talking as he entered, jingling and fearsomely armed. He stood at the bar. The innkeeper took long, too long, in producing the bottle and glass. A silence, a huge mountain of silence, towered behind Trotta's back. He emptied his glass at a gulp. He could feel them all waiting for him to go. He would like to have told them that it wasn't his fault. But he found he could neither speak to them nor leave immediately. He did not wish to appear afraid and he drank down several glasses one after another. Still not a word. They might be making signs behind his back. He did not turn round. At last he walked out of the inn with the sensation of forcing himself past the hard rock of silence and a hundred eyes pricking the back of his neck like threatening lances.

When he got back to his men it seemed appropriate to give the order to fall in at once, though it was not more than ten o'clock in the morning. He felt bored and he had also learned that boredom demoralizes troops, whereas rifle drill raises their morale. In a flash, the column stood in front of him drawn up in the correct double file and suddenly, no doubt for the first time in his military life, it occurred to him that these men's precise limbs were lifeless parts of a dead machine engendering nothing. The double file stood rigid, everyone held his breath. But Lieutenant Trotta, who had just experienced the heavy, ominous silence of the workers behind his back at the inn, realized that there can be two kinds of silence; and perhaps, he continued to think, there may be all kinds of different silences, just as there are so many kinds of noise. When he entered the inn, no one had ordered those men to fall in; all the same, they had suddenly become silent. And from their silence emanated an ominous, mute hatred, just as sometimes silent electric sultriness of an unspent storm emanates from the pregnant and immeasurably silent clouds.

Lieutenant Trotta listened. But nothing emanated from the

dead silence of his rigid lines. One stony face stood beside the next. Most of them were a little like his batman Onufrij. They had wide mouths and heavy lips which could scarcely close and narrow, bright, expressionless eyes. And as he stood in front of his troops, poor Lieutenant Trotta, in the blue radiance of a day in early summer, amid singing larks, chirping crickets, and the buzz of flies, nevertheless felt that he could hear the dead silence of his men more distinctly than all the voices of the day and he became convinced that he did not belong here. But if not here, where? He asked himself this while his men awaited further orders. Where do I belong? Not with those workmen at the inn. Sipolje, perhaps? To the fathers of my fathers? Ought I to be holding a plow and not a sword? And the Lieutenant left his men drawn up at attention. "Stand easy!" he shouted at last. "Ground rifles! Dismiss."

And everything was as it had been before. Soldiers lay about behind the rifle stacks. From the distant fields drifted the peasant women's songs. And the soldiers replied to them with the same songs.

The constabulary came marching from the town; three reinforced files, accompanied by District Mayor Horak. Trotta knew him. He was a good dancer, a Silesian Pole, a good citizen and good company at the same time and although no one had ever seen his father, he reminded them of him. And his father had been a postman. Today, as was required of him on duty, he wore the black-and-green uniform with violet facings, and a sword. His short fair mustache stood out golden as wheat, and from afar you could smell the powder on his plump rosy cheeks. He was as jolly as a Sunday procession. "My orders," he told Lieutenant Trotta, "are to break up the meeting at once. Please have your men alert, Lieutenant." He arranged his policemen round the waste land in front of the factory where the demonstration was to be held.

Trotta answered, "Yes," and turned his back on him.

He waited. He would have liked another Ninety Percent but could not manage to get to the inn again. He watched sergeant, corporal, and lance corporal vanish through its doors and come out again. He lay down in the grass beside the road and waited. The day advanced, the sun rose higher; the peasant women's songs ceased in the fields. It felt to Lieutenant Trotta that an immeasurably long time had elapsed since his return from Vienna. From those far-off days he only had an image of the woman who by now might be in the south, who had forsaken him, betrayed him, he thought. Here he was, lying by the roadside in the frontier garrison, waiting, not for the enemy but for the strikers. They came. They came from the direction of the inn. Their song preceded them, it was one the Lieutenant had never heard before. It had scarcely been heard in these parts. It was the *Internationale* sung in three languages. District Mayor Horak knew it professionally. Lieutenant Trotta could not make out a word of it. But to him its rhythms were like the vocalized silence which he had before felt at his back. Solemn excitement possessed the jolly District Mayor. He ran from policeman to policeman, pencil and notebook in hand. Once more Lieutenant Trotta gave his order, "Fall in."

Like an earthbound cloud the demonstrators advanced, past the staring, twofold fence of Jaeger. The Lieutenant was overcome by an ominous presentiment of the end of the world. He remembered the colorful magnificence of the Corpus Christi procession and for a brief instant he imagined that the dark cloud of rebels was advancing toward that procession. For the space of a single swift second the faculty of seeing in images descended upon him, so that, exalted, he saw the ages roll toward each other like two rocks, and he himself, the Lieutenant, was crushed between them.

His men shouldered arms; while over there, raised on invisible hands, there emerged the head and body of a man, above the dense black and continually moving mass of people. This hovering body became the near-exact center of the mass. Its hands were raised into the air. From its mouth rang incomprehensible sounds. The crowd yelled. Next to the Lieutenant, pencil and notebook in hand, stood Mayor Horak. Suddenly he closed his book and crossed the street between two glittering policemen to the edge of the crowd.

"In the name of the law!" he shouted. His clear voice was louder than the speaker's. The meeting was dispersed. For a second there was quiet. Then a single cry burst from the crowd of people. White fists came up beside the faces, each face was flanked by two fists. The police drew together into a cordon. In another minute the semicircle of people was in motion. It surged forward into the police, shouting.

Trotta gave the order, "Fix bayonets!" He drew his sword.

He could not see that his weapon glittered in the sunlight and cast a fleeting, playful, provoking reflection onto the shady side of the street, where the crowd had gathered. The knobs of the gendarmes' helmets, their bayonet points, were suddenly submerged in the crowd.

"Proceed toward the factory, forward march!" Trotta commanded. The Jaeger advanced, and toward them flew dark lumps of iron, brown sticks, and white stones. There was whistling, hissing, panting.

Horak, swift as a weasel, had come running up beside the Lieutenant. "For God's sake, Lieutenant," he was whispering, "tell them to shoot."

"Platoon halt," commanded Trotta and, "Fire!"

The Jaeger, in accordance with Major Zoglauer's instructions, fired their first round into the air. After this there was complete silence. For a second all the peaceful sounds of a summer midday were heard. And through the dust raised by the soldiers and the crowd, and through the faint burning smell of spent cartridges came the benevolence of the brooding sun. Suddenly a woman's sobbing voice cut through the noonday. And since some of the crowd were under the impression that this screaming woman had been hit, they again started hurling their crude missiles at the soldiers. These fell, at first sporadically, followed by more and more, until at last the whole crowd was flinging them. A few front-line Jaeger sank to the ground while Trotta still stood there, rather hesitant, his left hand gripping his sword, his right fumbling in his revolver case. He heard Horak's whisper beside him, "Fire, for God's sake, get them to fire!"

In a single second hundreds of incomplete thoughts and images passed through Lieutenant Trotta's excited brain, some simultaneously, and confused voices in his heart bade him first to be merciful and then to be ruthless, told him what his grandfather would have done in such a situation, threatened him with instant death and at the same time set death before him as the only possible and desirable end of this battle. Someone raised his hand. He thought an alien voice was giving the order, "Fire!" a second time and he could see that now the barrels of his guns were trained on the demonstrators. A second later he knew no more. For that part of the crowd which appeared to give way had in fact only made a detour and was rushing upon the Jaeger from behind, so that Trotta's men stood between the two groups. As the Jaeger fired their second volley, stones and slats full of nails came hurtling down on their backs. Hit on the head by one of these missiles, Lieutenant Trotta sank to the ground unconscious. They hit his body with all sorts of objects. Now the Jaeger were firing at random into their assailants on every side until they forced them into flight. The whole thing had taken scarcely three minutes. When, marshaled by the sergeant, they formed up again, wounded soldiers and workers lay in the dust of the road.

It took a long time for the ambulances to come. Lieutenant Trotta was carried to the little garrison hospital. There they diagnosed a fractured skull and fracture of the left collarbone; and it was feared that he might contract brain fever. An obviously arbitrary coincidence had decreed that the grandson of the hero of Solferino should break his collarbone in the skirmish; though, apart from the Emperor perhaps, none of his contemporaries could have known that the Trottas owed their success to a fractured collarbone.

Three days later brain fever did set in. They would certainly have communicated with his father had not the Lieutenant on first reaching the hospital and immediately after regaining consciousness begged the major urgently on no account to let his father know what had happened. True, he was now unconscious again and there was even some reason to fear for his life, but the major decided nevertheless to wait. So it was not until two weeks later that the District Commissioner heard about the rebellion on the frontier and his son's unfortunate part in it. He first learned about it from the newspapers in which left-wing politicians were careful to advertise it, since the Opposition had made up its mind that the army, this Jaeger battalion, and in particular Lieutenant Trotta, who had so wantonly given the order to fire, should be made responsible for these dead men and their widows and children. Proceedings seemed actually to threaten the lieutenant. That is to say, some kind of official investigation, arranged to keep Opposition circles quiet, and entrusted to the military authorities, would be used as a lever for rehabilitating and perhaps even conferring some distinction on the accused. All in all, the District Commissioner was somewhat perturbed. He wired his son twice and Major Zoglauer once. By this time the Lieutenant was better. Though still unable to move in bed, his life was no longer in danger. He wrote a short account to his father. And he was not concerned about his health, all he could think was that once again the ground in front of his feet was strewn with dead. He had made up his mind to leave the army at last. Occupied with thoughts of this kind, it was impossible for him to see and speak to his father, though he longed for him. In a sense, he was homesick for his father. The army was no longer his profession. Much as he loathed the occasion which had brought him to the hospital, he welcomed his illness because it postponed any need to make decisions. He gave himself up to the dismal reek of carbolic, the bleak whiteness of bed and walls, the pain, the daily changing of bandages, the stern and motherly concern of the nurses and the boring visits of eternally jocular fellow officers. He reread a few of the books recommended by his father once for summer reading; he had read nothing since he had been a cadet. Every line he read reminded him of his father, of the quiet summer Sunday mornings, of Jacques, of Bandmaster Nechwal, and of the Radetzky March.

One day Captain Wagner came to see him, sat by his bedside for a long time without saying much, got up, and then sat down again. With a sigh he eventually pulled out a document and asked the Lieutenant to sign. Trotta signed. It was a bill for fifteen hundred kronen. Kapturak had insisted on Trotta's signature. Captain Wagner became very animated, told a long, intricate story about a race horse which he intended to get hold of dirt cheap and enter for the Baden stakes, told a few more anecdotes, and then left suddenly.

Two days later the head surgeon came, pale and worried, to Trotta's bedside and informed him that Captain Wagner was dead. He had shot himself in the frontier woods. He left a farewell letter addressed to all his brother officers, and heartfelt greetings to Lieutenant Trotta.

The Lieutenant did not think about the bills or about the consequences his signature might have. He became delirious. He dreamt, and spoke in his dreams; the dead were calling him and it was time to depart from the earth—old Jacques, Max Demant, Captain Wagner, and the unknown killed workmen stood in a row and called him. But between him and the dead stood an empty roulette table, around which the ball, spun by no hand, twirled on and on forever.

His delirium lasted two weeks. It was a welcome excuse for
the army authorities to put off their inquiry, while informing
certain political quarters that the army, too, had had its victims,
and that the first responsibility had lain with the civil authorities, that the gendarmery should have been reinforced in time.
A voluminous dossier about the case of Lieutenant Trotta
grew as the various departments sprinkled it with a few more
drops of ink, as if they were watering flowers. At last the
whole affair was submitted to His Majesty's Military Cabinet,
and some unusually circumspect Chief Judge advocate learned
that this Lieutenant Trotta was the grandson of that hero of
Solferino, long since, indeed, passed into oblivion, but nonetheless in former intimate relationship with the person of the
Supreme War Lord. It was therefore plain that the case of the
Lieutenant might arouse interest in the highest places. It would
be wiser to wait before beginning any investigation.

So that, at seven one morning, the Emperor, just back from
Ischl, had to busy himself with the case of a certain Carl Joseph,
Baron Trotta von Sipolje. And since the Emperor was old,
though refreshed by his stay in Ischl, he could not understand why the name should make him think of the Battle of
Solferino, and he left his desk and walked with the short steps
of age up and down his plainly furnished study, up and down,
until at last the old valet, waiting outside, grew perturbed, then
really uneasy, and knocked at the door.

"Come in," said the Emperor. And seeing it was the valet,
he asked, "What time will Montenuovo be here?"

"At eight o'clock, Your Majesty."

It was still only half past seven. The Emperor found this
state of uncertainty intolerable. Why, why should "Trotta"
remind him of Solferino? And why couldn't he remember what
the connection was? Had he really grown so very old? Since
the Emperor's return from Ischl, this question of his exact age
had never ceased to be in his mind. For it suddenly seemed to
him odd that, though, of course, you have only to subtract the
year of birth from the current year to find out how old you
are, still, all the years begin with January, whereas his birthday
was August 18th. Now, if only the years started with August,
or if, for instance, he had been born on January 18th, that
would have been simple. But as it was, it seemed impossible
to know definitely whether one was eighty-two and so in one's

eighty-third year, or eighty-three and in one's eighty-fourth year. And the Emperor did not wish to inquire. People had so much to do and really it made no difference at all whether one were a year younger or older, since, even if he had been younger, he could not have told why this blessed "Trotta" should make him think of Solferino. The Lord High Steward would be sure to know. But he wouldn't be here until eight o'clock. The valet, perhaps . . .

The Emperor paused in his walk and asked the valet, "Tell me, do you know the name 'Trotta'?"

The Emperor wanted to address his valet familiarly, as usual, but this was a point of world history and the Emperor felt a certain respect for any man whom he questioned on a point of history.

"Trotta?" said the Emperor's valet. "Trotta?"

The valet, too, was old, and vaguely remembered a history reading lesson entitled "The Battle of Solferino." Then, like a sunbeam, memory lit up his face. "Trotta!" he cried. "Why, that was the cavalry lieutenant who saved Your Majesty's life!"

The Emperor went back to his desk. All the jubilant birds of Schönbrunn were twittering outside his study windows. It seemed to the Emperor that he was young again and he could hear the clatter of muskets, he could feel himself gripped by the shoulders and pushed to the ground. And right away the name "Trotta" was quite familiar, as familiar as the name Solferino. "Yes, yes," the Emperor said, with a little gesture, and he wrote across the edge of the Trotta dossier, "Settle favorably".

He rose again and went to the window. The birds sang, the Emperor smiled at them as though he could see them.

Chapter 15

The Emperor was an old man. He was the oldest emperor in the world. Around him, drawing closer and closer, death reaped and reaped. The whole field was bare. Only the Emperor, like a forgotten silver wheatstalk, stood waiting. His clear hard eyes had for many years been gazing absently into a deserted distance. His head was bald, like a rounded desert, his whiskers were white, like a pair of snowy wings. The wrinkles in his face were a tangled thicket, dwelling place of the decades. His body was lean and his back slightly curved. Indoors he walked with short steps. But as soon as he entered the streets, he tried to stiffen his thighs, make his knees flexible, his feet light, and his back straight. He filled his eyes with artificial benevolence and with the true characteristic of Imperial eyes: they appeared to look at all who looked at him and to greet everyone who greeted him; in reality, however, the faces only glided and floated past them and they gazed straight at that delicate, fine line on the horizon which divides life from death, a line always visible to old men's eyes, even if houses, forests, or mountains obscure it. People thought Francis Joseph knew less than they did because he was so much older than they were. But he may have known more than a great many of them. He saw the sun setting in his Empire, but he said nothing, he knew that he would die before its downfall. Often he feigned innocence and acted delighted when people gave him elaborate explanations of matters he understood quite well. For with the slyness of the very young and the very old, he enjoyed misleading people. He rejoiced in the vanity which persuaded them that they were cleverer than he. He concealed his wisdom in simplicity, since it does not become an emperor to be as wise as his advisers. Better far to seem simple than wise.

When he went out shooting he knew quite well how they set the game before his gun so he only aimed at the creatures they drove in front of him, though he could have brought down others equally well. It does not become an old emperor to show that he has seen through a trick, and that he can shoot better than a gamekeeper. When people told him a story he always pretended to believe it, for it does not become an emperor to confront people with an untruth. When people smiled behind his back he pretended to know nothing about it. It does not become an emperor to know that people smile about him, and, indeed, their smiles are foolish so long as he refuses to notice them. When he had a temperature and people trembled for his life and his physician lied to him that his temperature was normal, the Emperor would say, "That's all right, then," though he knew quite well that he had a temperature. For an emperor does not accuse his doctor of lying. Besides, he knew that it was not yet time for him to die. There were many restless nights when he was worried by high temperature of which his doctors knew nothing. For sometimes he was not well and no one noticed it. And at other times they said he was ill when he was well, and then he would pretend to be ill. When they thought him kind he was indifferent, and where he seemed cold, his heart bled. He had lived long enough to know that it is foolish to tell people the truth. So he did not begrudge them their illusions and believed less in the continuance of his world than any gossip who told stories through his vast empire. For it does not become an emperor to vie with gossips and worldlings. So the Emperor held his peace.

Although his holiday had done him good and the physician was satisfied with his pulse, his lungs, and his breathing, since yesterday he had had a cold. It did not occur to him to draw attention to it. They might prevent his attending the autumn maneuvers and he wanted to see a day's maneuvers again. The document concerning the man who had saved his life, whose name he had forgotten again, had reminded him of Solferino. He did not like wars, for he knew that one loses them, but he loved the army and war games and uniforms, maneuvers, parades, the grand march past, and company drill. It vexed him now and then that the officers' hats were higher than his own, that their trousers had neat creases and that they wore patent-leather shoes, and the collars of their tunics were far too high. Many, indeed, were even clean-shaven. Not long ago he had come across a clean-shaven officer of the militia and the sight had troubled him all day. But if once he showed himself among them, they knew quite well what was regulation and what mere swagger. He could court-martial some of them. For in the army an emperor may do anything, in this army even the Emperor was a soldier. How he enjoyed the fanfares, though he pretended it was the tactical plans that engrossed him. For it annoyed him in his weaker moments, although he knew that God Himself had set him on the Apostolic throne, to think he was not a front-line officer, and he bore a grudge against staff officers. He remembered how after Solferino he had shouted like a sergeant-major at the straggling men when they had lost discipline and how he got them back into line. He was convinced—though to whom dare he say so?—that ten good sergeant-majors are of more use than twenty generals on the staff. He longed for the maneuvers.

So he decided not to let them see his cold and to use his handkerchief as sparingly as possible. No one was to be forewarned; he wished to surprise the maneuvers and the whole district with his decision. He took pleasure in the despair the civil authorities would feel at not having taken adequate measures to protect him. He was not afraid. He knew quite well that the hour of his death had not yet come. He spread consternation. They tried to persuade him not to go. He remained obdurate. One day he stepped into the Imperial train and went steaming eastward.

In the village of Z., not ten miles from the Russian frontier, his quarters had been prepared in an old Schloss. The Emperor would rather have stayed in one of the cottages assigned to the officers. But for years they had not allowed him to enjoy authentic military life. Only once, for instance—and, as it happened, during that same disastrous Italian campaign—had he ever seen a real-live flea in his bed, but he had told nobody. For he was the Emperor. And an emperor does not mention insects. That had been his view even in those days. They closed his bedroom windows. During the night he could not sleep, though everyone set to guard him was asleep. The Emperor got out of bed in his long pleated nightshirt and, softly, softly, so as not to wake anyone, he unlatched the high narrow windows. He stood there for a while breathing in the freshness of the autumn night and watching the stars in the deep-blue sky, the soldiers' glowing red campfires. He had once read a book about himself which contained the sentence, "Francis Joseph I is no romantic." They write that I'm no romantic, the old man thought, but I love campfires. He would like to have been a lieutenant, to have been young. I may not be in the least romantic, he thought, but I should like to be young. If I'm not mistaken, the Emperor thought further, I was eighteen when I came to the throne. "Came to the throne"—it seemed a daring phrase to him; just now he found it hard to think of himself as "the Emperor." To be sure, there it was, printed in this book, which they had given him with the usual respectful dedications. Without doubt, he was the Emperor Francis Joseph I. In front of his window the infinite, deep-blue night glittered with stars. Under it stretched the wide, flat land. They said that these windows faced northeast, so he was looking toward Russia. But of course he could not see the frontier of his realm. At this moment the Emperor Francis Joseph would like to have seen the frontier of his realm. His realm! He smiled. The night was curved and blue and immense and full of stars. Thin and old, the Emperor stood at the window in his white nightshirt and he seemed very insignificant to himself in face of the immeasurable night.

The humblest of his soldiers on patrol in front of the tents was more powerful than he. The humblest of his soldiers! And he was the Supreme War Lord. Every soldier swore before God Almighty faithfully to serve Francis Joseph I. He was sovereign by the grace of God and he believed in Almighty God, behind the glittering star-studded blue of the sky. He concealed himself, the Almighty, the Inconceivable: they were His stars which glittered in the sky and it was His sky which vaulted the earth; and part of the earth, namely the Austro-Hungarian Monarchy, He had allotted to Francis Joseph I. But Francis Joseph I was a thin old man standing by the open window, afraid that any moment his guards might catch him out of bed.

Crickets chirped. Their voices, endless as the night, inspired him with the same reverence as the stars. Now and then it seemed to the Emperor that the stars themselves were singing. He shivered a little. But still he was afraid to close the window, he might not manage it as smoothly as before. His hands trembled. He remembered that once before, long ago, he had come to see maneuvers in this district. This room, too, emerged from forgotten times. But he did not know whether it was ten, twenty, or even more years ago since then. He felt he was floating on the sea of time, not toward any goal, but at random, on the surface of the waters, often beaten back to the rocks which seemed familiar to him. Someday, somewhere he would sink. He sneezed. Yes, his cold. So long as he hadn't wakened anyone. He listened. Nothing stirred in the anteroom. Cautiously he closed the window again and groped his way back to bed on his thin feet. With him he took the image of the blue starry sky. He preserved it under his eyelids. He fell asleep, night arched above him, as if he were lying in the open.

He woke, as he always did in the field (that was what he called maneuvers) punctually at four in the morning. Already his valet was in the room. He knew that outside the door the equerries were in attendance. Yes, he would have to start the day. He'd scarcely get a minute to himself all day long. But at least he'd outwitted them during the night and had had a good quarter of an hour at the open window. He thought of this slyly stolen pleasure and smiled. He chuckled at the valet. The orderly had just come into the room and froze on the spot, taken aback by the Emperor's chuckle, by His Majesty's braces which he was seeing for the first time in his life, and by the still untidy rather rumpled whiskers, between which the smile played like an old and tired little bird. He was taken aback by the Emperor's sallow complexion and the skin on his bald scalp which was scurfy. He did not know whether to smile with the old man or to wait in silence. And suddenly the Emperor started to whistle. He was actually rounding his lips, his whiskers moved a little closer together, and the Emperor whistled a well-known song, a little out of tune. It sounded like the reedy piping of a shepherd. And the Emperor said, "Hojos is always whistling that. I'd like to know what it is." But neither valet nor batman knew, and a little while later, when he was washing, the Emperor had already forgotten the song.

It was a heavy day. Francis Joseph looked at the slip listing the day's engagements hour by hour. The only church in the place was Greek Orthodox. A Catholic priest would say mass first, then a Greek priest. He found church functions more trying than anything else. He had the feeling that he was called upon to make a special effort before God. And he was so old. God might have excused me some of it, the Emperor thought. But He is even older than I am and his decisions seem as unfathomable to me as mine do to the soldiers in the army. And where should we all be if every subordinate began to criticize his superior? Through the high windows the Emperor watched God's sun rise. He made the sign of the cross and knelt down. For countless years he had seen the sunrise. Almost every day of his life he had been up earlier than the sun, as a soldier gets up earlier than his officer. He was familiar with every kind of sunrise, the joyous, fiery daybreaks of summer, the desolate mists around late-winter suns. And though he could no longer remember dates, had forgotten the days, months, and years when good or ill had come upon him, he could still recall each morning which had ushered in an important day in his life. He remembered how one had been overcast, another bright. And day after day he had made the sign of the cross and knelt, as some trees open their leaves every morning to the light, whether they are days of gathering storm or of the felling axe, or of the deadly frost of spring, or days full of peace and warmth and life.

The Emperor rose. His barber came. Regularly every morning he held up his chin and his whiskers were trimmed and neatly brushed. The cool metal of the scissors tickled the lobes of his ears and his nostrils. Sometimes it made the Emperor sneeze. Today he sat at a little oval mirror, watching the movements of this barber's bony hands with pleasurable excitement. After every little hair that dropped, after each scrape of the razor, each tug of brush and comb, the barber skipped away and breathed, "Your Majesty," through shaking lips. The Emperor did not hear this whispered word. He could only see that the man kept moving his lips, dared not inquire, and concluded that the man must be a little nervous.

"What's your name?" he asked. The barber had corporal's rank, though he had served only six months in the Landwehr in which, however, he served his colonel impeccably, winning the approbation of all superiors. He now sprang back to the door in one leap, elegant as his trade demanded, yet soldierly too. It was a leap, a bow, a jerk to attention all in one. The Emperor nodded benignly.

"Hartenstein," the barber said.

"Why do you jump about so?" asked Francis Joseph.

But he received no answer. The corporal approached again timidly and finished his work as quickly as he could. He wished himself miles away, back in the camp.

"Don't go yet," said the Emperor. "I see you're a corporal. Served a long time, eh?"

"Six months, Your Majesty," breathed the barber.

"Hm, and you're a corporal already? In my time," said Francis Joseph, as any veteran might have said, "in my time, it wasn't so easy to get on. Still, you're a smart-looking soldier. Would you like to stay in the army?"

Hartenstein had a wife and children and a prosperous little business in Olmütz and he had tried once or twice to simulate arthritis in order to get himself discharged at the earliest possible moment. But he couldn't say, "No," to His Majesty. He said, "Yes, Your Majesty," and knew in that moment that he had messed up his whole life.

"Well, that's all right then. So now you're a sergeant. Only don't be so nervous."

Good. The Emperor had made a man happy. Excellent, excellent. He had done excellently by this Hartenstein. Now the day could start. His carriage was waiting. They drove slowly up the hill to the Greek church at the top. A gold double cross sparkled in the morning sun. The military band played "May God keep him" and the Emperor stepped down and entered the church. He knelt in front of the altar, moved his lips, but did not pray. He kept thinking of the barber. Almighty God could give the Emperor no such sudden proofs of his benevolence as he had just given a corporal, and it was a pity. King of Jerusalem—it was the highest rank which God could confer upon a sovereign. Francis Joseph was already King of Jerusalem. A pity, the Emperor thought. Someone came to whisper in his ear that the Jews out in the village were also expecting him. He had completely forgotten the Jews. Oh, the Jews as well, thought the Emperor, distressed. All right, let them come. But we must make haste or we won't be in time for maneuvers.

The Greek priest hurried through his mass. The band struck up "May God keep him" again. The Emperor came out of church. It was nine o'clock in the morning. At nine-twenty the field day was due to begin. He decided to mount at once and not get back in his carriage. The Jews could just as well be received on horseback. The carriage was sent back and he rode to meet the Jews. At the end of the village where the highroad opened out, leading on to the headquarters and the maneuver ground, they swarmed toward him, a dark cloud. Like a field of strange black grain stalks in the wind, this congregation of Jews did obeisance to the Emperor. He saw their bent backs from the saddle. Then he rode up closer and made out the long, fluttering beards, silver, pitch-black, or flame-red, stirring in the light autumn wind. Their long bony noses seemed intent on finding something on the ground. In a blue cloak, the Emperor sat on his white horse. The whiskers on his cheeks shone in the silvery autumn sunlight. White mists rose from the fields around him. The leader of the Jews approached the Emperor, in the black-bordered white prayer shawl of the Jews and with fluttering beard. The Emperor paced his horse. The old Jew's feet went slower and slower. At last he seemed to be standing still and yet moving. Francis Joseph shivered a little. He stopped so suddenly that his horse reared. He dismounted. His suite did likewise. He went on foot. His brightly polished boots were covered with the dust of the country road and lines of heavy gray slime formed along the edges. The black crowd of Jews eddied toward him. Their backs rose and fell. Their coal-black, flame-red, and silver-white beards waved in the gentle breeze. The patriarch stopped three paces from the Emperor. In his arms he bore a large purple Torah scroll decorated with a gold crown, its little bells softly jingling. Then the Jew lifted the Torah scroll toward the Emperor. And his widely bearded, toothless mouth gabbled in an incomprehensible language the blessing which Jews utter in the presence of an emperor. Francis Joseph inclined his head. The delicate haze of an Indian summer drifted above his black cap, ducks screeched in the air, a cock crowed in a distant farmyard. All else was quiet. A somber muttering rose from the crowd of Jews. Their backs bent lower still. Infinite, cloudless, the silver-blue sky spanned the earth. "Blessed art thou," said the Jew to the Emperor, "who shalt not see the end of the world." I know it, Francis Joseph thought. He offered the old man his hand. He turned. He mounted his white horse.

He trotted away to the left, across the hard clods of autumn fields, followed by his suite. The wind carried to his ears a remark made by Captain Kaunitz to a friend riding at his side: "I couldn't make out a word that Jew was saying." The Emperor turned in his saddle. "Well, my dear Kaunitz," he said, "he was speaking only to me." And he rode on.

He knew nothing of the purpose of these maneuvers. He knew only that Reds were fighting Blues. He made them explain all the details. "I see, I see," he kept repeating. It amused him to make them think he was trying to understand and couldn't. Fools, he thought. He shook his head. But people thought his head was shaking because he was so old. "I see, I see," said the Emperor over and over again. Operations were already fairly far advanced. The Blues' left wing, which stood that day about two and a half miles from the village of Z., had been in retreat for two days before the cavalry thrust of its Red opponents. The center held the ground surrounding P.—hilly country, hard to attack, easy to hold, but exposed to the danger of being surrounded if the Reds once succeeded, as today they would make every effort to, in cutting off the Blues' two wings from their center. But though their left was in retreat, the Blues' right was not giving way; on the contrary, it continued slowly to advance, showing at the same time a tendency to extend at last, and envelop the enemy. This the Emperor thought was a very banal kind of situation. Had he been commanding the Reds, he would have tried to entice this impetuous drive of Blues by retreating further and further, and attempting to make them concentrate their strength on the outer extremity of his lines until at last he could have found an exposed position between their forces and the center. But the Emperor said nothing.

He was distressed by the monstrous fact that Colonel Lugatti from Trieste, vain as, in his unshakable opinion, only Italians can be, had his greatcoat collar cut far too high, higher even than a tunic collar ought to be, and that further, to display his rank, he wore this unspeakable high collar coquettishly open. "Tell me, Colonel," the Emperor asked, "where do you have your greatcoats made? In Milan? Unfortunately, I've forgotten the names of the tailors there." Staff-Colonel Lugatti clicked his heels and buttoned up the collar of his greatcoat. "Now, you might be taken for a

lieutenant," said Francis Joseph. "You look young, yo
know." And he set spurs to his horse and galloped off toward
the hilltop on which, after the line-up of old-fashioned battles,
the generals were posted.

He was resolved, should it take too long, to cut short "the
engagement," since he wanted so much to see the march past.
Francis Ferdinand would never do that. He'd have been sure
to take sides, Blue or Red, start ordering them around and
would, of course, always win. Where was the general nowadays
who would care to defeat the heir to the throne? The Emperor
let his old, pale-blue eyes stray over the faces. A vain lot, he
thought. A few years back it would have annoyed him. But
not today, not today. He did not know exactly how old he was,
but when they stood around him like this he felt he must be
very old indeed. Sometimes it felt as though he were drifting
away from people, off the earth. They all grew smaller and
smaller the longer he looked at them. Their words reached
his ears as if from an immense distance and died again, an
indifferent echo. If somebody had an accident he saw quite
well the efforts they made to break the news as gently as
possible. They didn't know that he could bear anything.
Great sorrows were familiar to his spirit and new ones came
to join the old, like long-expected brothers. He no longer got
so violently angry. He no longer rejoiced too greatly. He no
longer suffered so deeply. Now he got them to cut short the
"engagement" so that the march could begin. Regiments of
every branch of the service drew up on the unending plains,
unfortunately in field-gray, another new-fashioned notion
which was not to the Emperor's taste. Scarlet cavalry breeches
still glowed, above the dry yellow of stubble fields, and broke
through the infantry-drab like fire from the clouds. The
narrow glint of the swords flashed in advance of marching
columns and double columns. Red crosses on white background shone behind the machine-gun divisions. Like ancient
war gods on their heavy wagons, the artillery came rolling
along, and the fine dun and chestnut horses pranced in strong
proud discipline. Through field glasses Francis Joseph saw
the movements of each separate line and for a few minutes
he felt proud of his army, and for a few minutes felt regret at
losing it. For he saw it already dispersed and dashed to pieces,
split up among the many nations of his monarchy. For him

the great golden sun of the Habsburgs was setting—shattered against the primeval basis of the universe into sunballs which, as isolated stars, would be set to shine on independent nations. It'll never suit them to be ruled by me, thought the old man, there's nothing to be done about it, he added to himself. For he was an Austrian.

So, to the consternation of all chiefs, the Emperor descended from his hillock and began inspecting the lines, almost regiment by regiment. He picked out a rank here and there, examined their new haversacks and bread bags, pulled out an occasional tin of food, and wanted to know what it contained, noticed an expressionless face here and there and inquired about the family, occupation, and home of its owner, and scarcely heard some of the answers. Sometimes he stretched out his old hand and patted a lieutenant on the shoulder. Soon he reached the Jaeger battalion in which Trotta was serving.

It was a month since Trotta had left the hospital. He stood at the head of his platoon, pale, thin, and indifferent. But as the Emperor approached him, he began to notice his indifference and regretted it. He felt as if he were shirking a duty. The army no longer meant anything to him, nor did the Supreme War Lord. Lieutenant Trotta was like a man who has lost not only his home but also his homesickness for it. He felt sorry for this white-bearded old man who came inquisitively closer and closer to him, fingering packs and breadsacks and tins of food. The Lieutenant would have welcomed the intoxication which had overcome him on all the festive occasions of his military life at home, on summer Sundays on his father's balcony, at every parade, when he got his commission, or even, only a few months ago, at the Corpus Christi procession in Vienna. Nothing stirred in Lieutenant Trotta as he stood five paces away from his Emperor, nothing except pity for an old man stirred in his thrust-out breast. Major Zoglauer rattled out the official formula. Something about him displeased the Emperor. He had the suspicion that things were not all they should be in the battalion this fellow commanded and he resolved to look more closely into it. He stared attentively at the expressionless faces, pointed to Carl Joseph, and asked, "Is he ill?"

Major Zoglauer related what had happened to Trotta. The name struck Francis Joseph as something at once familiar and annoying and he remembered the incident as it had been reported in the document; while behind it, that long-forgotten incident at the battle of Solferino came to life. He could still plainly see the captain who, in that ridiculous audience, had stubbornly begged to have the patriotic reading lesson suppressed. Reading lesson No. 15! The Emperor recollected the number with all the pleasure he experienced at just such trivial proofs of his "excellent memory". His temper improved visibly. Major Zoglauer seemed less unpleasant.

"I remember your father well," said the Emperor. "He was very unassuming, the hero of Solferino."

"Your Majesty," said the Lieutenant, "it was my grandfather."

The Emperor took a step back, as if pushed aside by the tremendous lapse of time which had suddenly come between himself and this young man. Yes, yes, he could remember the number of a reading lesson but not the monstrous number of years he had lived through. "Oh," he said, "really. So that was your grandfather? I see, I see. And your father's a colonel, isn't he?"

"District Commissioner in W."

"I see, I see. I must remember that," added Francis Joseph as a kind of apology for the slip he had just made.

He stood a little while longer in front of the Lieutenant, but he saw neither Trotta nor the others. He no longer wanted to inspect the lines but would have to continue so that people did not notice how afraid he was of his own age. His eyes looked out again as usual into the distance where the frontiers of eternity are just perceptible. So he did not notice the crystal drop which appeared at the end of his nose and that everyone was staring at in fascination, until it fell at last into his thick silvery mustache, where it remained invisibly embedded.

And everyone felt relieved. And the march past could begin.

PART THREE

Chapter 16

Various significant changes were taking place in the household and life of the District Commissioner. He noted them in rather grim amazement. Small indications which, in fact, struck him as immense, convinced him that all around him the world was changing, and he thought of its destruction and Count Chojnicki's prophecies. He was looking for a new servant. Recommended to him were many younger and obviously worthy men whose records were untarnished. They were men who had done their three years' service in the army and even attained the rank of lance corporal. He took on one or two of them on trial. But he kept none of them. They were called Karl or Franz, Alexander or Joseph, Alois or Christoph. He tried to call them all Jacques; after all, the genuine Jacques had really been called something else and had only assumed his name and had lived his whole long life with honor as Jacques, as many a famous poet has assumed a name under which he has written immortal songs and poems. But after a few days it became obvious that these Aloises, Alexanders, Josephs, and so on did not want to answer to the illustrious name of Jacques. The District Commissioner considered their re-calcitrance not mere offense against obedience and against the established world order; it was also an insult to the irrevocable dead. So it didn't suit them to be called Jacques! These hope-less fools, lacking in experience, intelligence, and discipline. The dead Jacques lived on in his master's memory as a servant of exemplary character, indeed, as the pattern of human excellence. But even more than the recalcitrance of the serving men, the irresponsibility of their former employers and the authorities who had given such miserable specimens favorable references astonished Herr von Trotta. If it had been possible for a certain Alexander Cak to belong to the Social Democratic

Party and yet become a lance corporal in his regiment, then one could despair not only of that regiment alone but of the whole army. Cak was a name he never wished to forget, a name which could be enunciated with a certain amount of spite, so that it sounded as if Cak were being shot if the District Commissioner so much as mentioned him. In the District Commissioner's opinion, the army was the only remaining reliable force in the state. To the District Commissioner the whole world consisted of Czechs, a people he considered to be recalcitrant, obstinate, and stupid, the originators of the concept "nation". There might be many peoples, but certainly no "nations". And over and above this, he received scarcely intelligible remissions and memoranda from the government concerning greater tolerance toward "national minorities," one of the phrases Herr von Trotta loathed most of all. "National minorities" were merely more extensive aggregations of "revolutionary individuals". Indeed, he was surrounded by nothing but revolutionary individuals. He felt them to be multiplying in a positively unnatural, inhuman fashion. It had grown quite clear to the District Commissioner that the loyal element was becoming increasingly infertile. They produced fewer and fewer children, as census statistics, which he occasionally consulted, proved. He could no longer conceal from himself the terrible thought that Providence itself was displeased with the monarchy and since, in the accepted sense of the term, he was a practicing if not a very devout Christian, he inclined to believe that God was punishing the Emperor. Indeed, gradually he gave himself up to all sorts of strange reflections. The dignity he had assumed since the first day of his appointment to W. had certainly aged him at once. Not even when his whiskers were still jet-black would it ever have occurred to anyone to think of Herr von Trotta as a young man. But only now did the inhabitants of the little town of W. begin to say that the District Commissioner was getting old. He had had to relinquish a number of old familiar habits. Since old Jacques's death, for instance, and his own return from the frontier garrison, he had given up his walk before breakfast for fear that one of the many suspect and impermanent individuals who served him might have forgotten to put the mail on the breakfast table or to open the window. He loathed his housekeeper. He had always loathed her, but had managed occasionally to speak to her. Now that Jacques no longer waited at his table the District Commissioner said nothing at all, for the pointed words had really been intended for Jacques's amusement and had, in a sense, been attempts to win his approbation. Only now that the old man was dead, Herr von Trotta realized he had talked solely at Jacques, like an old actor who knows that a seasoned admirer of his art is sitting in the stalls. And if he had always eaten quickly, now he tried to leave the table after the first few mouthfuls. It seemed indecent to enjoy garnished roasts while worms were devouring old Jacques in his grave. And even if he did occasionally direct his gaze upward, in the hope, and with a kind of inborn devoutness, that the dead man was in heaven and able to see him, all the District Commissioner ever saw was the familiar ceiling of his room. For simple faith had deserted him long ago and his senses no longer obeyed the dictates of his heart. It was all very depressing.

Sometimes on weekdays the District Commissioner even forgot to go to his office. It might, for instance, happen that on a Thursday he would put on his black Sunday coat to go to church, and it was not until he was outside that he noticed from various unmistakable indications of weekday activities that it was not Sunday, and he turned back and changed into his ordinary suit. On the other hand, he sometimes forgot to go to church on Sunday, though he stayed in bed later than usual and did not remember that it was Sunday until Nechwal's band appeared under his balcony. There was garnished roast, as on every Sunday, and afterward the bandmaster came for coffee. They sat in the study. They smoked cheroots. Bandmaster Nechwal, too, was looking older. Soon he would retire. He went less frequently to Vienna and such stories as he still had to tell sounded stale even to Herr von Trotta. He still missed their point but knew the sound of them, just as he knew the look of so many people whose names he nevertheless did not know.

"How are you all?" Herr von Trotta asked.

"Thank you, all very fit."

"Your wife?"

"Very well indeed, thank you."

"And the children?" For the District Commissioner still did not know whether Nechwal had sons or daughters and continued the habit of twenty years by still prudently inquiring after "the children".

"My eldest boy is a lieutenant," Nechwal answered.

"In the infantry, of course?" said Herr von Trotta, as was his custom, and remembered for a moment that his own son now served with the Jaeger and not with the cavalry.

"Oh yes, the infantry," said Nechwal. "He'll be coming to stay with us soon. I hope you will allow me to introduce him to you."

"Please do, please do. I shall be delighted," said the District Commissioner.

One day the young Nechwal came to call. He was serving in the Deutschmeister regiment, had had his commission for a year and looked, thought Herr von Trotta, "like a fiddler".

"He's so like you," said Herr von Trotta, "almost the image," though really the young Nechwal took after his mother more than the bandmaster. By "fiddler" the District Commissioner meant a certain cool, unmistakable self-possession; a short blunt nose, over a little, twiddling blond mustache, like a pair of curly brackets pulled horizontal; well-shaped doll-like little ears which might have been made of china; and neat, fair hair parted down the center. "He's a jolly-looking fellow," said Herr von Trotta to Herr Nechwal. "And how do you like the service?" he asked the young man.

"As a matter of fact, District Commissioner," replied the bandmaster's son, "I find it rather boring."

"Boring! In Vienna?" asked Herr von Trotta.

"Yes," young Nechwal said. "You see, District Commissioner, if you're serving in some little garrison, you never notice you haven't got any money."

The District Commissioner felt insulted. It was such shocking form to mention money. And he was afraid that young Nechwal might be hinting at Carl Joseph's better financial position. "Though my son serves on the frontier," said Herr von Trotta, "he's always managed very well. In the cavalry, too." He stressed it. For the first time ever he felt embarrassed that his son had left the Uhlans. People like Nechwal would certainly not crop up in the cavalry. And the thought that this bandmaster's son might imagine himself in any way young Trotta's equal caused the District Commissioner almost physical distress. He decided to show up this "fiddler". He scented sedition. The boy's nose had a kind of Czech twist to it. "Do you like serving?" asked the District Commissioner.

"As a matter of fact," said Lieutenant Nechwal, "I can think of jobs I should enjoy more."

"How's that? Enjoy more?"

"A more useful job," said young Nechwal.

"Isn't it useful to fight for your country?" asked Herr von Trotta. "Assuming, of course, that one has a bent for the useful." It was obvious that he gave sarcastic emphasis to the word "useful".

"But we don't fight," said the Lieutenant. He narrowed his eyes until they vanished almost completely, and in a way which seemed quite insufferable to the District Commissioner. The Lieutenant's upper lip curled over shining gums so that his little mustache touched his nose—and the nose, Herr von Trotta thought, was like the broad snout of some animal. A thoroughly revolting fellow, thought the District Commissioner. "Times have changed," young Nechwal continued. "All these different nations won't hang together for long."

"Indeed?" said the District Commissioner. "And how do you come to know all this, Lieutenant?" Yet as he spoke, the District Commissioner knew quite well that his scorn was pointless, that he was a veteran drawing his powerless sword against the enemy.

"Everyone knows it," the boy said, "and says it."

"Says it?" repeated Herr von Trotta. "Do your brother officers say such things?"

"Oh yes, they do."

The District Commissioner said no more. He suddenly felt that he was standing on a high mountain peak and opposite him stood Lieutenant Nechwal in a deep valley. He was very small, Lieutenant Nechwal. But though he was so small and stood so low, he was right all the same. The world was no longer the old world. It was about to end. And it seemed quite in order that an hour before the end of the world the valleys should prevail against the summits, the young against the old, the foolish against the reasonable. So the District Commissioner was silent. It was a summer Sunday afternoon. The yellow Venetian blinds filtered the golden sunlight into the study. The clock ticked. Flies buzzed. The District Commissioner remembered that summer's day on which his son Carl Joseph had come home to him in the uniform of a lieutenant of the cavalry. How long ago was that? A few years. But in those few years it seemed to the District Commissioner that things had moved too fast. As though the sun had risen and set twice a day and every week had two Sundays and every month sixty days. So that the years had all been double years. And Herr von Trotta felt himself betrayed, as it were, by time, though it had offered him double measure. It was as if eternity had delivered spurious years in duplicate, instead of genuine ones of twelve months. And although he despised the lieutenant down there, opposite him deep down in his miserable valley, he did not trust the peak on which he stood. Oh, it was most unjust. Unjust! Unjust! For the first time in his life the District Commissioner felt himself to be the victim of an injustice.

He wanted Dr Skowronnek, the man with whom he had been playing chess every afternoon for the past few months. A regular game of chess was one of the changes that had occurred in the District Commissioner's life. He had long known Dr Skowronnek, but no more or less than any other regular patron of the café. One afternoon they had found themselves sitting face to face, each half covered by a voluminously spread newspaper. As if at a word of command, they had put down their papers at the same instant and their eyes had met. At the same instant they realized that they had both been reading the same item of news. It was an account of a summer fair in Hietzig where a butcher, Alois Schinagel, had, thanks to his supernatural gluttony, remained victor in a meat-eating contest and had been awarded the gold medal of the Hietzig Champion Eaters' Association. The eyes of both men had simultaneously said, We both enjoy meat, but what an idiotic, newfangled notion to award people gold medals for that sort of thing. Whether there is love at first sight has never really been established. But friendship, friendship at first sight, between middle-aged gentlemen, of that there can be no doubt. Over the edges of his rimless pince-nez, Dr Skowronnek gazed at the Commissioner. As he did so, Herr von Trotta took off his own. He raised his pince-nez to the doctor. The doctor came over to his table.

"Do you play chess?"

"Yes, I do," said the District Commissioner.

They never needed to arrange to meet. Every afternoon they

226

met at the same time. They arrived simultaneously, their habits seemed to be governed by a general harmony. During the game they scarcely spoke. Nor did they feel the need for conversation. Sometimes their bony fingers met on the narrow board, like people in a little square, jerked away and returned home again. But slight as these encounters were, the fingers, as if endowed with eyes and ears, perceived everything about each other and the men to whom they belonged. When Dr Skowronnek's fingers had brushed a few times against the District Commissioner's, it was as though they had known each other for many years and that they had no secrets from each other. And so one day, gentle conversation began to surround their game and remarks about the weather, the world, politics, and people floated over their hands, which had long been familiar with each other. A remarkable man, the District Commissioner reflected on Dr Skowronnek. An extraordinarily sensitive person, thought Dr Skowronnek about the District Commissioner.

For most of the year Dr Skowronnek had nothing to do. He worked four months out of every twelve as a spa physician in Franzensbad and his world view was based solely on the confidences of his women patients. For the women told him everything that worried them and there was nothing which did not worry them. Their health suffered from their husbands' profession as well as from their lack of attention; it suffered from the general malaise of the times, from the cost of living, political crises, the constant menace of war, from the newspapers their husbands insisted on subscribing to, from the unfaithfulness of lovers, from the indifference of men but also from their jealousy. So Dr Skowronnek gained insight into many different kinds of people, and their private lives. He knew their kitchens, their bedrooms, their inclinations, passions, and failings. And since he believed only three-quarters of all the ladies told him, in the course of time he achieved an excellent knowledge of the world, of more use to him than his medical science. Even when he was talking to men, he smiled the skeptical yet benevolent smile of a man who is not surprised by anything he hears. A sort of distancing kindness shone on his puckered-up little face. And indeed, he liked people as much as he despised them.

Had Herr von Trotta's simple mind gauged this sly kindness

in Dr Skowronnek? Be that as it may, he began to trust and esteem him as he had not trusted anyone apart from Moser, the companion of his youth. "Have you been here long, in our town, Herr Doktor?" he asked.

"Ever since I was born," said Skowronnek.

"What a pity," answered the District Commissioner ,"what a pity that we are only just getting to know each other."

"I've known you for a long time, District Commissioner."

"And I've seen you about," replied Herr von Trotta.

"Your son was here once, a few years ago."

"Yes," said the District Commissioner. "Yes, I remember."

He thought of the afternoon when Carl Joseph had come with his letters to the dead Frau Slama. A wet afternoon. In summer. It had been raining. The boy stood at the bar drinking bad cognac.

"He's changed his regiment now," said Herr von Trotta. "He's serving at B. on the frontier, with the Jaeger."

"He must be a source of great pleasure to you," said Dr Skowronnek. He meant "worry".

"Yes," said the District Commissioner. "Of course." He got up quickly and left the doctor.

For some time now he had considered confiding all his worries to Dr Skowronnek. He was getting old, he needed a listener. Every afternoon he made up his mind anew to speak to Dr Skowronnek. But he never could manage to formulate a phrase which might have led to confidences. Every day Dr Skowronnek sat expecting it. He could feel the time was ripe for the District Commissioner to speak to him.

For several weeks Herr von Trotta had been carrying a letter from his son in his breast pocket. It was up to him to reply to it, but Herr von Trotta could not bring himself to write an answer. And so the letter grew heavier and heavier, a veritable load in his pocket, until it began to weigh on his heart. For Carl Joseph had written to tell him that he was thinking of leaving the army. It came at the very beginning of the letter. "I'm thinking of leaving the army. . . ." As soon as the District Commissioner read this, he had stopped to glance down at the signature to make quite sure Carl Joseph had written it. Then he had taken off his reading glasses and laid them aside, and the letter with them. He had sat back in his chair. He was in the office. The day's official correspondence had not been opened. They might all have been the most urgent letters, demanding immediate attention, but Carl Joseph's few opening words had disposed, in the most unsatisfactory manner, of the official business of the day. On no other day in all his life had the District Commissioner's official duties been influenced by personal factors. And, however modest and humble a servant of the state he might be, his son's contemplating leaving the army had much the same effect on Herr von Trotta as if the whole of the Imperial and Royal forces had informed him of their decision to disband. Everything, everything in the world seemed to have lost its meaning. The end of the world was at hand.

When at last, in spite of it all, the District Commissioner set himself to deal with the official correspondence, it was with the sensation of discharging some vain, anonymous act of heroism of the kind performed by wireless operators on sinking ships. It was a full half hour before he finished his son's letter. And the District Commissioner replied as follows:

My dear Son,
    Your letter has shaken me profoundly. I must wait a little before letting you know my final decision.
                                                    Your Father

Carl Joseph had never answered this letter. Indeed, his usual letters home ceased, so that for some time now the District Commissioner had had no news at all of his son. He hoped each morning for a letter, the old man, knowing all the while that none would come. Every morning he felt not as if an expected letter were missing but as if the day had brought its expected and dreaded silence. His son kept silent. But his father could hear these silences. Each morning it was as if, all over again, his son were refusing to obey him. And the longer Carl Joseph's letters failed to arrive, the harder it became for the District Commissioner to write the expected answer. And though first it had seemed almost to go without saying that he should simply write forbidding him to leave the army, gradually he began to feel that he no longer had any right to forbid him anything. He was considerably discouraged, the District Commissioner. His whiskers grew more and more silvery. His temples were completely white. His head sometimes sagged upon his chest until his whiskers drooped on the starched shirt front. He would fall asleep, suddenly, in his chair, wake with a start a few minutes later, and imagine he had slept for hours. Particularly since he had given up some of his old habits, he had lost his exact sense of the passing of time. For the hours and days had existed only in order to maintain these habits, and now they were like empty vessels which could no longer be filled and which needed no attention. Only for his chess in the afternoons did the District Commissioner appear punctually.

One day he received a surprising visit. He was sitting over papers in his office when he suddenly heard the well-known raucous voice of his old friend Moser and the office porter's futile attempts to keep him at bay. The District Commissioner rang the bell and had the professor brought in.

"A good day to you, sir," said Moser. Wearing no overcoat and carrying his portfolio, Moser in his slouch hat did not have the appearance of a man come straight from a railway station after a long journey. He might simply have stepped across the road. And the District Commissioner was seized with the frightening thought that Moser had decided to settle in W. The painter went back to the door, turned the key, and said, "Just so that no one disturbs us, my dear fellow. It might injure your career." Then, with slow, broad strides he went up to the desk, embraced the Commissioner and imprinted a resonant kiss on his bald head. That done, he sank into the armchair next to the desk, laid his hat and portfolio on the floor in front of his feet, and said no more.

Herr von Trotta was equally silent. He knew now why Moser had come to see him. For three months now he had sent him no money. "You must excuse me," said Herr von Trotta. "You shall have it at once. You really must excuse me. I've been so worried recently."

"I can imagine," said Moser. "That son of yours is expensive. I see him every other week in Vienna. Seems to be having a good time, our lieutenant."

The District Commissioner rose. His hand went to his breast pocket. He felt Carl Joseph's letter. He went to the window. He asked, with his back to Moser, his eyes on the old chestnut trees in the park, "Have you spoken to him?"

"We have a drink together whenever we meet," said Moser. "He's very generous, your son."

"I see," echoed Herr von Trotta. "He's very generous." He hurried back to the desk, pulled out a drawer, counted some notes, pulled a few out, and gave them to the painter. Moser stowed the money away in his hat, between the worn sweatband and the felt, and got up to go. "One moment," said the District Commissioner. He went to the door, unlocked it, and said to the attendant. "Show the Herr Professor the way to the station. He's going to Vienna. His train is due in an hour."

"Your servant," Moser said with a bow. The District Commissioner waited a few minutes, then he took his hat and stick and went to the café.

He reached it a few minutes late. Dr Skowronnek was already at their table, and had set out the chessmen on the board. Herr von Trotta sat down.

"White or black?" asked Skowronnek.

"I won't play today," said the District Commissioner. He sent for a cognac, drank it, and began. "Doctor, I want to confide in you about something."

"Please do," said Skowronnek.

"It's about my son," began the District Commissioner. And so, in his official flat, somewhat nasal voice, he spoke of his worries as if he were speaking of official matters to an official adviser. His worries were classified, so to speak, under the headings "main" and "subsidiary". Point by point, in brief paragraphs, he related to Dr Skowronnek the story of his father, of himself, and of his son. When he had finished, they found themselves alone in the café. The greenish gas jets were already hissing monotonously in the billiard room above empty tables.

"And so, there it is," concluded the District Commissioner.

There was a long silence between the two men. The District Commissioner dared not look at Dr Skowronnek. And Dr Skowronnek dared not look at the District Commissioner. They sat with eyes cast down as if they had found each other in a disreputable action.

Skowronnek said at last, "Perhaps there's a woman behind it? Why should your son want to be in Vienna so often?"

Indeed, the District Commissioner would never have thought of a woman. Now he himself could not imagine how he had failed to think of something so obvious. Everything, though to be sure it did not amount to much, that he had ever heard of the fatal influence which women exert over young men suddenly crowded his mind, and at the same time liberated his heart. If nothing worse than a woman had made Carl Joseph decide to leave the army, the thing, though bad, and possibly hard to remedy, was at least normal and intelligible, and the end of the world no longer a matter of sinister, hidden forces against which nothing could avail. A woman, he thought. But no. He had heard nothing of any woman. And so he said in his official style, "I've heard no rumors of any female."

"Female?" repeated Dr Skowronnek and smiled. "It might conceivably be a lady."

"Do you mean," said Herr von Trotta, "that my son may be thinking seriously of marriage?"

"Not necessarily that," said Dr Skowronnek. "Even ladies don't have to be married." He realized that the District Commissioner had one of those simple minds which, so to speak, needed to be sent to school. And he decided to handle him like a child about to learn its mother tongue. He said, "Well, let's not worry about the ladies. Really, they aren't so very important. For one reason or another, your son doesn't want to stay in the army. And I can understand it."

"You can understand it?"

"Certainly. No young officer in our army can feel really satisfied with his profession if he thinks at all. He feels that war is his only chance, and yet he knows very well that war means the end of the monarchy."

"The end of the monarchy?"

"Yes, Herr von Trotta, the end. I'm sorry. Let your son do as he wishes. He may be better suited to some other profession."

"Some other profession . . ." echoed Herr von Trotta. "Some other profession," he said again. There followed a long silence. Then, for the third time, the District Commissioner said, "Some other profession." He tried to make himself familiar with these words, but they remained as foreign to him as the expressions "revolutionary" and "national minority". And it occurred to the District Commissioner that he would not have to wait long for the end of the world. He thumped his bony fist on the table, the round cuff clattered, the green lamp above the little table shook a little and he asked, "What other profession, Doctor?"

"He might perhaps," said Dr Skowronnek, "be able to get a job on the railways."

The next moment the District Commissioner had an image of his son in the uniform of a ticket collector, with a clipper in his hand to punch the tickets. The phrase "be able to get a job" sent dread into his aged heart. He was cold. "I see. You think . . ."

"That's all I can think of," said Dr Skowronnek. And since now the District Commissioner was getting up, he too got up and said, "Let me come with you."

They walked through the park. It was raining. The District Commissioner did not open his umbrella. Now and again from thick masses of leaves heavy drops splashed down on his shoulders and his hard hat. It was dark and quiet. Each time they came to one of the rare lamps whose silver heads stood shrouded in dark foliage, the two men bent their heads. When they came to the park gates they hesitated for a moment. Dr Skowronnek said suddenly, "Good-by, Commissioner." And Herr von Trotta crossed the street alone to the massive arched doorway of the District Commissioner's Residence.

On the stairs he ran into his housekeeper. "I shall not be eating today, dear lady," he said to her, and went on quickly. He would have liked to climb them two at a time, but felt embarrassed, and walked in the usual dignified manner into the office. For the first time since he had been in charge of the District he sat in his office in the evening. He lit the lamp with the green shade which was as a rule lit only on winter afternoons. The windows were open. Rain was drumming hard against the tin sills. Herr von Trotta pulled a sheet of yellowish foolscap from his drawer and wrote:

Dear Son
I have decided, on mature reflection, to allow you to determine your own future. I ask you only to let me know what you decide.
Your Father

Herr von Trotta sat for a long time in front of his letter. He read the sentences a few times over. They sounded like his last will and testament. Previously, it would never have occurred to him to consider his functions as a father more important than his official duties. But now that by writing this short letter he had ceased to be responsible for his son, it

233

seemed to him that his life had little meaning, that now he must also cease to serve the state. What he had just done was not dishonorable, and yet he felt as if he had insulted himself. He left the office, the letter in his hand, and went to the study. Here he lit every lamp—the standard lamp in the corner, the hanging lamp on the ceiling—and he stood beneath the portrait of the hero of Solferino. He could not see his father's face clearly. The portrait disintegrated into a hundred oily highlights and streaks of paint; the mouth was a faint red line, the eyes two black fragments of coal. The District Commissioner climbed on a chair (he had not stood on a chair since he had been a boy), held his pince-nez in front of his eyes, stretched, and stood on tiptoe. He just managed to make out Moser's signature down in the right-hand corner of the portrait. With some difficulty he got down, stifled a sigh, retreated backward, to the opposite wall, bumping himself violently and painfully on the edge of a table, and began to examine the portrait from a distance. He extinguished the ceiling lamp. And in the profound dusk he felt he could see his father's face glow with life. It advanced upon him and retreated, seemed to recede into the wall, to be staring in through an open window, from distances impossible to gauge. Herr von Trotta felt a great exhaustion. He pulled up an armchair face to face with it, sat down, and undid his waistcoat. He could hear the diminishing drops of the ceasing rain beat a hard irregular rhythm against the windowpanes, and from time to time he heard the wind rustling the old chestnut trees opposite. He closed his eyes. He fell asleep, still holding his letter in its envelope, his hand motionless over the arm of the chair.

When he woke, full daylight was streaming in through the large rounded study windows. The District Commissioner saw first the portrait of the hero of Solferino, then felt the letter in his hand, saw the address, read his son's name, and got up, sighing. His shirtfront was crumpled; the wide, claret-colored tie with white spots had worked itself to the left; and for the first time since he had worn trousers, Herr von Trotta noticed horizontal creases in those he had slept in. He looked at himself in the mirror for a while. And he saw that his whiskers had a ragged look, that a few miserable gray hairs curled on his bald head, and that his bushy eyebrows were as devastated as if a minute storm had swept through them. The District Commissioner glanced at the clock. And since his barber was almost due, he hastened to get undressed and quickly slip into bed in order to feign a normal morning. Still he kept hold of the letter. It was in his hand all the time he was being soaped and shaved and, later, when he was washing, the letter lay on the slab beside the basin. Not until he sat down to breakfast did Herr von Trotta give the letter to the office porter with instructions that it was to go by the next government mail.

He went to work as usual. And no one would have had cause to remark that Herr von Trotta had lost his faith. The devotion with which he disposed of the day's business was not less meticulous than on other days. But it was devotion of a totally different order. It was merely a devotion of the hands, the eyes, even the pince-nez. And Herr von Trotta was like a virtuoso in whose soul the fires of genius are all burnt out, but whose fingers, thanks to the skill of years of habit, strike the right notes with dead precision. Still, as has been said, no one noticed.

Sergeant-Major Slama came in the afternoon as usual. "Tell me, my dear Slama," Herr von Trotta asked him, "did you ever marry again?" He did not know himself why he asked the question today and why the private life of the Sergeant-Major should suddenly concern him.

"No, Herr Baron," said Slama. "And I never intend to."

"Ah, you're right there," said Herr von Trotta, although he could have given no good reason why the Sergeant-Major was right in deciding not to remarry.

It was the time at which he went every day to the café and he set out as usual. The chessboard was already on their table. Dr Skowronnek and he arrived together. "Black or white, Commissioner?" asked the doctor, as every day.

"It doesn't matter," said the District Commissioner, and they began to play. Herr von Trotta played with close attention, almost with devotion, and he won.

"You're turning into quite a chess champion," said Skowronnek.

The District Commissioner felt truly flattered. "I might have become one, perhaps," he replied. And he thought it would have been better if he had, that everything would have been better some other way. "By the way," he said after a time, "I've written to tell my son he must do as he likes."

"I'm sure you're right," said Dr Skowronnek. "One can't make oneself responsible. No human being can be responsible for another."

"My father was for me," said the District Commissioner, "and my grandfather for my father."

"It was different in those days," answered Skowronnek. "Not even the Emperor is responsible today for his monarchy. It almost looks as if God were refusing to be responsible for the world. It was easier in those days. It was all so certain. Every stone lay in its proper place. The streets of life were decently paved. The houses were all roofed. But now, Commissioner! Now the paving stones are all lying around haphazardly in dangerous little heaps all over the street, the roofs have holes in them, so that the rain pours into the houses, and everyone has to find out for himself which street he really wants to go down, and what kind of house he is trying to get into. When your father said you'd never make a landowner and told you to become a civil servant he was right. You've become a model civil servant. But you were wrong to put your son into the army. He is not a model soldier."

"Yes, yes," Herr von Trotta agreed.

"So it's better to let things slide. When my children refuse to obey me, I only do my best not to look undignified. It's all I can do. Sometimes I go and look at them when they're asleep. Their faces are like the faces of strangers. I scarcely recognize them. And I realize that they really are strangers. They belong to a time which is yet to come, which I shall not see. My children are still quite young. One is eight, the other ten, and when they're asleep they have rosy round faces. And yet there is much that is dreadful in their sleeping faces. I sometimes feel it's the cruelty of the age to which they belong. It's the future which comes to them in their sleep. I don't want to have to live in it."

"Yes," said the District Commissioner, "yes."

They played a second game of chess, but this time Herr von Trotta lost. "I shan't be a champion," he said mildly, reconciled to his failings. Today, also, they sat on late. Those voices of the quiet greenish gas globes were hissing and the café was empty. Again they went back through the park. This time it was a radiant evening and the usual strollers passed them. They talked of the rainy summer and how lovely it had been last year, and said that the winter would be a hard one. Skowronnek crossed the street with Herr von Trotta. They stood in the doorway of the Residence.

"You were quite right," Dr Skowronnek said, "to send your son that letter, Commissioner."

"Yes, yes," agreed Herr von Trotta. He went into dinner to dispose quickly and silently of half a fowl with salad. His housekeeper eyed him covertly, rather anxiously. Now that Jacques was dead, she passed the plates herself. She left the dining room before him with a little curtsy of the kind she had executed thirty years ago as a little girl in front of her headmaster. The District Commissioner waved her away as one shoos off a fly. Then he got up and went to bed. He felt tired, almost ill; in his mind the previous day had become as unreal as a distant dream, but its grief still weighed upon his limbs.

He fell quietly asleep, believing that now the worst was behind him. He did not know, old Herr von Trotta, that fate spun bitter grief for him as he slept. He was old and tired, death was ready for him, but life still refused to let him go. Like a cruel host, life kept him at the table because he had not drunk to the dregs the bitter cup that stood prepared for him.

Chapter 17

No, the District Commissioner had not drunk to the dregs the bitter cup that stood prepared for him. Carl Joseph received his father's letter too late—that is, at a time when he had long since made up his mind to answer no more letters and to write none. As for Frau von Taussig, she sent him wires. Her telegrams reached him once a fortnight, deft little swallows, sent to call him to come to her. Then Carl Joseph dashed to his wardrobe, took out his gray suit of civilian clothes—his better, more important, and secret existence—and changed. Immediately he felt at home in the world he was about to go to; he forgot his army life.

Captain Jedlicek of the First Jaeger had replaced Captain Wagner in the battalion, a decent fellow of gigantic physical proportions, massive, merry, and mild, like all giants, and open to all fair speaking. What a man! They knew as soon as he arrived that their tricks would never get the better of him; and that he was stronger than the frontier. You could rely on him. He broke all military rules in such a way that it looked as though he had overturned them. He was the sort of man who could easily have invented a whole new set of rules and had them accepted and carried out. He spent vast sums of money, but money came flowing in to him from all sides. The others lent it to him, or let him have their signatures, pawned their rings and watches for him, wrote home on his behalf to fathers and aunts. Yet not precisely because they loved him. Love would have brought them closer to its object, and Jedlicek seemed not to care for intimacies. On sheer physical grounds it would not have been easy. His height, his girth, the force of his personality were enought to keep them all at such a distance that he never found it hard to be good-tempered. "You go along," he said to Trotta. "I'll be responsible." He accepted the responsibility. And he could shoulder it. And every week he needed money. Lieutenant Trotta got it from Kapturak.

Lieutenant Trotta himself needed funds. It seemed inadequate to go to Frau von Taussig without money. It would have been like arriving unarmed at an armed camp. What foolhardiness! Gradually he stepped up his requirements and the sums he took with him, though he always returned reduced to the very last penny, and resolved again and again to take more next time. Sometimes he tried to account for the money he spent. But he never succeeded in recollecting individual items, and the laws of simple addition often failed him. He could not keep accounts. The little notebooks in his pocket could bear witness to his disconsolate efforts to keep things in order. Endless columns of figures covered each page. But they became confused and intermingled, he lost control of them, they galloped away from under his eyes, to return the next minute transformed, quite unrecognizable. Nor did he understand the rates of interest. What he lent disappeared behind what he owed like a hill behind a mountain. Nor did he understand Kapturak's calculations. And though he did not trust Kapturak's honesty, he mistrusted his own mathematics even more. In the end, every figure bored him. Once and for all, with the desperate courage of impotence, he relinquished attempts at calculations.

He owed Kapturak and Brodnitzer six thousand kronen. This sum seemed immense even to him with his poor head for figures, when he compared it with his monthly pay (and even of that a third was regularly deducted). But gradually he accustomed himself to thinking of the figure six thousand as a powerful but familiar enemy. In hopeful moments it even seemed to him that the sum was diminishing and losing its power. On bad days it swelled and gained new strength.

He went to Vienna to Frau von Taussig. For weeks he had undertaken these brief fugitive visits like sinful pilgrimages. And like the pious pilgrims who enjoy their pilgrimage for its own sake, making a distraction, even an adventure of it, Lieutenant Trotta associated the goal of his pilgrimage with its setting, with his longing for the free life he imagined it to be, with the civilian clothes he put on, and with the charm of the forbidden. He loved his journeys. He loved the ten minutes' drive in a closed cab to the station during which he imagined himself unrecognized. He loved the feel of the borrowed hundred-kronen notes in his pocket, his for today and tomorrow, his alone. No one could see that they were borrowed and

239

already beginning to grow and swell in Kapturak's ledgers. He loved the civilian anonymity in which he passed through and left the Nordbahnhof in Vienna. No one recognized him. Officers and privates passed him by. He neither saluted nor took salutes. Sometimes his arm raised itself of its own accord for the military salute. Quickly he remembered his civilian clothes and let it drop again. His waistcoat was a source of childish joy. His fingers would keep wandering through the pockets for which he had no use. In vanity they caressed the knot of his tie above his waistcoat; it was the only one he owned, Frau von Taussig had given it to him. In spite of countless efforts, he could never manage to tie it properly. The dullest detective would have known Herr Trotta for an officer in civilian clothes at first glance.

Frau von Taussig stood waiting on the platform. Twenty years ago (she thought it was fifteen, for she had denied her age for so long that now she was certain the years had passed her by uncompleted), twenty years ago she had stood just as today waiting at the Nordbahnhof for a lieutenant, though he had been in the cavalry. She stepped onto the platform as into a rejuvenating bath. She plunged into the acrid savor of coal dust, the steam, the screech of shunting engines, the insistent clanging of signal bells. She wore a short traveling veil. She imagined it had been the fashion fifteen years ago. Really it was twenty-five years ago, not even twenty. She loved waiting on the platform. She loved the moment when the train came roaring in and she caught sight of Trotta's absurd little dark-green hat at the carriage window, his adorable perplexed young face. For she made Carl Joseph younger, like herself, more foolish and naïve, just like herself. She opened her arms to receive him the instant his foot was on the platform, just as she had opened them fifteen, that is twenty, years ago. Out of the face she was wearing today shone the young rosy, unwrinkled one she had worn twenty, that is fifteen, years ago: a girl's face, sweet and rather hot. Around her throat, its skin already creased in two deep lines, she had hung that thin and childish gold chain which twenty (i.e. fifteen) years ago had been her only ornament. She rode, just as she had driven fifteen (i.e. twenty) years ago, with the Lieutenant by her side, to one of those small hotels in which stolen love blossoms in little creaking heavens, in poorly furnished heavens, paid for by the hour.

Then followed their walks: those delicious quarters of an hour beneath the young green of the Wienerwald, sudden little tempests of the blood. Their evenings in the rosy twilight of opera boxes, behind drawn curtains: caresses well known, but still unexpected, for which the experienced yet unsuspecting flesh waited. The ear was familiar with the music heard many times, but the eye was familiar with only fragments of the scenes. For Frau von Taussig had preferred always to sit behind the curtains of her box or to keep her eyes shut at the opera. Caresses born of these sounds, entrusted by the orchestra to the man's hands, ran like ice and fire along her skin—long-desired, eternally youthful handmaidens, gift bearers—often before received, yet forgotten, so that they seemed only to to have been dreamt of. Quiet restaurants opened to them, quiet dinners began in corners where the wine they drank seemed also to have grown, ripened by the love which shone here eternally through the darkness. Then came their partings, their last embraces in the afternoon, hurried on by the ruthless watch on the bedside table, yet accompanied by, and already full of, the joys of their next encounter. Then the rush to catch the train, the very last kiss at the carriage door, the hope, relinquished always at the very last moment, of traveling back together.

Tired but sated with all the sweets of love, the joys of the world, Lieutenant Trotta arrived back at his garrison. His servant, Onufrij, had his uniform ready for him. He changed in the back room of the restaurant and drove to the barracks. He went to the company office. Everything in order. Nothing unusual had occurred. Captain Jedlicek was as pleased with life, as merry, exuberant, and fit as ever. Lieutenant Trotta felt relieved and at the same time disappointed. In a secret corner of his heart he had been hoping for a catastrophe which would have made continued service in the army impossible for him. He would have gone straight back to Vienna. But nothing had occurred. And so there would be twelve more days to wait, imprisoned by the four walls of the barrack yard, in the desolate little streets of this town. He glanced at the dummy targets around the walls of the barrack grounds. Little blue men, riddled with shot and repainted, they looked like a row of malicious dwarfs to the Lieutenant, the household spirits of these barracks, threatening him with the very weapons that had pierced them, targets no longer, but dangerous marksmen. As soon as he had reached the Hotel Brodnitzer, he entered his bare room and flung himself down on the iron bedstead. He resolved not to return to the garrison from his next leave.

But he was not the man to carry out this resolution and he knew it. And so, in fact, he lived in the expectation of some unlooked-for stroke of luck that might one day fall from the skies and set him free from the barracks for good: to set him free both from the barracks and from the necessity of having to leave them of his own free will. He could take no other step towards freeing himself except to stop writing to his father and to leave unopened the last few letters that had arrived from him, with a vague intention of opening them some other time. Some other time.

The twelve days went by. He opened his wardrobe, looked at his civilian clothes, and waited for her telegram to come. Usually it came to him at dusk, shortly before nightfall like a homing bird. But today it did not come, not even when dusk had turned into night. The Lieutenant would not turn on any lights, he did not want to acknowledge the night. Open-eyed, fully dressed, he lay on his bed. All the familiar sounds of spring wafted through the open window: the deep-throated noise of the frogs and, above it, its high-pitched, clearer reverberation, the chirping of crickets. This was broken at intervals by the distant call of a night jay and the songs of boys and girls in the frontier village. At last the telegram arrived. It informed the Lieutenant that he could not come this time. Frau Taussig had been called away to her husband. She would soon be back but was not sure when. The message ended with a "thousand kisses." The number offended the Lieutenant. She ought not to have been miserly, he thought; she could just as well have wired a hundred thousand. It occurred to him that he owed six thousand kronen. Compared with them, a thousand kisses seemed inadequate. He got up from the bed to close the wardrobe door. There, neat and straight, a well-pressed corpse, dangled the free, civilian Trotta. The wardrobe door slammed shut. A coffin, dust to dust.

He opened the door into the passage. Onufrij was always there, silent or softly humming or holding his mouth organ against his lips, his hands around it to muffle the sound. Sometimes he sat on a chair, sometimes he squatted in the threshold.

He could have left the army a year ago. He stayed on voluntarily. His village, Burdlaki, was in the neighbourhood. Whenever the Lieutenant went away, Onufrij would go home to his village. He took a cherrywood stick and a white handkerchief with blue flowers into which he wrapped mysterious objects, slung the bundle onto the end of his stick, shouldered it, accompanied the Lieutenant to the station, waited until the train had left the platform, stood at attention and saluted, even if Trotta was not looking at him out of the carriage window. Then he began to walk to Burdlaki, along the narrow path through the swamp between the willows, the one safe path on which there was no danger of being sucked in. Onufrij was back in good time to meet Trotta. And he sat down outside Trotta's door again, silent or humming, or playing the mouth organ between his hands.

The Lieutenant opened the door into the passage. "You can't go to Burdlaki this time. I'm not going away."

"Right, Lieutenant." Onufrij stood up in the whitewashed passage, a stiff, straight dark-blue streak.

"You're to stop here," repeated Trotta. He thought Onufrij had not understood him.

But Onufrij only repeated, "Right, sir," and, as though to prove that he understood more than was credited him, he went downstairs and came back with a bottle of Ninety Percent.

Trotta drank. The bare room became more tolerable. The unshaded electric blub on its twisted wire with swarming moths around it, shaken by the night breeze, cast dreamy swaying reflections on the shiny, brown surface of the table. Carl Joseph's disappointment gradually mellowed to a comfortable grief. He struck a kind of bargain with his woes. Everything in the world was unutterably sad today, and he, the Lieutenant, was the nucleus of this miserable world. It was for him the frogs croaked so dismally and for him the grief-stricken crickets lamented. For him the spring filled itself with such sweet, gentle melancholy grief; for him the stars stood so unattainably high in the heavens and to him shone their light in such frustrated longing. The infinite grief of the world was in perfect harmony with the suffering universe. Behind the deep blue vault of his sky, God Himself looked down in pity on him. He opened the wardrobe again. There, dead forever, dangled the free Trotta. Beside that free self hung Max Demant's sword, his dear friend's sword. In his trunk lay old Jacques's memento, the petrified root, by the side of the late Frau Slama's letters. On the window ledge lay no fewer than three unopened letters from his father, who might himself be dead by now. Alas, Lieutenant Trotta was not only sorrowful, he was bad, a thoroughly bad character. Carl Joseph returned to the table for another glassful and gulped it down. Out in the passage Onufrij had just begun a new tune on his mouth-organ. It was the well-known song "Oh, our Emperor"— "*Oj nash, cisar, cisarewa.*" Trotta knew the first few words in Ukrainian, not more. He had not succeeded in mastering the local language. He was not only a thoroughly bad character, he had a foolish, exhausted mind. In short: he had messed up his whole life. His chest felt constricted, tears welled up in him, soon they would start into his eyes. And he drank another glass to make their passage easier. They gushed forth at last. He spread his arms across the table, pillowed his head and sobbed bitterly. He cried for about a quarter of an hour. He did not hear that Onufrij had stopped his playing and that there was a knock on the door. He only raised his head as the door slammed. And he saw Kapturak.

He managed to force back his tears and to say in a sharp voice, "What are you doing here?"

Kapturak, cap in hand, never moved from the threshold. He was not much taller than the door handle. His sallow gray face had a smile on it. His clothes were gray. He was wearing gray canvas shoes, streaked with the fresh gray, glossy slime of the neighborhood. A few little gray curls intertwined on his minute head and were plainly visible. "Good evening," he said with a little bow. At the same time his shadow on the white door behind him darted up and crumpled again immediately.

"Where's my batman?" Trotta asked, and, "What do you want?"

"So, you haven't gone to Vienna this time?" began Kapturak.

"I don't go to Vienna at all," Trotta said.

"You haven't asked for money this week," said Kapturak. "I've been waiting for you to come along. I wanted to ask about you. I've just been in Captain Jedlicek's room. He isn't in."

"Oh, isn't he," said Trotta indifferently.

"No," said Kapturak. "He's not at home. Something's happened to him."

Trotta heard quite plainly that something had happened to Captain Jedlicek, but he inquired no further. First of all, he was not inquisitive. (Today he was not inquisitive.) And second, it seemed to him that such a tremendous amount had happened to him that he could not concern himself with anyone else. Third, he did not feel the least inclined to listen to Kapturak. Kapturak's very presence annoyed him. Only he hadn't the power to do anything against the little man. A vague, a very vague, recollection of the six thousand kronen he owed his visitor kept recurring to him, a painful recollection. He tried to suppress it. The money, he tried to convince himself, has nothing whatever to do with his being in here. There are two of them, quite different people. The one who lent money is not here. The other one, in my room, wants to tell me some stupid story about Jedlicek. He stared at Kapturak. For some moments it seemed to the Lieutenant that his visitor was disintegrating and coming together again in vague gray blotches. Trotta waited until Kapturak was completely in one piece. It needed a certain effort to make quick use of the moment of full reintegration: there was constant danger that the little gray man would dissolve again.

Kapturak came a step closer to him, aware, it seemed, that his visibility was doubtful, and said, rather louder this time, "Yes, something's happened to the Captain."

"Well, so what's happened?" said Trotta dreamily, as if he were asking in his sleep.

Kapturak took another step toward the table and, holding his hands in front of his mouth, he whispered with a rustling sound, "They've arrested and deported him on suspicion of espionage."

Hearing this, the Lieutenant rose. He stood, both hands leaning on the table. He scarcely felt his legs. He felt that he was standing on his hands. He almost dug them into the table. "I don't want to hear anything about it from you," he said. "Get out."

"I'm sorry, that's impossible, impossible," said Kapturak. He was standing close to the table now, next to Trotta. He dropped his head as if he had a shameful admission to make and said, "I must insist on part payment."

"Tomorrow," said Trotta.

"Tomorrow," Kapturak repeated. "Tomorrow it might not be possible. You see what surprises each day brings. I've lost a small fortune with the captain. How do I know I shall ever set eyes on him again? And you're his friend."

"What are you saying?" asked Trotta. He lifted his hands off the table and suddenly felt steady on his feet. He realized that Kapturak had said something monstrous, though true. Monstrous because it was true. Carl Joseph had a simultaneous vision of the one episode in his life in which he had been a danger to others. He now wished himself armed as he had been then with pistol and sword, his men behind him. This little gray man was much more menacing than the crowd had been. To compensate for his own impotence, he worked to fill his heart with alien rage. He clenched his fists. He had never done it and he felt he could never actually be formidable, only at best appear so. A vein stood out on his forehead, his face grew red, his eyes became bloodshot, his gaze became glazed. He succeeded in looking really threatening. Kapturak was wincing away.

"What was that you said?" repeated the Lieutenant.

"Nothing," said Kapturak.

"Go on, repeat it," commanded Trotta.

"Nothing," Kapturak answered. Again he disintegrated into indistinct gray blotches. Lieutenant Trotta was filled with the immense fear that the little man was possessed of the spectral faculty of dis- and re-integration at will. And the irresistible desire to experience the substance of Kapturak took hold of Lieutenant Trotta like the uncontrollable passion of a discoverer. From the bedpost behind him dangled the sword, his weapon, the defender of his domestic and military honor. And strangely enough, at this moment, a magic instrument, too, designed to reveal the laws governing evil spirits. He felt the glittering sword behind him, a strong, magnetic force emanated from the weapon. And attracted, as it were, by this magnetism, he took a leap backward, his eyes still fixed on the melting and reintegrating Kapturak, until his left hand had closed over the scabbbard, his right, in a flash, stripped the blade so that while Kapturak leapt away to the door, dropping his cap, which lay in front of his gray canvas shoes, Trotta pursued with glinting steel. And without realizing what he was doing, the Lieutenant set the swordpoint to the breast of the gray apparition, sensed the resistance of cloth and flesh along the length of the blade,

246

and felt relieved, because at last it seemed evident that Kapturak was a human being; yet the Lieutenant could not manage to sink his point.

It was only an instant. But in that instant Lieutenant Trotta heard, saw, and smelled everything alive on earth; the voices of the night, the stars in the sky, the light of the lamp, the objects in the room, his own shape—as though it were not he that owned it, as though it were hanging there in front of him; the dance of the midges round the light, the damp breath of the swamps, and the cool night breeze. Suddenly Kapturak spread his arms out. His scrawny little hand clutched left and right at the doorway. His bald head with its little gray curly hairs sank on to his shoulder. At the same instant he set one foot in front of the other, and twisted up his absurd gray shoes into a knot. And behind him on the white door there formed, under Trotta's staring eyes, the wavering shadow of a cross.

Trotta's hand shook and he dropped the sword. It fell, with a gentle jangling moan. Kapturak dropped his arms. His head slid off his shoulders and tumbled forward on his chest. His eyes were shut. His lips were trembling. There was silence. The midges fluttering round the light could be heard and, through the open window, frogs and crickets, and the barking of a dog close by. Lieutenant Trotta lurched. He turned around. "Sit down," he said, pointing at the only chair in the room.

"Yes," said Kapturak. "I'll sit down." He crossed briskly to the table, as briskly, Trotta felt, as though nothing had happened. The point of his toe touched the sword on the floor. He bent to pick it up. As if it were his duty to tidy the room, he carried the naked sword over to the table between two fingers, picked up the scabbard, sheathed the sword, and hung it in its place on the bedpost, without looking at the Lieutenant. He circled the table and sat down opposite the standing Trotta, of whose presence he then became aware. "I'll stay only a moment to recover," he said. The Lieutenant said nothing. "A week from today, at this time, I must ask you to repay me the whole sum," Kapturak continued. "I don't want to do business with you. You owe me seven thousand two hundred and fifty kronen in all. I must further inform you that Herr Brodnitzer has been outside the door and has heard everything that has taken place. You know, I think, that Count Chojnicki is not expected back so early this year—in fact, he may not come at all. I should like to go, Lieutenant." He got up, went to the door, bent down, picked up his cap, and glanced round again. The door shut after him.

The Lieutenant was now completely sober. Just the same, it all seemed like a dream to him. He opened his door. Onufrij sat on his chair as always, though, he realized, it must be very late by now. He looked at his watch. It was half past nine. "Why aren't you in bed?" he asked.

"Because of your visitor," said Onufrij.

"Did you hear it all?"

"Yes," said Onufrij, "I heard everything."

"Was Brodnitzer here?"

"Yes, sir," Onufrij confirmed.

There could be no doubt of its really having taken place, just as Lieutenant Trotta had experienced it. So, in the morning, he would have to report the whole affair. The other officers were not yet back. He went from door to door; their rooms were all empty. They were sitting in the mess, discussing the case of Captain Jedlicek, the gruesome case of Captain Jedlicek. He would be court-martialed, dishonorably discharged, and shot. Trotta strapped on his sword, took his cap, and went downstairs. He would have to wait around for the others down there. He paced up and down in front of the hotel. This business of the captain, oddly enough, preoccupied him more than his own with Kapturak. He felt he could discern the sly machinations of dark powers. It struck him as uncanny that Frau von Taussig should have had to go to her husband on this of all days. Gradually he perceived how all the fatalities of his life could be interconnected, as if they were manipulated by an invisible puller of strings, whose aim it was to annihilate the Lieutenant. It was clear, clear as the nose on your face, as the saying goes, that Lieutenant Trotta, the grandson of the hero of Solferino, in part caused the destruction of others and was in part himself drawn down into the abyss by them; and, in any case, he was one of those luckless beings on whom an evil power has cast its evil eye.

He paced the empty street. His steps resounded in front of the drawn blinds of the brightly lit café where music was playing, where cards pattered down on the tables, and where a new nightingale sang and danced instead of the old one, but performed the same songs and dances. There would certainly be no officers in there today. And, in any case, he didn't care to go in to look for them. For Jedlicek's shame was also his, although for a long time now he had loathed the army. The captain's shame was the shame of the whole battalion. Lieutenant Trotta's military upbringing was strong enough to make him doubt whether after this any officer of his battalion would dare show his face again in uniform. Jedlicek! He had been so big and strong and gay and gone through such a lot of money. He took everything on his broad shoulders. Zoglauer liked him, all the men liked him. They had all felt him to be stronger than the swamp and the frontier. And he had been a spy! Music came from the café. Cups chinked, chattering voices swelled, to die again in the nocturne of never-wearying frogs. It was spring. But Chojnicki was not coming. The one man whose money might have saved him. It was far from being six thousand kronen now. It was seven thousand two hundred and fifty. To be paid a week from today, at the same time. If he didn't pay, they'd be sure to fabricate some connection between himself and Captain Jedlicek. He'd been his friend. After all, hadn't they all been friends with him? But anything could be expected from the unfortunate Trotta. Fate, it was fate! A fortnight ago at this time he'd been a carefree young man in civilian clothes. At about this time he'd met Moser and had a drink with him. And today he envied Professor Moser.

The sound of familiar steps came round the corner. All those staying in the Hotel Brodnitzer were returning home. They all came home together, a silent pack. He went to meet them. "Oh, you haven't gone away then?" said Winter. "You've heard the news? Awful, isn't it? Horrible." They went upstairs, one after the other without a word, each trying to be as silent as possible. They almost crept upstairs. "All into Number Nine," ordered First Lieutenant Hruba. It was his room, the largest in the hotel. With lowered heads, they went into Hruba's room.

"We will have to do something," Hruba began. "You saw Zoglauer. He's in despair. He'll shoot himself. We will have to do something."

"Nonsense," said Lieutenant Lippowitz. He had joined the army rather late, after two terms as a law student, and he never quite shed the civilian; they treated him with the shy, rather mocking deference due to reservists. "We can't do anything about it," said Lippowitz. "Except keep quiet and get on with our jobs. He isn't the first. And, unfortunately, he won't be the last in the army, either."

Nobody answered. They realized that they couldn't do anything. Yet each had hoped that, once they got together in a room they might hit on all kinds of clever expedients. Now, however, they all realized that only fear had driven them together, because each one of them had been too afraid to stay alone, within his own four walls, with his fear. And they also saw that it did not help them to herd together and that even herding with all the others—each was still alone with his own affair. They raised their heads, looked at one another, and let them sink again. They had all sat together like this before, just after Captain Wagner's suicide. Now they were all thinking of Captain Wagner, Jedlicek's predecessor. Each wished that Jedlicek had shot himself as well. Then they all began to suspect that Wagner, too, their dead comrade, had only shot himself to escape arrest.

"Look here," said Lieutenant Habermann, "suppose I force my way in to him and shoot him?"

"Well, first of all, you'd never get in," Lippowitz answered. "And second, they'll have arranged for him to shoot himself. As soon as they've got it all out of him, they'll give him a revolver and lock him up."

That's right, that's what they do," cried several. They breathed more freely. They were beginning to hope that by this time Jedlicek would have blown his own brains out. They felt that it was their own intelligence that had just worked out this very reasonable custom of military justice.

"I almost killed someone this evening," said Lieutenant Trotta.

"Who? What for? Why?" they all asked.

"You all know him, it was Kapturak," he began. He told them about it slowly, searching for words; and, as he came to the end, found it impossible to explain why he'd dropped his sword. He felt that they would never understand him. In fact, they were not following him.

"I'd have done him in," exclaimed one of them. "So would I," said another. "And I", a third.

"Well, it's not that easy," Lippowitz chimed in.

"That bloodsucker, that Jew," someone said. And they all

250

stopped talking, because they remembered that Lippowitz's father was also a Jew.

"Well, I suddenly saw a cross on the door behind him," Trotta said, feeling surprised that, as he said it, he should be thinking of Max Demant and his grandfather, the white haired king of all publicans. "I suddenly saw a cross on the door behind him."

One of them laughed. Another said coldly, "You were drunk."

"Oh, stop," Hruba ordered at last. "All this will have to go to Zoglauer in the morning."

Trotta looked at one face after another; tired faces, weary faces, excited faces, faces which even in their tiredness and excitement were provocatively gay. If only Demant were alive now, Trotta thought. I could talk to him, to the grandson of the white-bearded king of publicans. He tried to leave unobtrusively and went to his room.

Next morning he reported the incident. He described it in the military language which, ever since his childhood, he had used to deliver reports and describe events—his mother tongue. But he was well aware that his report was incomplete, that in fact he had omitted the essentials, that between the incident as he had experienced it and the words in which it was described there was a wide mysterious gap, like a strange territory. Nor had he forgotten to mention the shadow of the cross which he thought he had seen. And the Major smiled just as Trotta had expected him to smile, and asked, "How much had you been drinking?"

"Half a bottle," said Trotta.

"Well then," remarked Zoglauer. He had smiled for only an instant, the harassed Major Zoglauer. It was a serious matter. Serious matters were unforunately piling up. A serious matter which would have to be referred to higher authority. One might wait, though. "Have you got the money?"

"No," said the Lieutenant.

And for a moment their eyes met helplessly, in that empty, impotent state of miserable people who dare not admit even to themselves that they are impotent. Army regulations don't tell you everything. You could read them through from cover to cover and back to front, they didn't tell you everything, by any means. Had the Lieutenant done the right thing? Had he

251

been a bit impetuous? Was the fellow who'd lent him a small fortune within his rights in demanding repayment? And even if the major summoned all his officers and asked their advice, who could have told him? Who could be wiser than the commander of the battalion? And what on earth was wrong with this wretched lieutenant? There'd been trouble enough in getting that strike business hushed up. Misfortune upon misfortune accumulated on Major Zoglauer's head. Woe to Trotta! Woe to his battalion. The major felt like wringing his hands, if only it were possible to wring one's hands on duty. Even if every officer in the regiment were to contribute on Trotta's behalf, they'd never be able to scrape up that amount. And, unless he paid, things would become still more involved.

"What on earth did you need all that for?" the major asked, and then he remembered that he knew. He waved his hand. He didn't want any details. "You must write home to your father," said Zoglauer. It seemed to him a brilliant idea. And so the report came to an end.

Lieutenant Trotta went back and sat down and began to write to his father. But he found he couldn't manage without a drink. So he went downstairs into the café and asked for pen, ink, and paper, and a Ninety Percent. He began. What a difficult letter! What an impossible letter! Carl Joseph started a few times, screwed up the paper, began again. Nothing comes harder to a lieutenant than to give an account of matters which concern him and which imperil his position. This circumstance afforded sufficient proof that Lieutenant Trotta, who had disliked the army for so long, still had enough military ambition left not to want to let himself to be turned out of it. And quite unconsciously, as he strove to make the complex business clear to his father, he was transformed again into Cadet Trotta who long ago on his father's balcony had yearned to die for Habsburg Austria to the strains of the Radetzky March. So strange, so mutable, and so confused is the human soul.

It took Trotta over two hours to get the thing down on paper. It was late afternoon. The gamblers were gathering in the café. With them came Brodnitzer, its proprietor. His politeness was unusual and frightening. His bow to Trotta as he passed was so low that Trotta knew at once it was intended to be a reminder of the incident with Kapturak and of Brodnitzer's own function as an authentic witness. Trotta went to look for Onufrij. He stood in the hall shouting Onufrij's name down the stairs. But Onufrij did not answer his call. Brodnitzer came and said, "Your servant went off early this morning."

So Trotta had to carry his own letter to the station to mail it. Only while he was on his way did it occur to him that Onufrij had absented himself without leave. His military training dictated anger. He himself, the Lieutenant, had often been to Vienna without leave, and in civilian clothes. Perhaps the fellow was simply taking after his master. Perhaps, Trotta further reflected, he's got a girl waiting for him. I'll lock him up till he's blue in the face. Even as he thought it, he realized that the thought was not really his at all, and not seriously intended. It was a mechanical phrase forever ready in his military mind, one of those innumerable mechanical phrases which take the place of thoughts in military minds and anticipate decisions.

But no, his man Onufrij did not have a girl in the village. He owned four and a half acres of land, inherited from his father and looked after by his brother-in-law, and twenty gold ten-kronen ducats, buried in the soil, to the left beyond the huts, on the path which led to their neighbor Nikofor. The man Onufrij had risen before daybreak to brush and polish the Lieutenant's boots and uniform; he had stood the boots outside the door and hung out the uniform on the chair. He took his cherrywood stick and set out on the march for Burdlaki.

He went along the narrow path on which the willows grew, the only path that indicated the dryness of the ground. For these willows absorbed all the damp of the swamps. On either side of the narrow path rose gray, multifarious and ghostly mists which constrained him to make the sign of the cross. Ceaselessly and with trembling lips, he muttered the Lord's Prayer. Yet he was cheerful. Now, on his left, came the huge slate roofs of the railway sheds, and the sight reassured him somewhat, since they were there, just where he had expected them to be. So he made the sign of the cross again, this time in gratitude, to God, Whose mercy had permitted the railway sheds to remain in their usual places where he had expected them. He reached the village of Burdlaki an hour after sunrise. His sister and brother-in-law were already in the fields. He entered his father's hut, in which they lived.

The children were still asleep in their cradles, slung from

the ceiling by stout ropes on thickly coiled iron hooks. He took a spade and a rake from the vegetable patch behind the house and set out in search of the third willow on the left in front of the hut. Outside, he stood with his back toward the door and his face toward the horizon. He took some time making certain that his right hand was the right and his left the left. Then he went out towards the left, to the third willow, in neighbor Nikofor's direction. Here he began to dig. From time to time he glanced about him to be sure that nobody was watching. No. No one saw what he was doing. He dug and dug. The sun rose so fast that he felt it must be midday already, but it was only nine o'clock in the morning. At last he heard a ringing sound: the iron of his spade had struck against something hard. He threw down the spade and began gently stroking the loosened earth with his rake, lay flat on his belly, and with all ten fingers scraped aside the loose crumbs of damp soil. First he touched a linen handkerchief, felt for the knot, and pulled it out. There was his money. Twenty gold ten-kronen ducats.

He did not allow himself time to count them. He stowed the treasure in his trouser pocket and went to the Jew who kept the village inn in Burdlaki, a certain Hirsch Beniower, the only banker on earth known to him personally.

"I know you," said Hirsch Beniower, "and I knew your father, too. Do you need sugar, flour, Russian tobacco, or money?"

"Money," said Onufrij.

"How much do you want?"

"A lot," said Onufrij, and spread his arms as wide as they would go.

"Good," said Beniower. "Let's see how much you've got." And Beniower opened his big book. In this book it was written that Onufrij Kolohin owned four and a half acres of land, and Hirsch Beniower was willing to lend him three hundred kronen on it.

"Let's go to the mayor," said Beniower. He called his wife to tend the shop and went with Onufrij Kolohin to the mayor. There he gave Onufrij the three hundred kronen and Onufrij sat down at a worm-eaten brown table and began to sign his name on the document. He took off his cap. The sun was already high in the sky. It managed to send its piercing rays even through the small windows of the peasant hut where the mayor of Burdlaki discharged his office. Onufrij sweated. On his low forehead beads of perspiration stood out like glassy swellings. Each letter Onufrij wrote made a crystalline swelling stand out on his forehead. They trickled down falling like tears wept by Onufrij's brain, until at last his name stood signed and witnessed on the document. So, with twenty gold ten-kronen pieces in his trouser pocket and three hundred one-kronen paper notes stuffed in the pockets of his tunic, Onufrij Kolohin began his way back.

He came to the hotel in the afternoon and went into the café looking for his master. When he caught sight of Trotta he waited in the midst of cardplayers as unconcerned as if he were standing in the barrack square. His whole broad face shone like a sun. Trotta gazed long at him, tender-hearted but looking severe.

"I'll lock you up till you're blue in the face," he said, the Lieutenant's mouth obeying the dictates of his military brain. "Come up to my room," said Trotta, and he got up and the Lieutenant climbed the stairs. Onufrij followed just three steps behind him. They stood in the room.

Onufrij, still wreathed in smiles, reported, "Lieutenant, here's some money," and drew his whole fortune out of his breeches pocket and the pockets of his tunic. He put it on the table. There were traces of silvery-gray slime on the crimson handkerchief which for so long had wrapped twenty gold ten-kronen ducats under the earth. The blue notes lay next to the handkerchief. Trotta counted them. Then he undid the bundle. He counted the gold coins. He laid the notes with the coins on the handkerchief and knotted the bundle again. Then he returned it to Onufrij.

"I'm sorry, I mustn't take your money," said Trotta. "It's against army regulations. If I took this money from you, I would be turned out of the army and reduced to the ranks. Do you understand?"

Onufrij nodded his head.

The Lieutenant stood there, holding the bundle. Onufrij kept nodding his head. He stretched his hand out and took the bundle. It swung in the air for a while.

"Dismiss," said Trotta and Onufrij departed with his bundle.

The Lieutenant remembered the autumn night in the cavalry

garrison when he had heard Onufrij's thudding feet behind his back. He also thought of those grotesque "Scenes" of army life, little green, clothbound volumes which he had read in the hospital library. They had abounded in faithful servants, untutored peasant lads with hearts of gold. And although Lieutenant Trotta never had the slightest taste for literature— the word, if he happened to hear it, made him think of *Zrinyi* a drama by Theodor Körner, and nothing else—he had always felt a dull resentment against the gentle melancholy of those little books with their golden-hearted characters.

Trotta was not sufficiently experienced to know that even in real life there are untutored peasant lads with hearts of gold and that a lot of truth, however clumsily rendered, is put into badly written books.

Lieutenant Trotta, in fact, had not had much experience of anything.

Chapter 18

The District Commissioner received his son's unhappy letter on a fresh and sunny spring morning. Herr von Trotta balanced the envelope on his palm before he opened it, for it seemed heavier than any letter he had ever received from his son. There must be at least two sheets, an unusually long letter. Its bulk moved his ageing heart to perturbation, paternal anger, delight, and at the same time presentiment. The hard cuff around his old hand clattered a little as he opened the envelope. With the fingers of his left hand he steadied his pince-nez, which seemed to have got rather shaky these last few months, while with his right he held the letter rather close to his face so that the lower edges of his side whiskers rustled against the sheets of paper. The obviously hurried writing shocked Herr von Trotta as much as the extraordinary contents of the letter. Even between the lines the District Commissioner looked for some hidden subject for alarm. Because it seemed to him that what was written in it did not convey the full disaster, and he realized that he had been waiting for some terrible news day after day, for many days, especially since Carl Joseph had ceased to write. That was why he remained calm when he put the letter away. He was an old man of a past generation. Old men, in those days before the great war, were far more foolish than the young of today. But in the crises which were calamitous to them and which would in the times we are living in be dismissed with a quick joke, these brave old gentlemen maintained an heroic calm. Nowadays the notions of honor—personal, family, and professional—by which Herr von Trotta lived, are the nearest relics of childish, superstitious legends. But in those days Austrian District Commissioners like Herr von Trotta were less shocked by the news of the sudden death of an only child than by an even seemingly dishonorable action. In those days an officer of the Imperial and Royal Army who had refrained from killing the man who impeached his honor be cause he happened to be in debt to him, was a misfortune according to the tenets of an age which now lies as if buried under the fresh grave mounds of those killed in the war. Indeed, such a man was more than a misfortune. He was a disgrace— to his progenitor, to the army, and the monarchy. So that at first Herr von Trotta's fatherly emotions were less stirred than, so to speak, his official heart. Go, it admonished, lay down your office at once, retire before your time. You have nothing more to expect in your Emperor's service. In the next instant, his paternal heart protested loudly. It's the age we're living in, it's the frontier garrison, it's your own fault, your son's decent and honorable, only, unfortunately, weak. You've got to help him.

You've got to help him. The name of Trotta must be kept unsullied, and above reproach. On that point, the Commissioner's two hearts were in full accord, the official reinforced the fatherly. So the first thing to do was to raise some money. Seven thousand two hundred and fifty kronen! Those five thousand florins allotted years ago by the Imperial bounty to the son of the hero of Solferino had long since melted into thin air, together with that hero's legacy. The District Commissioner had spent them on one thing or the other, on household expenses, Cadet School fees for Carl Joseph in Moravian Weisskirchen, on his horse, on Moser, on various charities. Herr von Trotta had always made a point of appearing richer than he was. He had all the instincts of the gentleman. And in those days (and even perhaps at the present time) no instinct could be more expensive. People so cursed know neither how much they possess nor what they are spending. They dip into an invisible well. They never keep accounts. They are convinced that their purses can never fail their generous impulses.

For the first time, then, in a life which had lasted so many years, Herr von Trotta found himself confronted with the seemingly impossible task of raising a relatively large sum of money without delay. He had no friends, except those former students and schoolfellows who, like himself, now sat in government offices and with whom he had had no contact for years. Most of them were poor. He knew old Herr von Winternigg, the richest man in the district. Slowly he began to accustom himself to the gruesome thought that tomorrow or the day after, or even today, he would have to ask Herr von Winternigg for a loan. Herr von Trotta's powers of imagination were by no means vivid. Yet he managed to get a clear and agonizing vision of every step along this petitioner's calvary. And for the first time in his long life he realized how hard it is to be helpless and yet remain dignified. In a flash insight descended on him, blasting the pride he had guarded and fostered with such care; his inheritance, which he had intended to be his legacy, was gone. Already he felt humbled, like one who has for many years gone on fruitless begging visits. Pride had been the stout companion of his youth and later his support in middle age; now the poor old District Commissioner was deprived of it. He decided to write at once to Herr von Winternigg. He had hardly begun the letter when it became clear that he did not feel up to the task of writing to announce a call which, strictly speaking, had to be described as a begging visit. And old Herr von Trotta had the feeling that unless he stated the real object of his visit at the beginning of his letter, he was involving himself in a kind of deception. It was impossible to find suitable words for such a request. So he sat on and on, pen in hand, considering, polishing every phrase, and crossing out every sentence. He might, of course, telephone Herr von Winternigg. But ever since the office had boasted a telephone (it had been installed only two years ago) Herr von Trotta had used it only for official calls. He could not see himself stepping up to that large, rather sinister-looking brown box to twist a handle and ring a bell and begin a petition to Herr von Winternigg with the really dreadful word "Hello", an expression which was like an insult to Herr von Trotta, a kind of unseemly, childish rallying cry, totally unsuited to a serious man's important discussion of serious matters. Meanwhile, it occurred to him that his son must be waiting for his answer. A telegram perhaps; but what message should the District Commissioner send? WILL DO WHATEVER I CAN MORE LATER, for instance? Or: WAIT PATIENTLY FURTHER NEWS? Or: TRY OTHER MEANS IMPOSSIBLE HERE? Impossible! The word struck long and terrible echoes. What was impossible? To save the name of Trotta from disgrace? That would have to be possible. It would not be allowed to be impossible! He paced his office from end to end, just as he had his study on Sunday mornings, when he had tested young Carl Joseph. One cuff was behind his back, the other clattered as he walked. Then he went down into the yard, impelled by the sudden notion that the dead Jacques might still be sitting in the shade of the beams. The yard was empty. The window of the cottage in which Jacques had lived was wide open and his canary still perched on the ledge. It sat and chirped. Herr von Trotta turned back at once, took hat and stick, and went into the town.

He had made up his mind to do a most extraordinary thing: namely, to go and see Dr Skowronnek at his house. He crossed the little market place, turned down the Lenaugasse, and examined every house for a name plate since he did not know the doctor's number. In the end, he had to go into a shop and ask for Skowronnek's address, though it struck him as the height of indiscretion to get this information from a stranger. But Herr von Trotta had the strength of mind and the confidence to survive this ordeal and entered the house which had been pointed out to him. He was shown through the hall into the garden and found the doctor reading a book under a large sunshade.

"Good Lord!" Skowronnek exclaimed. He was well aware that something most unusual must have occurred to make the District Commissioner come to his house.

Herr von Trotta accomplished a whole series of involved apologies before he began. Then he told his story, sitting on a bench in the little garden with downcast eyes and scraping the point of his stick through bright pebbles on the narrow path. He handed the doctor Carl Joseph's letter. He said no more, suppressed a sigh, and took a deep breath.

"My savings amount to two thousand kronen," said Dr Skowronnek, "and I hope, Commissioner, you'll allow me to place them at your disposal." He said it very rapidly, afraid that the District Commissioner might interrupt him; and in his embarrassment he picked up Herr von Trotta's walking stick, and himself began scraping the gravel path for, having said so much, he could sit no longer with idle hands.

Herr von Trotta said, "Thank you, Doctor. I accept. I'll give you a written acknowledgement and, if you'll allow me, I'll pay it back to you in instalments."

"There's no question of that," said Dr Skowronnek.

"All right," said the District Commissioner. He found it impossible to utter the unnecessary words which politeness had always prompted him to speak to strangers. Suddenly he was pressed for time: the few days still at his disposal were shrinking away to nothing.

"Now, as for the rest," continued Skowronnek, "that you can only get from Herr von Winternigg. Do you know him?"

"Slightly."

"Well, Commissioner, there seems no other way . . . . But I think I can tell you the sort of man he is. I once attended his daughter-in-law. He is what people call inhuman. And he might, Commissioner, well, he might just refuse to lend it to you."

Skowronnek was silent and the District Commissioner took back his stick. And it was very quiet. The only sound they could hear was the ferrule scraping in the gravel.

"Refuse me, you say," the District Commissioner whispered. "I'm not afraid of course," he said out loud. "But if he does?"

"Well," said Skowronnek, "if he does, there's something much more out of the way. It keeps coming into my head, though it might be really too fantastic. But perhaps for you, in your case, it is hardly too extraordinary. Well, I think I should go straight to the Old Man—I mean the Emperor! After all, it's more than just a question of money. There's always the danger —you'll forgive my putting it so bluntly—that your son may . . . " Skowronnek wanted to say, "Get kicked out." But he said, "May resign from the army."

And having said it, Skowronnek felt ashamed. So he added, "Perhaps it's a childish idea. Even while I was thinking, it occurred to me that you and I are nothing but a pair of over-grown schoolboys, discussing an impossible escapade. Yes, although we're both so old and burdened with care, there's a kind of bravado in the idea. Forgive me."

But to Herr von Trotta's simple soul there was nothing childish about Dr Skowronnek's suggestion. Every document he drew up or signed, every trifling instruction passed on to his Assistant Commissioner, or indeed even to Sergeant-Major Slama, set him directly under the outstretched scepter of the Emperor. Nor did it seem in the least unusual that the Emperor should have spoken to Carl Joseph. The hero of Solferino had shed his blood for him; so had Carl Joseph, in a sense, in a minor fray against turbulent and suspicious individuals, the disorderly elements. And according to Herr von Trotta's simple notions, it was not in the least an abuse of the Emperor's bounty that he, the Emperor's servant, should go to Francis

Joseph as any child in need might go to its father. However, Dr Skowronnek felt disturbed, and began to doubt the District Commissioner's sanity, when the old man exclaimed, "Doctor, what a splendid idea. Nothing simpler."

"Not quite as simple as all that," said Skowronnek. "You haven't much time, you know. You can't get a private audience in two days."

The District Commissioner saw the force of that, and they decided he must begin with Herr von Winternigg. "And risk a refusal," said the District Commissioner.

"And risk a refusal," Dr Skowronnek repeated.

The District Commissioner set out at once to Herr von Winternigg. He went in a cab. It was midday. He stopped at the café for a brandy. He felt that he was undertaking a most unseemly errand. He had eaten nothing, he would be disturbing old Winternigg at luncheon. But he had no time. The thing had to be settled this afternoon. The day after tomorrow he would see the Emperor. He stopped his cab outside the post office, went in, and, with a steady hand, wrote a telegram to Carl Joseph: SHALL BE ARRANGED GREETINGS FATHER. Now he was quite convinced that all would be well. Impossible as it seemed to scrape up the money, it was even more impossible that the honor of the Trottas should be impugned. Yes, the District Commissioner imagined that his father's spirit, the spirit of the hero of Solferino protected and accompanied him. And the brandy fired his elderly heart. It beat a trifle faster, but he was quite calm. He paid off his cab at the gates of Winternigg's villa, dismissing the driver with a benign finger, his customary salutation for his inferiors. He smiled benevolently at the footman. Holding his hat and stick, he waited.

Herr von Winternigg came, minute, shrunken and sallow. He held out his dry little hand and sank into a capacious armchair, almost vanishing in the green upholstery. His colorless eyes were turned on the big windows. No expression enlivened them—or, rather, the eyes themselves concealed any expression. They were two dim little mirrors which showed the District Commissioner only his own little reflection. More fluently than he had expected, with well-turned apologies, he explained why it had been impossible to announce his visit in advance. Then he said, "I'm an old man, Herr von Winternigg." He had had no intention of saying that. Winternigg's wrinkled yellow eyelids blinked once or twice; the District Commissioner had the sensation of addressing an ancient shriveled bird which could not comprehend human speech.

"I'm sorry," Herr von Winternigg said, nonetheless. He spoke very softly. His voice had no more timbre than his eyes had expression. He exhaled as he spoke and revealed a surprisingly powerful set of teeth, pale-yellow teeth, a strong, protective fence guarding his words. "I'm sorry," said Herr von Winternigg, "but I have no ready cash."

The District Commissioner got up at once. Winternigg, too, sprang to his feet. He stood, short and sallow, in front of the District Commissioner, hairless before a silvery pair of side whiskers and Herr von Trotta seemed to grow and himself could feel that he was growing. Had his pride been sacrificed? In no way. Was he humbled? No, not at all. He had to save the honor of the hero of Solferino, as that hero had had to save the Emperor's life. Begging visits were quite simple. Contempt: for the first time Herr von Trotta's heart filled with real contempt, contempt almost as great as his pride. He took his leave. "Good day to you," he said in his accustomed, haughty, nasal voice, the voice of officials. He went on foot, went back in his shining silver dignity, slow and erect, down the long avenue which led from Winternigg's villa into the town. The avenue was empty. Sparrows hopped across the way, blackbirds piped and old dark-green chestnut trees flanked the path of the District Commissioner.

At home, he picked up the silver bell for the first time in months. Its light voice hurried through the whole house. "My dear lady," said Herr von Trotta to Fräulein Hirschwitz, "I should like my trunk packed in half an hour. My uniform, if you please with the cocked hat and the sword, the tail coat, and the white tie. If you please. In half an hour." He took out his watch, it opened with a snap. He sat in the armchair and shut his eyes.

His full-dress uniform hung in the wardrobe on five pegs: tails, waistcoat, breeches, cocked hat, and sword. Piece by piece, it came stepping out of its own volition, assisted merely by the careful hands of Fräulein Hirschwitz. The big brown canvas-covered trunk lined with rustling tissue paper gaped open and, piece by piece, received the uniform. The sword obediently entered its leather case. The tie wrapped itself in a light tissue-paper veil. The dazzling gloves rested in the lining of the waistcoat. Then the trunk closed and Fraulein Hirschwitz went to announce that all was ready.

And so the District Commissioner left for Vienna.

He arrived in the late evening. But he knew where to look for the men he needed. He knew the houses in which they lived, the cafés where they ate. So Government Councilor Smekal, and Privy Councilor Pollak, and Chief Imperial Audit Councilor Pollitzer, and Chief Municipal Councilor Busch, and Metropolitan District Councilor Leschnigg, and Police Councilor Fuchs—each of these, and others of their kind—saw the strange-looking Herr von Trotta enter and each felt perturbed and very surprised to see how old he had grown, although he was much the same age as they were. Yes, he looked positively reverend. They were almost afraid to call him by his Christian name. For, in truth, he was much older than they. On that evening he was seen in many places; almost simultaneously he hovered around them, like a ghost, they felt, a ghost of the old times and of the old Habsburg monarchy. The shades of history escorted him, and he himself was a silver phantom of history. Extraordinary as the words he spoke might sound to them, his strange intention of securing a private audience with the Emperor at two days' notice, he himself, this prematurely aged and at no time youthful Herr von Trotta, looked odder still. And by degrees they began to feel that there was nothing surprising in his proposal, and it all seemed perfectly in order.

In Montenuovo's office, the office of the Comptroller of the Household, sat Gustl, the lucky one whom they all envied, though they knew that once the Old Man was gone and Francis Ferdinand had succeeded to the throne, the glory of Gustl would come to an ignominious end. They were only waiting to see it happen. Meanwhile, Gustl had got married, married one of the Fuggers—he, plain middle-class Gustl, who had sat on the third bench in the left-hand corner, whom they'd all had to help in exams, and whose "luck" they had followed with the bitterest remarks for the last thirty years. Gustl had a handle to his name and a place in Montenuovo's office. He was Hasselbrunner no longer, but *von* Hasselbrunner. His job was child's play, whereas they all had to spend their days dealing with burdensome and highly complex official matters. Hasselbrunner! He alone might perhaps be able to do something.

So, by nine the next morning, the District Commissioner had taken up his stand outside Hasselbrunner's door in the offices of the Comptroller of the Household. Hasselbrunner, they told him, was out of town, but might be back that afternoon. Smetana, whom he hadn't been able to find the previous day, happened to come by, and Smetana hastily apprised of the circumstances, knowing as ever, was full of suggestions. Hasselbrunner might be out of town, but Lang had the office next to his. And Lang was a most obliging fellow. This set the District Commissioner off on his fruitless errands, from one government office to the next. He had no inkling of the secret laws which governed the Imperial and Royal Government Service in Vienna. Now he became acquainted with them. In obedience to them, the office porter would be surly until he took out his card and then, on perceiving his rank, would become obsequious. Higher officials, without exception, welcomed him with the tenderest regard. Each and every one seemed prepared, in the first quarter of an hour, to sacrifice his career, indeed his life, for the District Commissioner. Not until the next quarter of an hour did their eyes become troubled and their faces fall. And infinite regret crept into their hearts, paralyzing their wills, and each one of them said, "If only it were anything else! But of course, oh, with pleasure! But this, my *dear* Baron Trotta, well, even for one of us, need I say more? To you, of all people?" Such protests fell on Herr von Trotta's heedless ears. He passed through cloisters and courts, up to the third floor, then to the fourth, and down again to the first. Then he decided to wait for Hasselbrunner. He waited until midday, when he learned that Hasselbrunner had not left town, but had only stayed at home.

And so, in the Trotta's name, in defense of their honor, the intrepid Commissioner forced his way into Hasselbrunner's house. Here at last he found a gleam of hope.

Hasselbrunner, Herr von Trotta at his side, went out in search of X and Y. It was a question of pushing onward to Montenuovo. By about six that evening they had succeeded in discovering one of his intimates, seated in that famous pastry shop in which the light-hearted, sweet-toothed Imperial dignitaries might sometimes be found in the afternoon. There, for the fifteenth time that day, Herr von Trotta learned that his intentions were impossible to fulfil. He remained unmoved.

The silent dignity of his years, the odd, slightly crazy determination with which he spoke of his son and of the dangers that threatened his name, his solemnity in speaking of his late father as "the hero of Solferino" and not otherwise, of the Emperor as "His Majesty" and not otherwise, all had their effect on his listeners; until even they began to feel that Herr von Trotta's project was justified and not extraordinary. This District Commissioner from W. went so far as to say that if it should prove the only way, he, the son of the hero of Solferino, an old servant of His Majesty, would fling himself down, like a common porter from the market, in front of the carriage which drove the Emperor from his palace at Schönbrunn to the Hofburg every morning. He, Franz von Trotta, a District Commissioner, had to put the whole matter right. By this time, his task of saving the honor of the Trottas with the Emperor's help had so inspired him, that his son's misfortune, as he privately thought of the whole affair, had at last given significance to his long life. Yes, this task alone made his days significant.

It was difficult to infringe the prescribed ceremonial. This they told him fifteen times over. He answered that his father, the hero of Solferino, had infringed the ceremonial. "Look," said the District Commissioner, "this is how he grasped His Majesty by the shoulders to force him to the ground." He, who, as a rule, repressed a shudder in the presence of any violent or unnecessary gesture, started himself to grasp the shoulders of one of the gentlemen to whom he was describing the scene and attempted to re-enact then and there the historic rescue. No one smiled. And they did their best to devise a formula by which ceremony might be circumvented.

He went into a stationer's shop to buy a sheet of regulation foolscap, a small bottle of ink, and a steel pen with an Adler point, the only kind he could write with. Then, with a quick hand but in his usual flowing "copper-plate" which conformed to the rigid rules of "hair and shadow," he drew up the prescribed form of petition to His Imperial and Royal Apostolic Majesty, not for an instant doubting, or at least not permitting himself to doubt, that the matter would receive attention in some way favorable to the petitioner. He would have wakened Montenuovo himself in the middle of the night. In the District Commissioner's opinion, his son's affair had, in the course of the day, become the affair of the hero of Solferino and so, of the Emperor: in a sense, the affair of his country. He had hardly eaten since his departure from W. He looked more worn and haggard than usual, reminding his friend Hasselbrunner of one of those exotic birds kept in the Schönbrunn gardens, which represented nature's attempt to reproduce the physiognomy of the Habsburgs in the animal kingdom. Indeed, the District Commissioner reminded all who had seen him of the Emperor Francis Joseph himself.

These gentlemen in Vienna were not by any means used to the degree of resolution with which he confronted them. They, whose habit it was to dispose of far more serious contingencies with epigrams light as feathers, coined in the café of the Residency, saw in old Herr von Trotta a character not only from a geographically but also historically remote region, a specter of Austrian history, admonishing their consciences to patriotism. The unfailing irony of their comments at every sign of their own approaching destruction died on their lips for the space of an hour, and the name of Solferino aroused their awe and reverence, the name of that battle which had first heralded the decline of the Habsburgs. They were forced to shudder a little at the sight and words of this strange District Commissioner. Perhaps they were already aware of the specter of death which a few months later was to grasp them all. And on the back of their necks they felt the chill air of death.

Altogether, Herr von Trotta had three days. And he succeeded in the space of a single night in which he neither slept nor touched food or drink, in infringing the gold-and-iron laws of ceremony. Just as the name of the hero of Solferino had vanished from the schoolbooks of the monarchy, so, too, that of the hero's son was absent from Montenuovo's archives. Apart from Montenuovo himself, and the Emperor's valet, who had only recently died, no one remembers how District Commissioner Franz von Trotta was received at Schönbrunn early one morning by the Emperor, shortly before His Majesty's departure to Ischl.

It was a lovely morning. All night the District Commissioner had been adjusting his full-dress uniform. He kept his window open. It was a bright summer night. From time to time he went over to the window. He could hear the sounds of the sleeping city and the crowing of cocks in distant yards. He smelled the

267

breath of summer. He saw the stars on the patch of night sky as he listened to the regular footsteps of the policemen on their beat. He waited for daybreak. For the tenth time he went to the mirror to rearrange the bow of his white cravat above the wings of the stick-up collar, flick over the gilt buttons of his coat with a white cambric handkerchief, polish the gold hilt of his sword, brush his shoes, comb out his whiskers, force down again the few remaining wisps of hair upon his bald head, since to him they never seemed to lie neatly enough, and dust his swallow tails. He took up his cocked hat, stood at the mirror, and kept repeating, "I beg Your Majesty's clemency for my son." He saw in the mirror how his side whiskers stirred as he said it and he thought it unseemly. So he began rehearsing the words in such a way that not a hair should move as he was saying them, and yet they should be clearly audible. He felt not in the least fatigued. He went back to the window, like a man who takes another look at the sea. And he stood there, waiting for the sunrise, as men long for a ship that will take them home. Yes, he longed to go home to the Emperor! There he remained, until the gray twilight of morning brightened the sky, the morning star sank, and the confused voices of birds announced sunrise.

Then he switched off the lights in his room. He pressed the bell beside the door. He sent for the barber. He took off his coat again. He sat down. He had himself shaved. "Twice," he told the sleepy young man, "and shave me both ways." Now his chin glistened pale-blue between the silver whiskers on his cheeks. The alum crystal tingled, the cool powder dusted his throat. His audience was at eight-thirty. Once more he brushed the black-and-green dress coat, and said once more in front of the mirror, "I ask your Majesty's clemency for my son." He locked his door. He put on his white gloves, smoothed out the fingers, stroked down the kid, paused for a last glance in the big mirror on the landing between the hall and the first floor and tried to catch a glimpse of his profile. Cautiously he proceeded on his way, down the red carpet of the staircase, scarcely touching it with the tips of his toes, emanating a silvery dignity, a whiff of powder and eau de cologne, and the sharp smell of boot polish. The hall porter bowed very low. The carriage drew up outside the swinging doors. Herr von Trotta flicked the cushions and sat down. "Schönbrunn," he ordered.

He sat bolt upright throughout the drive. The horse's hoofs clattered gaily down freshly washed streets and the hurrying, white bakers' boys stood to watch the carriage pass like the *pièce de résistance* in a procession. Herr von Trotta rolled toward the Emperor. He asked his coachman to pull up at what seemed to him a fitting distance. And, with dazzling gloves at the side of his black-and-green tailcoat, picking his way carefully to keep the dust of the drive from clouding the sparkling polish of his boots, Herr von Trotta proceeded up the straight avenue which terminates in the palace of Schönbrunn. Above him, the morning birds sang joyfully. The scent of lilac and jasmine overwhelmed him. Here and there, from the white of chestnut candles a tiny petal fluttered down on him, and he nipped it off his coat with thumb and forefinger. Slowly he climbed the shallow, polished steps, already white in the morning sunshine. The guard presented arms; District Commissioner von Trotta entered the palace.

He waited. As etiquette prescribed, a Gentleman of the Household came to inspect him. His coat, his gloves, his breeches, boots, were impeccable. No fault could possibly have been found with Herr von Trotta. He waited. He was waiting in that spacious anteroom which led directly out of the Emperor's study. Through its six tall arched windows, their blinds half drawn—though they were already opened for the day—the riches of an early summer morning came drifting in with sweet scents and the excited voices of the birds of Schönbrunn. But the District Commissioner heard nothing. Nor did he seem to heed the gentleman to whom the discreet task of informing His Majesty's visitors of certain prescribed rules of deportment was entrusted, and who neglected his duty in face of such unapproachable, silvery dignity: he let the words die on his lips. Two gigantic sentries stood like statues on either side of high white doors with their gilt moldings. Bare except for one broad crimson strip of carpet, the golden-brown parquet reflected indistinctly the lower half of Herr von Trotta —the gilt tip of the scabbard, the dark breeches, the undulating shadow of the tailcoat. He got up. With timid, noiseless steps, he walked on the carpet. His heart was thumping but his soul was at peace. At this instant, five minutes before the audience with the Emperor, he felt he had known these rooms for years; that every morning without fail he himself had given the

Emperor Francis Joseph a full account of yesterday's events in the Moravian District of W. The District Commissioner was at home in his Emperor's house. At most, he was a trifle pre-occupied by the thought that perhaps it would be well to pass his fingers once again through his side whiskers, and that now there was no longer time to take off his white kid gloves.

No Imperial Minister, not even the Comptroller himself, could have felt less constraint than Herr von Trotta. From time to time a little wind bellied out the sunny blinds, and patches of summer-green came into Herr von Trotta's field of vision. The birds sang louder and louder. A few heavy flies were already buzzing in the foolish belief that it was midday. Little by little, the full warmth of the summer day made itself felt. The District Commissioner remained in the middle of the room. His right hand held the cocked hat to his hip; his left, in its dazzling glove, rested on the gold hilt of his sword. His face was rigidly set towards the doors behind which his Emperor sat. Thus he stood for two minutes. Through the open windows came the light, clear chime of distant clocks. Suddenly the double doors divided. And, head erect, with prudent, silent, and yet unfaltering steps, the District Commissioner advanced. He bowed very low, remained a few seconds with his face toward the parquet, his mind a blank. And when he straightened his back, the doors were closed.

In front of him stood the Emperor Francis Joseph at his desk, and to the District Commissioner it seemed as if his elder brother were standing at the desk. Francis Joseph's whiskers were tinged with yellow, especially around the mouth, otherwise they equaled Herr von Trotta's in whiteness. The Emperor was in general's uniform, and Herr von Trotta in the uniform of a District Commissioner. They were like two brothers, one of whom had become an emperor and the other a district commissioner. Very human, like all that followed in this audience between Herr von Trotta and his sovereign (of which the archives give no record), was Francis Joseph's gesture, just at this instant. For he feared there might be a drop at the end of his nose and drew out a handkerchief from his breeches pocket, and passed it lightly across his mustache. Then he glanced down at the memorandum. Aha! Trotta, he thought. Yesterday he had had the necessity for this sudden audience explained to him, but had not paid much attention.

For months now the Trottas had never stopped importuning him. He remembered at the last maneuvers having spoken to the youngest member of the family. That one had been a lieutenant, a strangely pale lieutenant. This one, of course, must be his father. And the Emperor had forgotten again whether the young man's father or his grandfather had saved his life at the battle of Solferino. Had the hero of Solferino suddenly become a District Commissioner? Or could this be the son of the hero of Solferino? He leaned on both hands across the desk.

"Well, now, my dear Trotta?" he asked, for it was part of his Imperial duty to surprise people by knowing their names.

"Your Majesty," said the District Commissioner and made another low bow. "I ask Your Majesty's clemency for my son."

"Oh, and what is your son?" inquired the Emperor to gain time and not at once betray the fact that he was unfamiliar with the Trotta family history.

"My son is a lieutenant serving with the Jaeger at B."

"Oh, indeed" said Francis Joseph. "Is he really? That's the young fellow I saw at the last maneuvers. A nice young man." And since this confused him a little, he added, "You know, he nearly saved my life. Or was that you?"

"Your Majesty," observed the District Commissioner, bowing again, "that was my father, the hero of Solferino."

"How old is he now?" asked the Emperor. "The Battle of Solferino, wasn't that the one there was a reading lesson about?"

"Yes, Your Majesty."

Now the Emperor clearly recollected the audience with that odd captain and, just as he had done long ago when the queer captain came into his presence, Francis Joseph walked around his desk, a few paces forward toward his visitor, and said, "Come closer, won't you?"

Herr von Trotta approached. The Emperor extended a lean trembling hand, an old man's hand with small blue veins and little lumps on the finger joints. Herr von Trotta took the Emperor's hand and bowed. He would have liked to kiss it. He did not know if he dare hold it, or whether he ought to let his own so rest in it that his sovereign could at any moment withdraw his hand if he felt inclined. "Your Majesty," he said for the third time, "I ask Your Majesty's clemency for my son."

They were like two brothers. A stranger catching sight of

them at this moment might have taken them for brothers. The snowy hair on their cheeks, their sloping shoulders and similar build gave each the feeling that he stood face to face with his mirror image. The one felt he had changed into a District Commissioner, the other, that he had changed into the Emperor. To the Emperor's left hand and the Commissioner's right, the two high windows were open, also hung with curtains yellow as sunshine.

"It's a nice fine day," said Francis Joseph suddenly.

"A lovely day," said the District Commissioner.

And while with his left hand the Emperor pointed to the window, the District Commissioner's right took the same direction. Now Francis Joseph was almost certain that this was his mirror image.

Suddenly the Emperor remembered that he still had a lot to attend to before his departure to Ischl. And so he said, "Very good. It will all be settled. What's he been up to? Debts? They shall be settled. Don't forget to remember me to your father."

"My father is dead, Your Majesty."

"Oh, dead?" said the Emperor. "Pity. pity," And he lost himself in memories of the Battle of Solferino, and went back to sit at his desk, pressed the bell knob and no longer noticed Herr von Trotta, who left with bowed head, his left hand on his sword-hilt, cocked hat held high to the right thigh.

Morning birdsong filled the room. For all his high opinion of birds, privileged among God's creatures, still, deep in his heart, the Emperor did not altogether trust them, just as he did not trust artists. And, according to the experience of the past few years, the twittering of birds had frequently been the occasion of one of his small lapses of memory. Quickly he scribbled a note, "Trotta affair," on the document. Then he sat waiting for the daily visit of his Comptroller. It was just striking nine. He would be coming.

Chapter 19

Lieutenant Trotta's awkward business was shrouded in solicitous silence. Major Zoglauer remarked only, "The highest quarters have intervened on your behalf. Your father has sent the money. That's all we need say about it." After which Carl Joseph wrote to his father. He reported that any threat to his honor had been averted by direct intervention from high places. He begged forgiveness for the unconscionably long time during which he had been silent and had not answered the District Commissioner's letters. He was touched and moved. And he made an effort to give his gratitude due expression. But he had no words for remorse and melancholy and longing in his limited vocabulary. It was an acrimonious piece of work. When he had written the letter, the following sentence occurred to him: "I'm thinking of applying for leave so as to be able to ask your forgiveness in person." For formal reasons, he could not add this felicitous phrase as a postscript. So the Lieutenant set about rewriting the letter. It took him an hour. The rewriting had improved the style of the letter, and with that the whole thing seemed to him to be settled, the whole disgusting business over and done with. He himself was amazed at his phenomenal luck. The grandson of the hero of Solferino could always rely on the old Emperor. No less pleasing was the now established fact that his father had money. Now that there was no longer any threat of getting thrown out of the army, he was in a position to leave it voluntarily and to live in Vienna with Frau von Taussig. He might perhaps even become a civil servant and wear civilian clothes. He had not been to Vienna for a long time. He had heard nothing from her. He missed her. He had a Ninety Percent, which made him miss her even more, at that consoling pitch of longing which permits a few tears. Recently, tears had been close to the surface in Lieutenant Trotta. He surveyed the work of his hands once more with great satisfaction, slipped it into an envelope, and with a light heart inscribed the address on it. As a reward, he ordered a double Ninety Percent.

Herr Brodnitzer brought it in person and said, "Kapturak's gone."

A lucky day, no doubt about that. That little man, who might have continued to remind the Lieutenant of one of his worst hours, had been removed. "Why?"

"Well, they just turned him out."

So far did the hand of Francis Joseph reach, the arm of the old man who had talked to Lieutenant Trotta with a glittering drop at the end of his Imperial nose. So far did the memory of the hero of Solferino extend.

Within a week of Herr von Trotta's audience, they had got rid of Kapturak. An august hint to local authorities had also led to the closing of Brodnitzer's gambling rooms. Nobody mentioned Captain Jedlicek now. He was engulfed in that engimatic silent oblivion from which a man could no more hope to return than from the grave. He was submerged in the military penal prisons of the old monarchy, in the dungeons of Austria. If his name happened to occur to one of the officers, it was immediately banished. Most of them succeeded in doing this thanks to their natural faculty for forgetting. A new captain came. A certain Lorenz, a plump, stocky, good-natured man with uncontrollable inclinations to negligence in matters of dress and bearing—always ready (though it was forbidden) to take off his tunic and have a game of billiards, giving you a view of his sometimes patched and slightly sweaty shirt sleeves. He was the father of three and the husband of a harassed looking wife. He settled down quickly. They got used to him immediately. His children were as alike as triplets and would come in a trio to fetch him at the café.

Gradually, the nightingales ceased to come from Olmütz, Hernals, and Mariahilf. Now the café band played only twice a week. Even so, its verve and fire had deserted it, and, for want of dancing girls, it played classical music—but rather to lament than to revive the warm bygone days. The officers started getting bored again unless they were drunk. When they drank they became melancholy and felt deeply sorry for themselves. The summer was very sultry. They had two breaks during morning drill. Rifles and privates sweated. The notes from the bugles sounded dull and listless in the clammy atmosphere. A thin, flat haze, like a veil of silver lead, spread itself across the sky. It hung over the swamps and even muted the ever-active din of the frogs. The willows did not stir. The world longed for a breeze. But the winds were all asleep.

Chojnicki had not come back this year. They were angry with him as if he were a defaulting entertainer under contract to the army every summer. But to liven things up in this desolate garrison, Captain Count Zschoch of the Dragoons had the really brilliant idea of organizing a large summer fête. The notion was especially brilliant because the fête would serve as a rehearsal for the great centenary celebrations of the regiment.

The regiment's hundredth anniversary was not due for another year; but it seemed that this exuberant regiment could not contain itself for a whole ninety-nine years without a fling of some kind. Everyone said what a brilliant idea it was. Colonel Festetics agreed and started to believe that he had been the first to think of it. The Colonel had begun his preparations for the great centenary display weeks ago. Every day in his spare time he sat in the regimental office dictating the respectful letter of invitation which, in six months' time, was to go to their honorary colonel, a minor German prince, unfortunately of a somewhat obscure collateral branch of the family. The style alone of this courtly missive demanded the joint effort of Colonel Festetics and Captain Zschoch. Sometimes they got involved in violent arguments on questions of style. The Colonel, for instance, thought the phrase "and so the regiment permits itself most submissively . . ." quite in order; whereas the Count considered "and so" to be wrong and "most submissively" not *de rigueur*. They had resolved to achieve two sentences a day and they managed that. Each dictated to a secretary, Colonel Festetics to a lance corporal, Captain Count Zschoch to a one-year volunteer. Then they compared their sentences, praising each other to the skies. Then the Colonel locked up the rough drafts in the big regimental cupboard to which he alone had the keys. They were placed on the top of the plans, already completed, for the great review and gymnastic display of officers and men. All the plans lay next to the large mysterious sealed envelopes containing secret orders in the event of mobilization.

So after Captain Zschoch had announced his brilliant idea, they interrupted the drafting of the letter to the prince and set to work sending similar invitations to the four corners of the earth. These plainly worded invitations required less stylistic precision and were completed within a few days. The only arguments concerned questions of precedence. Captain Count Zschoch differed from Colonel Festetics in his opinion that the first invitations should be sent to the higher-ranking people. "All at the same time," said the Colonel. "That's an order." And although Festetics belonged to one of the best Hungarian families, Count Zschoch saw in this the plainest evidence of democratic leanings in his Colonel, due no doubt to the fact that he was Hungarian. He grimaced and sent the invitations all at the same time.

The mess superintendent was called in. He had the address of every officer on the reserve list, as well as of those on the retired list. They were all invited. So were the closest relatives and friends of the Dragoon officers. These were informed that this would be a kind of dress rehearsal for the centenary celebrations. It was a way of letting them know that there was the prospect of meeting the Honorary Commandant of the regiment, that prince of an obscure collateral branch. Some of the people invited came from much older families, but they nevertheless attached some importance to meeting this diluted prince. Since it was to be a garden party, it was decided to make use of Chojnicki's little wood. His "little" wood differed from Chojnicki's other woods in that nature herself, as well as the owner, apparently intended it to be used for occasions of this kind. It was a young plantation of nice little pines and offered coolness and shade, smooth paths, a few little clearings ideal for covering with planks and converting into dance floors. So the little wood was used. Once again, Chojnicki's absence on this occasion was regretted. Nevertheless, he was invited, in the hope that he would not be able to withstand an invitation to the party of the regiment of Dragoons, and that perhaps, as Festetics put it, he might even bring some decent people with him. The Hulins were asked, and the Kinskys; the Podstatzkis, the Schünborns, the Albert Tassilo Larisch family, the Kirchbergs, the Weissenhorns; and the Babenhausens, the Sennyis, the Benkyös, the Zuschers, and the Dietrichsteins. They all had some connection with the Regiment of Dragoons. Captain Count Zschoch, taking a last glance at the list, sat back and said, *"Donnerwetter! Himmelherrgottsakra!"* and he repeated this original remark a number of times.

It was unfortunate but unavoidable that the unpretentious officers of the Jaeger battalion would have to be asked to such a grand occasion. We'll show them their place, thought Colonel Festetics, and Captain Count Zschoch was of precisely the same opinion. They looked at each other with angry eyes as they dictated these invitations, the one to his corporal, the other to his one-year volunteer. Each took care to make the other responsible for having had to ask the Jaeger battalion. Their faces brightened when they reached the name of Baron Trotta von Sipolje. "Battle of Solferino," observed the Colonel. "Hm," said Captain Zschoch. He was convinced that the Battle of Solferino had taken place in the sixteenth century.

All the regimental clerks were set to twining garlands of red and green paper. Orderlies sat on the pine stumps in the little wood stretching wires from tree to tree. Three times a week the Dragoons were excused from morning drill. Instead they "did lessons" in barracks. Here they were taught how to comport themselves in the presence of illustrious guests. For the time being, half a squadron was placed at the cook's disposal. The peasants learned to polish kettles, set trays, hold wine glasses, and turn the spit. And every morning Colonel Festetics would descend severely on the kitchen, inspect the cellars and the mess. A pair of white cotton gloves had been issued to every private who seemed at all likely to come into contact with the guests. Those whom the sergeant-major's caprice had selected for this onerous distinction had to parade before the Colonel every morning with outspread hands in white cotton gloves. He inspected the gloves for fit and cleanliness and durability of seams. He was in high spirits, transfigured by hidden sunshine. He admired his own energy and he demanded admiration. He developed extraordinary powers of imagination. He had at least ten ideas a day, where previously he had managed quite well on one a week. These flashes of new insight not only concerned the celebrations; they touched on fundamental problems of existence—for example, the rules of squadron drill, accouterment, and even strategy. In the course of these days it became clear to Colonel Festetics that he could quite easily be a general.

Now the wires stretched from tree to tree, and the next thing to do was to hang the festoons. So they put them up experimentally. The Colonel inspected; undoubtedly, Chinese lanterns were also required. But since, in spite of mist and sultriness, there had been no rain for a long time, a storm might break any day. The Colonel therefore posted sentries whose duty it was to unhook the garlands and lanterns at the least indication of an approaching storm. "The wires, too?" he prudently asked the Captain, well aware that even great men enjoy help from their advisers. "The wires will be all right," said the Captain. So they left them on the trees.

No storm broke. The haze and sultriness continued. On the other hand, they gathered from a number of refusals that an aristocratic club in Vienna was holding its celebrations on the same Sunday. Some of the people invited were torn between their desire for all the latest gossip first-hand (and the club ball was the only place to get it) and the enjoyment and adventure which a visit to the almost legendary frontier promised. This exotic prospect was as seductive as gossip—the chance of finding out who were really one's friends and enemies, the opportunity of according favors or obtaining them. Some promised to wire at the last minute. Such replies and the prospect of dealing with telegrams almost completely deprived Colonel Festetics of the confidence he had recently acquired. "This is disastrous," he said. "It is disastrous," said the Captain. And they hung their heads.

How many rooms ought they to get ready? A hundred? Would fifty do? And where? The hotel? At Chojnicki's? But unfortunately he was not there and had not even replied. "Chojnicki's unreliable, I never have trusted him," said the Captain. "You're quite right," said the Colonel. There was a knock, and the orderly announced Count Chojnicki.

"Marvelous to see you," they both exclaimed. He got an enthusiastic welcome. The Colonel felt that his inspiration was failing him and now he needed help. Captain Count Zschoch, too, felt that his imagination was exhausted. They took turns embracing their friend, three times over. Each waited impatiently for the other's embrace to be achieved. Then they ordered brandy. All the cares that had weighed them down were transformed into charming, graceful ideas. Chojnicki, for instance, suggested casually, "Perhaps we'd better say a

hundred rooms, and if fifty aren't used, so much the worse."
With one voice they exclaimed, "Brilliant!" and fell to
embracing their friend all over again.

There was no rain during the last week before the party.
The paper festoons, the Chinese lanterns, hung unscathed.
Sometimes the sergeant and four privates, camped at the edge
of the wood like pickets, their alert eyes spying toward the
west for the lines of the celestial enemy, would be alarmed by
the faintest rumble or hint of distant thunder. In the evening,
a glint of pale sheet lightning sometimes streaked livid across
the dun-colored mists which lay piled along the western
horizon which cushioned the fiery ball of the setting sun.
Storms occasionally broke in the distance, as in another world.
In the wood the dry earth crackled with brittle pine needles
and strips of withered bark from the pine trunks. The piping
of the birds was dull and sleepy. The soft sandy soil sent out
heat waves between the trees. The festoons stayed on the
wires.

On Friday a few guests arrived. Telegrams had announced
them. The officer on duty met them. The excitement in both
barracks mounted hourly. In Brodnitzer's café Dragoons and
Jaeger consulted, for no good reason except to add to the
pandemonium. No one wanted to stay by himself. Impatience
drove one to the other. They whispered, and found themselves
revealing a lot of secrets which they had kept private for years.
They trusted each other implicitly, they loved each other.
They sweated in harmony and common expectation. The
celebrations covered the horizon like a great festive mountain.
They were certain that it was more than a mere distraction,
that it meant fundamental changes in their lives. At the last
minute, their professional work filled them with misgivings.
Of their own accord, the celebrations began both to entice
and threaten them. They darkened the sky and filled it with
light again. The men brushed and ironed their full-dress
uniforms. Even Captain Lorenz dared not venture so much
as a game of billiards. The slippered ease in which he had
hoped to end his army career was gone forever. He eyed his
full-dress tunic distrustfully, he was like a fat old dray horse
which has stood for months in the cool shade of its stable and
finds itself suddenly faced with a string of trotters.

Sunday dawned at last. They had fifty-four guests. "*Donner-*

wetter, Saperlott!" said Count Zschoch a number of times. He had always known the kind of regiment he was serving in; but now, confronted by fifty-four exalted names, he felt he had never been sufficiently proud of it. The celebrations were due to begin at one o'clock with an hour-long parade in the barrack square. They had borrowed two army bands from larger garrisons. These were to play in the little wood on two round wooden open bandstands. The ladies sat in the covered baggage carts, summery dresses laced with stays, in hats like cartwheels on which stuffed birds made their nests. Though they felt the heat, they smiled, each a gay, refreshing breeze. They smiled with lips and eyes, and with bosoms encased in aromatic, tight-hooked bodices, with their lace gloves which reached to their elbows, with their minute handkerchiefs in their hands with which, at regular intervals and very delicately indeed, they would dab their noses. They sold champagne and sweets and tickets for the lucky wheel which the mess superintendent himself was to operate, and little colored bags of confetti with which they were covered and which they tried to blow away with roguishly pursed lips. Nor did they lack paper streamers. These coiled around their necks and ankles, hung down from the trees, transforming the natural pines into artificial ones. Their green was so much thicker and more satisfying than anything nature could supply.

Above the little wood, meanwhile, the long-expected storm had begun to gather. Thunder came nearer and nearer, but was drowned by the military bands. Evening enveloped tents, carriages, confetti, and dancing couples. The Chinese lanterns were lit, and nobody noticed that sudden puffs of wind made them wave about more violently than was safe for festive lanterns. The sheet lightning which lit up the sky more and more fiercely was not yet as brilliant as the fireworks one platoon was setting off behind the wood. If they noticed it at all, everyone was inclined to mistake this lightning for a failed rocket. Suddenly someone exclaimed, "There's going to be a storm!" And the rumor began to spread throughout the little wood.

So they got ready to leave and go, on foot, on horseback, or in carriages, to Count Chojnicki's house. All the windows were wide open. The gleam of candlelight streamed into the broad avenue in powerful fanlike flames, gilding the ground and the trees so that the leaves looked like metal. It was still early, but the cohorts of moving clouds joining forces on all sides were darkening the sky. Carriages, horses, and guests, brightly clad women and even more brightly colored officers, gathered in front of the Schloss gates, in the wide avenue, and on the graveled oval in front of the gates. Their mounts, held at the bit by orderlies, and the carriage horses tugging the reins of harassed coachmen, became impatient; the wind, like an electric comb, rippled their glossy coats, and they neighed anxiously for their stables, scraping the gravel with nervous hoofs. The unrest of nature and beasts communicated itself to the people. The excited shouts which a moment ago they had been hurling at each other died on their lips. Everyone looked anxiously at doors and windows. The high double wings were open, and they started to enter the house in groups.

Whether they were too involved with the manifestations of the storm which, though not exceptional, nevertheless made people restive, or whether they were distracted by the confused sounds of the two military bands which were beginning to tune their instruments in the house, nobody heard the swift gallop of the orderly who was hurrying toward the drive and who pulled up with a sudden swerve on the gravel. Dressed in his uniform, with his polished helmet, his cartridge belt, and the rifle slung across his back, the white sheet lightning playing around him and against a gloom of purple clouds, he was not unlike a stage messenger of war. The Dragoon dismounted and asked for Colonel Festetics. He was told that the colonel had gone inside. A moment later he came out, received a dispatch from the orderly, went back into the house. He stopped in the round outer hall where there was no ceiling light. A footman came up behind him holding a branched candlestick. The Colonel tore open the envelope. The footman, although he had been trained from early youth in the great art of service, could not control his suddenly trembling hand. The candles which he held guttered wildly. Without having in any way attempted to read over the Colonel's shoulder, the text of the dispatch—a single sentence, scribbled in huge blue pencil—obtruded into the visual field of his well-bred eyes. It would have been equally impossible not to have sensed through closed eyelids the flashes, which glittered now in quicker and quicker succession in every corner of the sky, as to have averted his gaze from the terrible large blue-penciled letters. HEIR TO THE THRONE REPORTED MURDERED AT SARAJEVO.

The message made its impact as a single word on the Colonel's consciousness, and on the eyes of the footman standing behind him. The Colonel dropped the envelope. The footman bent, holding the candles in his left hand, to retrieve it with his right. When he straightened up again he found himself staring into the face of Colonel Festetics, who had turned toward him. The footman stepped back. He held his candles in one hand, the envelope in the other and both his hands were shaking. The reflection of the flickering flames alternately lit and obscured the Colonel's face. This normally ruddy face, embellished by a gray-blond mustache, turned first violet then chalk-white. His lips quivered a little, his blond mustache twitched. Apart from the footman and the Colonel, there was no one in the hall. From within the house came the first muffled waltz of the military band, the ring of glasses, and the murmur of voices. Through the door which led outside they saw the reflections of distant lightning and heard the faint rumble of distant thunder. The Colonel stared at the footman.

"Did you read it?"

"Yes sir," the footman answered.

"Well, keep your mouth shut," said Festetics, putting his finger to his lips. He left. He lurched slightly. Or perhaps the flickering candlelight made his walk appear unsteady.

The footman, curious now and as excited by the Colonel's command to silence as by the gory information he had just come by, stood waiting for another servant to take his candles so that he might make his way into the rooms and there perhaps get more detailed information. Besides, though he was an intelligent, reasonable, middle-aged man, gradually he began to feel uncomfortable in this round hallway, scantily lit by his candles, plunged into even darker brown gloom after every streak of the violent blue-white lightning. The air was heavy and surcharged; the storm delayed. To the footman's mind there seemed a supernatural connection between the storm and the message. He reflected that at last the hour was arriving in which supernatural forces wished to manifest themselves clearly and cruelly to the world. So he crossed himself, holding the candlestick in his left hand. At this instant Chojnicki came out, looked at him in some surprise and asked if he felt so frightened of the storm. It wasn't only the storm, said the footman. For though he had promised to say nothing, the load of complicity grew too heavy for him. "Well, what else is it?" Chojnicki asked. Colonel Festetics, said the man, had just received terrible news. And he quoted it.

Chojnicki told him first to draw the thick curtains across the windows which by now had all been closed against the lightning, then to have his carriage brought. He was going into town. But while they were setting his horses between the shafts, a cab arrived, its dripping hood pulled forward, from some place where the clouds had already burst. Out of it, an attaché case under his arm, stepped that jolly district mayor who had quelled the demonstration of striking brush manu-facturers. He first offered the information that it was raining in the little town, as if this were his express purpose in coming. After which he told Chojnicki that the Heir to the Throne of the Austro-Hungarian Monarchy had probably just been shot dead in Sarajevo. Some travelers who had arrived three hours ago had been the first to spread the news. Then there had come a mutilated telegram in code from the Home Office. Further inquiries were still unanswered. Obviously, the thunderstorm had interfered with telegraphic communication. In addition, since this was Sunday, there would be only a skeleton staff in the government offices. But in the town, and even in the villages beyond it, excitement seemed to be increasing. In spite of the rain, people were standing around in the streets.

As the mayor told his story in hurried sentences, they could hear the drag of dancing feet from the house, the bright tinkle of glasses, and from time to time a burst of deep-throated male laughter. Chojnicki decided first to assemble a few of his guests whom he considered influential, prudent, and not yet drunk, in one of the more distant rooms. Making a number of excuses, he shepherded them into the room he had in mind, introduced the district mayor, and gave his news. Among those initiated were the colonel of the regiment of Dragoons, the major of the Jaeger battalion, their adjutants, some bearers of illustrious names, and, among other Jaeger officers, Lieutenant Trotta. There were not many chairs in the room, so some propped themselves up against the walls and a few exuberant, unsuspecting men sat down cross-legged on the carpet. But they remained where they were, even once they had learned everything. Some may have been frozen with horror; others again were simply drunk. The rest were naturally indifferent to any outside event and were, so to speak, paralyzed by good breeding: it was unseemly to incommode their bodies simply because a catastrophe had occurred. Some had not even removed the confetti from their heads and shoulders. This clownish decoration intensified the horror of the news.

In a few minutes the little room was stuffy. "Let's open a window," somebody said. Someone else unlatched a high narrow pane, leaned out, and in the next instant came bounding back. A livid white streak of lightning of exceptional intensity plunged down into the park beyond the window. It was impossible to see just where it had struck, but they could hear the rending of splintered wood. Black, heavy branches crashed to the earth. Even the indifferent, jovial squatters sprang to their feet, the slightly drunk began to totter and grow pale. They were genuinely surprised they were still alive. They held their breath and stared at one another with round eyes as they waited for the thunderclap. It came after a few seconds. But eternity itself had been crammed in the space of time between lightning and thunder. They tried to get nearer one another. They formed a compact knot of bodies and heads around the table. For the moment their faces all looked fraternally alike, no matter how various in feature. This might have been their first thunderstorm. Trembling, they waited until the short crack of thunder had died away. Then they breathed a sigh of relief. And while heavy clouds torn by flashes of lightning poured themselves down with a jubilant and deafening din outside the windows, the men resumed their original positions.

"We ought to break up the party," said Major Zoglauer.

Captain Zschoch, a few stars of confetti still in his hair, the remnant of a pink streamer around his neck, sprang to his feet. He was outraged, as captain, as count, as a Dragoon in particular, as a cavalryman in general, and above all as himself, a superior person—in brief, as Zschoch. His thick eyebrows bristled, forming two menacing palisades of spikes. Their points turned on Major Zoglauer. The big, pale, foolish-looking eyes, which seemed to mirror things their owner happened to observe years ago and seldom those which were in front of him, now expressed the arrogance of the Zschoch line, an arrogance of the fifteenth century. He had almost forgotten the lightning, the thunderclap, the fearful news, and, indeed, all the events of the last few minutes. He was able to remember only the efforts he had made with these celebrations, his brainchild. Nor could he hold his liquor: he had drunk champagne, and there were beads of sweat on his short snub nose.

"This news is not true," he said. "It just isn't true. Let anyone prove to me that it *is* true! It's a stupid lie, it's obvious from the word 'reported' or 'rumored' or whatever the political jargon is."

"Rumor is quite enough," said Major Zoglauer.

Here Herr von Babenhausen, a cavalry captain in the reserve, joined in the altercation. He looked hot and fanned himself with his handkerchief, pushing it into his sleeve and pulling it out again. He detached himself from the wall and came up to the table; he screwed up his eyes. "Gentlemen," he said, "Bosnia's a long way off. I attach no importance to rumors, I ignore them. If it *is* true, we'll know soon enough."

"Hear, hear!" cried Baron Nagy Jenö, the one in the Hussars. Though of undeniably Jewish origin (his grand-father had been a Jew in Oldenburg), Baron Nagy Jenö, whose title had been purchased by his father, considered the Magyars the noblest race in the monarchy and, indeed, on earth, and took immense and successful pains to forget his Semitic ancestors by taking on all the defects of the Hungarian gentry. "Hear, hear!" he repeated. He had come to the point of loving or loathing spontaneously all that seemed to further or retard the national policy of Hungary. He had hardened his heart against Francis Ferdinand because of the rumors that the Heir to the Austrian Throne favored Slavs and disliked Hungarians. And Baron Nagy had not come expressly to the frontier celebrations to have his enjoyment interfered with by a mere rumor. He considered it a betrayal of the whole Magyar race if he, one of its members, allowed himself to be prevented by a rumor from dancing the czardas here, as his nationality obliged him to. He screwed in his monocle more firmly—as he always did when national sentiment was indicated, just as an old man will tighten his hold on a walking stick before setting out on his wanderings—and said, in Hungarian-German, which sounded like a kind of lachrymose lisp, "Herr von Babenhausen is quite right. Perfectly right. If the Heir to the Throne really is murdered, there'll always be someone else to sit on it."

Herr von Sennyi, of purer Magyar extraction than the Baron, and suddenly worried by the thought that a Jew was exceeding him in Hungarian national feeling, stood up to say, "The Heir to the Throne may have been murdered, but, well, first we have no definite news, and second, how does it concern us?"

"It has something to do with us," said Count Benkyö, "but he hasn't—it's only a rumor."

Outside, the deluge continued steadily. The blue-white streaks of lightning were fewer, the thunder more distant.

First Lieutenant Kinsky, reared in Moldavia, suggested that the Heir to the Throne had been a poor bet for the monarchy, supposing that "had been" was the right way of putting it. He agreed with the last two speakers. This rumor could only be taken for what it was worth. They were all so far from the place where it was said to have occurred that nothing could really be checked. Anyway, they would hear the whole truth only after the party was over.

At which point Count Battyanyi, slightly drunk, began speaking to his compatriots in Hungarian, which no one else could understand. The others all stood staring at the speakers in some consternation. But the Hungarians seemed prepared to go blithely on all evening, perhaps it was one of their national customs. Although not understanding a word they said, the others could see plainly from their faces that gradually they were forgetting everyone else. At times they burst out laughing. The others felt slighted, less because there was laughter at such a moment than because they could not ascertain the cause of the laughter. Jelacich, a Slovene, lost his temper. He loathed Hungarians as much as he despised the Serbs. He loved the monarchy. He was a patriot. But he stood there, his hands outspread and helpless, holding his patriotism like a banner which he had to deposit somewhere and for which there seemed to be no safe cranny. Some Slovenes, and their cousins the Croats, lived more or less at the mercy of Hungary. All Hungary separated Captain Jelacich from the Emperor Francis Joseph, Vienna, and Austria. At Sarajevo, almost on his native soil, and perhaps at the hands of just such a Slovene as Jelacich, the Heir to the Throne had met his death. If now the captain should start to defend his murdered prince against the sneers and gibes of these Hungarians (since he alone in the room could understand them), they might tell him that it was his own people who had struck the blow. And, indeed, he was feeling rather guilty. He did not know why. For a hundred and fifty years his family had faithfully and devotedly served the Habsburg dynasty. Yet his two half-grown sons were talking of the independence of Southern Slavs and hiding their pamphlets from him, pamphlets which might have been written in hostile Belgrade. Yet he loved his sons. Every day at one o'clock when his regiment passed the gates of the grammar school, they ran out to him, through the heavy brown doors of their school, with tousled hair and laughter on their parted lips; and paternal affection made him dismount and put his arms around them both. He winked at the fact that they were reading seditious newspapers, was deaf to their doubtful political talk. He was intelligent and could see that he stood helpless between his forebears and his progeny, who seemed destined to be the begetters of an entirely new race of men. They looked like him, they had his eyes, their hair was the same color as his, but their hearts beat to a different rhythm, their brains harbored alien thoughts. They sang strange songs he had never heard. At forty, he felt like an old man whose sons are incomprehensible as great-grandchildren.

All that makes no difference, he thought now, and he went to the table to strike it with the flat of his hand. "We must ask you, gentlemen," he said, "to continue your conversation in German."

Benkyö, who had just said something, stopped and answered, "I'll say it again in German, if you like. We all agree, my countrymen and I, that we ought to be glad the swine's done for."

Everyone sprang to his feet. Chojnicki and the jovial district mayor went out of the room. The guests remained alone. They had been given a hint that dissensions within the army must have no witnesses. Beside the door stood Lieutenant Trotta. He had drunk a good deal. His face was pale, his body limp, his gums dry, his heart empty. He knew he was drunk, and yet, to his own amazement, the usual beneficent haze in front of his eyes was lacking. On the contrary, things seemed to be sharply outlined, as if he watched them through clear, smooth ice. These faces, never seen until today were, he felt, well known to him. This whole occasion was familiar, it was the realization of something he had often seen in his dreams. The country of the Trottas was falling to pieces, disintegrating.

At home, in the Moravian district town of W., Austria perhaps still existed. Every Sunday Herr Nechwal's band played the Radetzky March. Once a week, on Sundays, Austria existed. That forgetful old gentleman, the Emperor, with the white whiskers and the crystal drop on the end of his nose, and old Herr von Trotta were both Austrians. Old Jacques was dead. The hero of Solferino was dead. The regimental surgeon, Dr Demant, was dead. Get out of the army, he had said. I will, the Lieutenant thought. My grandfather got out, too. I'll tell them, he thought further. He was impelled to some kind of action, just as he had been years ago in Frau Resi's establishment. Was there no portrait to be rescued? He felt his grandfather's somber gaze at the back of his neck. He took a step toward the middle of the room. "I know," he said, and still knew nothing at all. "I know," he repeated and came forward another step, "that the Archduke and Heir Apparent, His Imperial Royal Highness Francis Ferdinand, has been murdered."

He was silent. He compressed his lips. They formed a thin pale-pink line. In his small dark eyes sparkled a bright, almost white, light. His black untidy hair overshadowed his low forehead, darkening the cleft between the eyebrows, the angry cleft, the Trotta legacy. He bent his head. His fists were clenched at the end of his slack arms. Everyone looked at his hands. If they had known the portrait of the hero of Solferino, they would have thought it was old Trotta come to life.

"My grandfather," Trotta began again, and again felt the old man's eyes behind him, "my grandfather saved the Emperor's life. And I, his grandson, will not stand by and allow the dynasty of the Supreme War Lord to be insulted. These gentlemen are behaving outrageously." He raised his voice. "Outrageously," he yelled. He had never heard himself shout. Unlike the others, he never bellowed at his men. "Outrageously," he repeated. His own echoes rang in his ears. The drunken Benkyö lurched across to the Lieutenant.

"Outrageously!" yelled Lieutenant Trotta.

"Outrageously!" Captain Jelacich echoed him.

"If anyone says another word against the dead man, I'll shoot him down," continued Trotta. He felt in his pocket. And, since the drunken Benkyö started muttering something, he shouted, "Silence!" in a voice which seemed not to be his, a thundering voice, perhaps the voice of the hero of Solferino. He felt at one with his grandfather. He himself was the hero of Solferino. It was his own portrait which was fading under the study ceiling.

Colonel Festetics and Major Zoglauer got up. For the first time since the existence of an Austrian army, a lieutenant was telling majors and colonels and cavalry captains to hold their tongues. No one now believed that the murder of the Archduke was merely a rumor. They could see the Heir to the Habsburg dynasty in a bright red steaming pool of blood. They also feared that they would be seeing blood at any moment in this room. "Tell him to stop," whispered Colonel Festetics.

"Lieutenant Trotta," said Zoglauer, "leave us."

Trotta turned back toward the door. At that instant it was thrust open. Guests pushed their way into the room, confetti and paper streamers on their hair and shoulders. The door remained open. They could hear women laughing in the other rooms and the music and the gliding feet of the dancing people. Someone shouted, "The Heir to the Throne has been murdered!"

"Play the Funeral March," shouted Benkyö.

"Yes, the Funeral March," several repeated.

They crowded through the door. In the two large rooms in which up to now there had been dancing, the two bands, conducted by the smiling bright red bandmasters, struck up Chopin's Funeral March. A few guests wandered round and round in time to it. Paper festoons coiled on their necks, their hair was dotted with confetti. Men, in civilian dress and in

289

uniform, escorted ladies. Unsteadily, their feet obeyed the macabre, stumbling rhythm. For these bands were playing without music and were not being conducted but merely accompanied by the slow loops which the bandmasters traced in the air with their ebony batons. One band sometimes fell behind, strove to catch up with the other, and jumped the beat. The guests walked round the empty, gleaming, polished parquet floor. They walked round and round one another, each a mourner behind the corpse of the one in front, with the invisible corpse of Francis Ferdinand and of the monarchy in their midst. They were all drunk. Those who had not had enough to drink found their heads reeling with the never-ceasing circumambulation. Gradually, the bands increased their pace and the ambling legs of the guests began to march. Drummers drummed incessantly and the heavy sticks of the big drum rattled like a pair of brisk young drumsticks. Suddenly the tipsy drummer clashed down on his silver triangles and, as he did, Count Benkyö pranced for joy. "The swine's done in!" the Count shouted in Hungarian. But they all knew what he had said as well as if he had spoken German. Some began to hop. The crashing bands kept speeding up the Funeral March. The triangle's bright silvery intoxicated chime pierced the blare of instruments.

In the end, Chojnicki's footmen were sent to put away the instruments. Smiling, the players allowed their instruments to be taken from them. Fiddlers sat goggling after their fiddles, cellists after their cellos, hornplayers after their horns. Some stood working their bows across the unanswering cloth of their sleeves, rocked by the beat of such inaudible melodies as might still be sounding in their drunken heads. When they removed one drummer's percussion instruments, he continued to brandish his drumsticks in the air. The bandmasters, who had drunk most of all, were finally dragged away, each between two footmen, like their instruments. The guests laughed. Then there was silence. No one uttered a sound. All stayed where they were and did not stir. Bottles were cleared after the instruments. Those who were still holding half-filled glasses had them taken away.

Lieutenant Trotta left the house. On the front-door steps sat Colonel Festetics, Captain Count Zschoch, and Major Zoglauer. It was no longer raining. There were only drops from the clouds which had thinned out and from the eaves of the roof. Wide white sheets had been spread over the steps for the three men to sit on; they might have been sitting on their own shrouds. Jagged raindrops stiffened their dark-blue backs. The remnant of a paper streamer clung, damp and permanently adhesive, round the neck of the Captain.

The Lieutenant took up his position in front of them. They did not move. Their heads were bent. They were like a martial group in a waxwork show.

"Major," said Trotta to Zoglauer, "tomorrow morning I shall ask to send in my papers."

Zoglauer got up. He held out his hand and tried to say something but could not utter a sound. Light began to fill the sky, a gentle wind tattered the clouds and, in the shining silver of brief night, already touched with a trace of morning, their faces were plainly seen. The Major's thin face was all in movement. Wrinkles thrust into one another, the skin twitched, his chin strayed here and there, seemed almost to oscillate. Little muscles tightened over the cheekbones, eyelids fluttered, cheeks quivered. All had been set in motion by a turmoil of confused, unutterable, and unuttered words. A trace of madness flickered across his face. Zoglauer pressed Trotta's hand second after second, for an eternity. Festetics and Zschoch continued to cower motionless on the steps. There was a scent of elder. They could hear the gentle drip of the rain and the soft rustling of the damp trees; and sounds of beasts, struck dumb by the storm, had timidly begun to come to life again. No music sounded in the house. Only people's voices came through closed windows from behind drawn blinds.

"You're young, you may be right," Zoglauer said at last. It was the stupidest, poorest part of what he had been thinking during these seconds. The rest, a vast, confused coil of reflections; he swallowed again.

It was long past midnight. But in the town people still stood about the streets, on the wooden pavements, talking outside their houses. They fell silent when they saw the Lieutenant passing.

By the time he reached the hotel, the sky was graying. He opened his cupboard. He packed two uniforms, his civilian suit, his underclothes, and Max Demant's sword. He went to work slowly, to use up the time. He looked at his watch to see how long each gesture took him. He prolonged his gestures, fearing the gap he would have to fill until he went to barracks.

Morning came. Onufrij brought his parade uniform and his brilliantly polished boots.

"Onufrij," Carl Joseph said, "I'm leaving the army."

"Yes sir," said Onufrij. He went out, down the passage, packed his things in a colored handkerchief, slung it on the thick end of his stick, and laid the bundle ready on his bed. He decided to go back home to Burdlaki: the harvesting would soon be starting. Now there was nothing to keep him in the Imperial and Royal Army. They called that sort of thing desertion and you could get shot for it. But the police came to Burdlaki only once a week and you could hide. Many others had done it, Panterleimon, Ivan's son; Grigorij, the son of Nikolai; pockmarked Pavel; carroty Nikofor. Only one had ever been caught and hanged, but that was a long time ago.

As for Lieutenant Trotta, he presented his request to resign his commission during officers' report. He was given instant leave. In the barrack yard he said his farewells to brother officers. They did not quite know what to say to him. They stood around him in a hesitant ring until Zoglauer at last found the proper farewell formula. It was extremely simple: "Good luck." The others echoed it.

Carl Joseph stopped at Chojnicki's. "I've always got room," said Chojnicki. "I'll come and pick you up."

For a second Trotta thought of Frau von Taussig, and Chojnicki guessed and said, "She's joined her husband, this time he won't get over it so easily. They may keep him on as a permanent patient. I don't blame him. I envy him. I've just been to see her, you know. My dear man, she's aged, aged."

Next morning at ten o'clock Lieutenant Trotta arrived at the District Commissioner's Residence. His father was sitting in the study. He was visible the instant the door opened, sitting opposite the door, under the window. Through the green blinds the sun cast narrow strips of light on the dark-red carpet. A fly buzzed, the clock ticked on the wall. It was cool, shady, drowsy with summer, just as it had been during vacations. Nevertheless, today a new, indeterminate radiance lay upon the objects in this room. One could not be sure what caused it. The District Commissioner got up. He himself was the source of this new light. The pure silver of his beard tinged the greenish twilight and the reddish glow of the carpet. The mildness of an unknown, perhaps unearthly light emanated from him, the light of a day which was already breaking in the earthly life of Herr von Trotta, just as earthly mornings begin to dawn when the stars of night are still shining. Many years ago, when he had come home from Moravian Weisskirchen for vacations, the whiskers on his father's cheek had been one small, black, divided cloud.

The District Commissioner stood at his desk. He waited for his son to come across to him, laid down his pince-nez on a document, and opened his arms. They kissed quickly. "Sit down," said the old man and pointed to the same armchair in which Carl Joseph the cadet had perched on Sunday mornings from nine to twelve, his cap on his knees, the sparkling snow-white gloves on the cap.

"Father," said Carl Joseph, "I'm leaving the army." He waited. He felt at once that as long as he was sitting he could explain nothing. So he got up to face his father at the other end of the desk and stared across at the silvery whiskers.

"After the terrible catastrophe," his father said, "which befell us all the day before yesterday, such an act amounts to desertion."

"The whole army's deserted," replied Carl Joseph. He left the desk. He began walking up and down the room. His left hand behind his back, his right reinforcing what he was saying. Many years ago the old man had walked up and down like that. A fly buzzed, the clock ticked. The streaks of sunlight brightened on the carpet; by now the sun must be high. Carl Joseph interrupted his narrative and looked at the District Commissioner. The old man was sitting with his hands half hidden in round, stiff, glossy cuffs, and hanging limply from the arms of the chair. His head sank on to his chest and his beard rested on his lapels. He's young and foolish, his son was thinking, a dear, silly, young fool with white hair. Perhaps I am his father, the hero of Solferino. I've grown old, he's only lived a long time. He walked up and down and began explaining. "The monarchy is dead, dead!" he shouted and stood still.

"So it would seem," murmured the District Commissioner.

He rang, and instructed the office porter, "Tell Fräulein Hirschwitz that luncheon will be twenty minutes late."

"Come," he said, got up, took his hat and stick. They went into the park. "A little fresh air will do us no harm," said the District Commissioner.

They avoided the kiosk where the blond young lady sat dispensing soda water with raspberry syrup. "I'm tired," said Herr von Trotta. "Shall we sit down?" For the first time since his appointment to the District of W. he sat down on an ordinary bench in a public park. He drew aimless figures and lines on the ground with his stick and said, while doing it, "I went to see the Emperor. I didn't really intend to tell you. The Emperor himself saw to that business of yours. Now, not another word about it."

Carl Joseph slipped an arm through his father's. He felt again the thin paternal arm: the arm on which, years ago, his had rested as they strolled one evening through Vienna. This time he did not withdraw his hand. They got up together and went home arm in arm.

Fräulein Hirschwitz came in her gray Sunday silk. A streak of her high-piled coiffure above her forehead had taken on the hue of this festal gown. She had improvised a Sunday meal: noodle soup, a roast of veal, and cherry dumplings. But on these the Commissioner wasted not a single word. He might have been consuming an ordinary, weekday cutlet.

Chapter 20

A week later Carl Joseph said good-by to his father. They embraced in the hall before he got into the cab. To Herr von Trotta demonstrations of affection were out of place on a railway platform in front of casual observers. Their embrace was fleeting as usual, surrounded by the drafty shadows in the hall and the coolness of the flagstones. Fräulein Hirschwitz was waiting on the balcony, completely in control of herself, like a man. In vain Herr von Trotta had tried to explain to her that she need not wave. She seemed to consider it a duty. Though it was not raining, Herr von Trotta opened his umbrella, the slight overcast seemed sufficient justification for doing so. Under the protection of the umbrella, he got into the cab, so that Fräulein Hirschwitz could see nothing at all from the balcony. He said nothing. Not until his son was in the train did the old man raise an admonitory finger. "I think," he said, "it would be best if you asked to resign for health reasons. It's not wise to resign from the army without some good pretext."

"Very good, Papa," said the Lieutenant.

Just before the train was due to move out Herr von Trotta left the platform. Carl Joseph watched him go, straight-backed with his rolled umbrella, its ferrule pointing upward, like a drawn sword. He did not turn around again, old Herr von Trotta.

The Lieutenant received his discharge. "What will you do now?" the others asked him. "I've got a job," said Trotta. They asked no more.

He inquired about Onufrij. He was told in the regimental office that batman Kolohin had deserted.

Lieutenant Trotta went back to the hotel. Slowly he changed. First he unbuckled his sword, the emblem and weapon of his honor. He had dreaded this moment. He was surprised he managed it without feeling melancholy. On the table stood a bottle of Ninety Percent, but he didn't need a drink. Chojnicki was coming to pick him up; already his whip cracked under the window. Now he entered the room, sat down and watched.

It was afternoon, three o'clock was striking from the clock tower. All the rich voices of summer drifted in through the open window. Summer itself was calling Lieutenant Trotta. Chojnicki, in a pale-gray suit with his light-tan shoes and yellow driving whip, was the messenger of summer. Carl Joseph rubbed the dull sheath of his sword with his tunic sleeve, drew it, breathed on the blade, polished the steel with his handkerchief, and put the sword in its case. It was like a corpse-washing. He took it out again before he strapped the sword box in his trunk and weighed it on his palms. Then he buried Demant's sword next to it. He read the scratched inscription under the hilt. GET OUT OF THE ARMY, Demant had told him. Now he was getting out.

Frogs croaked, crickets chirped. Just under the window, the bays whinnied and tugged gently at the light carriage, its axles creaked. Trotta stood in his unbuttoned tunic, the black-rubber neckband gaping out beyond the green facings on the collar. He turned and said, "The end of a career."

"The career itself is over and done with," said Chojnicki.

Trotta took off his coat, the Emperor's coat. He spread the blouse flat across the table as he had been taught at cadet school: first he turned back the stiff collar, folded the sleeves and put them into the cloth. Now it was time for the lower half; he turned it up, and the tunic was a little mound, the gray moiré lining was opalescent. Then came the trousers, folded twice, and Trotta put on his gray civilian suit, but kept the belt as a last reminder of his career (he had never been able to cope with braces). "My grandfather," he said to Chojnicki, "must have packed up his uniform one day, more or less as I'm doing."

"Most probably," Chojnicki said.

The trunk was still open, with Trotta's military self lying in it, a regulation corpse, correctly folded. It was time to close the trunk. A sudden stab of pain assailed the Lieutenant; his throat contracted, tears were in his eyes, he turned and tried to speak to Chojnicki. At seven he had been in the institution, at ten a cadet. He had been a soldier all his life. The soldier Trotta must be buried and mourned. You don't lower a corpse into the earth without shedding a few tears. It was a good thing Chojnicki was there.

"Have a drink," Chojnicki said, "you're becoming melancholy." Then he got up and locked the Lieutenant's trunk.

Brodnitzer himself came to carry it down to the carriage. "Herr Baron," Brodnitzer said, "it was a pleasure to have you in the hotel." He stood beside the carriage, hat in hand. Chojnicki was holding the reins. Trotta felt a sudden affection for Brodnitzer. "Farewell," he wanted to say. But Chojnicki was clicking his tongue, the horses tugged at the reins, they raised their heads and their tails at the same time, and the light high wheels of the carriage went crunching through the sandy street, so soft it might have been a bed.

They drove between the swamps echoing with the noise of frogs.

"Here's your house," said Chojnicki.

It was a little house on the edge of a wood, with green blinds like those on the windows at home. In it lived Jan Stepaniuk, an underforester, an old man with a long mustache the color of tarnished silver. He had served twelve years in the army. He said "Herr Leutnant" to Carl Joseph, brought home again to his military mother tongue. He was wearing a coarsely woven linen shirt with a narrow collar, embroidered red and blue. The wind puffed out the wide sleeves of the shirt and made his arms look like wings.

And here Carl Joseph stayed.

He was determined not to run into any former comrades. He wrote letters to his father, by flickering candlelight, sitting in his wooden room, writing on yellow, fibrous, official paper, spacing his beginning four digits off the top edge of the paper, his text two off the side. They were as alive as leave permissions.

He had little to do. He would enter the name of the day laborers into a heavy, leatherbound, black ledger and the requirements of Chojnicki's guests. He added up figures, with good intentions, but incorrectly; he reported on the state of the poultry, the fruit, the pigs which they bought and sold, of their few acres of yellow hops, of the oast house, which was rented yearly to a commission agent.

He knew the local speech now and could tell, more or less, what the peasants said to him. He bargained with the red-haired Jews who were already beginning to buy wood for the winter. He learned the different values of birch, fir and pine, lime and maple. He scraped and pinched. Like his grandfather, the hero of Solferino, he counted out hard silver coins with bony fingers every Thursday when he went into town to the pig market to buy saddles and hames, yokes and scythe blades, grindstones and sickles, rakes and seed. If he saw an officer passing, he lowered his head, though it was an unnecessary precaution. His mustache had thickened and proliferated; the hard black bristles stood so densely on his cheeks, you could scarcely recognize him. They were getting ready for the harvest; the peasants stood outside their huts, grinding scythes on the round, brick-red grindstones. In every village stone was whirring against steel, drowning the song of the crickets. At night the Lieutenant sometimes heard music and noise from Count Chojnicki's new Schloss. He absorbed these sounds into his sleep with those of the nocturnal crowing of cocks and dogs barking at the full moon. At least he was content, alone, at peace. It was as if he had never led any other life. If he could not sleep, he would get up, take his stick, and walk in the fields, through the many-voiced chorus of night, waiting for the dew and the gentle song of the wind proclaiming day. He felt as refreshed as after a full night's sleep.

Every afternoon he walked into surrounding villages. "Praised be Jesus Christ," the peasants would say to him. Trotta would answer, "For ever and ever amen." He walked with bent knees like them, like the peasants of Sipolje before him.

One day he walked through the village of Burdlaki. Its tiny church tower pointed like a villager's forefinger at the blue sky. It was a quiet afternoon. Cocks crowed sleepily. Midges clustered and hummed all down the village street. A black-bearded peasant suddenly came out of his hut. He stood out on the road and said, "Praised be Jesus Christ."

"For ever amen," said Trotta and was about to walk on.

"Herr Leutnant, it's Onufrij," said the bearded peasant. His beard muffled his whole face, it spread out thick like a black fan.

"Why did you go and desert?" asked Trotta.

"I only went back home," said Onufrij.

No point in asking such foolish questions. He understood Onufrij well. He had served his lieutenant as the lieutenant had served his Emperor. Now the fatherland no longer existed. It was crumbling to bits. "Aren't you afraid?" asked Trotta.

No, Onufrij was not afraid. He lived with his sister. Every week gendarmes passed through the village, but never stopped to make inquiries. They were all Ukrainian peasants like Onufrij. If no one lodged a written declaration with the sergeant-major, he had nothing to worry about. In Burdlaki people did not lodge declarations.

"Good luck, Onufrij," said Trotta. He went on along the winding street, which all at once opened out into fields, and Onufrij followed as far as the bend. He could hear the tread of the military hobnailed boots on the gravel on the road. Onufrij had taken his army boots with him. He was on his way to the Jew Abramtschik, who kept the village inn. You could get best quality soap there, and brandy, cigarettes, tobacco, and stamps. This Jew had a flaming red beard. He sat in the archway of his inn and radiated over two kilometers of the road. When he gets old, Carl Joseph thought, he will be a white-bearded Jew like Max Demant's grandfather.

He had a drink, bought stamps and tobacco, and went on. From Burdlaki his road led past Oleksk, to the village of Sosnow, then to Bytok, Leschnitz, and Dombrowa. He went the same way every day. Twice he had to cross the railway line: two railway gates, striped a faded black and yellow, and glass signals, continuously clattering in the signal boxes. They were the gay voices of a world which no longer concerned Baron Trotta. That world was extinguished, as were the years in the army, as if he had never done anything but walk across fields and country roads, stick in hand, and had never had a sword at his side. He lived as his grandfather, the hero of Solferino, had lived, and his great-grandfather, the pensioner at Laxenburg, in the castle park, and perhaps like other nameless ancestors and the peasants of Sipolje. He took the same road always, past Oleksk, to Sosnow, to Bytok, to Leschnitz, and Dombrowa. These villages lay in a ring round Chojnicki's Schloss. He owned them all. From Dombrowa a willow path led on to Chojnicki's. It was still early. If he went a little faster, he would get there before six o'clock and would not meet any former comrades. Trotta walked in quick strides. Now he was standing beneath the windows. He whistled. Chojnicki came to the window, nodded, and came out.

"Well," Chojnicki said to him. "It's come this time. There's a war on. We've been expecting it long enough. Even so, we won't be ready for it. It seems as if the Trottas aren't destined to live long in peace. My uniform's ready. I expect we'll both be wanted in a week or two."

Never, it seemed to Trotta, had nature been so peaceful. At this hour you could look straight into the sun as, visibly, it sank westward. A violent wind came to receive it, rippled the small white clouds in the sky and the wheatstalks on the ground, caressed the scarlet faces of the poppies. A blue shadow drifted across green meadows. Toward the east the little wood disappeared in deep violet. Stepaniuk's low house, where he lived, gleamed white at the edge of the wood, its windows burnished with evening sunlight. The crickets increased their chirping. The wind carried their voices into the distance; there was silence and the fragrance of the earth.

Suddenly there was a faint hoarse honking from above. Chojnicki raised his hand. "Do you know what that is? Wild geese. They're leaving us early. It's still midsummer. They can hear shooting already. They know what they're up to."

It was Thursday, the day for a small party. Chojnicki turned away. Trotta walked slowly back to his little house with its glowing windows.

That night he could get no sleep. At midnight he heard the hoarse honking of the geese. He got up, dressed, and went outside. Stepaniuk, in his blouse, lay on the threshold, his lighted pipe burnt faintly red. He was stretched flat on his back and said without moving, "I don't seem able to get any sleep."

"The wild geese," said Trotta.

"That's it, geese," confirmed Stepaniuk. "Never in all my life have I heard geese so early in the year. Listen, listen to that!"

Trotta stared up at the sky. The stars glittered as always. Nothing else was visible in the sky. Yet, under the stars, the hoarse honking went on and on. "They're practising,"

Stepaniuk said. "I've been lying out here a long time. I can see them sometimes. It's no more than a gray shadow. Look, up there!" He pointed his glowing pipe at the sky. For an instant they both caught sight of the tiny white shadows of the geese under cobalt blue. They flew along like a bright little veil. "That isn't the only thing," said Stepaniuk. "This morning I saw hundreds of crows, never seen so many. They're foreign crows, from foreign parts. I think they've come across from Russia. We have a saying here, 'Crows are the prophets among birds'."

A broad silver streak lay along the northeastern skyline. As they watched, it brightened. The wind was rising. It carried a confusion of sounds from Chojnicki's Schloss to their ears. Trotta lay down on the ground beside Stepaniuk. He looked up sleepily at the stars and listened to the honking of the geese. He fell asleep.

He awoke at daybreak, feeling as if he had only slept half an hour, but at least four must have passed since he went to sleep. Instead of the twittering birdsong which usually welcomed the morning, today the black croaking of hundreds of crows fell on his ears. Stepaniuk sat up beside him. He took his cold pipe out of his mouth and pointed the stem at the surrounding trees. The huge black birds sat clumsily on the branches, an eerie windfall from the sky. They sat motionless, these black birds. Stepaniuk flung a stone at them, but the crows only flapped their wings a few times. They sat on the branches like growing fruits. "I'll have a shot at them," said Stepaniuk. He went inside to get his gun, came out, and fired. A few birds toppled down, the rest seemed not to have heard the crack of his gun. They all stayed on the branches. Stepaniuk picked up his black corpses; he had killed a good dozen. He carried his quarry indoors in both hands. Their blood dripped on to the grass. "Queer sort of crows," he said, "they're not budging. They're the prophets among birds."

It was Friday. In the afternoon, as usual, Carl Joseph went through the villages. The crickets were not chirping, the frogs were not croaking, only the crows cawed. They were sitting everywhere, on oaks, on birch trees, on the willows. They may come every year before the harvest, Trotta thought. They hear the peasants grind their scythes and get together. He walked through Burdlaki, secretly hoping to see Onufrij, but Onufrij was not there. The peasants stood outside their huts, whetting their scythes on the red grindstones. Sometimes they looked up from their work; the cawing of the crows worried them, and they fired dark curses at the dark birds.

Trotta came to Abramtschik's inn; the red-headed Jew sat outside, his beard gleamed. Abramtschik got up. He took off his black velvet skullcap, pointed upward and said, "The crows are here. They've been cawing all day long. Wise birds. We ought to take notice."

"Perhaps we ought, perhaps you're right," said Trotta and went on again by the usual willow path to Chojnicki's. He stood under the windows. He whistled. No one came.

Chojnicki was sure to have gone into town. Carl Joseph followed him there by the field path, through the marshes, to avoid meeting people. Only the peasants used this path. Some came toward him. The path was too narrow for two, you had to stand and let the other pass. All those whom Trotta met today seemed to be walking faster than usual. Their stride was longer. As they walked past him they greeted him more casually. They went with heads bent, like people who are filled with weighty thoughts. And suddenly, when Trotta could already see the customs barriers behind which the town began, the number of people increased. A group of twenty or more came along the path in single file. Trotta stopped. He could see they must be factory workers, brushmakers, going home to their villages. There might be some among them whom he had shot at. He waited to let them pass. In silence, one after another, they hurried along, each with a little bundle slung from a stick across his shoulder. Dusk seemed to come on more rapidly, as though these hurrying people increased the darkness. The sky was faintly overcast; the sun was sinking, a dim red ball; silver-gray mists rose from the swamps, straining toward the clouds, like earthly brothers striving to reach their sisters in the sky. Suddenly all the town bells began to ring. The men on the path stopped for an instant to listen and went on again. Trotta stopped one of them to ask him why the bells had begun to ring. "It's because of the war," he said without looking up.

"The war," Trotta repeated. Of course, there was a war: it was as if he had known it since daybreak, since yesterday

302

evening, the day before that, indeed for weeks, ever since he had sent in his papers; since the wretched celebrations of the Dragoons. It was the war for which, at the age of seven he had begun to prepare himself. It was his war, a grandson's war. The days for the heroes of Solferino were returning. The bells rang without stopping. He came to the customs barrier. The wooden-legged gendarme stood outside his little house surrounded by people, and on the door was a shining black-and-yellow poster; its opening words, black on yellow background, were legible even at a distance: TO MY PEOPLES.

Peasants in short, rank-smelling sheepskins, Jews in flutter-ing, bottle-green caftans, Swabian farmers from the German colonies in gray loden coats, Polish citizens, traders, craftsmen, government officials, surrounded the little customs house. On each of the four walls there was a poster in a different language. TO MY PEOPLES. Those who could read, read it out. Their voices mingled with the resounding bell peals. Some went from wall to wall and read the text in every language. As one bell ceased, another immediately began. Crowds were streaming out of the town on the wide streets which led to the station. Trotta went towards them into the town. It was dusk by now and, since this was a Friday evening, candles, alight in all the little houses of the Jews, lit up the pavements. Every little house was like a sepulcher. Death himself had lit the candles. Louder than on other Jewish holidays came the chanting from the houses in which they prayed. They were ushering in an extraordinary, bloody Sabbath. They rushed out through the dusk in dark swarms over the pavements, and gathered together at the crossroads, where soon their lamentations rose for those among them who were soldiers and were going to war in the morning. They clasped each other's hands, they kissed one another on the cheek, and when two embraced, as if this parting were their last, their two red beards became entangled so that the men had to use their hands to separate their beards. The bells tolled above their heads. Bugles from the barracks cut across the bells and the lamentations of the Jews. They were sounding lights-out. The last lights-out. Night was upon them. No stars shone. A dark, flat sky hung low and dismal over the town.

Trotta turned back. He tried in vain to get a lift. He went with long hurrying strides to Chojnicki. The gate stood open and there were lights on in all the rooms, just as there had been on the evenings of his large parties. Chojnicki, wearing uniform and helmet, came towards him in the hall, his cartridge belt already strapped on. He had ordered the carriage. His garrison was three miles away and he wanted to go there that same evening. "Wait, wait," he said. For the first time, thoughtlessly perhaps, or else it may have been the uniform, he addressed the Lieutenant in the familiar *Du*. "I'll take you to get your things, then back to the town."

They pull up at Stepaniuk's little house. Chojnicki sits down. He watches while Carl Joseph takes off his civilian clothes and puts on his uniform, just as he had watched a few weeks ago—but it is long ago—when Trotta was taking off his uniform. Trotta is returning to his own. He takes his sword out of its case and straps it on the belt. Its heavy gold and black tassels swish softly against the shining metal of the sword. He locks his trunk.

They have only a little time to say good-by. They pull up in front of the Jaeger barracks. "Good-by," says Trotta. Their handshake is a long one. Time seems to slip past almost audibly behind the coachman's broad, immovable back. It is as if a handshake is not enough. They feel the need for something more. "We always kiss," Chojnicki says. They embrace and kiss quickly. Trotta gets out of the carriage. The guard at the gate presents arms.

The horses tug at the reins, the barrack gates close behind Trotta. He stands for a minute and listens to the sound of Chojnicki's carriage wheels.

Chapter 21

That same night the Jaeger battalion marched northward in the direction of the Wolocyska frontier. It began to drizzle, then to rain, and the white dust on the road on which they marched was transformed into silvery-gray slime. It slapped around the boots of the soldiers and spotted the immaculate uniforms of the officers marching to their death in prescribed regalia. The long swords got in their way; their magnificent long-fringed black-and-gold tasseled sashes became entangled, sodden, caked over with hundreds of little mud globules. In the gray early-morning light, the battalion reached its objective, joined up with two other infantry regiments, and formed extended lines. There they waited two days, with no sign of war. Sometimes they heard stray shots to their right, in the distance. There were little border skirmishes between cavalry squads. Sometimes they saw wounded excisemen and here and there a dead scout. Ambulance men carried these wounded, like corpses, past the waiting lines. The war refused to begin. It hovered for days, as storms hover before they break.

On the third day came orders to retreat, and the battalion formed up for the march back. Both officers and men were disappointed. The rumor spread that two miles eastward a whole regiment of Dragoons had been cut up. Cossacks, so they heard, had already invaded the country. They marched west silently and glumly. It soon became obvious that an unprepared retreat was in progress. At crossroads and in market towns and villages they met a confused crowd of arms of all kinds. The army command sent numerous and conflicting orders. Most were concerned with the evacuation of towns and villages and the treatment of Russophile Ukrainians, priests and spies. Hasty regimental courts martial passed hasty sentences in the villages. Secret agents, whose reports could not be verified, came to accost teachers and

305

Greek Orthodox priests, officials, peasants, and photographers. There was no time. They had to retreat as fast as possible and also punish traitors as fast as possible. So that on the sodden roads, Dragoons, field artillery and ambulances, transport, Uhlans and infantry got entangled in helpless suddenly accumulated crowds; couriers galloped about, while the inhabitants of small towns took flight westward in endless, white-faced streams, laden with red-and-white striped mattresses, gray sacks, brown pieces of furniture and blue oil lamps. And all the while volleys of the hurried executions and sullen bugle calls accompanied the monotonous voices of the judge advocates. Wives of the murdered men huddled screeching for pardon under the mud-caked boots of officers, while red and silver flames burst from huts and barns, stables and hayricks. War, for the Austrian army, began with a series of courts martial. For days on end traitors, real or supposed, swung from the trees in village churchyards, to inspire the living with fear. But far and wide the living had taken to flight. Flames, stronger than the ceaseless, even drizzle of rain which ushered in the autumn of blood, surrounded these bodies as they dangled from branches whose leaves had begun to crackle. The old bark of ancient trees charred slowly, and tiny smoldering sparks crept up along the fissures like fiery worms, seizing the foliage; the green leaves curled, turned red, then black, then gray; the ropes broke; the corpses came thudding down with black faces and bodies unscathed.

One day they called a halt in the village of Krutyny. They had arrived there that afternoon; they were to go on westward the next morning before daybreak. That day the rain held off, and a pleasant late September sun spread silver light across wide fields in which stood harvests, the living bread not to be consumed now. The air was redolent of the Indian summer. Even the crows stopped their noise, deceived by the brief peace of the day and deprived of hope for their carrion. It was eight days now since the officers had changed their clothes. Their boots were waterlogged, their feet swollen, their knees stiff, the calves of their legs were sore, and their backs too painful to bend. They were billeted in village huts, where they tried to get clean clothes out of their baggage and wash in the thinly trickling village well. The Lieutenant could not sleep in the clear and still night; the only sounds were made by forgotten dogs in isolated farmyards howling in fear and hunger. He came out of the hut where he was staying and went down the long village street, following the direction of a church tower which pointed its Greek double cross up at the stars. The church, with its shingle roof, stood in the middle of a little graveyard, surrounded by slanting crosses, which seemed to sway in the moonlight. Before the high, gray, wide open churchyard gates three corpses were strung up—a bearded priest between two young peasants in sand-colored smocks with rough raffia shoes on their motionless feet. The priest's black cassock reached to his shoes and, from time to time, a night wind stirred them so they swung against the round edge of the cassock, like dumb clappers in a soundless bell, which, though no sound came, appeared to be ringing.

The Lieutenant approached the hanged men. He stood and examined their swollen faces. And he thought he recognized some of his own men in them. These were the faces of the people with whom he had drilled every day. The priest's rough, black, fan-shaped beard made him think of Onufrij's beard. That was how he last remembered Onufrij. And who knew, perhaps Onufrij was this priest's brother. Lieutenant Trotta looked around. No human sound was to be heard. In the belfry bats' wings rustled. Abandoned dogs yelped in abandoned farms. The Lieutenant drew his sword and cut down the three men from their nooses. Then he shouldered the corpses and carried them, one by one, into the churchyard. There, with his drawn sword, he began loosening up the earth in the narrow strips between the graves, until he felt he had made enough room for three corpses. Then he put all three down, shoveled earth over them with sword and scabbard, and stamped it down all around. Then he made the sign of the cross. He had not crossed himself since the last mass at the cadet school in Moravian Weisskirchen. He wanted to say an Our Father, but his lips only moved without producing any sounds. A nocturnal bird screamed. The bats flapped their wings. The dogs howled.

Next day, before sunrise, they marched on. The silver mists of the autumn morning shrouded the world. Soon the sun came up above them, glaring, hot as in midsummer. They began to get thirsty. They were marching through a deserted sandy neighborhood. Sometimes they thought they could hear water trickling, somewhere. A few men went running off in what seemed to be the direction of the sound but came back at once. No stream, no pond, no well. They passed through a few villages, but in these the wells were all stopped up with bodies of people killed and executed. The corpses hung over the wooden rims of the wells, sometimes doubled up over them. The men did not stop to look into the depths. They came back. And marched on.

Their thirst grew fiercer. They heard shots and lay down flat on the ground. The enemy had probably caught up with them. They crept on, pressed to the ground. Soon, they could see, the road began to open out and at the end of it glittered a deserted railway station; from this point railway lines started. The battalion reached the station running on the double. Here they were safe for a few kilometers. They were protected on either side by the railway embankment. The enemy—it might be a Cossack sotnia galloping along—was perhaps at the same elevation on the farther side of the bank. Suddenly someone shouted, "Water!" and in the next instant they had all caught sight of a well up on the ridge of the slope by a little signal box.

"Stop where you are!" commanded Major Zoglauer.

"Stop where you are!" repeated the officers. But they could not hold their thirsty men. Singly, then several at a time, they began scrambling up the slope; rifles cracked, men fell. Enemy horsemen beyond the slope were firing at the thirsty men and more and more thirsty men went scrambling up toward the fatal well. By the time the second platoon of the second company had come almost level with the well a dozen corpses lay about on the green bank.

"Platoon halt," commanded Lieutenant Trotta. He stepped out beside them and said, "I'll get you some water. All stop here. Hand up those buckets." They brought him two canvas buckets from the machine-gun section. He took a bucket in either hand. And climbed the embankment to the well. Bullets whistled around him, around his feet, his legs, and above him; they sang in his ears. He bent down over the well. Below, on the other side of the ridge, he could see two lines of aiming Cossacks. He was not afraid. It never occurred to him that he might be hit like the others. He could hear the bullets before they had been fired—at the same time he heard the opening drumbeats of the Radetzky March. He was standing out on his father's balcony. Down below, the military band was playing. Nechwal was just lifting his ebony baton with the silver knob. Trotta let the second bucket down into the well. The cymbals clashed. He raised his bucket. With a brimming bucket in either hand and bullets whizzing round his ears, he put out his left foot to start the descent. He came down two steps. Only his head was visible above the ridge. A bullet struck his skull. He took one more step and fell. The brimming buckets swayed and tipped and spilled their water all over him. Warm blood gushed from his head into the cool earth of the slope. From below he could hear the voices of Ukrainian peasants in his platoon in chorus, "Praised be Jesus Christ".

"For ever amen," he wanted to say. They were the only Ruthenian words he could speak. But his lips would no longer move. His mouth gaped open. His teeth shone white in the face of the blue autumn sky. Slowly his tongue grew blue and he could feel his body getting colder. Then he died. That was the end of Lieutenant Baron Carl Joseph Trotta von Sipolje.

So commonplace, so unsuitable for inclusion in readers designed for the use of pupils in Austrian Imperial and Royal primary and secondary schools, was the end of the grandson of the hero of Solferino. Lieutenant Trotta died, not with sword in hand but with two buckets of water. Major Zoglauer wrote to the District Commissioner. Old Trotta read the letter a few times over and let his hands drop. It fluttered down to the reddish carpet. Herr von Trotta did not take off his pince-nez. His head trembled and the trembling pince-nez, with its two little lenses, was like a glass butterfly fluttering on his nose. Two heavy, crystal tears dropped simultaneously from the eyes of Herr von Trotta, clouding the lenses, and ran their course into his side-whiskers. Herr von Trotta's body remained still, only his head trembled. It trembled backward and forward, to the left and to the right, and the pince-nez beat its glassy wings. So he sat at his desk for an hour or more. Then he got up and went, at his usual pace, to his house. He took out his black suit from the wardrobe, the black tie and strips of crape which he had worn for his father, round hat and arm. He changed. He did not look into the mirror. His head still trembled. He was doing his best to steady it, but the harder the District Commissioner tried, the more it shook. Still the fluttering pince-nez clung to his nose. At last he gave up all attempts and let his head tremble. He went, in his black suit with the crape armband, to Fräulein Hirschwitz's room, stood on the threshold, and said to her, "Dear lady, my son is dead." Quickly he closed the door and went to his office, from one subordinate's room to the next, only putting his trembling head around the doors and saying each time, "My son is dead, Herr So-and-So, my son is dead, Herr So-and-So." Then he took hat and stick and went out. Everyone greeted him and was surprised to see his head trembling. The District Commissioner stopped one person or another from time to time and said, "My son is dead." Nor would he wait for their flustered condolences but went straight on to Dr Skowronnek.

Dr Skowronnek was in uniform, a colonel in the Army Medical Corps; mornings in the garrison hospital, afternoons, as usual, in the café. He rose as the District Commissioner entered, saw his trembling head and the crape armband and knew everything. He took the District Commissioner's hand and glanced at the restless head, the fluttering pince-nez. "My son is dead," repeated Herr von Trotta.

Skowronnek held his friend's hand long in his, several minutes. They stood hand in hand. Then the District Commissioner sat down and Skowronnek put the chessboard on another table. When the waiter came the District Commissioner said to him, "My son is dead, Herr Ober." The waiter bowed very low and brought some cognac.

"Another," ordered the District Commissioner. At last he took the pince-nez off his nose. He remembered having left the letter with the news of his son's death on the floor of his office, and went back to look for it. Dr Skowronnek followed. Herr von Trotta seemed not to notice him. But he was not in the least surprised when Skowronnek, without knocking, opened the office door, entered, and remained with him. "Here is the letter," he said.

All that night and for many after, Herr von Trotta did not sleep. His head still trembled and shook among the pillows. Sometimes the District Commissioner dreamt of his son.

Lieutenant Trotta stood with his officer's cap held out to his father and said to him, "Drink, Papa, you're thirsty." The dream recurred again and again, more and more frequently. And gradually, the District Commissioner found a way of summoning his son every night and on many nights Carl Joseph came several times. So that now Herr von Trotta began to long for night and for his bed, and daylight made him feel impatient. When spring came and the days were longer, he kept his room darkened in the mornings, closed the blinds early, and so prolonged his nights by artificial means. His head did not stop trembling. He himself and everyone else got quite used to the constant trembling of his head.

The war seemed to concern Herr von Trotta very little. He took up a newspaper only in order to hide his trembling head behind it. There was never any talk of victories or defeats between him and Dr Skowronnek. Usually they played chess without exchanging a single word. One would sometimes say to the other, "Do you remember that game two years ago? You were just as inattentive then as today." It was as if they were talking of things that had taken place decades ago.

Many months had passed since the news of Carl Joseph's death, the seasons had returned and changed according to the old immutable laws of nature, though men, under the red veil of war scarcely seemed to be aware of the change, Herr von Trotta least of all men. His head still trembled and trembled, like a large but light fruit on too thin a stalk. The Lieutenant had rotted long since, or been devoured by carrion crows which swarmed above the bodies along the fatal railway lines, but to old Herr von Trotta it still seemed as if he had only yesterday received news of his son's death. And the letter from Major Zoglauer, who by now was also dead, lay in the District Commissioner's breast pocket to be taken out again every day, read again, and kept in its terrible freshness like grave mounds tended by loving hands. What, to old Herr Trotta von Sipolje, were those hundred thousand other dead, who by now had gone after his son? What concern of his were the confused and hurried orders which came week after week from his superiors? What, to him, was the end of the world which now he could perceive even more clearly than on the occasion he had heard the prophetic Chojnicki. His son was dead. His office terminated. His world had ended.

Epilogue

All that remains is to give an account of the last days of Herr von Trotta. They passed almost like one day. Time flowed past him, murmuring monotonously in a broad even stream. War communiqués and the many new regulations and special enactments concerned him little. But for the war, he would long since have retired. He stayed on because the war demanded it. And sometimes he got the impression that he was living a second, paler life while his first, real life, had ended long ago. His days, he felt, did not speed him toward the grave as other men's did. Petrified, like his own headstone, Herr von Trotta stood on the brink of days. Never had the District Commissioner looked so like the Emperor Francis Joseph. Sometimes he would even venture himself to make the comparison with the Emperor. He thought of his audience at the Imperial palace of Schönbrunn and, in the manner of simple old men talking of their mutual grief, he would say to Francis Joseph in his imagination, "What? Well now, if anyone had told us all this in those days. Two old fellows like you and me. . . ."

Herr von Trotta slept very little. He ate without noticing what they gave him. He signed official documents without having read them through. Sometimes he arrived at the café in the afternoons before Dr Skowronnek. Then he would take a foreign newspaper, three days old, and read news he was long familiar with. If the doctor happened to mention the latest news, he would only nod, as if he had known it all a long time.

One day he got a letter. It came from a certain, to him completely unknown, Frau von Taussig, who was serving as a voluntary nurse in the Steinhof Asylum in Vienna. She wrote to tell him that Count Chojnicki had returned insane from the front a few months ago and often spoke of the

District Commissioner. In his confused utterances he always insisted that he had an important message for Herr von Trotta. If by any chance Herr von Trotta thought of coming up to Vienna, a visit to the patient might possibly effect an unexpected improvement in his condition, since such recoveries had occurred in similar cases. The District Commissioner questioned Dr Skowronnek. "Everything is possible," said the doctor. "If you feel you can stand it—I mean, without too much strain. . . ."

"I can stand anything," said Herr von Trotta. He decided to go at once. Perhaps the patient might have something important to tell him about the Lieutenant. He might even have something from his son to give the father. Herr von Trotta went to Vienna.

They took him to the military section of the asylum. It was late autumn, a dull day. The asylum stood enveloped in the gray drizzle which for days had been soaking the world. Herr von Trotta sat in the blinding whiteness of a corridor looking out through a barred window at the denser but more delicate bars of rain, and thought of the slope under the railway line on which his son had died. He'll be getting soaked, the District Commissioner thought, as if the Lieutenant had died a few days before and his corpse was still quite new. Time passed slowly. People with deranged faces and gruesomely distorted limbs were taken past him down the corridor. But, though this was his first visit to an asylum, madness held no terror for the District Commissioner. Only death was terrible. A pity, he thought. If Carl Joseph had gone out of his mind instead of dying, I could have brought him round. And even if I hadn't managed that, could have come to see him every day. Perhaps his arm would have been as shockingly contorted as that lieutenant's who has just gone by. But it would have been his arm, and you can stroke a twisted arm and you can look into contorted eyes. So long as they are my son's eyes. Happy the fathers whose sons are mad.

At last Frau von Taussig came to him, a nurse like all the others. He noticed only her uniform, what did her face matter to him? But she stood and looked at him for a long time and said, "I knew your son."

Then he looked at her face. It was the face of a woman who has grown old but who was still beautiful. Her nurse's hat made her look younger, as it makes all women look younger because pity and gentleness rejuvenate women, as do the outward emblems of pity and gentleness. She's a society woman, thought Herr von Trotta. "How long ago did you know my son?" he asked her.

"Before the war," said Frau von Taussig. She took his arm to conduct him along the corridor, as she conducted her patients, and said very quietly, "Carl Joseph and I were in love."

The District Commissioner asked, "Excuse me, but was it on your account he got himself into that silly scrape?"

"Partly," said Frau von Taussig.

"I see, I see," said Herr von Trotta. "Partly." Then he squeezed the nurse's arm a little and added, "I only wish Carl Joseph could still get himself into scrapes on your account."

"We must go and see the patient now," said Frau von Taussig. For she felt tears welling up in her eyes and considered that it would be unseemly to cry.

Chojnicki was in a bare room; all furniture had been removed because he was sometimes violent. He was sitting on a chair with legs screwed into the floor. When the District Commissioner entered he got up and went towards his visitor. "Leave us, Wally," he said to Frau von Taussig, "we have important things to talk about."

They were alone. Set into the door was a spyhole. Chojnicki went to the door and covered the peephole with his back. He said, "Welcome to my house." For some strange reason his bald head appeared even balder to Herr von Trotta. From the patient's wide, rather prominent light-blue eyes a chill wind seemed to emanate, a frost sweeping over the drawn, sallow, yet at the same time bloated face, howling across the desert of the skull. From time to time the right-hand corner of his mouth twitched. He seemed to be forever trying to smile with the right-hand corner of his mouth; as though his whole faculty for smiling had shifted to the right-hand corner of his mouth, leaving the remainder of it bereft forever.

"Sit down," said Chojnicki. "I've sent for you to tell you something important. Not a word to anyone about it. You and I are the only ones to know. The Old Man's dying."

"How do you know?" said Herr von Trotta.

Chojnicki, still against the door, pointed a finger at the

ceiling, then put it to his lips and said, "I know from up there."

Then he turned and opened the door again. He called, "Sister Wally," and said to Frau von Taussig, who came at once, "The audience is over." He bowed. Herr von Trotta left him. He went back down the long corridor and down the broad stone steps.

"It may have worked," said Frau von Taussig.

Herr von Trotta took his leave and drove to see Herr Stransky, the minor railway official who had married a Koppelmann. The Stranskys were at home. They did not immediately recognize the District Commissioner. Then they welcomed him uneasily, dolefully, rather frigidly, it seemed to him. They gave him coffee and cognac. "Carl Joseph," said Frau Stransky née Koppelmann, "came to see us once, as soon as they made him a lieutenant. He was a dear boy!"

The District Commissioner stroked his whiskers and said nothing. Then the Stranskys' son came in. He limped hideously, it was awful to see. Carl Joseph did not have a limp, thought the District Commissioner.

"They say the Old Man's dying," said Railway Official Stransky suddenly.

Then Herr von Trotta got up at once and left. It was no news to him that the Old Man was dying. Chojnicki had told him, and Chojnicki had always known everything. He went to see his old friend Smetana of the Comptroller's office. "The Old Man's dying," said Smetana.

"I want to go to Schönbrunn," said Herr von Trotta. And he drove to Schönbrunn.

The palace of Schönbrunn stood enveloped in precisely the same relentless drizzle as the Steinhof lunatic asylum. Herr von Trotta went up to the avenue, the same avenue along which he had walked, long, long ago to the secret audience on his son's behalf. His son was dead. And the Emperor was dying. And for the first time since Zoglauer's letter, Herr von Trotta thought he could perceive that his son had not died arbitrarily. The Emperor can't survive the Trottas, he thought. They saved his life and he can't survive the Trottas.

He stayed outside. He stayed in the rain with the ragged crowd. A gardener from the Schönbrunn park in a green apron, spade in hand, came to ask them, "How is he now?"

315

And the onlookers outside the palace—foresters, coachmen, petty officials, porters, and pensioners like the father of the hero of Solferino—answered the gardener, "Nothing new. He's dying."

The gardener went away again, went away with the spade to dig up beds, the everlasting earth. The fine rain became denser and denser. Herr von Trotta took off his hat. The little crowd of court employees took him for one of themselves, or for a postman from the Schönbrunn post office. And one after another said to him, "Did you ever know the Old Man?"

"Yes," said Herr von Trotta. "He spoke to me once."

"Now he's dying," said a forester.

Just then a priest with the Blessed Sacrament was going into the Emperor's bedroom.

They had just taken Francis Joseph's temperature. It was 102·7. "I see, I see," the Emperor said to the chaplain, "so this is what it's like to die." He sat upright against the pillows. He could hear the unceasing rain through the windows and the crunch of people's feet on the gravel. It seemed to him that these sounds were alternately far away and near, and sometimes he was aware that it was the rain which caused the soft gentle trickle outside the window. But soon he had forgotten that it was the rain. He asked the doctor a few times, "Why is it murmuring so?" For he could not manage the word "trickling," although it was on the tip of his tongue. But after he had inquired for the cause of the murmuring, he believed that he was in fact hearing a murmuring sound. The rain murmured. People's feet outside on the gravel murmured. Both the word and the sounds it signified pleased Francis Joseph more and more. And besides it did not matter what he asked them, for they could no longer hear him. He was only moving his lips, but to him it felt as if he were speaking quite audibly, a little softly perhaps, but as distinctly as for the past few days. At times he was surprised they did not answer him. But soon he forgot both what he had asked and his surprise. So he gave himself up to the curious faint murmur of the world which went on living all around him while he died, and he was like a child which gives up its struggle against sleep, compelled by a cradle song and wrapped in it. He shut his eyes. After a while he opened them again and looked at the plain silver crucifix and the dazzling candles on the table waiting for the priest. Then he knew that the priest would soon be there. And he moved his lips and began, as he had been taught as a boy, "In contrition and humility I confess my sins. . . ." But they did not hear this either. He saw at once that the chaplain was there. "You've kept me waiting a long time," he said. Then he considered his sins. "Arrogance" occurred to him. "I've always been arrogant," he said. He went through his sins, one by one, as listed in the catechism. I've been Emperor too long, he thought. But it felt just as if he'd said it aloud. "All men must die; the Emperor dies." And at the same time it seemed to him that the part of him which had been imperial was dying. "The war is a sin, too," he said aloud. But the priest did not hear him. And Francis Joseph felt surprised again. Every day the casualty lists came, it had gone on since 1914. "Finish it!" said Francis Joseph. They did not hear. "I wish I'd been killed at Solferino," he said. They did not hear. Perhaps, he thought, I am dead already and am speaking as a dead man. That's why they can't hear me. And he fell asleep.

Outside, among the crowd, Herr von Trotta waited, the son of the hero of Solferino, hat in hand, in the steadily pouring rain. The trees in Schönbrunn park rustled and sighed, rain drove in gusts against them, softly, profusely, indefatigably. Dusk gathered. Inquisitive people came. The park filled. The rain never stopped. The waiting people came and went. Herr von Trotta stayed. Night fell, the steps were deserted, people had gone home to bed. Herr von Trotta stood close to the door. He could hear the sounds of carriages arriving and, sometimes, above his head, a window was opened. Voices called. The door opened and shut. Nobody noticed him. The rain streamed down steadily, gently, the trees rustled and sighed.

At last bells began to toll. The District Commissioner departed. He went down the shallow steps and back along the avenue to the iron gate, which was open tonight. He walked the whole long way back to the city, bareheaded, hat in hand. He met nobody. He walked very slowly, like a mourner. The sky was gray by the time he got to his hotel.

He went back home. It was raining in the district town of W. Herr von Trotta summoned Fräulein Hirschwitz and said,

317

"I'm going to bed, dear lady. I feel tired." And so, for the first time in his life, he went to bed during the day.

He could not go to sleep. He sent for Dr Skowronnek.

"Dear Dr Skowronnek," he said, "will you please tell them to bring the canary." They brought the canary across from Jacques's cottage. "Give it a bit of sugar," said the District Commissioner. So the canary got its bit of sugar. "A pretty pet," said Herr von Trotta.

"Pretty pet," Skowronnek echoed him.

Then the District Commissioner said, "Will you send for the priest, please? But come back, won't you."

So the doctor waited for the priest to come. Then he went back. Old Herr Trotta was lying quite still among his pillows. His eyes were half-closed. He said, "Take my hand, dear friend. Will you bring the portrait?"

Dr Skowronnek found the study, climbed a chair, and unhooked the portrait of the hero of Solferino. When he came back, bearing the portrait in both hands, Herr von Trotta was no longer capable of looking at it. Rain drummed gently against the panes.

Dr Skowronnek waited, the portrait of the hero of Solferino on his knees. After a few minutes, he got up and went to take Herr von Trotta's hand. He bent over the District Commissioner's chest, drew a deep breath, and closed the dead man's eyes.

It was the day on which they buried the Emperor in the Capuchin Vault. Three days later they lowered the District Commissioner's corpse into the earth. The burgomaster of W. made a speech. It began with the war, as all speeches did in those days. The burgomaster went on to relate how Herr von Trotta had given his only son to the Emperor and had, nevertheless gone on living and serving his country. Meanwhile, it drizzled steadily on the bare heads of all those gathered round the grave and there was a rustling, trickling off leaves, off sodden wreaths and dripping flowers. Dr Skowronnek, in the, to him, unfamiliar uniform of a territorial medical officer, was doing his best to stand smartly to attention, though he did not feel it in the least an appropriate attitude, or expressive of grief for the dead, civilian that he was. After all, death isn't a staff surgeon, thought the doctor. He was one of the first

318

to approach the grave. He declined the spade which a grave-digger offered him but bent his back to take a wet clod of earth, broke it up in his left hand, and, with his right, strewed handfuls on the coffin. Then he stepped back. It occurred to him that it was afternoon and nearly time for a game of chess. But now there was no one to play with. All the same, he decided to go to the café.

As they were walking out of the cemetery, the burgomaster offered him a lift in his carriage. Dr Skowronnek climbed into it. "I should like to have mentioned" said the burgomaster, "that Herr von Trotta couldn't have survived the Emperor. Don't you agree, Doctor?"

"I don't know," replied Dr Skowronnek. "I think perhaps neither of them could survive Austria!"

He asked to be dropped outside the café. He went to his usual table, as every day. There stood the chessboard, just as if the District Commissioner had not died. The waiter came to take it away, but Skowronnek said, "Leave it, please," and played himself at chess, smiling from time to time when he happened to look across at the empty chair, listening to the quiet autumn rain rustling, hissing, streaming outside the windows, trickling incessantly down the windowpanes.